Praise for Sherry Knowlton's

DEAD ON THE DELTA

"Every page of *Dead on the Delta* radiates Knowlton's love and knowledge of this unique part of our planet and highlights its potential for disaster. Knowlton's suspenseful book sets the beauty of the Okavango against the dangers that lurk there." —MICHAEL STANLEY, AUTHOR OF THE DETECTIVE KUBU SERIES, ALSO SET IN BOTSWANA

"Dead on the Delta is a gripping new adventure for Alexa Williams. Set against the backdrop of Botswana's Okavango Delta, Alexa faces brutal poachers and a frightening conspiracy that reaches all the way to the top of Botswana's elite. The situation comes to a head in a terrifying confrontation that requires all of Alexa's strength as she fights for her own survival. A satisfying read set in a gorgeous landscape." —MICHAEL NIEMANN, AWARD-WINNING AUTHOR OF THE VALENTIN VERMEULEN THRILLERS

"A well-balanced and intelligent thriller . . . Suspense and thriller fiction fans have plenty to look forward to with *Dead on the Delta.*" —INDEPENDENT BOOK REVIEW

★★★★ "Full of action, adventure, politics, and, of course, animals."
—MANHATTAN BOOK REVIEW

★★★★★ "Great cast of characters and a fantastic female lead. Now I want to read the other books in the Alexa Williams series." —SAN FRANCISCO BOOK REVIEW

"Knowlton has outdone herself. *Dead on the Delta* has perched itself in the top tier of my favorite mystery novels . . . Knowlton moves her courageous, savvy, and lovable heroine halfway across the world and takes her faithful readers along for the trip." —PAT LAMARCHE, AUTHOR OF *MAGIC DIARY* AND *STILL LEFT OUT IN AMERICA*

"In this suspenseful tale of international corruption and hatred, Alexa Williams once again proves a formidable heroine. The ins and outs of the book will keep you up for the night." —ALMA BOND, *MIDWEST BOOK REVIEW*

Praise for Earlier Books in the Alexa Williams Suspense Series

DEAD OF WINTER

". . . a searing tale of murder, love, and communal fear. From flying drones to police investigations and legal wrangling, *Dead of Winter* will keep you guessing and glued raptly to your reading chair." —GAYLE LYNDS, *NEW YORK TIMES* BEST-SELLING AUTHOR OF THE ASSASSINS

". . . a riveting mystery that will stick with you long after the last page is turned. . . . While addressing xenophobia, racism, and America's complicated history, *Dead of Winter* is the novel we need and the story we want." —J. J. HENSLEY, AUTHOR OF *BOLT ACTION REMEDY* AND *RECORD SCRATCH*

"Knowlton examines the explosive combination of ignorance and fear that results in hate and violence." —MATTY DALRYMPLE, AUTHOR OF THE LIZZY BALLARD THRILLERS AND THE ANN KINNEAR SUSPENSE NOVELS AND SHORTS

DEAD OF SPRING

"A lawyer who yearns for the quiet life proves a magnet for murder." —*KIRKUS REVIEWS*

"A suspicious suicide of a powerful politician takes on new meaning when Alexa Williams's investigations uncover corruption at the heart of the fracking industry. Highly recommended." —MARK LEGGATT, BEST-SELLING AUTHOR OF INTERNATIONAL THRILLER *NAMES OF THE DEAD*

"A spellbinding yarn jerked straight from today's frightening headlines." —KAY KENDALL, AUTHOR OF HISTORICAL MYSTERIES

DEAD OF SUMMER

"Alexa Williams is a sassy, alpha-female heroine. The plot is knotty, lots of will-she or won't-she, all woven into an intense battle of wits that heats up every page. While reading, I could almost see the credits rolling for the movie." —STEVE BERRY, *NEW YORK TIMES* AND #1 INTERNATIONAL BEST-SELLING AUTHOR

"Fans of Sherry Knowlton's *Dead of Autumn* will find summer to be an equally deadly season . . . a riveting, suspenseful read." —MELISSA F. MILLER, *USA TODAY* BEST-SELLING AUTHOR OF LEGAL THRILLERS AND ROMANTIC COMEDIC MYSTERIES

"Edgy and engaging." —HEIDI RUBY MILLER, AUTHOR OF THE AMBASADORA SERIES

DEAD OF AUTUMN

"*Dead Autumn* features a dead body harkening back to the crimes of an earlier era—there are conventions in genre writing that fans appreciate." —*LIBRARY JOURNAL*

"I recommend this book to anyone who loves mysteries or rural Pennsylvania."
—VAL MUELLER, AUTHOR OF *THE FAULKNER'S APPRENTICE* AND *THE CORGI CAPERS*

DEAD ON THE DELTA

Also by Sherry Knowlton

DEAD of WINTER
DEAD of SPRING
DEAD of SUMMER
DEAD of AUTUMN

BOOK 5 OF THE ALEXA WILLIAMS SERIES

DEAD
ON THE DELTA

SHERRY KNOWLTON

MILFORD
HOUSE
an imprint of Sunbury Press, Inc.
Mechanicsburg, PA USA

MILFORD HOUSE

an imprint of Sunbury Press, Inc.
Mechanicsburg, PA USA

For information about special discounts for bulk purchases, please contact Sunbury Press Orders Dept. at (855) 338-8359 or orders@sunburypress.com.

To request one of our authors for speaking engagements or book signings, please contact Sunbury Press Publicity Dept. at publicity@sunburypress.com.

FIRST MILFORD HOUSE PRESS EDITION: February 2021

Set in Adobe Garamond | Interior design by Crystal Devine | Cover design by Lawrence Knorr – Photo by Mike Knowlton | Edited by Jennifer Cappello.

Publisher's Cataloging-in-Publication Data
Names: Knowlton, Sherry, author.
Title: Dead on the delta / Sherry Knowlton.
Description: First trade paperback edition. | Mechanicsburg, PA : Milford House Press, 2021.
Summary: When Alexa Williams and her wildlife researcher companions happen upon a herd of elephants massacred at the hands of poachers in Botswana, Africa, they quickly find themselves wrapped up in a dangerous world of black-market activities and complicated conservation efforts, presenting them with complex landscapes--political and physical—which they must navigate successfully if they want to protect beloved animal species and escape with their own lives.
Identifiers: ISBN : 978-1-620064-33-7 (softcover).
Subjects: FICTION / Thrillers / Crime | FICTION / Suspense | FICTION / Mystery & Detective.

Continue the Enlightenment!

In wildness is the preservation of the world.

—Henry David Thoreau, *Walking*

The lion that kills is the one that does not roar.

—African Proverb

For Mike,
my travel companion on all of life's journeys,
with love.

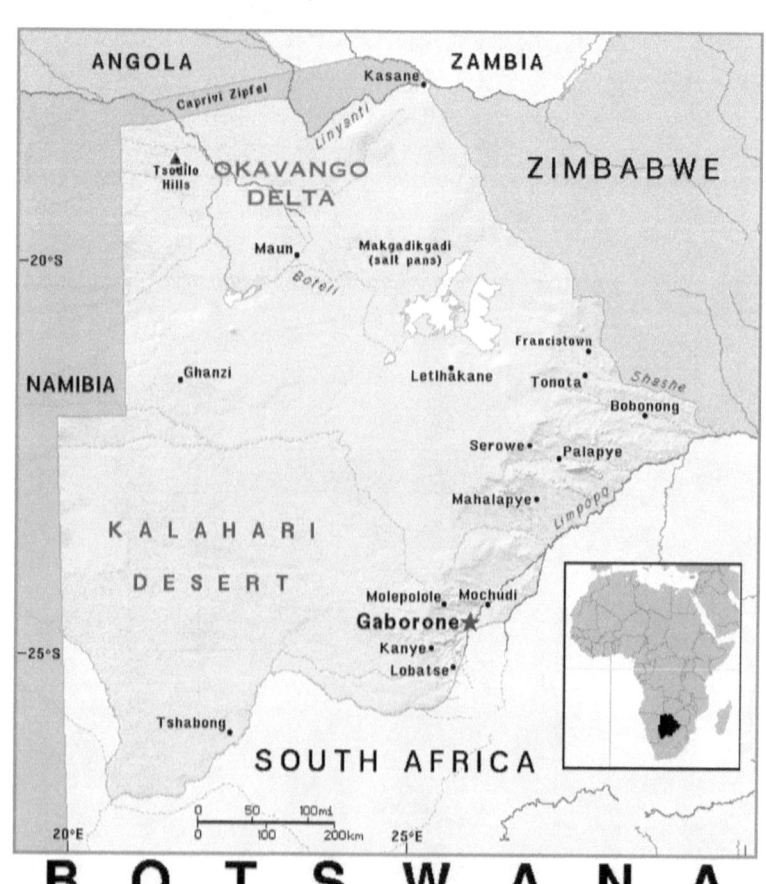

ANGOLA ZAMBIA

Caprivi Zipfel

Kasane

Linyanti

Tsodilo Hills

OKAVANGO DELTA

ZIMBABWE

Maun

Makgadikgadi (salt pans)

Boteti

-20°S

Francistown

NAMIBIA

Ghanzi

Letlhakane

Tonota

Shashe

Bobonong

Serowe

Palapye

Mahalapye

Limpopo

K A L A H A R I

D E S E R T

Molepolole

Mochudi

Gaborone ★

Kanye

Lobatse

-25°S

Tshabong

SOUTH AFRICA

0   50   100mi.
0   100   200km

20°E

25°E

B O T S W A N A

CHAPTER ONE

ACROSS THE RIVER, the big male raised his head and stared downstream, shifting from sleep to full alert in seconds. With a deep stretch and a shake of his mane, he rose and vanished into the underbrush. The dominant lioness nudged a sister dozing nearby with feet in the air. One by one, the big cats rose from their torpor. Within a few seconds, the entire pride melted into the mopane scrub, even the unruly cubs.

Placing a final mark on her simple drawing, Alexa dropped her sketchbook and pencil on the back seat and laughed. "Too bad we're not documenting the characteristics of lion tails instead of faces. I was this close to capturing the whisker patterns on the big female, then poof. They all disappear." The leaves of the huge ebony next to the vehicle rustled in the wind, prompting Alexa to raise her voice, "Did something spook them? This wind? A leopard?" She scanned the grassy riverbank with her binoculars but found nothing.

In the front passenger seat, Reese jotted a note on the clipboard in his hands, then turned with a grin. "*Lion Tales*. Sounds like the name of a kids' book."

Alexa groaned at the goofy pun.

Reese looked to Mokapi, beside him at the wheel. "We've had so little time to observe this group. Let's circle around and follow them. Maybe we'll figure out why they moved. I counted ten. How many did you see?"

"Ten. There should be two more young males in this pride." Mo cocked his head for a moment, then said, "Not sure why the cats moved. A smaller competitor, like a leopard, wouldn't bother the lions. Especially since the pride male is there. Let's rock and roll. Maybe we'll catch sight of them on the other side of the river." Mo flashed a broad smile. He reached for the key to start the Land Cruiser but then sat back. "Listen," he said in a sharp tone.

Alexa leaned her head out of the open window. She caught the loud chop-chop-chop of a helicopter just before the sound was swallowed up by the roar of an airboat rounding the bend of the river. Riding the current at full throttle, the boat carried a dozen men in camouflage, holding assault rifles.

She followed Reese's gaze as his head tilted skyward to look at the black helicopter. It swooped in to pace the boat, and both disappeared downstream. Heart hammering, Alexa asked, "What's going on?" The acrid stink of petroleum fuels floated on the dry breeze, fouling the loamy riverbank scent of vegetation, mud, and dung.

Mo responded in a wary voice, "Botswana Defence Force. The anti-poaching unit."

"Wow. I've been hoping for a chance to interact with the BDF." Reese's voice lifted. "Botswana has such an excellent track record for dealing with poaching, although I know there's been some controversy in recent months."

"They look like they mean business. Did you notice that none of them even acknowledged our presence? How weird was that?" Alexa placed the binoculars on the seat next to her as dust rose in the distance. "Vehicle coming," she cried.

"She's moving fast." Mo opened the door and swung his legs out to face the approaching vehicle. "Maybe more BDF? This isn't Department of Wildlife ranger territory."

Reese opened his door and climbed out onto the running board to watch. Alexa moved the binoculars aside and clambered across to the seat facing the road.

Expecting another safari vehicle, she gasped when a military transport truck flashed past, packed with more uniformed men gripping weapons.

Reese ducked his head back into the vehicle. "Mo, is a response like this typical for the unit? Between the boat, the helicopter, and the truck, I counted more than thirty soldiers."

The Motswana wildlife researcher, whose assigned territory included this game concession, shook his head. "We're not far from the Caprivi Strip. Poaching is an issue up here. Poachers slip over the Namibian border, usually at night. So, the BDF has targeted enforcement activities in this sector for years. They have a big camp a few kilometers from here. Still, I've never seen so many men respond to an incident. Let me find out if anyone knows what's happening."

Mo reached for the handset and fired off a series of what sounded like questions in Setswana. Standard procedure. The safari guide network relied on their radios to communicate animal sightings and to call for help in emergency situations. Following a burst of static, a male voice responded, speaking in an agitated tone.

Reese slid back into his seat, hanging on every word of the conversation. Alexa smiled at the look of intense concentration on her boyfriend's face. As if force of will would help him understand a language that he spoke only at the most rudimentary level.

She leaned back and slipped off her fleece jacket, tuning out the excited radio exchange. The early morning research drive had been promising. They'd come across the River Pride in their first hour in the field. Mo said that this family of lions often rested near the water after a nighttime hunt. Although Reese had pushed for a suitable viewing spot on the same bank as the lions, Mo had suggested parking here rather than risk disturbing the animals. He'd made the right call; it had been a good vantage point until the BDF onslaught drove the cats away.

After two and a half months in Botswana on this research project, Alexa had learned to treasure the cool mornings in the bush. Searching out big cats on the prowl as darkness gave way to golden dawn was thrilling. The predators became less active as the sun rose in the sky, settling into sleep through the heat of midday. Alexa was surprised at how much she'd come to enjoy the lion research and respect these animals. She especially loved watching the cubs tumble and play and the way the attentive mothers, even when they appeared to doze, kept a watchful eye on their young ones.

Today, the anti-poaching squad had shattered the morning's serenity for both the lion pride and Alexa. Despite the low-key response from Reese and Mo, the jarring intrusion had put her on edge. Seeing so many high-powered weapons this far off the grid in such a remote corner of the Delta made Alexa uneasy. Of course, these were soldiers charged with stopping poachers.

Mo clicked off the handset. "The guides aren't one hundred percent clear what's happening. Word is that JB from Kagiso found some evidence of poaching at first light. They called in the BDF. JB and the other camp guides are off-line now, so no one can confirm details. One fellow heard part of the radio message to the BDF and thought he caught the words 'carcass' and '*tau*.' But there was static. Could have said 'tau.' Could have said '*tlou*.'"

"So, dead lions or dead elephants? Either's terrible. It's critical we know if someone has killed a lion. Scum of the earth, poachers." Reese's voice rose in concern. "Can we find the BDF guys?"

After a moment's hesitation, Mo nodded. "Sure, boss. We can try. BDF is not so happy to have outsiders at poaching arrests, but we're researchers. And it could be lions killed."

"Yes. We're lion specialists. Let's do it." Reese looked at Alexa. "Are you okay with chasing this down? If the poachers hit any lions, we should document that."

"Go. Go." Alexa poured out the remaining tea in her tin cup and stuffed it into the open backpack at her feet as Mo swung the Land Cruiser over the grass and onto the road.

The sturdy vehicle lurched and bounced as Mo steered in the direction the military truck had vanished. Alexa peered ahead, trying without success to spot the truck's dust cloud. Every vehicle that traveled these sandy roads left a long trail of dust in the dry season. She shouted to the men in the front seat, "Either they turned off or they're so far ahead the dust has settled."

Reese grunted his assent, but Mo just nodded, his hands gripping the wheel.

They raced through changing territory. Tall stands of grass gave way to a low forest, the stunted trees gnarled as if in pain. Far to the right, a line of tall, leafy trees signaled the meandering path of the river. Warthogs and roan antelope trotted next to the vehicle as they passed.

In the back seat, Alexa braced to keep from flying out of the Land Cruiser, grasping the back of Reese's seat with one hand and the half-wall of the open SUV with the other. "Whoa," she gasped as her body left the seat and then slammed back down.

"Sorry. Pothole." Mo jerked the steering wheel to the right and rode in the grass beside the track for a few seconds before he careened back into the roadway. "I'm heading in the direction of Kagiso. If we don't see some signs soon, I'll radio again."

"Signs?" Alexa settled back in her seat, still holding onto the side of the rocking vehicle.

Reese shouted over the engine roar. "Vultures, hyenas, jackals. If there's a kill of some sort, they'd be heading toward it. Or we might be able to spot the BDF vehicles or helicopter."

Mo jammed on the brakes as a small herd of elephants emerged from a thicket and ambled across the road ahead. The pungent odor of dusty elephant trailed behind the plodding herd. A calf, probably about six months old, tripped on the bank, and one of the larger females steadied the youngster with her trunk. Wobbling, he followed the other big beasts across the savannah.

Pulling the Land Cruiser off the road, the researcher said, "Let me call in. See if we can pinpoint where they are."

"I thought they'd be on the river somewhere. Although I guess the soldiers could have left the boat and walked inland." Reese stood up to stretch while Mo worked the radio. He swung out onto the running board and stood next to Alexa.

"Are you all right back here?" He caressed her cheek. "Mo's been pushing forty kilometers an hour. That's pretty brutal on these roads."

Rubbing the base of her spine with one hand, Alexa laughed. "Yeah. It's gone well beyond African massage territory." Safari guides joked about the miserable roads, referring to the bumpy ride as an African massage. These last twenty minutes had been backbreaking, and she'd borne the brunt of it.

"Hang in there. If we go off-road, we'll have to slow down. Still, I'd like to get there soon. To see any evidence of poaching before it's disturbed." Reese frowned. "I've been thinking about the possibility that it's lion poaching. I think it's doubtful that this would be a big game hunt. Not like Cecil the Lion over in Zimbabwe."

"This is a photography-only concession, so big game hunting's not allowed, right?" Alexa asked.

"Exactly. The Botswana government would come down hard on illegal trophy hunting. So, it's unlikely that a hunting guide, a foreign hunter, or even a local villager would attempt a trophy lion kill here," Reese nodded. "What I've been afraid of is the type of lion poaching that has popped up in Mozambique and South Africa."

Alexa gave her boyfriend a sympathetic look. She loved that he was so passionate about protecting wildlife. He'd been immersed in big cat research for years. Although Africa Trust had hired her as a temporary employee, she was pretty much along for the ride on this four-month assignment in the Okavango Delta, getting what sometimes felt like a literal crash course in lion conservation. Her law practice at home hadn't prepared her for anything of this sort, but she'd learned a lot about the topic during this brief stint in Botswana.

"Someone condemned lion poaching at one of the Commission meetings I attended. More a statement of outrage. No real details."

"Yeah. It's pretty hard to process. The hot new thing is to kill lions for their teeth, tails, and paws. Some take the bones too."

"Revolting." Alexa winced.

"The stuff goes straight to the Asian market. For jewelry. Medicine. And, with the decline in the tiger population—partly due to poaching as well—they're substituting lion bones for tiger bones in tiger cake and wine. Might be other buyers out there, but the current consensus is that most lion products are going to Asia. Just like elephant ivory and rhino horn."

Mo finished his lengthy conversation and clicked off the radio. "I finally got through to one of the Kagiso guides. We're not far away. He confirmed there's a poaching incident. It's near a wide bend on the river. The road splits up ahead. After we take the left fork, it's just a few kilometers."

"Did he say what happened? Did they catch poachers in the act?" Reese swung back into the front passenger seat.

"He doesn't think so. Said that something big was discovered early this morning. He doesn't know much more—or wouldn't say on the open radio."

Mo drove the final kilometers at a cautious pace while Alexa and Reese kept their eyes on the horizon. Almost noon, as the sun approached its zenith, the temperature had risen at least ten degrees. Alexa was glad for the broad brim of her baseball cap as she scanned the skies for birds of prey.

"Hyenas." Reese pointed to three scruffy-looking brown animals trotting across an open plain far ahead of them. "Amazing that hyenas can smell blood from four kilometers away."

Alexa squinted at the sky in the direction the hyenas were headed. "There," she exclaimed. "Vultures. Wow. Tons of vultures."

When Reese spotted the circling birds, he pointed toward them with a glance at Mo.

Keeping his hands on the wheel, Mo nodded. "There's a track up here to the right. That should take us close."

When the research assistant downshifted and edged the front tires off the road, it took Alexa a few seconds to see any signs of a track. Ahead, the grass grew almost a foot tall. Then, she made out two tire-sized parallel lines that cut through the vegetation.

Reese peered through the open window as they wound through the grassland. "I think we're going in the right direction. A big vehicle has been through here very recently. The wheelbase is wider than the usual Land Cruisers and Land Rovers that pass through here. Some of the smashed grass has yet to spring back in place."

As they approached a line of teak trees, Mo stopped the vehicle and switched off the ignition. He and Reese both eased out onto the running boards and stood alert, listening.

"Over to the right," Mo whispered. "Voices."

Reese nodded as a shout rose beyond the fringe of forest, muted, as if carried from afar on the wind.

The men took their seats, and Mo turned the key, shifted into second gear, and veered off the fading track, driving toward the sound. The Cruiser lurched up, down, and sideways as Mo inched through the underbrush and trees.

Alexa jumped when a lone waterbuck leapt from behind a fallen tree and fled from their approach. She smiled as the graceful animal bounded away. When she turned back, Alexa was startled to see another group of hyenas to her right. The lead hyena stopped in its tracks and watched Alexa with flat eyes that bored directly into her own, as if the menacing beast were sizing up a rival for the meal ahead.

With effort, Alexa tore her eyes from the animal's implacable gaze and gasped as the vehicle went dark. Heart pounding, Alexa took a wild look around the interior; then she broke into laughter that balanced on the fine edge of hysteria. She'd been so focused on the hyena that she hadn't noticed they'd driven beneath a thick canopy of tall trees that blocked the sun.

"You okay back there?" Reese glanced back with a puzzled look.

"Yeah. I'm just a little nervous." Alexa's voice cracked with tension. She dreaded finding butchered lions. She'd grown so attached to the species in these weeks on the Delta. And she was still wary of the show of force that the BDF had displayed as it rushed to this poaching incident.

Mo slowed the Cruiser as he picked his way through gaps in the forest. When they were trailing lions or leopards, he would often plow right over saplings and dead branches. Alexa realized that, today, he was aiming for stealth as he yanked the steering wheel hard to the right to avoid a fallen limb. Ahead, the forest brightened, marking the far edge of the trees and, perhaps, the river.

"Stop a moment," Reese directed and raised his binoculars to his eyes. "Those trees on the far right. Filled with vultures. The ground ahead seems higher. I can see some small hills; maybe termite mounds. And I thought I caught a few glimpses of movement."

Alexa and Mo both peered through their field glasses. "It's too far to make out the details. Except for the shapes wheeling in and out of the trees. No doubt they're vultures," Alexa noted.

"I say we keep going." Mo's hesitant tone undermined his words. He licked his lips. "I expect the BDF to stop us as we get nearer. They often set up a loose perimeter around a site they're working on. We don't want this to turn into a 'Hotel California' situation."

"What? Oh, no. They have to let us leave. The worst that can happen—they'll turn us around." Reese took another look with his binocs. "Wish we knew what was going on. But let's proceed."

Alexa grinned at Mo's reference to the famous Eagles song; a big fan of American rock and roll from the seventies, the researcher peppered his conversations with lines from classic rock. But after a moment, her anxiety returned. Encroaching on a BDF investigation could be risky.

A few minutes later, they neared the tree line. The small termite mounds grew larger, and giant scavenger birds—vultures and marabou storks—clouded the sky. Hyenas and a few jackals paced just outside the shade of the trees. In a dance as old as the African continent, these death eaters were biding their time in anticipation of a feast.

"The number of scavengers here is very unusual. What in God's name could have drawn so many birds and beasts?" Mo asked as he crossed himself.

Alexa shivered. The bird noise was deafening. The flap of the nine-foot wings on the marabou storks thrummed a bass note to the incessant screeching of the multiple species of vultures. In horrified fascination, she couldn't take her eyes off the huge mass of birds.

"Jesus H. Christ," Reese swore in a strangled voice as the vehicle slammed to an abrupt halt.

Jolted by the dismay in his tone, Alexa forgot the birds and looked toward her boyfriend in alarm.

Reese and Mo were both riveted by something in front of the vehicle, which Alexa couldn't see from her spot behind the driver's seat. Without another word, the two men climbed out of the Cruiser and stepped forward. They both moved as if walking through deep water.

Taking rapid breaths, Alexa edged open her door with dread and followed the men. For a moment, she couldn't absorb the panorama in front of them. A sea of dusty termite-mounds gave off waves of heat in the noonday sun. The shimmering moguls of pale dirt dotted the entire field stretching toward the river. Then, Alexa's knees buckled as her eyes focused on the nearest mound. "Oh no. How? Who? What type of person could do something so vile?"

Tears streaming down his face, Reese grabbed Alexa's arm to keep her from falling.

Mo murmured under his breath, a series of rapid words that could have been a tribal chant or a prayer.

Shaking, Alexa studied the huge form at her feet: a dead elephant sprawled on her side in the dirt. Deep cavities, red with drying blood, were the only thing that remained of her lower face after the poachers had hacked out her tusks. Beneath the female's front feet lay a tiny elephant that could have been no older than six or seven months. The pattern of blood spatters on the baby's body revealed that it had been felled with scores of bullets.

"Why kill the calf?" Reese asked in a bitter tone. "It's not even old enough to have tusks."

Mo responded in a flat tone. "Easier not to have to deal with a baby mourning the loss of its mother. They needed to get the tusks out as quickly as possible."

Alexa gasped for breath as a band of grief tightened around her chest. Feeling like her heart might break, she tore her gaze from the tiny, brutalized elephant and looked out over the sloping riverbank. Fallen elephants with ravaged faces lay collapsed all across the grassy slope, many resting in pools of dried blood. What had looked at a distance like ant mounds were gruesome carcasses. The elephants died covered in drying, ghostly gray mud, as if they'd finished cooling down in the river just before they'd been slaughtered.

A fierce gust of wind whipped across the elephant graveyard. With a clench of her stomach, it hit Alexa that the pervasive odor was the beginning of mass decomposition in the hot sun. She'd thought the foul stench was coming from the vultures. She gagged and pulled her neck scarf up to cover her nose and mouth.

"My God," Reese said. "There must be twenty of them. Maybe more."

"The biggest kill I've ever seen. I can't believe it. In my country," Mo took off his hat and twisted it in his hands.

Reeling from shock, Alexa wiped tears from her eyes and muttered, "Pure evil. These people need to be stopped."

CHAPTER TWO

ALEXA STOOD OVER the two dead elephants before her, frozen by shock and revulsion. Wrapping her arms around her torso to control the shaking, she looked beyond the mother and baby and shuddered at the mass carnage.

Neither Reese nor Mo spoke. Reese's shoulders slumped; his tall frame hunched in distress. The distraught expression and ashen undertone of Mo's dark face made the slender man look more like a scared teenager than a respected wildlife researcher nearing thirty.

Still rooted in place, Alexa reached out to grab Reese's hand as she gazed at the field of fallen elephants, trying to grasp the scale of needless death.

"*Tsamaya kusa! Tsamaya!*" Mo's alarmed shout jarred Alexa. The research assistant flapped his hands and stomped the ground, facing down an approaching hyena.

When Alexa and Reese joined in waving their arms, the animal backed off. It stopped just a few yards away to pace back and forth.

"Damn," Reese barked. "What are we thinking? We're out of the vehicle, standing in the middle of a banquet for scavengers. We should get back in the Cruiser before one of these hungry bastards attacks us, or a big cat shows up."

Bastards? Reese must be shaken to the core to call the hyenas 'bastards.' How many times had the wildlife lover told her, "Every species has a role in nature, even the ugly ones, the nasty ones, and the ones that will kill you in an instant"? She grabbed his hand again on the short walk back to the Land Cruiser, not clear if the comfort was more for him or her.

Stopping by the vehicle doors, Reese gave her a searching look. "How are you doing? This is pretty rough. The senselessness of it all . . ." his voice trailed off.

"And the sheer number of elephants. How could anyone even begin to cart off all that ivory?" Alexa closed her eyes for a moment. "I'm okay. The shock is starting to fade." She flinched as a vulture flew by, almost at ground level, and landed on the carcass they'd just left. She tugged her hat down tighter.

As Alexa stepped onto the running board, Mo called out a warning from the driver's seat. "Incoming." He pointed to an SUV headed in their direction. "I was surprised that the BDF didn't stop us before we got this far. Looks like they've seen us now."

Reese hopped onto the running board next to Alexa. "They've had their hands full. Might have split up their force to send some soldiers to track the poachers. That would limit the number of men left to secure the site." His voice caught. "The dead ellies are spread out over such a big area."

As Alexa clambered into her seat, Mo muttered, "They will not be happy that we're here. Let me talk to them. If I need you, mention the Africa Trust and your 'friend,' the minister of Environment, Wildlife and Tourism. Hold on. I'm going to back out of here." He drove the Land Cruiser toward the oncoming vehicle.

"I met him once. I guess that makes us friends," Reese murmured.

As they drove away, Alexa looked back to see the lurking hyena swoop onto the tiny elephant and target its tender belly. She tore her eyes away when Mo slid the Land Cruiser to a stop next to the BDF SUV.

"*Dumelang borra*," he called in greeting.

The driver extended his hand, palm forward, motioning them to stay in the vehicle. Both soldiers exited their SUV, gripping assault rifles in their hands. The driver approached Mo's open window while the other soldier circled the vehicle and stood by the passenger side of the Land Cruiser.

Although they kept their guns pointed toward the ground, it would have taken less than the span of a heartbeat for the soldiers to aim and fire. Hands clammy and breath uneven, Alexa tried to follow the rapid conversation between Mo and the lead soldier with little success. In her short time in Botswana, the words of Setswana that she'd picked up were limited to the names of animals and basics like "hello" and "goodbye."

Now the soldier was shaking his head and saying, "*Tlou. Tlou.*" Elephant. Elephant.

Mo rejoined with a series of questions and the English words, "Africa Trust," but the man continued to shake his head.

Then, Mo held up his hand and said, "*Leta.* I must speak to my boss."

Alexa hung over the seat to listen as he told Reese, "They're jumpy. Twenty-nine elephants were killed by the poachers. He has orders to let no one into the site." Mo lowered his voice. "He's afraid he'll get in trouble because we got this far. I think he could be persuaded to call for guidance if you talk to him. I'm not sure how good his English is. I told him you are from the States and a minister with Africa Trust. Do you want to push it?"

Reese sighed. "Yeah. I'd really like to get more information about this for the Trust's elephant project. It's such a clusterfuck." He opened his door but halted when the second soldier raised his weapon. Reese raised both hands and shouted, "Can we can speak?"

Alexa tensed, fearing that Reese could be shot. She barely registered Mo's rapid translation of Reese's words to the lead soldier.

"Okay. He says to walk slowly," Mo told Reese, then slipped out of the Cruiser to join the conversation.

Alexa stayed seated under the watchful eye of the guy on her side of the vehicle. Looking at Reese towering over the driver, she figured three-on-one would exacerbate an already dicey situation. She couldn't hear what Reese or the other man were saying, but Mo had to translate the entire discussion.

Then, the lead soldier said, "Minister?" in a frightened voice.

Reese nodded.

The soldier gestured. "Come."

Reese and Mo jumped into the Land Cruiser.

"What's going on?" Alexa asked.

"Dropping the minister into the conversation lit a fire under the dude," Reese answered.

Mo put the Cruiser into gear and followed the soldier's SUV. "He must fear the government minister more than he fears his commander."

They drove in a wide arc around the field of fallen elephants toward a military transport vehicle. It was parked in the midst of several other vehicles painted in green camouflage. The insignia on the side marked all but one of the vehicles as BDF. The outlier was a Delta Wild Land Cruiser.

The soldier ignored the uniformed men who darted among the vehicles and led the researchers to a makeshift command station. Nestled under a big tree next to the river stood a folding table and chairs. Two men wearing uniforms with golden epaulets were huddled over the table with a third man in khaki.

"You stop here," the driver directed.

"Smart setup," Reese whispered. "Upwind from the dead elephants."

Mo shifted back and forth from one foot to the other, eyes riveted on the lead soldier as he spoke to the two men with gold braid.

"Hey. Isn't the guy in khaki Jack Spenser from Kagiso?" Reese peered toward the table.

"You are correct," Mo said. "I don't know him well. We once discussed the Northern Pride when the dominant lioness was gored by a buffalo. She recovered though."

Alexa studied the tall, rawboned man whom Reese had identified. Yes. He was the camp manager at Kagiso. She and Reese had met him on their original circuit through the game concessions that hosted the Africa Trust lion study.

"Come," the soldier said and walked them toward the men at the table.

Alexa dragged her feet as she followed Reese and Mo. The imposing man with the most gold on his shoulders glowered at them. In fact, his entire body vibrated with rage. She'd never seen anyone look so pissed.

She was surprised that, when he spoke, the man's tone was grim but his voice soft. "What a sad day for Botswana. I'm sorry you had to see this carnage." He held out his hand. "I'm Colonel Shonga, commander of the Botswana Defence Force wildlife operations. This is Major Bisi. I believe you know Jack. He's the point person for management of this concession."

Reese took the lead. "Yes. We've met. I appreciate you speaking with us. We're with Africa Trust and were doing research nearby. We'd like to gather some information. Perhaps be of assistance. What a tragedy."

"This is the worst we've encountered. There'll be hell to pay since the poachers slipped in right under our noses." The colonel straightened. "Maybe it's not a bad thing that you see what we're up against here in Botswana and the rest of Southern Africa."

A few hours later, the trio caught a Delta Wild plane to Noka Camp, where they were staying for the next leg of the research trip. Alexa stared at the Okavango Delta as it unspooled below, a kaleidoscope of tans and greens. Wide plains with grasses browning in the dry season. The Okavango River and its serpentine web of channels cutting through emerald-green reeds and papyrus. Stands of tall trees. All overlaid by a welter of narrow, sandy vehicle tracks and game trails. In this remote part of Botswana where she and Reese did their research, they had to fly in private planes from camp to camp. Going by land could take days. In some cases, direct land routes between camps didn't even exist.

The Delta region was carved into National Parks and government-owned concessions leased long-term to photo safari companies like Delta Wild. This land management model maintained the Delta as a wilderness for the wild animals that made the Okavango their home. Most of the through-roads were unpaved, some thick with the sand of the region.

While she watched the unfolding panorama below, Alexa's mind kept coming back to the elephant massacre. She had seen dead people. Some who'd died violently. Two men had died at her hands in self-defense. All those deaths had shaken Alexa to her core. It was somewhat surprising that the wanton murder of these elephants had affected her as much as some of the human deaths she'd encountered. Alexa pictured the baby elephant, its long lashes failing to conceal an eye gone dull with death. A tiny victim.

That was it. The common thread. These elephants were just as surely victims as Elizabeth Nelson, who Alexa had found dead in the woods near her cabin, or Cecily Townes, who'd been murdered in her own home. Senseless violence. Senseless deaths. The predatory nature of the crime and the perpetrators' disdain for the lives of their prey, whether human or animal, struck a common chord of outrage in Alexa. She went hot with anger. *These monsters should pay.*

As the pilot circled the runway to make sure it was clear of animals, Alexa stole a glance at Reese. He'd had his eyes closed for most of the flight. Two seats forward, Mo was looking out the window. She suspected that both were still having trouble processing the morning's tragedy too.

Back at their quarters near the staff section of Noka Camp, Alexa took a shower, glad for the solar-heated water. Long after she'd rinsed off the soap, she continued to scrub furiously at her arms and legs.

"Save some hot water for me," Reese called from the bedroom of the two-room tent. When he walked into the cramped bathroom, he stopped short. "Oh, sweetheart. No amount of scrubbing is going to wash away what we saw today." He caught Alexa's wrist with his hand.

"It was awful." Alexa's lip quivered and then the tears flowed. "They killed the babies too. Why? Why?"

Reese kicked off his boots and stepped into the shower fully clothed. He wrapped Alexa in his arms and murmured, "It was terrible. I know. I know."

Then, he reached around her to shut off the water and grabbed a towel. "Why don't you get dressed? Or maybe take a nap?" He kissed her damp forehead.

"I'm okay. We should see if we can get a snack." Alexa stepped out of the shower stall, wiping her face with the towel. "Why don't you take a shower and then we can run up to the dining tent?" She wasn't hungry, but afternoon tea might be a distraction.

She turned to hang her towel on a hook and giggled. Reese was still standing in the shower, his clothes dripping wet. "I guess you already took your shower. Plus, cleaned your shirt and pants. Remember, Noka is one of the camps that does laundry. I hear they have a perfectly good washer and dryer."

Reese laughed and unbuttoned his shirt cuff with an extravagant motion. He proceeded to disrobe in a goofy striptease, pausing between each piece of clothing to wring it out and hang it over the canvas stall.

"Lucky you're wearing quick-dry clothes." Alexa laughed.

"Except for these." Now completely naked, Reese twirled a thick wool sock in each hand.

"Take your shower," Alexa shouted and ran from the room, still chuckling. In the bedroom, she slipped on fresh clothes and stretched out on the queen-size bed, amused and comforted by Reese's efforts to distract them both from the morning's trauma. The overhead fan kept the small room cool, even though it was a warm afternoon outside the canvas walls.

As much as she fought it, her mind kept wandering back to the field of elephants. She'd seen dead animals, of course. Every day out here on the Okavango Delta, the resident animals played out a life-or-death struggle; eat or be eaten. The predators, like the big cats she and Reese were studying, organized their entire lives around the hunt. Find vulnerable prey. Take them down and gorge. Then rest up for the next hunt. The prey also focused on survival. Eat while the rains were good and the area rich with vegetation. When the dry season came and the Delta floodwaters with it, they tracked the revitalized plant life, making the most of the fresh flush of grazing. Then, when the Delta waters receded, they scraped for food again until the rains returned.

But the mass slaughter of elephants by poachers? Only humans could up-end the natural cycle by introducing a dark, savage element like this elephant kill. With that gloomy thought, Alexa closed her eyes and drifted into sleep.

"Wow, I guess I needed that nap you suggested more than I realized. Sorry I checked out on you like that. I hope you didn't mind missing tea," Alexa said, holding Reese's hand as they walked toward the dining tent.

"Don't be sorry. I wasn't that surprised when I got out of the shower and saw you dozing. I'm glad you got some rest after . . . that scene today. It was exhausting. I sat out on the deck and tried to read." He smiled. "I ended up closing my eyes for a few seconds too."

Alexa squeezed his hand. "Hope your nap was as dreamless as mine."

"It was. This morning's waking nightmare was enough for one day," Reese released her hand and guided her by the small of her back into the crowded canopy of the dining tent.

"Rough day, I hear?" Nick Fuller, the male half of the couple that managed the upscale Noka Camp, greeted Alexa and Reese at the entrance to the main lounge. "How about a gin and tonic to ease the stress?"

"You heard about the elephants? No gin for me. Maybe a glass of white wine. Do you have any of that Chenin Blanc?" Alexa asked just as Nick's fiancée, Emma, approached.

"Brilliant choice," Emma exclaimed and looked at Reese. "And you?"

"I'll stick with a beer. St. Louis, please."

Emma sailed off toward the bar.

Nick put a hand on Reese's shoulder, "We've placed you two next to us at dinner. I want to hear firsthand about this poaching. Hard to believe all the rubbish on the radio network this afternoon. Right now, I have to go meet and greet."

Alexa sank into a couch upholstered in Kuba cloth fabric, emotionally exhausted from the day's events, even after her unplanned afternoon nap. For a moment, she focused on the night sounds outside the open-air lounge. Covered only by a sweeping canvas roof, the large structure had no barriers to the velvety African dusk. As night fell, thousands of tiny bell frogs chimed in the reeds edging the channels that surrounded Noka Camp. She closed her eyes and smiled at the tinkling chorus. One of the camp staff brought their drinks, and Reese sat down beside her.

"Sounds like the elephant kill has hit the camp grapevine," Alexa said.

Reese ran a hand through his curly brown hair. "Not surprising. I bet the story hits the international news, especially since Botswana's so-called shoot-to-kill policy has gotten so much attention. No matter how controversial, their hardline policies have proved fairly successful in preventing poaching." He paused. "Up to now."

"No doubt this will affect the debate about those policies that's going on in the capital," Alexa replied.

A tall, wiry man with a shock of sun-streaked red hair plopped onto the chair across from them and said, "The international news? Already happened, *boet*. I read several articles online from Britain and the States before I met my safari group at Maun this afternoon. Bad news travels fast."

"Harry. Didn't expect to see you here." Alexa smiled at the tanned man, dressed like everyone there, in khakis—the uniform of African safari guides, camp staff, and travelers alike.

"You've been out in the field for a few weeks, right? I haven't seen you at Chapman's," he said.

Reese gave the South African-native guide, now Botswana citizen, a light punch on the arm. "Missed us, right? You don't like drinking alone?"

Harry winked at Alexa and said, "Not you, but I have missed your lady friend here. She elevates the conversation, shall we say."

Reese ignored Harry's flirting and said, "We have tomorrow here, then we fly back to Maun. I have to head over the border to Zimbabwe and check in with the project there on Monday."

"And I have a meeting with the Conservation Commission, which is drafting the new legislative proposals. So, I'm off to Gaborone." Alexa's expression brightened. "This poaching mess should light a fire under parliament."

"Don't bet on it, cupcake. Botswana politics are more complicated than the British Parliament and US Congress combined." The guide frowned.

"What are you telling your safari tour group?" Reese asked.

"About the poaching? The truth. Some unknown group of wankers cut down an entire family of endangered elephants so they could sell the tusks to another group of rich wankers in Asia. And that group of wankers will sell pieces of ivory to mostly Asian consumer wankers who care more about having a pretty trinket or getting it up for the ladies than the lives of gentle giants on a continent far, far away." Harry rose abruptly. "I have to get back to my flock. They're about to announce dinner."

The group of fifteen was seated at a single, long table, elegant with china and flickering candlelight. The ten people at the far end buzzed with anticipation at what the first day of their safari might bring. Alexa remembered how, on her first safari to Tanzania and Kenya, she'd been ecstatic to embark on the long-awaited adventure. Both informative and charming, Harry had the group well-in hand.

She whispered to Reese, "He's good at this."

"He should be. He's been guiding for more than ten years."

Emma turned back to the table after speaking to the lead waiter. "You're talking about our Harry, right? I'm thrilled that Delta Wild has assigned him back here to Noka for six weeks after he finishes with this group tour. He's lovely to have around. Guests go crazy for his whole dashing adventurer vibe."

"Darling, should I be jealous?" Nick asked in a droll voice. "After all, I spent years in the bush guiding big game hunts and then a few more guiding for Delta Wild. I can't think of a single time you've called me dashing."

Alexa raised an eyebrow. Nick was fit enough. The guy was probably in his late thirties, maybe early forties, and had that weathered look that comes from spending much of your life in the African sun. It was a look that she usually found attractive; but, in Nick's case, a whiff of the effete undercut the appeal. He always made her think of one of the snobbish aristocrats in a Jane Austen novel.

Laughing, Emma put her hand on Nick's. "Don't get your knickers in a twist, love. I'm yours, body and soul. But you're the dashing-yet-responsible camp manager now. That's a different role."

Reese asked, "Harry says the guests know about the elephant poaching?"

Emma moaned. "Yes. As you'd expect, they're upset. Such a perfectly awful thing to happen. Especially on their first day here. You saw the dead ellies, I hear?"

Alexa nodded. "It was pretty terrible. Hard to believe that people could just butcher those beautiful animals."

"Of course, you Americans lead such sheltered lives." Nick's tone was light but held an undercurrent of disdain. "Here in Africa, violence is not unusual."

Emma gave her fiancé a warning look. "Nick . . ."

Alexa bit her lip and thought. *Little do you know about the violence I've experienced. Reese has dealt with some pretty rough situations as well.*

Reese responded, his tone grim, "Many Americans aren't nearly as sheltered as you might think. Have you heard anything? Did the BDF find the poachers?"

"No. Those boyos are still on the loose. They're likely halfway across Namibia or Angola by now, heading for the coast," Nick said.

With a flick of her hand, Emma said, "Well, I hope we've seen the last of them. I would hate for more of our beautiful ellies to be killed. Not to mention the impact on bookings if guests start to worry about poachers."

Alexa sipped a spoonful of pumpkin soup. Despite its comforting warmth, she shivered. The prospect of running into ruthless armed poachers during their work out in the bush was something she hadn't even considered.

CHAPTER THREE

THE NEXT MORNING, Alexa, Reese, and Mo set off at dawn to track down the Noka Pride. Yesterday's fallen elephants haunted Alexa. In the gray half-light, every bush and termite mound they passed morphed into an elephant corpse. When Mo pointed out the lion pride in the distance, Alexa sighed with relief. The sight of three cubs scrambling over a fallen tree provided a welcome distraction for her overactive and gloomy imagination.

"Look behind the tree. They've taken down a kudu," Mo said.

Alexa grinned. "Not much left. How can you tell it's a kudu?"

"The horns. Can't you see the face?" Reese turned to find Alexa smirking. "I get it. You're joking."

"Hey. It was a rough day yesterday. We need a little bush humor."

Mo maneuvered the Land Cruiser close to the pride, which was focused on finishing the night's kill.

"They look very healthy," Reese observed.

"Lots of prey in this area, and they're easy to spot near the water at this time of year," Mo stopped snapping photos long enough to reply.

"I only see twelve cats. Didn't you say there are thirteen in this pride?" Alexa asked. "Oh wait. Over there comes a juvenile male."

"A little late to the party." Reese focused on the distant cat with his binoculars. "No. His face is smeared in blood. He's coming back for seconds."

In late morning, the research team left the now-sated lions to sleep off the feast and headed back toward Noka. When they approached a huge tree along a riverbank on the right, Mo backed in beneath it and said, "Time for some tea and coffee?"

All three scanned the branches above them for leopards before they left the vehicle. Mo unpacked a thermos of coffee and another of tea from a basket then set out cups and tins of scones and fruit on the hood of the Land Cruiser. While Reese and Mo talked about ordering some new equipment for the research project, Alexa kept an eye on a herd of impala grazing in the tall grass on the far side of the river. She nibbled on a scone and drank almost an entire cup of tea before she spoke. "This has been a much better morning than yesterday."

Reese snorted. "No, kidding." He scrunched the back of Alexa's neck in a playful squeeze.

"I wanted to tell you," Mo put his cup on the hood, "the guides were talking at dinner last night. Turns out those weren't the first poached elephants this season. Three elephants, all big bulls, turned up dead in Chobe; one in June, two in July. Authorities thought it was a random poacher, and they stepped up patrols in the National Park. The talk was that those kills could be related to yesterday's incident."

"Like practice runs?"

"Yes. Even though yesterday's massacre was quite some distance from Chobe itself."

Alexa asked, "This was the first you heard of it though? Doesn't news travel like lightning on the guide circuit?"

"Someone wanted it to stay quiet. Maybe because of those new laws you're working on?"

"Could be. It's been difficult to get the two sides together on the sanctions for poachers."

Mo nodded. "After what happened yesterday, the guides are so upset. Those who knew about the earlier poaching—they couldn't keep quiet any longer. Everyone is concerned."

"They should be. What doesn't make much sense—why pick Botswana's elephants? This country has one of the toughest anti-poaching programs on the continent."

Later that afternoon, Alexa stayed back at Noka Camp to work on her legislative project when Reese and Mo went searching for another nearby pride. All the camp guests were out in the field. Soon, the steady tap, tap, tap of hammers somewhere outside the canvas wall made it hard for Alexa to concentrate. Sighing, she escaped her cramped staff quarters and walked up to the main lounge to work. She'd no sooner opened the latest draft document when Emma approached.

"I'm interrupting, right?" the camp manager said as she perched on the couch across from Alexa.

"Not a problem. I was just getting started." For the most part, Alexa found Emma's constant cheeriness engaging. In her mid-twenties, the pale brunette was just a few years younger than Alexa. Something about her perpetual sunshine also seemed a bit naïve and made Alexa want to take the wide-eyed romantic under her wing.

Alexa closed her computer. "You don't mind if I hang out here, do you? It was pretty noisy back in our tent."

"Of course; stay here." Emma looked around the empty area with a grin. "It's not like you're disturbing anyone. We're doing some construction back there near your quarters. Building a new facility to house equipment. They try to work while the guests are off on a game drive or boat trip."

"Thanks. I have to review a document before my meeting in Gaborone next week."

"That's right. You're representing Africa Trust on a commission that's advising on the new conservation bill. Is that something you did in the States? Conservation legislation?"

Alexa set her laptop on the cushion beside her. "Not specifically, but I did chair a State committee that worked on sex-trafficking legislation. And I volunteer for an environmental organization at home.

"I'm finding the Commission interesting. A parliamentary environment is somewhat different than the way things work in the States. And, of course, the Tribal Council is a new aspect for me too. I hope the Commission wraps up its recommendations before we head back home so I can see the results of our work."

"Head back home." Emma sighed. "That sounds so lovely right now. Even Gaborone sounds wonderful, and I actually hate all the noise there. The hustle and bustle are just too chaotic for me."

Alexa frowned. "Are you getting tired of this whole camp manager gig? How long do you stay out here without a break? I love it in Botswana, but I have to admit I miss my dog, Scout; my family, my yoga classes . . ."

"Funny, sometimes it's the most mundane things I long for; like the morning mist rolling down the hill near my parents' cottage." Emma flashed a wistful smile. "I still love this job. I'm in real need of a rest though. We've been going nonstop with a completely full camp for nearly five months. Nick and I give each other a day off now and then, just to chill. He's flown into Maun and back a few times on his off days. Usually, I'm happy to just spend the day reading and relaxing by the pool. Now I've reached the antsy point."

"You get a long break, don't you? When's that?"

Emma's eyes brightened. "Yes. We get three months off starting at the end of September. That's the trade-off to all these months out here in the bush. Last time we spent most of the break with Nick's family in Zimbabwe. This year, I am going home for at least a month. Merrie Olde England."

"End of September. Just a month and a half away." Alexa's tone was encouraging.

"Righto. It will be here before we know it." Emma stood up. "I'll swan off so you can get to it. I have to go check on dinner arrangements. Can I send out a drink for you? Iced tea? Coca-Cola?"

"A Coke would be perfect," Alexa said. "I'll see you later." She spent a few minutes gazing out at the thick palms that covered the small island housing Noka Camp. Then, she picked up her laptop and plunged into the proposed legislative changes that the Commission would be discussing in a few days.

"You look tired, or is it unhappy? How was your afternoon?" Alexa asked Reese as they walked the well-trod path that led from the staff village across a small bridge to the dining tent. He had rushed into their room very late, with just enough time to shower and change. So, they hadn't had a chance to talk.

He drew Alexa in for a quick hug. "Sherlock Williams. You can always detect my moods, especially when I'm feeling down." His blue eyes darkened. "To answer your question, not a great afternoon in the field. We didn't find the Marula Pride until dusk. They weren't in any of the usual spots that Mo finds them. Not surprising, given all the activity out there. The lions could have been hiding from the commotion. Then, things quieted down, and three lionesses came out to hunt very late in the day. We'll have to come back up here to do a full observation."

"What kind of activity would make the cats hide? They're used to safari vehicles."

"BDF and Wildlife Services. A lot of bigger trucks. A helicopter circled overhead at one point."

Alexa brightened. "They've widened the search this far? Do you think they had a lead on the poachers?"

"Not from what Mo could learn from the guide network. Word was they found no trace of the poachers in the Kagiso or Chobe areas yesterday, so they were fanning out to the surrounding concessions. How did the poachers move all that ivory overnight? You'd think the BDF could track a transport truck. It would have to be quite large."

"Could have used a boat. The dead elephants were right by the river," Alexa suggested.

"Maybe. They expanded the search grid pretty quickly, so it seems they think the poachers have left the immediate area of the kill."

At the main camp, Alexa and Reese headed first to the lounge for a drink. The space that stood empty in the afternoon was packed with Harry's safari group, who were now chatting like old friends. Two other couples wearing country-club casual wear stood near the bar, looking a bit out of place.

Alexa scanned the room. "Is Mo joining us tonight?"

"Nah. He said he was going to eat with his guide buddies. He prefers the local cooking in the staff tent."

"Figured as much. He's a great researcher but doesn't seem too keen on socializing." Alexa smiled.

"Africa Trust pays him for the research, so that's the only thing I'm interested in. And yes. He is a great researcher. One of our best." With a thumbs-up, Reese headed toward the bar and called back over his shoulder, "Same wine as last night?"

Alexa nodded and considered approaching the country club quartet. Maybe put them at ease. She turned in their direction.

"Not so fast," Harry spoke at her shoulder. "The Texans can wait."

"They're Texans?" Alexa asked in an amused voice.

"Not blonde enough for Germans. And look at all the gold around the ladies' necks and arms. Texans or Russians for sure."

"How were your game drives today? Reese said there was a lot of BDF activity out there."

"Yeah. Lucky they clued in our drivers early, so we headed away from the search area."

"Any word on whether they caught the poachers?" Alexa glanced toward the bar where Reese was talking to the maybe-Texans.

Harry shook his head. "It would seem not. My group's off to the Moremi tomorrow, so we should be well away from the hubbub. I fear that the poachers are long gone." He frowned. "Watch out for our president to turn this incident into a call to restore more hunting concessions."

"What do you know that I don't, Harry? I would think the exact opposite. President Makwala has been all over the move to step up penalties for poachers and animal parts traffickers. Are you saying he has a hidden agenda?"

"*Bokkie*, everyone has an agenda, and they're not always that hidden. Our esteemed president was a partner in several of the old hunting concessions before he went into government. I've been here in Botswana long enough to know some of the history. I'm just saying, be careful that you don't swim too deep without understanding the political currents." Harry touched Alexa's arm and strode across the room to his tour group.

"You and Harry looked pretty intense." Reese handed Alexa a glass slick with condensation.

"He was giving me a heads-up about President Makwala. Apparently, he used to own hunting concessions. I get the idea that Harry doesn't quite trust the president's commitment to the new, no-big-game-hunting Botswana. Important to know for my work on the Commission." Alexa sipped the white wine, which had lost its chill. "I see you were chatting up the newcomers?"

"Yes. This is their first night on safari. They'll be staying at four Delta Wild camps over ten days. Never been to Africa before so they're both excited and scared. Especially the lady with the gray hair. She asked a lot of questions about lion attacks."

"Where are they from?" Alexa took another sip.

"Dallas," Reese answered and then clapped Alexa on her back after she snorted and choked on the wine.

Tonight, Emma had broken the diners into three groups. Harry's safari group and the four Texans sat at separate tables in the dining hall. Alexa and Reese sat with Nick and Emma on the deck outside the tented structure.

"What a gorgeous night." Alexa leaned back to take in the starry sky. No light pollution touched these remote Delta camps like Noka, so the stars shimmered like diamonds across the velvet black sky. Out in the nearby channel, a pod of hippos splashed and grunted.

Nick replied, "So, it is. We should have another eight weeks or so of this clear, dry weather. Then, we'll be on the cusp of the rainy season. When are you bringing your friends back here? Doing an official safari with them, if I recall correctly?"

"Mid-September," Reese said. "Not long after that, we'll be heading back Stateside. Hard to believe our time in Botswana is more than half over."

Alexa caught the sad note in her boyfriend's voice and bit her lip. She'd worried from the start that Reese would come here to Africa and want to stay. That old tension—Africa or Pennsylvania—again loomed over their relationship. Alexa was content with her life in Pennsylvania. A few years past, she'd returned to her hometown after years in New York City and a demanding job at a high-powered law firm. She'd chosen the serenity of a cabin in the woods, a partnership in the family law practice, and time for friends and family. When she'd met Reese, she thought she'd found everything she wanted.

Then, their relationship had hit a rough patch. Reese received a job offer on a wildlife project in Kenya, and he left for the country he'd learned to love in his first job after college. When he returned to Pennsylvania this past winter, they found their way back to each other. Reese moved into Alexa's cabin, and everything had clicked into place. She was happy with Reese, happy with her life.

Just a few months into this bliss, Reese's employer asked him to take on a special assignment. Africa Trust wanted him to spend four months in Botswana, filling in for a manager who needed surgery. Alexa had decided that, this time, she'd come along. For the experience. To show Reese that she understood his connection to African wildlife. Because she didn't want to spend four months without him. In fact, the package had seemed more like an all-expenses-paid safari than work—even though Africa Trust had even thrown in a temporary job for her. And the managing partner at Alexa's family law firm, her brother, Graham, had gladly rearranged schedules and assignments to smooth her four-month sabbatical.

Turns out that Alexa was loving this time in Botswana even more than she'd anticipated. Spending days outdoors, the focus on animals, living in a foreign country—she felt like, each day here, she got to unwrap an exciting new experience. But still she viewed this as an extended vacation. She would be happy to see home at the end of September.

She wasn't so sure about Reese's thoughts on returning to Pennsylvania. In her deepest heart, Alexa thought of Africa as a rival for Reese's affections. He'd left her for the lure of life in Africa once before. She could never be completely sure that Reese would choose her over the lions, the bush, and the siren song of life in the wild.

Almost as if she sensed Alexa's train of thought, Emma said, "Like I told Alexa earlier, I'm anxious to pop home to England for a visit later this year. But I'll be even more anxious to return to Botswana. You know that old saying, Africa gets in your blood. I believe it's true. When I came here for the hotel management internship, I could barely tear myself away at the end of the six months. I came back to Botswana right after I graduated, taking the first job I could get—an activities coordinator at one of the lodges in Chobe."

"Until I convinced her that she needed to experience a camp in the real bush." Nick smiled.

"And, of course, Nicky was right." Emma patted her fiancé's arm.

"Where do you call home?" Reese asked Nick.

"I've been in Botswana for more than a decade."

Alexa said, "You said something last night about guiding big game safaris in Zimbabwe?"

Nick hesitated, then overcame an apparent reluctance to discuss his personal life. "When I was born, Zimbabwe was still Rhodesia. My family were farmers there." His tone turned bitter. "You may know some of the story. Rhodesia was a British colony. We had a rough transition to independence, first with Britain then over a decade of internal strife. Guerilla warfare known as the Rhodesian Bush Wars.

"Finally, international pressure and civil unrest brought down the White-run minority government. I was just a newborn when the country transitioned to the new, Black-run government of Zimbabwe. From the start, the new government planned to take White-owned lands and give them to Blacks. To encourage Black farming. To right what were perceived as historical wrongs. Called it Land Redistribution. My family was under a lot of pressure to sell but held on. It got dangerous for a while, so they sent me to live with my uncle. He was wired into some big-time politician who had President Mugabe's ear. So, his land wasn't targeted, and his big game business thrived."

"Must have been a tough change in your life," Reese murmured.

"I did okay. My uncle took me under his wing and trained me. Gave me a guide job after university. My parents continued to work the farm. I went home to visit whenever I could." He grimaced. "They survived the Bush Wars and re-distribution, but their luck ran out with Mugabe's compulsory land reform . . ." Nick choked off the last word and dropped his fork.

Alexa hadn't quite followed Nick's litany of events in Zimbabwe history. She knew that Zimbabwe had long been a much less-stable country than Botswana and had been devasted economically under years of Robert Mugabe's dictatorship. That the country now had hope under new democratic leadership. So, she zoomed in on his last point. "Oh no," Alexa cried. "Did your parents lose the farm?"

Nick just stared at the table with no response.

With a sad expression, Emma shook her head. "Far worse. They were killed. A group of ex-soldiers, probably old ZANU rebels, killed Nick's dad and mum and ran off all the farmworkers. It was never prosecuted, like much of the violence during that time. A former colonel in ZANU took over the property soon after."

"ZANU?" Reese asked.

"Zimbabwe African National Union. It started as a militant group and morphed into a political party," Emma explained.

"I'm so sorry," Alexa told Nick.

"What a tragedy," Reese said, shaking his head.

Nick raised his eyes. "It's been years now. Don't know why this hit me so hard tonight, telling you about it. In a way, my uncle Duncan saved my life. If I had gone back to the farm, I would have been killed too." Nick straightened in his chair and gave a crooked smile. "So, that's the long answer to where I spend my holidays. I spend my free time with Uncle Duncan. Emma often goes with me, of course.

"Speaking of my uncle, he had some news about poaching when I rang him up today. He says there have been a few incidents on the outskirts of Hwange. There are huge elephant populations over there, what with the boreholes. Nothing as big as yesterday at Kagiso."

Reese muttered, "I'll see what I can find out about it when I'm in Zim next week. Hope the authorities here and across the border can track these poachers down."

"Oh, lovely," Emma interrupted. "Our first course."

On the short walk back to their room, Alexa said to Reese, "Well. Tonight's conversation just goes to show you can never know what someone else has experienced in life."

"Yeah. Nick comes across as . . ." Reese paused as if searching for the right word. "A bit of an upper-class lightweight. I had him pegged as one of the types I encountered in Kenya: post-Colonial and still, after all this time, longing for the past. Guess I underestimated him."

"Makes you reconsider," Alexa replied. "I was a little pissed last night at his remark about soft—no, 'sheltered'—Americans. Turns out he might have a point. My parents and yours are alive, well, and enjoying their homes without threat. Still, it rankles me how dismissive and, in a weird way, condescending, his remark was. Not everyone in the States has an idyllic life."

"That's for sure."

Alexa slowed and tuned into the pulsing darkness around them. The camp was totally open to the wild, so they had to be alert for animals on the prowl, especially at night. Something rustled in a nearby tree. In the distance, the low, grunting roar of a lion rose on the wind. Talking more to herself than to her boyfriend, Alexa whispered, "I love Botswana. I love Africa, but the undercurrent of violence; sometimes I can feel it in the air. Tonight, that violence is hard to ignore."

Pulling her sweater tight, she hurried to catch up to Reese.

CHAPTER FOUR

SLINGING HER BACKPACK over a shoulder, Alexa closed the door of the Land Cruiser and walked onto the wide front porch.

Sophie called out from behind the open cargo door of the vehicle, "It's locked. Everyone is out in the field today." The petite Africa Trust office manager dragged a cloth bag filled with office supplies from the vehicle and hurried up the steps, keys dangling from her fingers.

Reese followed with a duffel bag in each hand. "Thanks for picking us up, Sophie. Is anyone expected in tonight?"

Sophie replied as she opened the door and they walked into a big foyer, "Nobody's here until Monday. And we have the staff meeting on Thursday, so we could have a full house then. Take advantage of the quiet and enjoy your weekend alone." She flashed a smile.

Alexa replied, "Time on our own sounds great. Staying at the camps is wonderful. I'm so glad that Delta Wild donates our housing and meals when we're out in the field. All the staff at the camps are so accommodating." She sighed. "But sometimes it's nice to have a meal without having to be sociable."

"Ah, yes." Sophie giggled. "I don't know if I could do all that chit-chat every night. I'm more like the bush baby who likes to be on her own after dark, hiding in my little cozy home."

Reese peered at the young manager. "Yes. Your eyes are big and round, just like a bush baby's. I see the resemblance now."

Sophie cracked up. Still laughing, she said, "I'll be in the office. Sally made some soup and stocked up on fresh provisions. She'll be back Monday morning at nine."

Reese said, "We'll be gone by then. Alexa flies to Gaborone on the first flight out. And you arranged a seat for me on the Delta Wild plane to Hwange, right? We won't need a ride. We'll take the small car and leave it at the airport."

Sophie nodded and walked toward the door that led into the two side rooms that Africa Trust used for its Maun office. The rest of the house was home base for the research staff who moved throughout the Botswana bush. Many stayed here when they came in from the field.

"Thanks. I'll stop in soon and catch up on everything else. You leave at noon today, right?" Reese took a few steps toward the back of the house, where the project manager's suite was located.

"Yes. At noon sharp. I must meet my friend."

"Later, Sophie," Alexa called as she followed Reese toward their suite.

A splash out on the Thamalakane River startled Alexa, who was half-dozing on the screened-in porch that overlooked Maun's main river. Turning toward the noise, she watched two mokoros glide past. She raised her hand in a wave when she recognized the polers standing in the back as boatmen from a resort upstream. Likely, the couples in each of the narrow dugout canoes were guests of the resort. Alexa enjoyed the occasional glimpses she'd had of the Sundowner Resort's mokoros since they still used the original wooden version of the boats. Most camps in the Delta had converted to lighter, more durable fiberglass. However, mokoros were rare here on the Thamalakane. The majority in the Maun area plied the shallower Delta waters near Boro. Small motorboats were the more common mode of river traffic behind their lodging here.

Now fully awake, Alexa glanced at her watch. Four o'clock, which meant ten in the morning at home. She strolled inside to find Reese. As usual, he was sitting on the living room couch, hunched over a computer with piles of papers scattered on the seat around him.

Alexa walked to the back of the couch, leaned over, and kissed her boyfriend on the crown. "Hey. It's late enough that we can call Melissa and Jim. Saturday morning there. They might be home."

"Okay." Reese sighed. "Sophie gave me all of the reports from the field. She's done a great job of putting the data together. Now I'm trying to find any trends by pride, by region, by total study area. It's slow going." He turned and flashed Alexa a smile. "A break sounds great."

A few minutes later, they were huddled in front of Alexa's laptop, talking to her best friend, Melissa, in Pennsylvania. Alexa missed her bestie and looked forward to her upcoming visit. While she'd made several connections with people here, her time in Botswana had been short and much of it on the road in Gabs and various camps. None of her new Botswana friendships compared to the bond she'd shared with Melissa since their school days.

"You are both so tan and healthy-looking." Melissa beamed.

"Lots of outdoor time; lots of fresh air. What can we say?" Alexa giggled. "You and Jim will be here soon. Those few weeks will fly by. We can't wait."

"Where is your new husband?" Reese asked.

"Working. He's been pulling weekend shifts lately. You know how crowded the parks get over the summer, so he's been super busy. My assistant has been covering the gallery on Saturdays so I can stay home with the boys. I'm getting tons of photos of the two of them. I'm thinking of doing an exhibit: The Mastiff and the Frenchie."

"Ansel and Scout are still getting along okay?"

"Best buddies. Ansel will be distraught when his big friend leaves. Just a minute." Melissa turned away from the screen and cooed, "Scout, come here and see who's on Skype."

Soon the screen filled with the huge head of Alexa's English mastiff, Scout.

"Hey, buddy. Are you being a good boy for Melissa? I miss you," Alexa said to the dog.

Scout whined.

Off-camera, Melissa laughed and said, "I swear he recognizes your voice. Maybe even your face. His whole body is wagging."

Reese leaned into the screen. "See you soon, Scout. Be a good boy."

"All right. My turn. Go play with Ansel." Melissa reappeared on the screen. "We're counting the days until we leave. Victoria Falls, Ebony Camp, and then we'll be on your doorstep. I'm almost finished packing. Already."

Alexa said, "We're anxious to see you. Make sure you pack bug spray with DEET. And a fleece. It's still cold here in the mornings."

"That sounds heavenly. It was ninety-five here yesterday. The dogs huddled near the air-conditioning vents most of the day. Today's a little more bearable."

"In the dry season here, ceiling fans are the most you'll need—even at the hottest point in the afternoon," Alexa replied.

Melissa giggled. "Thanks for the packing tips. You sound like old Africa hands. I hope you won't be bored on our safari."

"No way. We're thrilled to have a chance to play tourist." Reese laughed. "It will be nice to focus on animals other than lions and leopards."

"Tough life," Melissa retorted.

Alexa laughed. "We'll let you go. I know Mom has emailed you about picking up Scout. They'll be home from Italy next week."

"Yep. It's all under control. Also, Jim stopped by your cabin a few days ago. Everything looks good. Deidre is taking good care of the place. She even planted your window-boxes with impatiens. Worked out well that she came back here to volunteer this summer."

Alexa grinned. "It did. Her aunt would be proud that Deidre's carrying on the family advocacy tradition with RESIST." Alexa's smile darkened as she remembered finding Cecily Townes, the crusader against sex trafficking, dead in her home—and the danger that had ensued for Alexa and Melissa.

Meanwhile, Reese said, "Thanks to both of you for watching Scout, keeping an eye on the cabin. We owe you big time. I might even have to help Jim with that Corvette engine to pay you back."

"Don't get me started on that car," Melissa mock-growled.

"Talk to you soon. Give Scout an extra ear-rub for us. Bye." Alexa ended the call at Melissa's farewell, already missing her friend. The thought of impatiens blooming at the cabin made her both happy and sad.

Reese put his arm around her. "Homesick?"

"Maybe just a little. Especially when I see Scout. I miss Melissa and my family." She grinned. "Don't get me wrong. I'm having a wonderful time here. Having a vacation from the nine-to-five routine is great. I'm enjoying the legal and political work on the Commission. And helping with wildlife research is so different from family law. It's hands-on. Out in the bush. The animals are fantastic." She kissed Reese on the tip of his nose. "I can see why you love this."

Reese's face lit up. "It's amazing, right? Kenya is great, but Botswana is even better. I feel bad that poor Gary needed shoulder surgery. But I love being back in the field for a few months. You get it now, right? Why I love Africa and its wildlife so much?"

Alexa listened to her boyfriend with mixed emotions. This exuberance Reese had for the wild was one of the things she loved about him. He never approached life in half-measures. He was all in.

Still, Alexa experienced a twinge of that old unease. She hadn't needed to hear Reese wax poetic about Botswana to wonder if she was going to lose him again to Africa's siren call. That fear had been building in the back of her mind for a few weeks.

Lost in these thoughts, Alexa replied into an awkward silence. "I do get why you love it." She smiled. "It's beautiful. There's a sort of primal drama that plays out in plain view in the wild. That daily struggle of life and death. It can be seductive and intoxicating. Even in the cities, like Gaborone, you sense that you're not far from that elemental rhythm of the bush. It doesn't seem as, umm, settled is maybe the word, as at home."

Reese nodded, but then Alexa frowned. "I find it a little frightening sometimes." She remembered her unease the previous night in the dark of Noko Camp. "The violence. In the space of a single breath, an animal can slip from one side of the 'kill or be killed' equation to the other. Look at those elephants. They lived a peaceful life, only worrying about guarding their tiniest babies against predators." Her tone turned from sad to angry. "Then, boom! Humans—animals they encounter every day without harm, slaughter them as they're resting for the night."

Reese wrapped his arms around her. "I know. It pisses me off too. The whole idea of killing a beautiful animal for its ivory—for trinkets—is outrageous. But, the Defence Force is good. They may still track the poachers down. I'm sure they're on high alert in case those bastards try again." He paused. "I like to think of the poachers as an anomaly. Angry men who've been cut out of the human herd and have lost their souls, their humanity. Most people in Botswana—heck, most people in the world—want to preserve the elephants and all the wild animals in Africa."

Alexa stood and gave Reese a sad smile. "You have a big heart, Michaels."

"What do you mean?"

"You work every day to help preserve lions and other big cats whose numbers are slowly dwindling due to man's encroachment, to habitat loss, to hunting. And yet you can still believe that mankind has these animals' best interests at heart."

"I absolutely believe that." Reese nodded and ran a hand through his curly brown hair.

"I know." Alexa leaned over to give him a quick kiss. "And I love you for it. Now, I'm going back to the porch to read. Have fun finishing your reports."

The next morning, Alexa opened her eyes to the smell of bacon cooking. Reese's side of the bed was empty, so she eased through the mosquito netting and padded toward the kitchen in bare feet.

Clad in a faded Middlebury College tee and cut-off sweatpants, his feet bare, Reese turned from the stove with a smirk. "Good morning, sunshine. I knew it. Bacon works every time."

Alexa grinned. "Yep. Woke me out of a dead sleep." She looked at the open cartons of eggs, milk jug, and bowls on the counter. "This looks like a major production."

Reese finished transferring the bacon to a platter and swooped over to give Alexa a kiss. "French toast. A complete Sunday breakfast. I've sliced some mango. On the table. And hot water for tea."

"French toast? What a treat. Is there syrup?"

"Maple syrup, no less. Sally has stocked this kitchen with almost anything we'd need."

"Need help?" Alexa stepped back to take a look at Reese's smudged tee shirt and rumpled hair. "I'm not sure who's winning here, you or the French toast."

Reese wiped his forehead, leaving a smudge of batter over his right eyebrow. "Contrary to appearances, I have everything under control. Why don't you clear off the table on the porch so we can eat there?"

"Okeydokey." Alexa gathered napkins and silverware, then filched a piece of bacon before she ran out the door, giggling. "I wouldn't dream of interrupting a master chef at work."

"This is sooo good." Alex beamed at Reese. "I can't remember the last time we had French toast."

"I do. The morning we hiked up to Tumbling Run. Our last hike at home before we flew here." Reese reached over and stroked Alexa's hand. "Remember how Scout jumped into that big pool under the first waterfall?"

"I miss the big beast."

"Me too. Especially the way he bumps his chin on the bed to wake me up first thing in the morning. Not."

Alexa laughed. "He's decided that you're the best companion for morning walks. Just like you're the best bacon chef."

"It won't be long before we see the gigundo dog again. However, we should talk about more immediate issues. Like today," Reese said. "We're in civilization for a change. Want to sally forth and check out the world of men?"

"What? No lions or leopards?" Alexa laughed. "Sure, let's go to the market at Motsana. I want to buy some baskets to take home."

Reese steered the Land Cruiser down the long dusty road that was Maun's main street, slowing for the donkeys and cows that meandered into their path. "It's easier out in the bush. I don't have to remember to drive on the left," he complained.

"Fewer bumps here though. And it is an actual paved road. So, there are trade-offs," Alexa replied as she took in the now-familiar hodgepodge of shacks made from corrugated tin, concrete block houses, rickety restaurants, and make-shift merchandise stands they passed. Dotted in between were long stretches of vacant land, well-kept stucco homes, cute little guest houses, modern chain grocery and retail stores, and entrances to several high-end river lodges. Even after more than two months in Maun, Alexa was fascinated by the stream of people they passed, wearing everything from jeans to khakis to tribal dress.

They drove for almost ten minutes more until Alexa spied a roundabout and said, "This is our turn, right?"

Reese found an open spot amidst the motley cars and SUVs parked in the cultural center's parking lot. "I guess we weren't the only ones with this idea," he muttered as he turned off the engine.

"It's the place to be," joked Alexa, looking at the packed open-air market. As the gateway to the Okavango Delta, Maun was a real crossroads for tourists on safari, backpackers and campers, guides, bush pilots, park personnel, and townies who liked living on the edge of the vast, wild waterway. It was a frontier melting pot, a little like America's Wild West of old.

As they walked toward the vendor booths, Alexa smiled at a group of children playing tag in the dust. Two little girls wore bright native dress. Except for the varying tones of their skin, the four boys looked almost identical in shorts and t-shirts. The last child, a tiny girl with a mass of red curls, looked like she was dressed for church in a crisp pink gingham dress.

Following Reese into the milling crowd of adults, Alexa laughed when they passed a booth hawking baseball caps. "Check this out. Disco Mickey Mouse." She pointed to a garish silver cap with a Mickey logo on the brim.

"A touch of the old USA," Reese chuckled. "Disney's one of our main exports."

"Like the KFC in Maun. Who would've thought?" Alexa took her boyfriend's arm and steered him toward the basket-maker's stall. "Sophie says this lady has the best baskets. Let me go there first. Then we can browse the rest of the booths. I wonder if there are mangoes anywhere?"

Reese rolled his eyes. "Well, if they're the best baskets, you definitely need to buy some."

"Do you have *pula* in case I need it?"

"I have some, but you know everyone in Maun takes US dollars," Reese replied then pointed to a sign next to the baskets. "Including this lady."

Alexa bought seven baskets woven of fine reeds in various colors. Slipping them into her canvas shopping bag, she spoke over her shoulder to Reese. "These will make great gifts for my mom, your mom, Kate, Melinda, Melissa, and Haley. Plus, one for me." It wasn't until Alexa turned that she discovered Reese was not there. Scanning the crowd, she located him a few booths down talking to two men whose backs were to Alexa.

When she reached Reese, his two companions turned to greet her. The sturdy guy with thick blonde hair exclaimed, "Well, if it isn't the Darling of the Delta."

"Hello, Piers."

The taller man rolled his eyes at Alexa and shook his head. "*Dumela*, Alexa. I apologize for this one. He does not reflect well on the honored profession of Delta Wild guide. Perhaps I will report him for misconduct when we return to camp." He grinned.

"You do that, Baruti. I'll sign a complaint if they want." Alexa linked her arm through Reese's and flashed an arch smile. "This guy's the only one who can call me darling."

"What she says." Reese grinned.

"Are you both on leave at the same time?" Alexa asked. "How will your camp survive without you?"

Piers said, "Baruti is starting his month's leave, but I'm just popping down to Jo-burg for a few days. It's my mum's birthday, and Dad is throwing her a big bash. We both head out of Maun tomorrow morning."

Reese looked at Alexa. "Piers and Baruti say that there's been another poaching incident. Upstream on the Thamalakane."

"Oh no. As big as the one near Kagiso?" Alexa cried in distress.

"No. Luckily, only four dead," Baruti said.

Reese sighed and shook his head. "Small mercy."

"Yes," Piers responded. "What concerns me is how close this was to Maun. And, once again, they got away without being spotted. Without BDF even knowing that poachers were in the area. These people are ruthless. And they're getting bolder."

"It's terrible," Alexa moaned. "How many more elephants will they kill before they're stopped?"

Baruti shook his head. "All the guides and management at Delta Wild are quite upset about the elephant poaching. I know that's true for people from the other camps too."

Piers nodded. "Yeah, it angers us. Elephant populations are high here in Botswana, but I don't have to tell you that they're in trouble on the continent. Plus, wholesale death of any species messes with the Delta ecosystem . . ." His voice trailed off and he donned a sheepish grin. "I know I'm preaching to the choir."

Alexa bit her lip. "I just can't get the image of those dead elephants out of my head. If you had seen the babies . . ."

Baruti frowned. "Poaching's a particularly nasty business. Piers and I borrowed a boat to head upriver this afternoon. We're going to check out this latest incident. We want to see this for ourselves."

"If the BDF is still there, they may not welcome you." Reese glanced at Alexa. "At first, they weren't very happy to see us when we crashed the site at Kagiso."

Alexa nodded. "The sight of all those dead elephants inspired us to do everything we can to help track down these poachers. We're going to spread the word to the entire Africa Trust research team to keep an eye out for strange people, suspicious behavior."

"It's a fine line though," Reese said. "These poachers could be dangerous. I don't want any of our researchers running into something they can't handle. Same thing is true for you folks."

"We, at least, have some training on dealing with dangerous situations," Piers replied. "Although our trip today is more about seeing what's happening."

Baruti asked, "Why don't you come with us upriver? Maybe having researchers with us will calm the BDF soldiers."

"Good idea," Piers enthused. "Can you imagine how frustrated these BDF boyos must be? They're known around the world for their success against poachers. Now, they're losing elephants at every turn. You met some of the officers though?"

"We met Shonga himself."

"Well then. We need you two to smooth the way."

Reese gave Alexa a questioning look.

"Sure," she said. She could see from the expression on his face that Reese was anxious to make this unexpected trip. "Our only plan for the rest of the day is dinner at Chapman's."

"Righto then." Piers smiled. "How about we pick you up from Chapman's dock around one o'clock? We'll be back well before time for sundowners."

CHAPTER FIVE

ALEXA LOUNGED NEAR the prow of the aluminum motorboat. A safety cushion cradling her back, her eyes scanned the shallow channel and the marshy grassland that stretched out on either side of the river. Reese and Baruti sat in the stern, flanking Piers, who manned the helm. A canvas roof shaded the small boat from the afternoon sun.

She had mixed emotions about this spur-of-the-moment boat trip into the wild. Being on the water was a great way to spend a Sunday afternoon, but when the destination was the site of another elephant kill, the day lost some of its magic. A cloud scudded over the sun, casting the water in shadow. As the vista turned dark, Alexa abruptly remembered that book she'd read in college, *Heart of Darkness*. Wasn't it about an outsider traveling up an African river to see a colonel about ivory? Intrigued by the thought, she gave a baffled shake of her head. The parallels were just a little too weird—although Colonel Shonga didn't strike her in the least as a madman.

Still, it was telling that she continued to regard herself as an outsider, especially in an area that boasted a healthy mix of natives and expats, old and new. Her few weeks on safari in East Africa a couple of years ago had given Alexa some minimal preparation for this Botswana adventure. Although each day she settled more easily into the rhythm of life here, Alexa still felt a bit out of her depth. For Reese, Botswana was new, but African wildlife research was a job he'd done in the past. He didn't fully grasp that, no matter how much she embraced the experience and even relished that feeling of being a little off-balance, Alexa was still adjusting.

When Piers made a sharp swerve to avoid a crocodile surfacing ahead, Alexa had to grab a roof support to avoid falling. The engine noise scattered a herd of impala on the bank, the sun emerging just as the skittish antelope sailed across a small channel in flight. Smiling at the animals' grace, Alexa turned to Reese, who flashed her a thumbs-up sign.

Making his way forward, he sat down and kissed Alexa's hand. "Doing okay? Every time I glanced up here you looked lost in thought."

She was tempted to reply, 'the horror, the horror,' but Reese had no clue that she'd been ruminating on nineteenth-century classic literature. Suppressing an ironic smile, Alexa said, "Doing fine. We've never been this far up the river, have we?"

"No. Baruti says the channel narrows in a few minutes, and soon we'll dock. They've arranged for a mate, one of the guides from a nearby camp, to pick us up and take us through a gate in the buffalo fence. Then to the poaching site."

"I'm not looking forward to another gruesome scene." Alexa shuddered at a vision of more hacked-up elephant carcasses.

"Piers and Baruti got an update from their guide friend. Although these dead ellies were just discovered, they were killed some time ago. Not a fresh kill."

"Time for the scavengers to do their work," Alexa muttered and breathed a silent sigh of relief. An old carcass, even from just a few weeks past, would be mostly skin and bones. Not the heartbreaking scene they'd witnessed at Kagiso.

No sooner had Reese returned to his seat than the surroundings changed. The wide marshlands gave way to tall reeds and grasses. Piers lowered the boat's speed as they plunged into a narrow opening in the towering vegetation. Alexa recognized the tall plants, typical of the Okavango Delta, as mostly floating reed beds and lacy papyrus. This channel was so slender that she could have reached out and touched the reeds as they passed. Dragonflies and small birds flitted across their path. A few minutes later, the river widened to a bed of water lilies, and Piers headed for the bank on the right.

"*Dumela*." A tall man in khakis slipped out of a safari vehicle to greet them. "You made good time." Piers handed his friend the rope, and the man secured it around a sturdy sapling. As they scrambled onto the bank, Piers yelled, "Reese, Alexa, this is Wilson."

Wilson nodded at Alexa as he shook Reese's hand. "You came to see the bad business? I hear that you saw the worst of it at Kagiso. We all need to help catch these criminals."

"Kagiso was terrible. You're right. We, too, want to see these poachers behind bars," Reese replied. Piling into Wilson's vehicle, they drove along a narrow sand track that curved away from the river and the marshes. After a few minutes' ride, the guide stopped the vehicle at a wide gate. A six-foot fence stretched out into the distance on the left and right. "Can you unlock it, mate?" He handed a key to Piers, who slipped open the gate and then secured it after the vehicle passed through.

"This is only the second time I've seen one of these buffalo fences. Do they work?" Reese asked.

Baruti grinned. "Yes and no. They keep the cattle out of the Delta and prevent disease exchange with the wild herd animals. They keep a lot of elephants from destroying farmers' crops. Yet, you saw the impala along the river. The fences can't contain all the native animals. And they really mess with the migrating herds."

"The debate on these things has raged for years," Piers added. "Back in the day, the powers that be erected them to make sure the cattle complied with European Union beef standards. For sales. That killed off huge numbers of migrating zebra and wildebeest because it interrupted their access to seasonal food and water. In reaction, they did away with many of the fences. Now, they're talking about putting more up."

Alexa said, "I'm on a commission in the capital that's offering advice on wildlife conservation policy. There were some who wanted to add these fences to our list of issues to consider. In the end, the chairman decided we had too much on our plate already. I suspect some of the NGOs will advocate for a new effort to discuss the fences."

"Problem is, there's no perfect answer. For years, the government has been very pro-wildlife, pro-tourism. With elections on the horizon next year, rumors are the tribes have been putting on pressure to change some of the policies, to become less pro-West, as they see it. Who knows what might happen?"

"Yes, the elections are driving the pace of our commission too."

Reese interrupted, "Vehicles ahead."

Slowing, Wilson came to a complete stop when two BDF soldiers stepped into the road and motioned a halt.

"Turn around, please. This area is closed for an investigation. There can be no access."

Wilson, Piers, and Baruti spoke over each other in reply. Alexa didn't follow the conversation in Setswana, but she could read its arc through tone of voice. The guides' original confidence took on a pleading note while the soldiers' calm voices became more adamant and commanding.

Alexa's shoulders slumped. Although she'd had reservations about this trip, they'd come this far. It would be a shame to turn around without seeing what damage the poachers had done here.

Reese must have been getting the same read. He raised a skeptical eyebrow at Alexa, and with a shrug, leaned forward to address the two men from BDF. "Sorry to interrupt, but is Colonel Shonga on-site?" He nodded toward Alexa and continued, "When my colleague and I met with him at the Kagiso incident last week, he asked us to assist in the search for these poachers. So, when we heard about this new discovery, we asked our friends to bring us up here to collect information.

"Oh, sorry. I'm Reese Michaels, head of the Africa Trust Wildlife Research Project. We're based in Maun and throughout the Delta."

The two soldiers exchanged a glance.

"Wait one moment," the shorter one said to Reese in a respectful tone. He marched a few feet away, turned his back, and spoke into a handheld radio. Ending the conversation, he walked to Reese's window. "Colonel Shonga asks that you report directly to the main tent. Just keep driving on this road and you'll see it." He nodded at his partner, and both stepped back to allow the vehicle to pass.

Piers turned to Reese and hooted, "I knew it would help to bring you along. Friends in high places and all that."

Reese ducked his head. "Africa Trust has developed a good working relationship with the government here. And the colonel seems like a good guy."

Wilson shook his head. "There are many who would not agree with that description of Colonel Shonga. He's made a lot of enemies with his laser focus on wildlife. Some say he loves the wild creatures more than people. And that the shoot-to-kill policy has been too unyielding, taking down village boys who were just night fishing or hunting to feed their families."

Alexa asked, "Would you agree?"

"No, I believe his heart is in the right place."

Baruti nodded, "If we don't act now to save the wildlife, it will be too late."

"Righto, brothers." Piers slapped the seat beside him. "We need more men like Colonel Shonga. The jury's still out on his boss, the general. And this president. But Shonga is a right one."

Two BDF soldiers who were waiting out front ushered them to the back of a large open tent that had been erected in a grassy area. Alexa would have called it a canopy rather than a tent, but she wasn't going to quibble terminology with the BDF. As they approached, Colonel Shonga rose from behind the table where he'd been studying maps.

"Welcome," he said. "This one is not so bad as when we last met. But, any loss to poaching is unacceptable."

Reese replied, "Thanks for giving us access to the site. We were in Maun when we heard about this latest discovery. These gentlemen are all Delta Wild guides who helped us get here." He introduced the trio of guides and added, "You've met Alexa, of course."

The colonel turned to the guides. "I'm glad to see you all here. I've just been speaking to your Delta Wild CEO and officials at the other camps throughout the Delta. We're asking for all the guides to help BDF when you're in the field. If you see any signs of poaching or anything that looks suspicious, notify us. Avoid direct confrontation. These men are dangerous. We've set up a radio call sign to contact us immediately."

He looked at Reese and Alexa. "When I was in America, I saw posters about terrorism in the New York subway: 'If you see something, say something.' We will borrow that phrase to ask the entire country to be alert and help us catch these devils. And we are going to contact all the research projects and other NGOs to assist as well. You had suggested this when we spoke at Kagiso."

Reese nodded his head, "Absolutely, sir. Everyone should work together. What we're fighting against is powerful. The lure of big money. What's the going rate on the black market for these tusks?"

"About fifteen hundred US dollars, per kilo. There are some reports that it's gone higher recently. These four elephants appear to have been young adults, so each of their tusks weighed maybe thirty kilos."

Reese whistled. "Just shy of four hundred thousand dollars for a night's work, and maybe two and a half million for the herd at Kagiso."

"Likely more. At Kagiso, there were some older cows that could have had tusks well above the norm. Since our elephant population has been so well protected, the matriarchs and older bulls have been able to live long lives and grow massive tusks. A real prize for these outlaws."

Alexa asked, "Can you tell us if you've made any progress on catching the poachers? Do you think it's the same people here as at Kagiso?"

"We cannot know for certain, but the methodology here is similar. We have some leads we are following, but these people are unusually skilled. I have confidence we will track them down, however, I fear it may not be the quick success that BDF has had in the past."

The colonel turned to his aide. "Joseph, can you show these people the carcasses?"

As the group followed Joseph, Colonel Shonga called out, "I know you'll respect our evidence-gathering process, but if you have any observations to share, stop back as you leave."

Joseph led them across the dusty track where they'd left their vehicle and up a small ridge on the other side. Alexa was surprised when he stopped at the top and pointed to a group of people clustered several yards away at the bottom of the slope. Not much farther beyond, she caught a bright flash; the gleam of sunlight on water.

"Is that the same river we came in on?" she asked.

Wilson nodded. "Yes. The river takes a long loop through narrow channels after the dock and then emerges into these grasslands. They skipped fencing through the loop because the water is so deep and the reeds are so thick. Not many animals pass through that natural barrier."

Reese, Baruti, and Piers plunged down the slope toward several desiccated carcasses. The tension in Alexa's shoulders disappeared when she saw that scavengers had left little but the tough skin and ears. Of course, the natural predators could not have been responsible for the four elephants' missing tusks. Only man could have separated those from the animals and carried them away.

Joseph turned back toward the tent. "I'll leave you now." He pointed at the tall man below who was walking toward Reese. "The captain is in charge of the evidence gathering."

Wilson helped brace Alexa as they descended the steep slope, then he hurried off to join Reese and his fellow guides.

Alexa hung back, reluctant to hear the bitter details of this herd's death. Seeing the dried carcasses wasn't as disturbing as the fresh slaughter of the huge herd at Kagiso. Because she wasn't distracted by blood and ravaged faces, Alexa considered the bigger picture. These poachers. These criminals. How could they waste life so carelessly? All to sell ivory to Asia for trinkets and carvings. Gasping, Alexa clenched her hands into fists and shook with a sudden fury.

Trying to calm down, she pivoted and stalked back up the hill, away from the investigators and her companions. Stopping for several deep breaths, Alexa looked toward the river. Even from this distance, she could see large gouges in the ground at the edge of the water.

That's how they took the ivory away, she speculated. She did the mental conversion. Thirty kilos equaled sixty-six pounds. A tusk of that size would leave a clear path as it was dragged through the marshy ground.

She climbed back up to the road and dug her binoculars from the backpack she'd left in the vehicle. Then, she trudged once more to the top of the small ridge for the best vantage point. With the binocs, Alexa could see broken stems of marsh grass and deep, muddy grooves trailing toward the water. Several yards up the slope, a rope stretched between two stakes to block off the area, making it clear that the BDF investigators were examining the riverbank.

Alexa scanned the water beyond. From this height, she could appreciate the way the channel snaked through the tall reeds, widening into more open areas and narrowing before it disappeared into towering vegetation. Looking far to the left, she could see the roof of their boat at the dock. She swept her gaze to the right too fast and, for a moment, the field of vision through the high-powered lenses wobbled.

Dizzy, she pulled the binoculars from her eyes. "Rookie move, Williams," she snickered. "After all these weeks, you should have Binoculars 101 down pat." Raising the glasses again, she continued her idle scan, stopping abruptly at a flash of silver to the right of a stand of papyrus. Earlier, she'd thought the gleam that had caught her attention was the water. But this river was an opaque, dull brownish green. Was this a BDF boat searching for poachers?

Alexa steadied the binocs to locate the metallic flash; to find a boat. There it was. Strange. The two men sitting in the open jon boat weren't wearing the camouflage uniforms of the BDF. They were dressed in drab tans and browns. Both wore hats. At this distance, Alexa couldn't make out their faces. Something about the shiny baseball cap one wore teased at her brain, but she couldn't figure out why.

Suddenly, the man in the rear of the boat started the outboard motor. The forward man's gaze was focused on the riverbank. As Alexa heard the distant chug of a motor, a BDF Land Cruiser drove along the bank toward the cordoned-off area. She watched it rumble along the water's edge with her naked eye for a few seconds, then saw Reese and the guides coming back up the hill.

When she raised the glasses to check on the boat, it had vanished.

CHAPTER SIX

ALEXA HURRIED TO catch up with Reese, who'd made a beeline for the only open table at Chapman's. Steeling herself to the din of voices, she squeezed past a server with an overloaded tray of drinks and narrowly avoided crashing into a tall man in a crisp linen suit who'd stopped dead in her path.

"Wow. This place is hopping," she said to Reese as she slipped into the chair across from him.

"Sorry I abandoned you, but this looked like our only chance to grab a table."

"You looked just like a lion on the hunt, identifying the prey and zooming in before it disappears," Alexa teased.

Reese scanned the crowded restaurant. "Is it a Botswana holiday or something?"

"I don't think so. Just the usual suspects, but maybe more than most nights." She glanced around at the tables filled with outdoorsy-looking types, most in their twenties or thirties. Men outnumbered the women, and in the mix of animated faces, white had a slight edge over the many shades of brown. Here and there were faces she recognized. Tad Dorsey, a colleague on the Commission she'd be attending tomorrow, was at one of the rowdier tables. Across the room, two Delta Wild guides were flirting with an attractive wild dog researcher.

She leaned forward so Reese could hear her. "Every time I come in here, it reminds me of a saloon in one of those old Westerns. I know that most of these folks are wildlife guides, wildlife researchers like us, and other people who work in camps on the Delta." She lowered her voice. "I like to think there are shady diamond dealers and soldiers of fortune here too."

Reese laughed. "You're right. Maun is a bit like a modern-day frontier town. Although, people tell me it's tame compared to a few years ago."

Alexa picked up her menu and then put it back down. "I know what I want. A burger and fries."

"Me too. Their burgers taste just like American burgers."

Alexa replied, "Now all we need is a server. Pretty is on duty. I saw her coming in." She looked around the room for their usual waitress but stopped short at the sight of a man leaning on the bar.

"What did I tell you?" She angled her head toward the man. "Diamond dealer or soldier of fortune? White linen is a bold choice for the dust of Botswana's dry season. I nearly rear-ended him a few minutes ago and was terrified I'd smudge his jacket."

"Okay. I'll play." Reese feigned confusion. "You're talking, obviously, about the tall Black guy at the bar. The one in the white suit?"

"Yes, Captain Obvious," Alexa sighed. "The one talking to the guy whose back is to us. Is there another person in this entire restaurant wearing a white suit?"

"Doesn't really look like a soldier. This isn't the right part of the country for diamonds. Given the color choice, have you considered man of the cloth, or maybe he's a doctor?" Reese choked on stifled laughter.

Alexa giggled and feigned a frown. "You're not playing the game right. I'm looking for mysterious and exotic."

As Reese opened his mouth to reply, the man in white leaned over to speak into his companion's ear. Face tight, he slapped a fistful of pula onto the bar and stalked toward the door. The second man swiveled on his barstool to face the room, then slid his feet to the floor.

"Is that Nick?" Alexa gasped.

"It is," Reese replied in a matter-of-fact tone.

Adjusting his shirtsleeves, Nick walked out of the room with his head down.

"Weird. He never mentioned that he was coming to Maun when we were at Noka," Reese said.

"I got the impression from Emma that he often hops into Maun for a day here and there, leaving her to run the camp on her own. Maybe he needs a break from the bush. Maybe he has a drinking problem. Or a woman on the side."

"Or he's having a secret affair with a diamond-dealing soldier of fortune who only wears white linen," Reese suggested in a mock-breathless tone, then laughed. "Of course, they may have just struck up a conversation at the bar and disagreed about politics or something."

Alexa saw Pretty approaching to take their order. "You're right. Just because they spoke doesn't mean Nick and Mr. Clean even know each other. My imagination always runs wild in this place. I tell you though. If I were Emma, I'd think twice about a lifetime commitment to old Nicky boy."

As Reese turned toward Pretty with a wide smile, Alexa's heart lifted. This man was brilliant, kind, passionate, and strong. He was a guy you could trust with your heart and your future. Poor, sweet Emma. Nick paled in comparison to a man like Reese. Sooner or later, she was sure the naïve British expat would see through Nick's act.

Tired from the trip upriver and the late night at Chapman's, Alexa slept during the entire hour-and-a-half flight to Gaborone. Still yawning, she took a taxi to her meeting, with a quick detour to drop her bag at a nearby hotel. By the time she climbed the stairs of the gleaming new building on the University of Botswana campus, Alexa was alert and looking forward to the workgroup session.

"Ah, Alexa, welcome. We are expecting two more before we start." Dr. Simon Kopo, the chairman of this working group, greeted as Alexa took an empty seat. The wiry, gray-haired man taught environmental sciences at the university and had been asked by the minister of Environment, Wildlife and Tourism to head the Conservation Commission.

As Alexa gathered her notes, she looked around the room. Today's meeting was the wildlife policies subgroup of the larger Conservation Commission. Although she'd participated for just two months, she had gotten to know most of her colleagues in the workgroup. They represented Botswana-based conservation groups, a few Southern African regional groups, and four international organizations that were registered in Botswana, including Africa Trust. There were also citizen and tribal representatives.

When Reese had been asked to fill in for Gary, the Botswana executive director for Africa Trust, he'd finagled Alexa into the package deal with the argument that she was better qualified to substitute for Gary on the Commission. She'd chaired a Pennsylvania state government committee on sex trafficking and was active in environmental causes at home. Working in another country at such a high level and learning about the conservation issues Botswana faced had been a fascinating process.

After a few minutes passed, Dr. Kopo looked at the clock on the wall and said, "Let us begin. I hope you all have a copy of the draft sent out last week?"

The eleven attendees nodded just as an older woman in bright traditional dress bustled into the room. "I'm so sorry to be tardy," she said as she eased her colorful bulk into a chair.

"No problem, Mrs. Nkala. We're glad that you can attend today's important meeting. We were just about to begin the introductions. Shall we go around the table, as customary?"

Alexa looked around the room again. Only one of the organizations was represented by a substitute at today's meeting, but the professor was a stickler for protocol.

After everyone announced their name and organization, Dr. Kopo cleared his throat and continued. "As you know, the clock is ticking. The minister has asked that the Conservation Commission provide him with a written report no later than the end of August. He wants his staff to review our recommendations before parliament meets in October and takes up changes to current conservation laws. This group has a unique chance to help guide Botswana in making even greater progress to preserve our wildlife as both a national treasure and an economic resource. After diamonds, tourism is our most important economic driver. Despite the importance of wildlife tourism, there are forces at work to restore big game hunting, reduce penalties for poaching, and endanger the health of our wildlife resources. We've had battles about these very issues in this room." The typically low-key academic's voice had risen during his remarks, and as he said the word 'battle,' he glared at the tribal representative.

The official from the Subia tribe, its people mostly herders, was supposed to represent all the tribes here. Not an easy job. The tribes often disagreed among themselves and, even more often, with the rest of the workgroup. Sometimes, Alexa thought it unclear exactly whose position the tribal official was pushing.

When the tribal rep looked down at the table, Kopo continued: "I'm sure many of you have heard about a large-scale poaching incident just last week near the Namibian border. Almost thirty elephants shot and brutalized for their tusks. Make no mistake, ladies and gentlemen. The work we are doing here is vital."

Dr. Kopo's words moved Alexa, who considered herself a strong advocate for the conservation of animal species that were declining and disappearing in

Africa—hell, worldwide. Witnessing the barbarity of elephant poaching with her own eyes made the issues this group had been discussing very real and very urgent.

In a calmer tone, the chair continued, "The minister says that he will share our report with the president before sending it to the members of parliament and the Tribal Council. Therefore, today's meeting is critical. I would like to walk out of here today with a final working group report to share with the entire Conservation Commission tomorrow."

As Dr. Kopo paused, a muffled groan came from the table across from Alexa. Frowning, she guessed who was responsible even before she observed everyone glaring at Tad Dorsey. A hothead, Dorsey was an environmental activist with the Southern Africa Wildlife Alliance, referred to as SAWA. Alexa was certain that none of the hard-fought compromises in this nearly final document went far enough for Dorsey. He'd been outspoken, bordering on rude, in all the meetings she'd attended.

"You have a comment, Mr. Dorsey?" Dr. Kopo asked in a mild tone.

"Not now. I'll wait until we walk through the recommendations," Dorsey replied. Then he muttered under his breath, "But this falls far short. Far, far short."

Diego from International Elephant Rescue caught Alexa's gaze and rolled his eyes. She stifled a smile. Diego had worked on committees like these in several African countries and was both an advocate for reform and practical enough to understand the need for compromise.

Dr. Kopo continued, "I propose we discuss any comments the entire group may have on the draft. Rather than go line by line, let's deal with each of the major issues: anti-poaching rules, trafficking of wildlife and wildlife parts, and enhanced enforcement."

Two long hours of posturing and bickering later, Alexa was relieved to hear Dr. Kopo announce a break. She took her cup of tea onto a small outdoor balcony to get some fresh air. A few seconds later, Diego and Destiny from Batswana Conserve joined her.

"At this rate, we'll be here until midnight," Diego groused.

Destiny shook her head, then giggled, bouncing her mass of tiny braids. "If Tad Dorsey had stayed home, we would be finished by now."

Alexa laughed. "That might be a bit of an exaggeration," she said. "All right," she amended in response to the looks that Diego and Destiny gave her. "A very tiny exaggeration."

She took a sip of tea. "Seriously though. The recommendations are coming together well. We have a consensus on the biggest items. Most of what Tad's pushing comes from frustration with South Africa and Zambia. He should realize Botswana legislation can't solve those other countries' issues with lion farms and the sale of animal parts to Southeast Asia. Most of his hot-button issues aren't even problems here. Yes, it's good to anticipate and prevent them. But there's a solid argument for not focusing on problems that don't exist in Botswana."

Alexa shuddered as she thought about Reese's description of the farms in neighboring South Africa, in which lions were raised for big game hunts. When the operators had expanded their market to sell amputated paws, teeth, and bones to Southeast Asia, they'd revved up demand in a market that poachers leapt to fill. So, lions had been added to the list of species they targeted.

Diego replied, "I'm worried about how the larger commission will treat the poaching penalties section. With the enhanced enforcement recommendations, we've all but formalized a shoot-to-kill policy for the BDF. I know we've had in-depth discussion about the moral and legal implications, but it's controversial. You know the neighboring countries have been giving the president a hard time about the alleged fishermen who've been shot by BDF, even though most of them were caught in the act. A few of the tribes aren't happy about it either."

One of Dr. Kopo's assistants popped his head outside. "We're reconvening in a few minutes."

Alexa finished her tea in a quick gulp. "You're right. Enhanced enforcement is going to be a big issue tomorrow. I want to get more tea before we sit down. See you in there."

As Alexa took another cup of tea from a student server, Mrs. Nkala sidled up. "There you are, Ms. Williams."

"Alexa, please."

"I have been searching for you, Alexa. I was intrigued by our conversation at the last session. About your experience writing sex-trafficking legislation in the States. I was hoping I could call upon you for advice. You know that I am trying to strengthen our laws on this horrible practice, as well as Botswana's scourge of HIV/AIDS. They are connected, of course."

"Yes. I believe everyone in Botswana knows of your passion for these issues, *Mma*."

"Dear, most people just call me Mama."

"How can I help, Mama?" Alexa asked the woman known as 'Mama Botswana' for her activism against HIV/AIDS. Botswana had the third-highest prevalence of AIDS in the world with a twenty-five percent infection rate among adults.

"I was hoping that you would spend a few hours with me this evening discussing these issues. If you are free, of course."

Alexa shrugged her shoulders. "I have no real plans. When would you like to meet?"

"Come to my home for dinner. I'll send my driver for you at six."

"Fine. I'm at a hotel, the—"

"We know where you are, dear. My driver, Big Boy, will collect you."

After the workgroup wrapped up, Destiny dropped Alexa at her nearby hotel. She dashed up to her room to change, glad that she'd thrown a nice outfit in her suitcase at the last minute.

Showered and dressed, Alexa paused in front of the room's floor-length mirror and smoothed the black sheath. "Wow. You clean up pretty good, Williams," she said aloud and tried to remember the last time she'd worn a dress. *That's right, an embassy party here in Gabs when the US ambassador had honored the Conservation Commission.* And she'd worn her one casual dress to dinner a few times at Chapman's. Other than that, Alexa's daily uniform was khaki pants or shorts and a khaki shirt. Alexa combed her fingers through her curls, which had lightened from honey brown to a streaky blonde in the African sun. Checking her watch, she smiled. Half an hour before Mama's car arrived.

Alexa moved a jacket from the corner chair and sat down, cell phone in hand. As she dialed Reese, she hoped she would reach him. Even though he carried a satellite phone, Reese rarely picked up a call if he was observing wildlife in the field.

"Hey." Reese's voice made Alexa smile. "How are things in Gabs?"

"Same as always. Hot. Noisy. The meeting went well. For the most part." Alexa paused. "There's one guy on the workgroup who's always a pain. He didn't disappoint."

"The guy from SAWA? Wasn't this supposed to be the final session? Certainly he's had his chance for input by now."

"Yeah. But Tad's one of those guys who thinks the definition of consensus is whatever he suggests." Alexa laughed at her own vitriol. "Still, we finished the recommendations. Dr. Kopo is pretty skilled at working the crowd. His assistants are putting the final touches on the document, and it will be presented to the larger commission tomorrow."

"You can fill me in on the details when you get back to Maun."

Alexa asked, "How's Zimbabwe?"

"Fine. We surveyed two prides. Tomorrow they want me to meet with the elders in a village outside the park. They've had some trouble with a lion wandering into the village. Lost some cattle. People are angry about the economic loss and worried their kids are in danger. They haven't shot the lion yet or tried to poison it. But, if we can't work out a solution, it's just a matter of time before they take action."

"How real is the chance this lion would harm someone?"

"Very real. I don't know yet why the lion is hanging around. Is he a young boy who's having trouble hunting on his own? An older guy with teeth problems who's cruising for easy prey like cows or goats? Either way, if a big cat becomes too comfortable with human activity, an unexpected lion-human clash often ends with a villager dead. And the stories about maneaters always surface in situations like this."

Alexa cried, "Maneater? Is that a real thing? Isn't there an old movie about that? Graham watched it all the time when we were kids. Scared me to death, but I thought it was just a story."

"Maneaters are rare. That movie, must have been *The Ghost and The Darkness*, was about a true but unusual incident back in the late nineteen hundreds in Tsavo, Kenya. Those two lions picked off railroad workers like they were chicken nuggets."

"Eww," Alexa groaned. "What an image. Cold, Michaels, cold."

"Sorry. A little bush humor. Probably not the best analogy since we're talking about dead men. Some accounts say the two lions killed well over one hundred people."

"But that was years ago."

"Maneaters still exist. About five years back, a lion in Tanzania killed thirty-five. And there have been a few isolated incidents in South Africa recently. Those seem to be more random. People in the wrong place at the wrong time. Lions take advantage of the unexpected opportunity for a meal."

"It is a scary thought. I already had a healthy respect for these big cats. I'll be even more cautious around them in the future."

Reese gave a soft laugh. "Caution is always good. These animals are built to be lethal. But, as I mentioned, maneaters are rare. That being said, it's human nature to fear the worst. And that's why we need to calm the villagers down and figure out what to do about this cat."

"Good luck," Alexa said. "I'm heading back to Maun after the session tomorrow. When do you expect to return?"

"Wednesday night. Depending on how this village meeting goes, I might have to fly back out here again after the staff meeting on Thursday. Maybe you can handle the final survey visit to Noka with Mo?"

Alexa rolled her eyes in exasperation. Reese was stretched thin, trying to handle a lot of projects. She expected to see less and less of her boyfriend in their last few weeks here. Not quite the romantic time together in Africa she'd expected. But they still had the safari at the end of the trip. That would be their time to enjoy Botswana and each other. "No problem. We can talk more on Thursday." She looked at the time. "Oh, I have to go. I'm having dinner with a colleague on the workgroup, Mama Nkala. Her driver is picking me up soon."

"Isn't that the famous AIDS activist? Wow."

"Yeah. I'm a little nervous. I don't really know her well. But it's a chance to see how the Botswana elite live. We haven't had much of a chance to socialize with local people in their homes."

"We're always out in the bush where the only socializing is in the safari camps. Tonight sounds like a cultural adventure. Have fun, Lexie. Talk to you in Maun, if not before."

Alexa grabbed her purse and a sweater and ran out the door.

In the lobby, the desk clerk nodded toward the door. "A car is here for you, Miss Williams."

As Alexa walked through the doors toward the gleaming black SUV, a man in a black suit with gold braid on the cuffs exited the vehicle. "Miss Williams? I'm Big Boy. Traffic should be light, so I estimate a fifteen-minute drive to Mama Botswana's compound." He opened the passenger door. "Please, miss. Settle in. I have bottled water if you like."

"Thank you." Alexa slid into the cavernous back seat, a little surprised at the luxury vehicle. This Mercedes looked just like the ones that cabinet ministers drove, although Mama Nkala held no formal government position.

Big Boy drove to the hotel exit gate, where he stopped and rolled down his window. "*Dumela*," he said.

"*Dumela, Rra*." Alexa could hear the response, but Big Boy's bulk blocked her view of the gate attendant. The unique Botswana tradition of descriptive names had truly hit the mark in Big Boy. This man was enormous.

As the SUV continued through the exit, Alexa caught a glimpse of the attendant. The man was peering through her window, a look of concern on his face. She raised her hand to wave but caught a reflection of her own movement in the darkened glass. The man couldn't see her through the privacy filter. Vaguely unsettled, Alexa leaned back and watched the lengthening shadows envelop the passing streets. As always, she was a little unnerved by how swiftly night fell in Botswana.

CHAPTER SEVEN

As THEY DROVE to Mama Nkala's home, Alexa reviewed what she knew about the legendary woman. Everyone here in Botswana was familiar with the basics. Nkala was beloved for her work in combatting HIV/AIDS. Botswana had been struggling to control its high incidence of the disease for years, with limited success despite free access to antiretroviral treatment drugs. Disproportionately infected with the disease, women revered Mama Nkala for speaking out on their behalf.

The nickname Mama Botswana had started here at home but was now recognized in human rights and public health circles around the world. When Alexa had first met Mama at a Conservation Commission meeting, she had immediately recognized her by reputation. She'd read about an awards ceremony at her own alma mater, Columbia University, where the school had honored Mama for her leadership in bringing the conversation about HIV/AIDS out of the shadows in Botswana.

Alexa's limited direct contact with Mama at the workgroup and Commission meetings had been casual and focused on the conservation issues at hand. She didn't remember how they'd wandered onto the topic of sex trafficking in one of their brief chats.

With her advocacy focus on HIV/AIDS, Alexa had thought Mama an odd choice to be a citizen representative on this particular commission. But Alexa had soon learned that Mama was quite knowledgeable and opinionated about wildlife and conservation issues. And Diego had clued Alexa in. He explained that, because of Mama's national stature and grassroots following, her endorsement of the Commission recommendations would go a long way toward smoothing acceptance of the report by President Makwala, parliament, and the Tribal Council.

Distracted by her thoughts, Alexa's attention had drifted from the drive. Now, she looked out the window to find that the SUV was traveling through one of the poorer sections of Gaborone. The houses were small with tin roofs. Most would more aptly be described as shacks. Despite the scarcity of working streetlights, the sides of the road were crowded with children playing in the dark and weary adults perched on stools and chairs in the dirt patches in front of their homes.

Alexa had expected that Mama Botswana would live in Extension Nine, an older, established neighborhood of Gaborone, home to the president's mansion and many of the city's upper class and prominent politicians. The presidential mansion dominated the quiet streets where huge homes nestled behind high walls, not far from more middle-class neighborhoods. Wondering where Big Boy was taking her, Alexa leaned forward with a frisson of disquiet to ask, "Are we heading out of town?"

"Not to worry, Miss Williams. We have just a few minutes more. Mama lives in Phakalane Estates, in a very fine house. Have you heard of this suburb? It sits just below the mountain where our first president, Seretse Khama, had his farm, Ruretse. Please, relax. We'll be there soon."

Remembering her earlier unease, Alexa tried to settle. She'd heard of Phaka-lane and was surprised to learn that Mama Botswana lived there. It was an enclave popular with the *nouveau riche* of Gaborone. Executives in Botswana's lucrative diamond business, some cabinet ministers, and other politicians. Construction magnates who had a hand in the capital city's booming real estate market. Well-heeled expats. An odd choice for a woman known for her charitable work.

Alexa chided herself. Was she bringing American perceptions to a country whose customs she didn't fully understand? A few butterflies churned in her stomach, a signal that she was more nervous about this unfamiliar social situation with a world-famous woman than she'd expected.

The SUV pulled up to a gatehouse where a uniformed man stepped out into a flickering pool of light. Then he nodded and waved the car through. Big Boy drove through a series of small streets, his progress slowed by periodic speed bumps. The houses all sat behind high walls and gates. Alexa noted that most had at least two floors, fairly rare even in Gabs. After a series of turns, Big Boy eased up to a massive gate that slid open as he approached. He pulled the

SUV to a stop in front of a large stucco house with a fountain splashing in the courtyard.

"We're here, miss. Let me open the door for you."

Big Boy ushered Alexa toward an ornately carved wooden door. "Thank you, miss. Dineo will take care of you from here. I have to park the car."

As the giant man backed down the steps, the door swung open to reveal a smiling woman. Before Alexa could digest the fact that she was wearing a starched white pinafore and traditional headdress, the woman nodded. "*Dumela*, Miss Williams. I'm Dineo. Mama is expecting you. Come right in."

Dineo led Alexa through a large, two-story foyer into a cavernous living room. "Miss Williams," she announced to the sole occupant of the room.

Mama Botswana used the wide arm of the cream leather couch to push to her feet. "Alexa," she exclaimed. "*Dumela*. Welcome. I hope your trip out here was smooth?"

Alexa clasped Mama's outstretched hand in greeting as she replied, "Quite smooth. I didn't know you lived out here in Phakalane. I'd heard about this hot new residential area in Gabs but didn't realize that it was so large." She looked around the stark white room decorated with huge local-style baskets and tribal art. "Your home is lovely."

"Ah, yes, Phakalane Estates. I don't take advantage of the golf course, but I needed more space for both entertaining and training AIDS volunteer groups. So, I sold my small home in the city and moved out here. There are trade-offs, like the distance to the Princess Marina clinic and the government complex. I use the commute for reading and phone calls.

"Please, sit. What would you like to drink? Wine, something stronger?"

Mama was wearing a raw silk caftan that looked like a Paris designer's idea of at-home wear.

Good decision to change into my little black dress.

"Sparkling water would be great if you have it?" Alexa lowered onto a chair upholstered in leopard fur. As Mama sank back into her seat, Alexa looked at the zebra skin rugs scattered across the floor. She gave the leopard-clad chair arm a surreptitious pat to make sure it was faux. It was. She breathed a sigh of relief.

Alexa said, "Thanks for inviting me to dinner. That was a long session today. If I'd stayed in my hotel room, I would have spent the evening reading over the workgroup recommendations again. And we'll have enough of that in tomorrow's Commission discussion. I hope our recommendations are accepted."

Mama snorted. "This is Botswana, dear. Nothing is ever accepted without talking it to death. Everyone will want to put their mark on these proposals before they go to our president. I admire Simon Kopo. He's run a good process. However, the man's no politician. And several of these issues are very controversial. I expect there will be some fireworks. And when it gets to parliament and the Tribal Council?" She wagged her head and raised her eyebrows.

"Which issues?"

"Enforcement. Shoot-to-kill, as some call it. Several of the penalties will be criticized as going too far. And there are many voices outside the Delta who believe the economics of hunting argue against a ban. But we'll know soon enough what tomorrow brings." She looked up as Dineo came into the room.

"Thank you, Dineo. We'll have dinner in, perhaps, ten minutes."

"Fine, Mama." Dineo handed her boss a drink in a martini glass and brought a glass of sparkling water with a slice of lime to Alexa.

"Thank you." As Alexa took a sip of the water, it occurred to her that Mama had never given a drink request to Dineo. Did the woman lurk outside the door or have an intercom in the room somewhere? She felt like she'd fallen into some weird African version of *Downton Abbey*.

Mama picked up the papers she'd been reading and waved them. "I was reviewing the latest longitudinal test results for Batswana patients taking antiretrovirals. The results are very promising, but we still need to convince more people to come into the clinics for testing and treatment."

Alexa pulled her attention back to Mama. "I read an article about the progress you've made in erasing the stigma of AIDS. What was the key to making people comfortable about coming forward for help?"

"I'm just the public face of many, many health professionals and volunteers who have been working on this problem for years. And your US embassy has been so generous in sharing America's expertise and resources to tackle the problem. Botswana is still a very patriarchal society. But our women came to the point where they said, enough is enough. We are dying. Our children are dying. We are ready to accept help. We want treatment. We want education on how to protect ourselves and prevent HIV.

"Many men have joined them, but not enough. Too many believe they are entitled to take their pleasure without accountability. That a sheathed spear diminishes their manhood."

Alexa asked, "Have the tribal leaders helped with education? I understand that the chiefs play a key role in the day-to-day lives of their tribes. Don't they administer justice for many routine and lower-level crimes?"

"Yes, and yes. But the tribal leaders vary in their educational levels and outlook on life. Some are more, what would an American call it?" She paused. "Progressive. Some are more progressive than others."

"Why are you now focusing on trafficking legislation?" Alexa asked.

"That's exactly what I want to discuss with you over dinner." Mama gestured toward a doorway at the back of the room. "I see Dineo is ready for us now."

Alexa followed Mama into an oversized dining room with a heavy mahogany table set for two. This room's walls were stark white, but large swatches of framed Kuba cloth gave the room a warmer feel. And an elongated light that spanned the length of the long table provided interesting black and brown texture.

"Another lovely room," Alexa murmured as she took a seat at the place setting across from Mama.

"A young decorator from Gabs helped me. I don't have the time for things like interior design. But, also, growing up in a one-room mud hut doesn't fully prepare you for decorating a spacious home."

"Is your home village nearby?" Alexa ladled a spoonful of creamy soup into her mouth. Pumpkin, of course.

"No, no. I was born in Rhodesia. My father was a freedom fighter against Ian Smith's repressive regime. When he was killed in the Bush Wars, my mother fled with my younger brother and me. The White man my mother worked for in Rhodesia arranged a job for her on his brother's farm. It was just over the Botswana border, so many of my formative years took place here in this country."

"Sounds like you had a lot of tragedy and turmoil in your childhood." Alexa couldn't imagine losing her father and then having to flee a war-torn country as a small child. *How does one live through that?*

"I was very young. Although I remember Papa, he was away a lot when I was a child. Fighting. And Rhodesia went through a lot of unrest. I was just a baby when the country declared independence and became Zimbabwe, but I was old enough to sense the anger and fear when the Bush Wars began. ZANU rebels fought against the White minority and Blacks who wouldn't break with the government.

"We had a much better life on this side of the border. Botswana was always a more secure place. We found refuge in the household of a kind man who treated me in many ways as his daughter. Even after my mother and her new husband died, he took care of my brother and me. And Botswana supplied me with a good education.

"My experience gave me an appreciation for the struggles of refugees and displaced persons. Politics and government in Africa can be volatile. Major conflicts and economic situations often force thousands of people from their homes into other countries, sometimes into refugee camps. These people are particularly vulnerable and become prey for human traffickers. As one of the more stable countries, Botswana has seen its share of immigrants seeking jobs, refugees, and victims of sex trafficking. Most of them funnel into Gabs or Francistown, but it's a problem elsewhere as well. The diamond mine communities, especially."

Alexa nodded and said, "I've not visited Francistown, but it's much smaller than Gaborone, correct?" She kept a polite expression on her face as she looked at the exquisitely presented lamb chops that Dineo had placed in front of her. Lamb was a frequent feature here in Botswana but not one of Alexa's favorite dishes. *At least it's not oxtail soup or goat*—both acquired tastes in Alexa's mind. Finding solace in that thought, she picked up a fork.

"Francistown is less than half the size of Gabs. Still, our second-largest city."

"I take it that all these people who've come into Botswana, whether voluntarily or trafficked, are exacerbating the AIDS problems?"

"Exactly. Their numbers increase the pool of people who can become infected. But, most important, these people are harder to reach for both education and treatment. Trafficking victims held in brothels are treated as chattel. They have no agency to do anything, let alone seek help for an HIV infection. This increases the spread of the disease. And then their handlers throw them out into the street when they become too sick to work." Mama paused to take a final bite of food, then laid down her knife and fork, English-style, on the plate.

Alexa stopped pushing the last few pieces of lamb around on the plate and laid her fork down too. "The Pennsylvania legislation that I helped develop focuses on strengthening the laws against trafficking, closing loopholes, penalties for traffickers, and funding for victim programs."

"Oh, but that will help. Anything to stop such a dirty business is an important goal in itself. Reducing victims coming into Botswana will also help in our fight against AIDS."

Alexa nodded in agreement. "I brought copies of the legislation. I'm not sure how easily a law for a state in the US will apply to Botswana. Still, I'm happy to walk you through the basic framework. After you and your team get a chance to study it, we can talk further if you want?"

"Excellent." As Mama replied, Dineo appeared in the room.

"Mama, you have an important phone call," Dineo murmured in her employer's ear.

"Fine." Mama looked at Alexa. "Please excuse me for a moment. Dineo will serve you dessert while I take this call."

Alone in the dining room, Alexa rolled her head to loosen the tension between her shoulders. Despite the casual atmosphere, this evening had kept her on the edge of her seat. She wasn't sure why. As she tilted her head back, Alexa studied the unique dining room light, hanging just above eye level. With a shock, she realized that the hundreds of cylinders that made up the unique work of art were actually porcupine quills. Hadn't Reese told her that the government had banned the collection of quills because it was endangering the prickly beasts? Alexa leaned forward to study the quills more closely. She'd just seen a display of quills found by the guides at one of the camps. These weren't plastic as she'd originally thought. These quills looked like the real thing.

After almost an hour of post-dinner discussion on Alexa's legislation, Mama wrapped up the evening and bid Alexa good night. Weary from the long day and the unfamiliar social situation, Alexa melted into the roomy back seat of Mama's SUV as Big Boy drove her back to her hotel. What a strange evening. She'd never spent so much uninterrupted one-on-one time with a world-renowned figure. She had to admit it was flattering to be treated as an expert by an international icon. Throughout Alexa's limited contact with Mama in their workgroup, she'd been a little awed by her reputation. Maybe that's why she was a bit off-balance tonight. Or maybe her unease came from lack of familiarity with Batswana customs, with being in a new social setting.

Mama Botswana was certainly an interesting and admirable woman. By all accounts, she'd made the lives of many thousands of HIV-infected Batswana better. Actually, saved lives. And she certainly brought passion to her causes. She seemed ready to take on sex trafficking with the same zeal she'd brought to reducing AIDS. After returning from her brief phone call, Mama had peppered Alexa with questions about the Pennsylvania law and its background. Just thinking about it made Alexa rub her temples, as if that would ease her overloaded brain.

She sat forward and pursed her lips. Wasn't it ironic that the woman known as Mama Botswana actually hailed from Zimbabwe? *I'd like to hear more of that story*, Alexa mused. Strange that in the space of a few days she'd heard from two very different Rhodesians whose lives were affected by the political turmoil and violence in that country. Nick was probably ten to fifteen years younger than Mama. He's White. She's Black. But both had their lives uprooted during the country's transition to independence.

Alexa's thoughts circled back to Mama. The woman's international reputation could best be described as the Mother Theresa of HIV/AIDS. However, the exquisitely decorated house in the ritziest enclave in the country didn't quite shout woman of the people. And the silk on that caftan was exquisite.

Alexa laughed to herself. *What a reverse snob you are, Alexa. Like rich people with designer décor and nice clothes can't be compassionate and caring?*

Big Boy took a sharp turn, and the parliament building slid by on their right. She considered Mama's prediction of fireworks at the big Commission meeting tomorrow. *Was she right? No doubt the woman knew more about the politics of Botswana than she.* Alexa frowned. After all the hard work they'd done in the workgroup, something about Mama's cavalier attitude toward opposition to the final recommendations bothered her.

Big Boy pulled into the hotel courtyard and hustled out to open her door.

"Thank you for the ride. Sorry to keep you working so late," Alexa said as she slid from the back seat.

"No problem, miss. *Bokoro.*"

"Good evening."

As Alexa walked toward the hotel entrance, she noticed the parking attendant watching. The man smiled and bobbed his head several times in an approving way. Alexa raised a hand in greeting, remembering the man's apparent concern earlier that evening. She shrugged her shoulders. Perhaps she'd read more into his expression than she should have. Maybe he was just a traditionalist, unused to seeing young women go out alone at night—especially in chauffeured cars.

Walking into the lobby, Alexa broke into a big smile. *Wait until I tell Reese that I had a private chauffeur named Big Boy. And went to a genuine Botswana mini palace.* She giggled as she imagined telling her boyfriend about the strange evening. Then, an image of zebra rugs and an over-the-top endangered porcupine quill chandelier flashed into her mind, and she stopped laughing.

CHAPTER EIGHT

"First, I want to thank all members for their hard work. I hope today's session will end our efforts as a commission. Our goal is to have sign-off on the complete set of proposals before we leave here today." Even though he spoke into a microphone, Dr. Kopo raised his voice to a near-shout to be heard over the chanting outside.

The crowd outside the auditorium had shocked Alexa when she'd arrived for today's meeting. All the earlier workgroup sessions had been low-key, attended only by members and a few staff from Dr. Kopo's office. Word must have gotten out that today's meeting was a critical one that could result in final recommendations to the government.

Dr. Kopo continued, "With this rash of elephant poaching incidents, these recommendations have taken on new urgency. Animals are dying, and our government needs stronger tools to combat the needless slaughter. Just last night, I learned of another incident in which a small family of elephants was found dead at the hand of poachers not far from Maun. This must stop."

An angry buzz swept through the auditorium. Nauseated, Alexa pictured the carcass of the baby elephant at Kagiso and shook her head in disgust. *Why hadn't the BDF arrested the poachers by now?*

After a long pause, the room quieted and Dr. Kopo spoke again. "I thought about simply opening the floor for discussion. On consideration, we will focus our conversation better if we know which provisions, if any, need further review." He gave a deprecating smile. "After all, if we agree on every single recommendation, our job is done. We can end the meeting very quickly."

From the chorus of titters among the attendees, Alexa judged that Dr. Kopo might be overly optimistic about instant consensus from two parallel groups that had been working independently for months. She was among those with questions, needing more information about the Economic Workgroup proposal for fee increases that could hurt photo safari outfitters.

Smiling as if unsurprised by the group reaction, Dr. Kopo said, "We'll do this as a secret ballot, then take a break while staff tally the votes. Your choice on each recommendation will be Adopt or Discuss, meaning adopt as presented or needs further dialog. We will spend our time on those provisions receiving a Discuss vote."

Alexa marked her ballot and had just enough time during the break to grab a cup of tea. Rushing back, she slid past Diego from Elephant Rescue and into her seat.

"Doesn't look like they're quite ready." He gestured to the front of the auditorium where a group of staffers clustered around a table.

"It would be great to have consensus on most of the topics," Alexa said.

"Define most." Diego raised an eyebrow. "My organization is okay with all but two of the economic recommendations in the draft. We'll see how this plays out. I might recommend that we all get a week to review the revised package before a final vote."

"That would be great, but I know Kopo is anxious because we're running up against the minister's deadline. I had dinner with Mama Botswana last night. She thinks the hunting ban and enforcement provisions will run into trouble."

"Hobnobbing with the Botswana elite, eh?" Diego ribbed Alexa. "We'll see if she's right . . ."

Dr. Kopo walked to the mic.

"Just about now," Diego finished.

"Ahem." Screech.

Alexa winced at the feedback from the microphone as Dr. Kopo cleared his throat.

"Good news. We have consensus on sixteen of the twenty recommendations." The academic paused and took a deep breath. "Perhaps the issues with the remaining four are minor." He twisted his mouth into a slight smile. "We shall see. They are Increased Tourism Taxes, Increased Concession Fees, Extending the Hunting Ban, and Broadening Authority for Situational Anti-poaching Enforcement Actions by Botswana Defence Forces."

"Mama was right," Alexa whispered to Diego. "Hunting and Enhanced Enforcement, aka 'Shoot to Kill.'"

Dr. Kopo said, "Judging from the comments, the ten-year extension of the Hunting Ban may be the most controversial recommendation. So, I suggest we tackle that one first." He nodded at a staffer, and the text of the recommendation flashed onto a video screen in the front.

He looked out over the group. "Comments or questions?"

The tribal representative on the Economic Workgroup stood first. "I see that the ban is meant to stop hunting safaris. No more loopholes that allow some outfitters to get permits through a lottery or petition to the government. Will Batswana be able to shoot lions or elephants that are killing their cattle or destroying their crops? We must be able to protect ourselves in the villages."

Dr. Kopo looked at the Subia tribe rep from Alexa's workgroup. "Can you address these concerns?"

As the Subia rep explained to the man that his concerns were taken care of in the proposal, Diego leaned over to murmur in Alexa's ear. "Dr. K has bigger *cojones* than I gave him credit for. He has the guy who fought hardest against this proposal defending it to his tribal counterpart. Smooth."

Nodding as if satisfied, the concerned tribal rep took his seat.

Dr. Kopo asked, "Other concerns?"

Tad Dorsey left the room, surprising since the hunting ban was one of his pet issues. Distracted by his exit, Alexa didn't notice Mama Botswana on her feet until the woman spoke.

Mama said, "Doctor. I know I voted to approve this resolution yesterday, but as a citizen representative, I must take the opinions of many into consideration. I did some reflection last night about who would be most impacted by banning all hunting safaris in Botswana. And, yes, the hunting outfitters will be hurt. But what about all the workers? The guides, the skinners, the cooks, all the people who depend on the business and the camps for employment? There's a proverb from Ghana that says, 'You should not hoard your money and die of hunger.' I want to make sure that we've thought this all the way through. Are we hoarding the animals at the expense of hungry people? An entire decade is a long time. So long that you and I may not even be around to see if this was a wise decision."

The auditorium broke out in an angry buzz at Mama's words. The astounded look on Dr. Kopo's face indicated shock at this eleventh-hour defection on one of the most critical recommendations.

At first, Alexa thought she'd misheard Mama in the racket from all the protestors shouting outside. As she continued to talk, the reality of her words sank in. Dismayed, Alexa remembered last evening's conversation. She'd taken Mama's remark about the hunting ban being controversial as a general observation. The woman had given no hint that she'd be the one leading the opposition.

Alexa bit her lip. Mama held considerable sway with the public. If she came out against this ban, it might not even make it past the minister.

Dr. Kopo's expression was thunderous. "I'm confused by this change in position, Mrs. Nkala. Especially since you voted to approve the recommendation just yesterday."

"As I said, I have modified my position after a thorough reevaluation of all the input I've received from individuals and citizen groups. And, after all, isn't today intended for further in-depth discussion?"

"What's going on here?" Alexa asked Diego.

He responded by shrugging and shaking his head. "I have no idea, but it's not good. And why wait until today? Did someone get to her?"

Alexa frowned. Mama Botswana didn't seem like a woman who could be easily pressured.

Dr. Kopo had called upon a workgroup member to respond. The man was refuting Mama's arguments one by one. The protest noise from outside had died down, so Alexa could hear his remarks clearly. Everyone in the auditorium was riveted by this dramatic confrontation.

Boom. Boom. Boom.

Alexa jumped as a series of crashes echoed through the auditorium. She gasped when a large swarm of people surged through the three sets of double doors at the side of the hall. As the crowd flooded the room, they chanted, "Back the Ban, Back the Ban. Stop Poaching Dead. Stop Poaching Dead." They carried an assortment of signs in English and Setswana, many of which she'd seen outside earlier in the day, including the phrases: *Ban Hunting. Stop Elephant Genocide. Save the Animals. Killing Is Not Sport. Photos Not Trophies. End Poaching Now. Make Poachers Pay.*

Up front, Dr. Kopo waved his hands in a futile motion for quiet. He shouted, "Order, please. Order, please. We must have order." Several male Commission members jumped from their seats and tried to wrest signs from protestors' hands as they stormed the stage. The slide on the large screen, which had displayed the language of the proposed hunting ban, had been replaced by the words *"Back the Ban"*—a sure sign that this flash mob had an orchestrated plan with help from the inside.

When police rushed into the auditorium holding guns with fat barrels, several women screamed. Through megaphones, the police shouted, "Exit the building now. Take your signs and leave."

Although none of the protestors complied with the police orders, Commission members leapt from their seats and streamed toward the exit doors.

"We need to get out of here," Alexa said to Diego. "This is going to get ugly."

"Agree. Those are tear gas rifles. Come on." Diego rose and ran away from the crowd toward the back of the big hall.

As Alexa hurried after him, she spotted the single door on the rear wall.

"I saw someone use this when I attended a concert here. Hope it's open," Diego gasped.

Hearing a burst of loud static, Alexa turned to take in the pandemonium onstage. She caught a glimpse of Tad standing at the podium, shouting into the squawking mic. Next to him, two women protestors threw their heads back and let out a series of ululations as they danced and thrust their signs in the air. A student led a battered Dr. Kopo from the stage. Blood poured from the professor's temple.

Popping noises and smoke filled the room. Tear gas! Alexa bolted toward Diego, who was waiting by the open door. She leapt through just as she felt her eyes sting. He slammed the door shut behind them.

After a fit of coughing, Diego peered at Alexa's reddened eyes. "Is it bad?"

"No, we got out just in time. Thanks." She raised a hand to rub a watery eye.

"Stop," Diego shouted and grabbed her wrist. "That makes it worse. Let's find some water and rinse out the tear gas. There has to be a toilet here somewhere."

A few minutes later, Alexa emerged from a small restroom, face still damp. "That's so much better. Can't imagine getting hit full blast with that stuff."

"It's not pretty. I got caught once by mistake between protestors and the police in Cameroon. Never found out what the protest was about. It took me days to recover from the tear gas though."

Alexa put a hand to her chest. "My heart's still racing. What a mess. Between Mama Botswana bailing on the hunting ban and that ass Tad Dorsey staging a protest—not quite how I expected today would go."

"Not quite," Diego echoed in a wry tone.

"Poor Dr. Kopo," she said.

"Order, please. Order, please." Diego mimicked the professor's outrage at the protestors.

"That's not fair," Alexa protested. But when she met his eyes, she gave a small giggle. A moment later, both were howling in uncontrollable laughter.

Alexa was the first to recover. "Oh, my. I needed that." She wiped her eyes. "Plus, it helped flush out the tear gas. I feel bad though. It looked like Dr. Kopo was hurt. He's an academic. I doubt he has any training in hand-to-hand combat with protestors."

"We should check on him and everyone else. And I should call my wife. This may already be on the news."

"My boyfriend's in the wilds of Zimbabwe. I doubt he'll hear about this for a while. But yeah. Let's get out of here. I'm pretty certain they won't reconvene the Commission today. Obviously, the hunting ban is unresolved. And we never even discussed the anti-poaching provisions. This could be a real setback for getting the report in front of parliament." Alexa sighed, concerned about the implications for improving Botswana's conservation policy and for the animals it would impact.

CHAPTER NINE

As DUSK DEEPENED, the crystalline tinkle of bell frogs by the river hushed. Even the bullfrogs stopped their deep croaking. In these chilly months, the frogs burrowed in early.

Alexa tucked the heavy blanket around her legs, still enjoying the screened-in porch as night fell. She'd been hoping Reese would join her at the house in Maun tonight, but he'd stayed in Zimbabwe for another village meeting. He planned to fly home tomorrow in time for the late-morning staff session.

None of the various staff who often crashed here at the Maun Africa Trust house had shown up tonight either. Sophie had given Alexa a run-down of the reasons. Most, like Mo, would be flying or driving in tomorrow morning. One was with a boyfriend. Another had a family emergency and would miss the meeting entirely. Alexa hadn't really absorbed all the details, leaping to the bottom line: She'd have the house to herself tonight. After the three-ring circus she'd just left in Gaborone, Alexa had been thrilled to have solitary time for yoga, breathing in the fresh air, and listening to the frog chorus on the Thamalakane.

After a short meditation practice, Alexa leaned back in the chaise longue and pulled the blanket to her chin. *Just a few more minutes before the cold drives me inside*, she thought.

Splash, bump, splash. When Alexa opened her eyes to pitch darkness, it took a moment to get her bearings. *Ah, still on the porch. I must have fallen asleep.* She shivered. *The cold woke me.*

Splash, scrape, splash. Alexa sat up straight, alarmed at the sounds coming from the river. Hippos waded out there from time to time, but they snorted and grunted. That scraping noise was man-made. Rustling footfalls now approached the house.

Heart pounding, Alexa rolled off the chaise and slipped into the house. As she moved back the dark hall, shuffling footsteps brushed past the open window in the bedroom suite that she and Reese shared. A gun cabinet in the office stored several rifles that staff sometimes carried for protection from animals in the field. But the office was in the opposite corner of the house. Tiptoeing toward the front rooms in her bare feet, Alexa ran through the list of moves she'd learned in basic Krav Maga.

Nah—she remembered how badly that had turned out last time. Her mouth went dry as she looked around for some sort of weapon.

A nightlight in the kitchen cast a faint glow into the hall ahead. There, by the coatrack! She grabbed a cricket bat from a bin of soccer balls and sports equipment just as a muffled thump hit the side of the house.

Alexa bit back a shriek and felt in her back pocket for her cell phone. Not there. She'd left it on the kitchen table after dinner. Backtracking a few steps, she rushed into the kitchen. She grabbed the phone, ready to dial 911. Then she remembered, *I'm in Botswana.* The emergency number was something else. *Maybe 999? Or 909?* She pulled up Sophie's number from her contacts, but before she could hit Send, footsteps rang across the front verandah followed by the creak of the front door.

Gripping the phone in one hand and the cricket bat in the other, Alexa crept toward the foyer. As she approached, the door that connected the foyer to the living quarters opened slowly. Bat raised, Alexa slid into position, pressing her back to the wall beside the door. When a man stepped through, she brought the bat down in a whoosh. It glanced off the man's shoulder as Alexa pushed by him and bolted for the front door.

"What the hell?" the man shouted. "Who? Alexa, is that you?"

Alexa had made it to the verandah but slowed at the sound of her name.

"It's Sammy." The man whined, "You could have really hurt me."

Chest heaving, Alexa turned and walked back into the house to confront the small man rubbing his shoulder, an aggrieved look on his face. Sammy, one of the Africa Trust researchers. A rush of anger replaced any lingering fear. "Hurt you? What are you even doing here? You scared me to death. Sophie said that no one would be sleeping here tonight."

"Found out about a free seat on a plane into Maun this afternoon, so, instead of waiting until tomorrow, I snagged it. I had dinner at Chapman's. Was going to take a taxi but some friends with a boat offered to drop me off on the way by. I didn't think anyone was here. Sophie said Reese would be in Zimbabwe until tomorrow morning. The house was dark."

"Reese, yes. But as you can see, I'm here. The house is dark because I was asleep."

"I'm sorry. I guess I frightened you." Sammy's expression turned sheepish.

"You think?" Alexa's breathing was returning to normal. "What was all that noise outside?"

"Noise?"

"Yes, something thumping against the side of the house."

"Oh, I stumbled over an old garden chair out there. It must have bumped the side of the house when I dragged it out of the way."

Alexa looked down at the cricket bat still clutched in her hand. "Did I hurt you? My aim was off a bit."

Sammy touched his shoulder. "I might have a bruise for a few days, but it'll be a reminder to knock the next time—and get the full details from Sophie." He cocked a smile. "But with a swing that weak, I won't be looking for you on the cricket pitch anytime soon."

"Lucky for you," Alexa retorted. She'd calmed down but was still annoyed. At Sammy for showing up so late and not knocking. At her own overreaction. She tried to muster a smile. "Well, if you're okay, I'm going to bed. That's where I was headed when you showed up. I'll see you in the morning. There's food in the refrigerator. Although you said you had dinner already, right?"

"Right. I'll be fine. I'm going straight to the bunkroom. I am sorry that I scared you. Goodnight." Sammy scuttled down the hall.

Alexa locked the front door and grabbed a bottle of water from the fridge. On the way to her room, she dropped the cricket bat into the sports bin. Still unsettled, she locked the door to her suite behind her, wedged a chair against the doorknob, and climbed into bed. She could buy the change in plans, the misunderstanding about Reese alone being in Zimbabwe. Still, something about Sammy's explanation didn't ring true. She didn't know the researcher that well, but he'd acted very jumpy. Jumpier than being clobbered by his boss's terrified girlfriend would explain.

When Alexa wandered into the kitchen the next morning, Sally, the middle-aged housekeeper, was preparing the staff lunch. "Did Sammy tell you about last night?" Alexa asked. "What a mix-up."

"Sammy? I have not seen him today." Sally poured Alexa a cup of tea. "Would you like some eggs?"

"No, toast is fine." Alexa eyed the stack of sandwiches the housekeeper was building on a nearby tray. "Looks like I should save room for lunch." Most of the Africa Trust staff regarded Sally as more a house mother than a housekeeper. She fussed over everyone and had taken Reese and Alexa under her wing from the moment they arrived in Botswana. Reese often said that Sally and Sophie were the real managers of Africa Trust Maun.

Alexa took her breakfast to the porch and browsed her emails. Her sister-in-law, Kate, had sent some photos of the kids at their summer home on the Outer Banks. The sun-kissed Courtney and Jamie looked like they were having a ball. Alexa had bought her beloved niece and nephew several presents for when she saw them again this fall.

By the time she'd finished her tea, staff was pouring in for the monthly meeting. Alexa wandered through the group, saying her hellos, and then continued onto the front verandah. Keeping a sharp eye out for snakes in the scraggly grass, she stepped around the corner of the house. As Sammy had mentioned, a rusted iron garden chair leaned against the outside wall. But he hadn't mentioned the fresh groove that gouged the sandy soil in a straight line from the river to the house. Why would Sammy drag a chair all that way?

As Alexa tiptoed toward the groove, Sophie called from behind her. "Are you asking for trouble, Alexa? I see cobras out here all the time." Her scolding tone changed. "Reese called from the airport. Do you mind picking him up so I can finish getting these reports together for the meeting?"

"No problem. Let me get the car keys." Alexa stepped back onto the verandah.

"What is it with walking out there in that poor excuse for a garden today? As I came into the office this morning, I had to warn Sammy about the cobras. Now, you." With a baffled shake of her head, Sophie brushed past Alexa and strode into the house.

Alexa sat in the corner, watching Reese with a bemused smile. She loved this side of him. He was in his element, interacting with these young staffers, who matched his enthusiasm for African wildlife. He was also a good manager, listening carefully as the researchers and data analysts ran through their monthly reports, asking questions to elicit fuller information.

Her attention drifted during a deep dive into statistical trends. The Climate Change Impact Study that this Africa Trust team was launching was important. Much of the detail they'd gathered for their biannual big cat count, the project that she was helping with, also would be fed into the Climate Change Impact Study. But she had little interest in the level of detail the group was tackling this morning.

Alexa tuned back in when Sammy launched his report. He was assigned to a territory near the Moremi, not that far from Maun. So, his story of catching a ride last night was reasonable. Today, he'd returned to the house just minutes before the start of the meeting with several bulging shopping bags, not unusual for the staff who spent several weeks at a time in the field.

Alexa still wondered what he'd been doing outside the house last night and then again this morning. Something about the whole incident struck her as sketchy. On the brief ride back from the airport, she hadn't had a chance to tell Reese about the frightening nighttime mishap. He'd been bubbling over about the negotiations with the Zimbabwe villagers on the rogue lion. And she didn't want to bring the Sammy encounter up in front of the young intern from Hwange, who'd arrived with Reese. Instead, she listened to Reese and the girl chatter about a camp staff soccer game for most of the drive.

In the end, Sammy's report was fairly routine. "Two new cubs were born to the Selemo Pride. The mother is the dominant female. We've seen a pair of new males in the area recently. Don't know yet if they're trying to establish territory or just passing through. We'll keep an eye on the situation over the coming months. The cubs should be fine for now, but there could be a battle between one of these new males and the pride male, Old One-eye. That would put the cubs at risk if a new male takes over the pride. That's it. Nothing else new," Sammy finished his report.

Reese smiled. "What about that new leopard? The one that came in from the west?"

Sammy responded, "Still there. He's gotten into a few spats with other established males. Now he seems to have carved out a niche in the east. He's a beauty."

"Glad to hear it," Reese responded before he turned to the entire staff. "Let's take a break for this lunch that Sally has been preparing for hours. Then, we'll fill you in on some recent developments in Hwange, and Alexa will bring us up to date on the Conservation Commission. I'd like to finish with a discussion on these poaching incidents. Get your ideas on what we might be able to do to help BDF."

As the group descended on the sandwiches and other goodies, Reese pulled Alexa out onto the verandah. "I don't feel like I gave you a proper greeting at the airport," he whispered and then drew her in for a long kiss.

Alexa grinned and then rose to her toes to kiss him again. "I think this quite makes up for any oversight, Mr. Michaels."

"You seem a bit distracted today. Is something going on?" Reese took Alexa's hand in his own.

"A few things. The final Commission recommendations going off track. What a mess. You'll hear the details in a few minutes. The other stuff . . . I'll fill you in tonight. Nothing urgent."

The front door opened, and the Hwange intern stepped out. "Oh, there you are," said the smiling blonde in a breathy voice. "Sandwiches are going fast. There may not be any left if you don't get through the line soon."

"Thanks," Reese said. "We'll be right in."

Alexa raised an eyebrow as the girl stepped back into the house. "Karla's from Denmark, right? Has she been involved in the village negotiations?"

"Only as an observer. She's a nice kid with real potential. I wanted to give her a chance to attend one of the monthly meetings. Especially since Ralph stayed at Hwange in case of another lion incident. Good soccer player too. Boy, the soccer game made me miss rugby."

"Hmm," Alexa murmured as she thought about the starstruck expression on the girl's face when she'd looked at Reese. And Karla's brief flicker of annoyance when she'd seen Alexa next to him. Then, she brushed the concern aside and said, "I didn't eat much at breakfast, so I really need one of those sandwiches. Let's get in there."

Late that evening, Alexa nestled her head onto Reese's shoulder and watched the mosquito netting above the bed sway in the soft breeze. "You must be exhausted after that marathon meeting today," she said. "I zoned out a few times, but you had to be engaged for every moment."

Reese grinned and kissed her hair. "Nerd alert. Loved every minute of it."

"What a surprise," Alexa replied in a droll tone.

"Seriously, this group is such a dedicated bunch of researchers." He paused. "Still, I have to admit I'm glad most of them took off after the meeting. Not sure I could have spent the entire evening talking shop too."

"The four who went out to dinner are back in the bunk rooms now. They're pretty quiet. Maybe because they're leaving early."

"Don't forget they're used to getting up at the crack of dawn to head out into the bush." Reese slid onto his side and looked into Alexa's eyes. "So, we'll have to be very, very quiet. We want them all to get their beauty rest."

"We need to be quiet? Was I talking too loud?" Alexa teased just before Reese brought his mouth down on hers in a hungry kiss. Her body arched and rose up to meet him.

"Talking isn't what I had in mind," he murmured.

In a flurry of rustling cloth, the two lovers disrobed then came together in a familiar cadence of mounting passion. Looking into Reese's deep blue eyes, Alexa stifled a scream as she reached her crescendo. With several deep thrusts, Reese reached his climax and collapsed into Alexa's arms.

In a husky voice, Alexa murmured, "Wow. Who knew that secret passion could be so, so . . ."

"Hot?" Reese whispered and kissed her cheek. "Perfect?" He kissed her other cheek.

"Yes, perfect." Alexa smiled. "I love you, Reese Michaels."

CHAPTER TEN

"Back on the *tau* trail." Alexa grinned at Mo as she threw her backpack into the Land Cruiser and climbed into the front passenger seat. She was back at Noka Camp while Reese returned to Zimbabwe to finish negotiations on the village lion problem. She knew her annoyance with Reese for spending so much time at Hwange on the lion issue was somewhat unreasonable, maybe even petty. It looked like the agreement would fund several lion-protector jobs in the village, which in turn could prevent the death of both locals and this wayward lion.

Still, Alexa couldn't help thinking about helpful Karla with the blonde hair and wide eyes glued to Reese's side in Zimbabwe. Meanwhile, he'd left Alexa on her own for this trip. She sniffed. *His loss*. At least she was at Noka, which had become one of her favorite camps.

Mo backed the vehicle out of the garage and headed out of camp. "I hope we can locate and log the pride we're tracking today. Tomorrow, we're scheduled to collar a new male up north."

"Is a vet coming?"

"Yes. He will arrive in late morning. This new pair of boys we'll look for is far from camp, on the northern border of the concession. We'll collar only one. We should prepare to stay out overnight. Unless we find these lions early, I don't want to risk a long drive back at night. It's also possible we'll need a second day to find them."

"Wow. This will be an adventure. I was involved in a collaring the first week Reese and I got here, but I was just an observer. And I've never camped out in the bush overnight. You have equipment I can use?"

"The Trust keeps several tents and sleeping bags at every concession. So, no problem. The vet is planning to stay for the extra day too."

Reese is going to be bummed that he missed out on this. Camping in the bush!
Alexa looked forward to the stories she'd have to share.

"You know where today's pride is?"

Mo seemed to be driving toward a specific destination. He hadn't hesitated as he took a series of new roads. "Earlier in the week, this family was hanging out near the edge of a lagoon. One of the guides spotted them in the same area yesterday, so we're going to try there first. This pride likes to hunt buffalo heading to the water, so they never seem to wander too far." He grinned. "Seeing buffalo knee-deep in the channel always reminds me of that Deep Purple song. They look like 'Smoke on the Water.'" Mo sang a few bars of the song.

Alexa laughed. "I don't know that one. You are obsessed with an era of rock and roll that was before my time. Sure, my parents played some of these songs, but I only know about half the ones you mention."

"They're before my time too," Mo said in a pedantic tone. "But I've studied American rock and roll. Extensively."

"I know." Alexa shook her head in amusement. "I know."

"The seventies were the best. Without question," Mo declared as he downshifted to cross a small stream.

Mo had made the right call. After checking several spots, they found the pride resting in the shade of a giant ebony tree about forty yards from a water crossing.

"Wow. Look at their stomachs. They fed during the night." Alexa gestured toward two lionesses sprawled on their sides. Nearby, four cubs slept in a rough circle around another female.

"Do you see any males?" Mo asked, scanning the area.

"No. Maybe they're still at last night's kill."

"Doubtful, since they usually get first seat at the table. But possible." He pulled the SUV into a spot with a clear view of the lions. "Let's get photos and do the complete documentation on the ones who are here. Then we'll track down the rest if they don't show up. Two additional sisters are missing too."

"Makes sense." Alexa reached for her camera and notebook.

The pair spent the next two hours documenting the three females and four cubs. By now, Alexa knew the routine well. Write a brief description of key characteristics of each cat, such as the torn ear of the female closest to the vehicle or the long scar on the right flank of the lioness sleeping with the cubs. Then, take photos of those characteristics along with making rough sketches. The whiskers and spots around each cat's mouth were critical to the individual description. Alexa had been surprised to learn that each cat has its own unique set of spots or whisker patterns that could be used, in conjunction with other noted characteristics, to identify individual lions and leopards. Using these markers, the Trust kept a database of all the cats they encountered.

Just as they were about to leave to search for the rest of the pride, one of the missing sisters joined the group. The cubs woke and ran to greet the newcomer. Alexa snapped a quick series of photos, trying to capture the youngsters' faces. Leopards, hyenas, unrelated male lions, and other animals all presented a threat to cubs in their first year of life. Many youngsters didn't make it. So, documentation for the young lions focused more on tracking their growth and survival. The research protocol delayed formal documentation until they had reached at least twelve months old.

When Alexa stopped shooting photos, Mo asked, "Finished?"

Alexa nodded and placed her camera into its case at her feet.

"How about we find a place downriver to have lunch? Afterward, we can head out to search for the missing males."

"Sounds good to me."

Mo drove some distance from the resting lions before he turned onto a track that led to the river. Alexa looked up to check the branches for leopards as he parked under a large tree. When they jumped out of the Land Cruiser, Mo got out their small cooler with lunch and drinks. Alert for animals, Alexa headed to the far side of the tree for a bathroom break.

When she returned, Mo had spread sandwiches and drinks on the small table that folded from the hood of the SUV.

"Wow," Alexa exclaimed, rubbing sanitizer into her hands. "Safari-style dining today." She grabbed a sandwich and bit into it, turning to watch a small herd of red lechwe graze across the river. In the distance, two young bull elephants were chest-deep in the river, feasting on tall grass along the bank.

The humans watched the elephants for a while in companionable silence before Mo said, "I was glad Reese spoke yesterday about being on the lookout for signs of poaching. When we're out in the field, everyone should be on alert."

"You did a good job of describing the terrible scene near Kagiso." Alexa's tone became somber. "I don't know if I'll ever get those images completely out of my mind."

"I'm very worried that they haven't found the poachers. In the past, BDF or wildlife rangers usually arrest poachers quickly. It's often local men caught in the act or easily traced. Others slip in from Namibia, Zambia, or Zimbabwe.

Some of those are caught before they make it back across the border. A few get away, but they're often identified and may be prosecuted in time. This is different. These people have struck several times, and then they vanish. They are very skilled. No one seems to have any idea who they are. What if they continue?" Mo paced back and forth, waving one hand, his half-eaten sandwich clutched in the other.

"There are five incidents so far, right? Reese and I visited the site of an older attack on four elephants not far from Maun. The terrible one we saw near Kagiso. And I've heard three separate reports from Chobe. I'm not counting the reports of dead elephants near Hwange. Reese asked around about them. No one thinks they're related to what's happening here in Botswana."

"Yes. I hear they think a bull elephant at Chobe was the first. The trial run. To figure out how to haul the ivory away. How to link up with a buyer. It's rumored that the Asians, mostly Chinese, Thais, and Vietnamese, have established routes to smuggle ivory and other animal parts out of Africa. The Ivory Ban has driven the trade further underground."

Alexa nodded. "I learned a little about the Asian smuggling routes in that workgroup I'm on in Gaborone. South African authorities broke one up a few months ago, but the experts who spoke to us believe there are several routes flowing through other countries."

"These elephant deaths really strike at my heart," Mo said in an anguished voice. "The elephant is the totem of my clan, so that means this animal is most sacred to me, to my father, to his father before him. This rash of elephant killings is an evil wind sweeping across the Delta. I fear that this evil still blows strong and will bring more destruction before it ends."

"I hope you're wrong, Mo. But the fact that the poachers have not been caught . . ." Alexa shook her head in dismay.

Mo fell silent and stared into the distance with a glum look.

Alexa let him have some space as she finished the last of her Coke and put the empty can back into the cooler.

"Hear that?" Mo cried.

Alexa listened, then caught the sound. Rruh, rruh, rruh. The unique roar of a lion calling for its pride.

Mo pointed away from the river. "Back there. Maybe it's the missing sister. Or the males." He packed the lunch leftovers into the cooler and hurried to stow them in the back.

Alexa folded the table on the grille of the Land Cruiser and climbed into her seat. Minutes later, they were driving toward the calling lion.

Noka Camp was quiet when Alexa and Mo returned in late afternoon. Near camp, they'd seen two vehicles full of guests not far from the entrance, heading out for their afternoon safari. Harry was the guide driving the first vehicle. Alexa smiled as she waved in passing. She'd forgotten he was assigned to the camp for a few weeks as a fill-in for guides on leave.

"Will I see you at dinner?" Alexa asked Mo as they left the garage.

"You know I like to eat with the staff and guides." Mo grinned. "Wholesome Batswana food, not that fancy Western stuff they make for the tourists."

Alexa laughed.

"How about we meet tomorrow after breakfast and pack what we'll need for the trip up north. I'll order food tonight from the kitchen. That way, we can be ready to leave soon after the vet flies in. I expect him in late morning."

"Fine. I'll catch you after breakfast." Alexa slung her backpack over her shoulder and headed toward the main tent. Accepting a glass of lemonade and two samosas from the staff who were clearing away the remains of afternoon tea, she made her way across the footbridge and down the path to her quarters.

Appreciating the quiet time, Alexa sat in a camp chair on the deck in front of her small tent. She'd been here several times now, so the place was familiar. She liked its location, tucked away in a grove of trees halfway between the island main camp and the village atmosphere of the staff lodging. Noka, like most of the other Delta Wild camps, kept a room like this for wildlife researchers, airplane pilots whose flight schedules had them overnighting at the camp, and company VIPs.

She picked up her notes from the day's field trip and read through them, clarifying details here and there. She'd found that sometimes her notes-on-the-go needed a little work, especially during hectic chases like this afternoon's. They'd careened through the brush off-road, tracking down the last lions in the pride. The call had been from a missing female. Soon after they'd located her, the two males had appeared. Getting the necessary photo documentation hadn't been easy though. The female kept a steady pace toward the rest of the pride, with the males following closely behind. Mo said the female's behavior showed she was close to a fertile period and that the dominant male would shadow her until she was ready to mate.

Eventually, Alexa and Mo had gathered enough photos and information about the three lions to complete their checklist. That concluded their documentation for the pride.

Alexa finished amplifying her notes and recorded the numbers of the photo sequence of today's lions for future reference. Then, she sat back and took in her surroundings. Looking at the vervet monkeys scampering through the canopy of trees overhead, she made a mental note to double-check the lock on the door when she left. Monkeys in your tent spelled disaster. At the edge of the staff village, a family of warthogs rooted in the underbrush. Over to the far left was the new building that workers had been pounding away on when she and Reese had been here two weeks ago. Today, it was quiet. In fact, it looked like they'd finished. She decided to stretch her legs after the long hours in the SUV and check it out.

Placing her camera, notebook, and empty teacup inside the buttoned-up tent, Alexa wandered down the steps and onto the dirt road leading toward the new building. Emma had said that it was built to store equipment. It was quite large. Alexa speculated that 'equipment' must mean things like boats and tractors and even Land Cruisers. The garage doors across the front were all closed. The place looked deserted.

Curious, Alexa decided to take a closer look. About forty yards out, she could see that the work was not fully complete. Several windows were propped up against a wall. Above them, the framework for the windows had been roughed in, but the openings were closed over with sheets of plywood.

A pygmy mongoose darted across the road ahead. Alexa smiled and rushed to the spot where it had crossed. The tiny creature had been headed for a fallen tree trunk where several other mongooses scurried in and out of the hollow log. Living this near the camp, they must have become habituated to people. Alexa's presence didn't seem to bother them.

After watching the mongoose activity for a few moments, a voice behind her shouted in a warning tone. She didn't catch the actual words.

Alexa looked around, alarmed. She'd forgotten one of the first rules of walking in the bush, even in camp: Keep an eye out for wildlife. She spun her head to check out the bush behind her, to the mongoose log, and then down the road toward her tent. Nothing.

"Hey!"

The shout had come from near the new garage. Alexa scanned the bush and trees in that direction. No elephants, no elands, no leopards.

"Hey, lady."

Panic abating, Alexa focused on the man who was shouting at her. He stood just outside a closed door at the side of the garage.

"Yes?" Alexa called and took a stride forward.

"No." The man held up his hand to halt her, then launched into an excited tirade in a language that Alexa could not understand. Setswana? He wore a tee shirt stained with paint, or maybe grease, and worn cargo pants. Perhaps a construction worker or a mechanic? She stifled a smile when she saw that he was wearing one of those silver Mickey Mouse hats she and Reese had seen in the Maun market. *Mickey must really be popular here in Botswana.*

When the man stopped speaking, Alexa took another step forward. "Sorry, do you speak English?"

He rushed toward Alexa, jabbing his arm forward, palm extended in the universal sign for halt. "No," he repeated, a scowl on his face. In heavily accented English he said, "Danger."

Adopting a calming expression and holding her hands up in surrender, Alexa took a few steps back. Retreat was the best option here. "No problem," she said. "I was just out for a walk." This guy could barely contain his anger. She didn't want to wind him up any tighter. "Sorry. I didn't realize this place was off-limits." She backed up a little farther and stopped.

The man made a shooing motion. "Danger. No."

With a wave, Alexa turned and headed back to her tent without stopping. When she made it to the deck, she sat in the chair and looked back toward the garage. Suddenly, she shivered.

Wow. For a hot second, she'd expected to be attacked by an animal. Damn that jerk for scaring her half to death. If he wanted to tell her that the garage was off-limits, why didn't he just walk out and tell her? *Although,* Alexa snorted, *I guess he doesn't speak English and I don't speak Setswana.* Or whatever. She'd heard enough Setswana by now to suspect that he was speaking something else. Maybe one of the tribal dialects. Regardless of the language differences, he was a rude, excitable little guy.

As Alexa reflected more on the encounter, her legal background kicked in. The irritable man was probably a construction worker just doing his job. His tee shirt and battered cargos set him apart from the camp staff who wore tan uniforms. It was clear from the boarded-over windows that the garage was still under construction. Who knows what work was still going on inside? And there would be huge liability issues if a camp guest or staff person were harmed on a construction site.

She'd let her fright about an animal cloud her encounter with the construction worker. It wasn't his fault. The real question: What was she doing standing in the bush, even in broad daylight, without staying alert for animals? *Alexa, Alexa. You may be getting a bit too nonchalant about living among wild beasts, many of which could finish you with a single strike. Didn't Reese just caution you about the danger of running into a lion? Other animals out here are just as dangerous. Stay alert. Time to up your game.*

With this pledge, Alexa went inside to change for dinner.

CHAPTER ELEVEN

"I'm so glad you're back." Emma wrapped Alexa into a hug. "Reese isn't with you on this trip?"

"No. He's in Zimbabwe, so I came here to Noka to help Mo on a few things. Thanks, as always, for finding me a room," Alexa replied.

"No problem. It's nice to see a friend among the daily onslaught of new guests. Of course, most of them are lovely and interesting people, but it's not the same as a familiar face for a lovely chat. Well, get yourself a drink. I have you with Nick and me at dinner. I also asked Harry to dine with us. You know he's assigned here for a while? He's always fun at the table." With that proclamation, Emma flitted toward the kitchen entrance.

Alexa wandered to the bar and ordered sparkling water as she surveyed the sea of khaki-clad guests. A large group of, perhaps, Germans. Maybe Dutch. Alexa couldn't easily differentiate between those two languages. Across the room, an American couple and their two teenage sons were riveted by their cell phones; Wi-Fi was only available to guests here in the main tent. And two older couples were slowly making their way toward the bar.

She nodded at them as she moved toward a bench on the edge of the tented room. After dining with Mama Botswana and spending intensive time with the entire Africa Trust staff, she was burnt out on socializing with strangers. Alexa looked out into the gathering dusk as she took a sip of her drink. In the distance, a nightjar trilled.

"May I?" said a deep voice she recognized.

"Harry, my favorite ginger." Alexa turned to smile up at the redhead. "I knew you were guiding here but thought that it was just for a week or so. Emma tells me you're here for much longer?"

The tall man eased onto the bench next to her. "I am. There are no group tours scheduled for the next several months. Usually, I take my break during this window. Teach a few Delta Wild guide courses. Do a little work on scheduling and programs at the Maun office. But they were in a jam here at Noka. Two guides are on leave. One quit and the new hires aren't fully trained. So, I'm here for most of the next two months. It's a nice change. Gives me the chance to learn the concession in-depth." He grinned. "Where's your better half?"

"Hwange, working with a village that has a rogue lion. I'm helping Mo." Alexa smiled. "Tomorrow, we're heading up north to collar a new male lion. Assuming Nick and Emma have no objection."

"On the border? I heard that two new males were seen up there. I've never been to that corner of the concession. Who's the vet coming in to help? Tale Dema?"

"That's the name. I've never met him. I've only been involved in one collaring project, soon after I arrived. Down south. A different vet flew out from Gabs." Alexa flashed Harry a sheepish look. "I'm a little apprehensive. I was really just an observer last time. I know that Mo's going to need my help after the cat is tranquilized."

"If you can find the cats."

"Right. Mo anticipates we'll be spending the night out there. That will give us a second day of tracking if we can't find them tomorrow."

"Sounds like an adventure."

"Exactly what I told Mo. Oh, there's Emma and Nick. Dinner can't be far away." Emma plunged into the group of Germans, slipping effortlessly into the socializing part of her job. Nick headed for the bar.

Harry bent toward Alexa's ear and murmured, "Excuse me for a moment, milady. I need to speak to old Nicky."

Alexa returned to her contemplation of the night outside the tented lounge, soothed by the chorus of frogs and crickets from the nearby channel. Then, one of the staff rang a bell and cried, "Dinner is ready, please."

As Alexa rose, Emma caught her eye and pointed to a table for four in the far corner. By the time she'd reached the table, Harry and Nick were already seated.

Nick spoke the minute Alexa sat down. "What's this about you and Mo going up north tomorrow? That's a fairly remote part of the concession. You know we always try to be accommodating to Africa Trust's research, but I'm a bit concerned about the two of you going so far off the grid."

"We'll have a vet with us too," Alexa replied, surprised at Nick's sharp tone.

Frowning, Nick leaned forward. "Harry mentioned that. Having a vet means you're going to be darting a lion. What if something goes wrong? We're short-staffed, and I can't be sending a crew out at short notice to help."

Surprised that Nick would push back so hard on a routine research activity, Alexa hesitated in order to compose an argument. Mo had expected the last-minute check-in with camp management to be proforma.

Harry jumped into the conversation. "I have an idea, Nick. My guests have an early flight in the morning. And I have no new guests scheduled for the next two days. I'm keen to see that part of the concession and these two new males. I could travel with the group."

Caught off-guard, Alexa took a moment to react. "Sure. I'd want to check with Mo to make sure we have enough equipment. But why not? The more the merrier." She turned to Nick.

Nick sighed. "I must say I'd feel better having Harry as part of your research party. Mo's a good chap, but I know nothing about this new vet. If you're going to be roughing it out there, wouldn't it be better to have a guide along?"

"Harry, you could also brief the other guides on what you find. That corner of the concession doesn't get much traffic. Although I guess someone was out there recently and spotted those new males."

"Otsile," Harry supplied.

"Right. He took a photographer out there to shoot photos of the dry riverbed. That's when they came across those lions. Wasn't it early last week? The lions might have moved on by now."

Alexa shook her head. "Maybe. Maybe not. If they're still there, we wanted to collar one so we can track where the pair goes next."

"It's settled then," Nick tapped the table with his palm. "Harry will travel with you and report back to me with an update on that part of the concession. Maybe I'll head out there myself in the near future."

"I'll let Mo and the kitchen know there'll be one extra for the trip." Harry smiled.

"Sounds like a plan." Alexa gave Nick a sweet smile, all the while chafing at his dictatorial tone. *Would he have intervened like this if Reese had been going instead of me?* She was pretty sure of the answer.

"A plan?" Emma said in a cheery voice as she pulled out a chair. "What have you been cooking up while I was organizing dinner?"

"The usual, dear. Exploration into the wilds," Nick answered. "Harry's going off with Alexa and Mo tomorrow to look for lions in the north."

"How fun." Emma clapped her hands. "A little different than your type of exploration, isn't it, Nicky? The pleasures of Maun are more down your alley."

"With all my duties here at the main camp and interfacing with headquarters in Maun, it's difficult to get out there in the bush as often as I'd like," Nick said in a stiff voice.

Alexa turned her attention to the soup in front of her and pretended not to notice Emma's snarky tone or to see Nick glare at his fiancée. Harry, too, appeared to be fascinated with spooning the cream of pumpkin into his mouth. Alexa had considered mentioning that she and Reese had seen Nick at Chapman's but let that pass.

After a brief silence, Harry turned to Alexa. "What's this we hear about the Conservation Committee session falling apart? Protestors stormed the castle or some such?"

She shook her head, a bemused expression on her face. "It was wild. The two workgroups were finalizing recommendations to the minister. Right in the middle of the session, when Mama Botswana was speaking, protestors burst through the doors and took over the stage. They were marching against any reinstatement of big game hunting and advocating stronger penalties for poachers."

In a breathless voice, Emma asked, "Did you get hurt? The news said that the protestors knocked around some of the Commission members."

"No. Lucky for me, I was sitting several rows back in the auditorium. When things turned nasty, a friend and I escaped through a back entrance. Dr. Kopo, the chair of the Commission, and several other people suffered some cuts and bruises. No one was badly injured."

"What about that Mama woman? She's quite famous in some circles," Nick said. "I've met her, actually."

"She is fine, far as I know. How do you know Mama?"

"'Know' is probably overstating it. A fundraising thing somewhere with my uncle. Years ago," Nick replied.

"SAWA led the protest, right?" Harry asked. "I've run into that jerk Tad Dorsey a few times in Maun. A real wanker. The guy fancies himself and SAWA as the African version of Greenpeace. But, acting up like this, they do more harm than good."

Nick interjected, "SAWA. That's the group. I read that an investigation's underway to determine if they're the ones poaching these elephants."

"What? That makes no sense," Alexa cried. "Tad might use extreme methods to get his point across, but SAWA's whole thing is protecting animals. Why would they poach elephants?"

"To create sympathy for the ellies and build public support for a strong response to poachers. In other words, to ramp up sentiment for strong poaching penalties. Genius, in a really sick way," Harry offered.

"Right. That's the theory this article laid out." Nick nodded.

Emma wrinkled her brow. "So, they kill the animals they want to save in an effort to protect the larger group of elephants in Botswana? Sounds pretty bonkers to me."

"What did Lenin say? To make an omelet, you have to break some eggs?" Harry snorted in mock derision. "So, they're not only wankers, they're Communist wankers."

"I still don't believe it. I've gotten to know Tad pretty well over the last few months. No doubt he weighs in on the extreme end of the scale. He can be a jerk. Like with the protest. Actually, he's almost always a jerk. However, I don't believe for a minute that he'd participate in the slaughter of elephants just to make a point."

"I guess the investigators will find out if you're right," Nick said as he buttered a roll. "I understand this Dorsey fellow and some other protestors are in jail. I think it's for the damage they did during the protest, not yet for poaching."

Alexa responded, "I got an email today from Dr. Kopo about the whole Commission situation. He's recovering from his injuries but is more concerned about the delay in issuing the recommendations. He said SAWA has been dropped from Commission membership, and he's working on a plan to wrap things up. He was a little vague about what the plan might be though." Alexa broke off to look at the woman standing next to her.

"Dessert?" asked the server.

The conversation over Bananas Foster became more desultory, with Nick, Emma, and Harry talking about recent animal sightings and camp activities. When the server returned with an offer of coffee or tea, Alexa rose.

"I'm going to turn in early." She grinned. "We're camping out tomorrow night in tiny tents. I need to stockpile sleep tonight. It's been a long time since I slept on the ground."

Harry jumped up. "I'm headed back to the staff village. I'll walk you to your tent first."

As they left the main area, Alexa asked, "What's up with Nick? I never dreamed he'd put up a fuss about Mo and me heading north."

"Not sure, but he's been a bit testy of late. That's why I told him about your trip. To pave the way. Seems that he and Emma are in a bit of a rough patch. That could be spilling over into camp business. Last week, I overheard him tear into the head chef over a minor problem."

"Thanks for the save. Although now you're committed to going with us tomorrow."

"No problem. I meant what I said. I'm trying to learn every corner of the concession while I'm assigned here." Harry chuckled. "I'd always heard American girls are princesses. Now I believe it. Have you seriously never camped out before? In a real tent?" He waved toward the line of guest tents. "Not like these luxury tents with beds and bathrooms."

Alexa spluttered. "You're calling me a princess? You are so, so wrong, my friend. In my teens and early twenties, I used to do a lot of backpacking. The Appalachian Trail—you've heard of that?"

Harry nodded. "Of course."

"It's very close to where I live, so I've done a lot of weekend, even week-long hikes on the Trail." She strayed into lawyer mode. "If you had listened closely to my statement, you'd know that I said, 'it's been a long time since I slept on the ground.' Not that I've never slept on the ground."

"My bad, princess. I sincerely apologize for doubting your wilderness credentials. Are there more like you in America? Perhaps I'll drop over the pond to check them out someday," Harry ribbed.

As they approached Alexa's tent, she scanned the area with her flashlight, still laughing at Harry. "Thanks for the escort."

"No problem. You know the rules. A guide has to accompany all guests to their tents at night. You're more guest than staff. Plus, princesses can't go anywhere without their royal guards." Harry had moved near enough for Alexa to see his slow, lazy smile.

For a moment, she looked into his eyes, so vivid she could see the green even in the dim glow of the flashlights. Then, she caught herself and stepped back. "Enough of the princess stuff. You know that in real life I'm a lawyer? Keep it up and I'll sue you," Alexa threatened over her shoulder as, grinning, she fled up the steps to the deck.

"Well good night then, Madame Attorney. I'll see you tomorrow." With a sweeping bow, Harry walked away.

"See you in the morning," Alexa called before she entered the tent. Still smiling, she reflected. If she weren't head over heels in love with Reese, Harry DeJongh would be a dangerously tempting man. *Surprising he hasn't already been snatched up by some discerning young woman.*

As she organized her clothes for the upcoming trip, Alexa hummed the song "Kumbaya," channeling her days at Girl Scout camp.

"Excited much?" she said aloud.

Yes, she was keyed up about this jaunt into the wild—and a little surprised at how comforting it was to have Harry join the expedition.

CHAPTER TWELVE

WITH EACH KILOMETER, the road became more challenging. They'd just driven through a long stretch of deep sand. Even with underinflated tires and low-range four-wheel drive, Alexa feared Mo would not be able to power through sand so deep. It was as if a long line of subterranean beasts were gnashing at the wheels, determined to stop the vehicle in its tracks. She rubbed her back, sore from the corkscrew motion of the Land Cruiser lurching through the soft powder. Dry stretches of terrain like this left no doubt that the Kalahari Desert was created from particles of rock and stone, honed by several millennia's flow of water through the Okavango Delta.

"Finally. This should be smoother." Mo wiped sweat from his forehead as the track turned into a dry riverbed. The hardpacked surface suggested that it had been years since water had flowed here.

From the front passenger seat, Harry said, "This must be a river that dried up after seismic activity, not seasonal rains. Guides talk a lot about the way earthquakes affect the Savuti Channel that fills with water for years then goes dry again. This could be similar, but more off the beaten track."

Tale, the vet, said, "I worked up here in the Delta about ten years ago. I've noticed a lot of changes since I've been back. Seismic activity. Climate change. Poaching. Even snare traps for bushmeat. On the positive side," he smiled at Alexa, "there are more researchers and more advocates for the wild."

Mo slowed the vehicle for a large herd of elephants munching greenery on the riverbank. A young male flapped his ears and trumpeted at them before returning to his meal.

"Don't be a cheeky boy," Mo murmured to the youngster as he edged the vehicle by the herd.

He continued driving for a few minutes, then pulled to a stop. Turning to the group, he said, "We've been driving for almost two hours. Based on Otsile's directions, we should leave the riverbed soon and head through some plains and forests. The place where he saw the lions is on the outer edge of the concession."

"So, we're entering lion territory?" Harry asked.

"Yes. We should be on the lookout for these two males as soon as we leave the riverbed."

Tale said, "When we find them, I'll need a few minutes to calculate the dosage for the tranquilizer and get set up."

Alexa chimed in. "Can you walk me through the collaring process one more time before we start? I need to know exactly what I'm supposed to do. I have several questions. Like, how do we keep the second lion away when his buddy's under?"

Mo smiled. "Let's find these bachelor boys first." He waved at the mid-afternoon sun. "We all know what lions are doing at this time of day."

"Sleeping," Harry supplied, "but they could bolt. Otsile says these boys were a little jumpy."

"We'll need at least an hour and a half from when we dart to when the lion wakes up. Timing depends a little on the cat's weight. We must finish the procedure, including making sure he's awake, before darkness falls," Tale said in a crisp, professional voice.

"Well, we'll take it as it comes. If we can find them soon and they don't run, we'll have plenty of time to set up, assign roles, and talk through the process. If they head out or we're too close to sunset, we'll discuss what to do. Agreed?"

Everyone nodded as Mo threw the vehicle into gear.

For three hours, they followed little-used, indistinct tracks and ventured off-road in several places, traveling through a changing landscape. Expanses of waist-high golden grasses and sprouting islands of scrubby palms gave way to stunted acacias and taller trees that rose over thick brushy areas. Everywhere they saw signs of elephant activity: the ever-present piles of dung and splintered branches left behind from the big animals' voracious grazing. Open to the elements, except for its canvas top, the Land Cruiser provided minimal protection from the heat of the afternoon. Alexa took frequent sips from her metal water bottle to stay hydrated as she bounced around the seat and peered into the distance for lions.

The area was rich with wildlife. In addition to elephants, there were herds of zebra, wildebeest, impala, kudu, tsessebe, and other antelope. They spotted a leopard in the crook of a huge tree as he watched a family of warthogs, unaware of their danger, grub for roots in the dirt. Graceful giraffes nibbled at thorny acacia leaves in one spot, and Cape buffalo stopped the SUV's progress by blocking the road at another. But no lions.

When Mo stopped at a sign that said *Leaving Noka Concession*, Alexa wiped the dust from her face with a wet handkerchief and asked, "What's the next move?" Her eyes burned from hours on the lookout for two big tawny cats in a landscape of tan grass and brush.

"Otsile told me that there's a big waterhole not far from where the river dips into the concession," Mo said and waved his hand to the left. "It's over that way. Did you notice the track that branched off a few minutes back? I think that could take us there. Otsile saw the lions along the road in this general area. It's possible they're still around and would come to drink at the waterhole in the evening."

Harry said, "I'm for the waterhole, mate. It's getting late. We need to find a place to set up camp before night falls. We don't want to set up next to a hyena's den and find out we have company during the middle of the night."

Mo laughed. "I think we'd smell a hyena den, even in total darkness."

"Ewww," Alexa groaned.

"Maybe not a hyena, but you take my point." Harry shook his head. "We need to choose a site near the waterhole but hidden from any animal traffic. And it's harder to set things up in the dark."

"I agree." Tale nodded. "You have a spotlight? If we don't see the lions before sunset, we can check out the waterhole tonight. If necessary, try the riverbank tomorrow early."

As they drove, Alexa studied the herds of impala and kudu for signs that a predator was nearby. A warning call. A group of animals frozen in place; gazes riveted on a spot in the distance. But nothing, even though the vast herds of grazing herbivores suggested this was prime territory to host lions. Soon, they entered a floodplain covered in short grasses. Then, a band of lush terrain indicated that they'd found the river.

Mo slowed the vehicle, and Alexa glimpsed a pool of water ahead. A small group of zebras looked up from drinking as they approached. After a moment, the animals dipped their heads back to the water.

"Is this Otsile's waterhole?" Harry asked. "Looks more like a pond left behind when the water level on the river fell."

"Probably part of the river system, but it must be Otsile's waterhole," Mo responded.

Tale said, "Look at the *motlhala*." He pointed to the jumble of tracks on the ground. "This spot gets heavy animal traffic. I'd like to check out the far side. That could be a good vantage point for us to use after dark."

"Good idea. Let's find a spot farther back to set up the tents, maybe behind that line of trees." Mo nodded toward a family of elephants lumbering toward the water. "Make sure we avoid elephant and buffalo pathways."

"These things are genius," Alexa exclaimed as she activated the pump. The folds of nylon blossomed into a fully formed tent, held up by air-inflated poles. "All those wasted years of feeding aluminum poles through slots on my dome tent."

Mo laughed. "Here's a hammer. You still have to tether it down with pegs, just in case the wind picks up." He and Tale had already set up the tent they planned to share.

Harry took the hammer and said to Alexa, "Let's tag-team the pegs."

Working together, it took only a few minutes to stretch out the tie-downs to Alexa's tent and fix them to the ground pegs. They did the same for Harry's.

As she carried a mattress pad and sleeping bag into her tent, Alexa smiled at the fact that the men had made sure her home for the night was in the middle of the three tents. Her kneejerk reaction was to protest the arrangement as sexist. Then, she chose to interpret it as a combination of chivalry and looking out for the rookie. After all, of the four people on this team, she was the only one who'd never roughed it in the wilds of Africa.

The day had been spectacular. Alexa had felt like an explorer voyaging into the unknown as they'd traveled farther and farther on their expedition into this remote corner of Botswana's wilds. For a moment, she missed Reese being here with her. But having her own adventure in the African bush was special too. Alexa grinned. *Maybe this lion expedition would give her some bragging rights with her wildlife-obsessed boyfriend.*

They'd chosen a campsite on a ridge not far from the water, tucked behind two small groves of trees. The tall trees acted as a screen. Animals at the pool could not see their row of tents. And all the well-trodden animal paths they'd scoped out earlier skirted the gap between the wooded copses.

When Alexa emerged from her tent, Mo said, "Is everyone okay with having dinner now? The kitchen packed some cold chicken and rice. There's soup in the thermos which might still be hot," he paused, "or at least lukewarm."

"Let's go for it." Alexa giggled. "I love lukewarm soup. I hope it's pumpkin."

"Yeah, I'd advise against starting a fire. If the lions come to drink, the sight or smell of a fire close by might spook them," Tale said.

Harry nodded. "Plus, it's pretty dry. I don't want to risk an open fire."

"I have a gel stove that we can use to heat water for coffee and tea tomorrow morning. There should be enough fuel to heat up soup, too, now that I think about it." Mo looked toward the Land Cruiser. He'd parked it next to the road after dropping off the equipment, not wanting to chance driving into the gullies near the bottom of the slope on their planned after-dark trip to the waterhole. Hidden by a small rise, the roofline was all that was visible of the vehicle.

"Lukewarm works for me," Harry said, and the others nodded.

Alexa frowned. "Limited gel fuel. No fire. I'm feeling cheated here. When Redford took Meryl Streep camping in *Out of Africa*, she bathed in a copper tub by the fire. Are you telling me that on my only night out here in the bush, I'm not going to get my copper tub moment?"

Harry laughed uproariously while Mo and Tale looked at each other with baffled expressions.

"You're just as good looking as Meryl Streep, gorgeous. Hate to tell you that you're not traveling with a Robert Redford—or even a Denys Finch Hatten—crowd. No baths this trip."

Taking pity on the obviously still-confused Mo and Tale, Alexa grinned. "Just kidding around, guys. Let's get dinner." As they drifted toward the Land Cruiser to get the food, Alexa studied Harry walking ahead of her. Some guys would know Robert Redford starred in *Out of Africa,* but how many would go to the next level and know the name of the real-life character he played in the movie. Fluke? Or did this guy have more depth than the smooth-talking flirt he played on the guide circuit?

A spectacular sunset gave way to darkness as they finished their makeshift dinner perched on camp stools. When Harry switched on a lantern, Alexa helped Mo pack the dishes into a steel box.

"Time to check out the waterhole," Mo said. "Who knows if the lions will show? It's always worth a try."

Tale nodded. "Agree. We can park on the other side of this tree line and see what wanders down for a drink."

"I brought a light with a red filter, so we'll have a backup red light if we need it." Harry fished a large flashlight out of his pocket and held it up.

"Can you give me a minute to throw on an extra layer of clothes?" Alexa asked. "It's getting cold."

"No problem." Mo smiled. "We have fleece blankets in the vehicle too. It's supposed to drop below four degrees tonight."

As Alexa dove into her dark tent, she mentally converted Mo's Centigrade temperature to Fahrenheit. Below forty degrees. It had been a good idea to bring long underwear. In the weak glow of a flashlight, she shucked her khakis, slipped into the long underwear, and redonned her shirt and pants. Grabbing a lightweight down jacket, she slid out of the tent, taking care to zip the front flaps completely closed.

Outside, the men waited for her, all holding warm jackets in their hands.

"Let's do this," Alexa said.

Tale switched off his solar lantern and placed it next to a tent. Harry shouldered a rifle that had been leaning against a stool. Mo carried the steel food box, which he planned to stash in the back compartment of the Land Cruiser.

As they headed toward the SUV parked by the road, Harry warbled the opening bars of "The Lion Sleeps Tonight."

Alexa giggled. "Keep your Wimowehs to yourself. We want the lions awake and cruising to the waterhole for a drink."

"I don't know any other lion songs," he protested as Mo and Tale laughed.

In the vehicle, the group quieted as Mo steered a wide loop around the deep line of trees that shielded their campsite from the waterhole. Driving off-road without headlights, he edged forward slowly. High clouds had come in at sunset, obscuring the rising moon. From the front passenger seat, Harry used a red-filtered spotlight to light a path through the tall grass. Here and there, a startled nightjar would rise into the air with a flurry of wings.

Although Alexa had been on a few nighttime game drives before, they had been on-road. This ride through the pitch-dark sea of grass was surreal and oddly seductive. The Land Cruiser swayed from side to side as Mo drove at a slow crawl, his passengers silent. Alexa closed her eyes for a moment to take in the cool breeze caressing her face and the powdery scent that rose from grass crunching beneath rolling tires. When she opened her eyes to the night, she could see nothing but inky darkness and the mesmerizing circle of red light that pulled them forward into the unknown.

At one point, Alexa sensed a large shape moving to the right of the vehicle just before a hippo shuffled in front of the Land Cruiser. Mo stopped until the beast passed. These big water creatures made their way onto land at night to graze and preferred a straight-line march to their destination.

"Would he attack us?" she asked.

Tale answered, "No. Hippos rarely attack vehicles. A word of advice though. Stay well away if you encounter one on the water or if you're walking. They're fast swimmers and even faster runners."

Mo repeated the standard safari joke about hippos. "Yes. If a hippo chases you, run in a zigzag. Or if you can run downhill, they will trip over their legs."

"Are the zigzag and running-down-a-hill things really true?" Alexa asked.

Harry replied, "You'd be better off climbing a tree or putting a termite mound or some other obstacle in the way. Those bruisers have bad tempers and deadly incisors; they'll kill you in an instant."

Continuing forward, Mo parked at the top of the hill that sloped down to the waterhole. Harry directed the spotlight toward the water and made a slow sweep of the pond. With the red filter, the light did not interfere with the animals' night vision. A group of five elephants stood knee-deep in the water on the far side, taking a long drink. Another larger herd waited their turn on the ridge nearby. After a while, several zebras pranced to a spot not far from the vehicle. They stuck to the water's edge, lifting their heads from time to time, on nervous watch for predators.

"They will leave quickly," Mo predicted.

Tale nodded. "Look at how skittish they are. Wonder why they're not with a larger herd."

"Hello. See that? The zebras just went on full alert." Harry swept the red light down the edge of the waterhole at the zebras and then up the far slope.

"There. At the top of the hill." Alexa leaned forward at the flash of red eyes.

"Oh, yes. *Tau*," Mo said with excitement in his voice. "Could it be one of the boys we seek?"

"Here comes another." A second pair of red eyes shone in the light as Harry shifted the beam farther back.

Alexa held her breath when the zebra herd, which had frozen in place, burst into a canter and headed away. The two lions paid no heed to the zebras' escape as they ambled to the pond. On the other shore, the elephants shuffled a bit, restless at the lions' approach. A female drew the smallest baby closer to her side. After a moment, the matriarch stood watch on the lions, and the rest of the herd resumed drinking.

Harry continued to train the spotlight on the two lions. They'd reached the edge of the waterhole and were circling its perimeter, coming closer to the SUV. Everyone fixed their binoculars on the pair.

"Nice manes. Our two males?" Tale asked in a hushed voice.

Mo replied, "Good chance. Neither seems to be collared. They both look young. Maybe in the two- to three-year-old range?"

A hush fell in the vehicle as the lions chose a place to drink. Alexa took some photos, knowing that they'd be grainy without a flash. If they couldn't find this pair tomorrow, at least they'd have a rough description for their database.

"Wow. The boy closest to us has a deep scar over his left eyebrow. It's very clear through the telephoto lens, even in the red light," she said.

"That makes it more likely that these are the two new males. None of the adult males in the nearest pride have facial scars." Mo's tone carried excitement. "I think we've found them."

Harry handed the spotlight to Mo. "Mate, can you handle this for a few minutes? My arm's going numb." As he rubbed his forearm, he said, "Let's watch which way they head when they leave. That will give us a direction for our search tomorrow."

"If we're lucky, they won't wander far tonight." Tale lifted his binoculars to his eyes again. "They're a little gaunt. No extension of their stomachs, so they haven't eaten today. I hope they don't disappear on a long hunt."

"Why aren't they taking down one of the animals here at the waterhole?" Alexa asked.

Tale said, "Element of surprise. These are two males. Fairly young ones at that. They don't have the strength in numbers of a pride. So, it's likely they prefer the stealth approach when they hunt."

About ten minutes later, the small herd of elephants left the water and plodded into the brush. The larger herd on the hill immediately made its way down the slope. The elephants approached with a slow, steady pace that kicked into high gear as they neared the water, many of them plunging into the pond with a splash. The commotion disturbed the two lions. The pair stopped drinking and eased back a few feet to watch the elephants. Then, a silent signal passed between the two cats, and they prowled back the way they came, toward the main river.

"As my wise grandmother often said, 'However long the night, the dawn will break,'" Mo chortled as he started the engine. "We've confirmed that these new boys exist. Today's search paid off. We'll track them tomorrow, starting at dawn. Time to get some sleep."

CHAPTER THIRTEEN

CRACK! A LOUD noise woke Alexa from a restless sleep. She opened her eyes and propped up on an elbow to listen. Even with the mattress pad, her hip and elbow ached from the hard ground. Shrugging off the sound as a dream or a falling branch, she settled back into her sleeping bag. Then, a series of loud reports split the night. Gunfire. She bolted upright, heart racing, and scrambled to pull on her shirt, pants, jacket, and shoes. She heard muffled voices to her right. Mo and Tale were awake too. In the dark, Alexa crawled to the door of her tent just as someone zipped it open from the outside.

Alarmed, Alexa drew back until Harry whispered. "Someone's shooting down by the waterhole. We need to find cover. No flashlights." From the direction of the waterhole, Alexa could hear elephants trumpeting amid more gunfire. Harry reached out a hand to help her to her feet—his other held a rifle.

Alexa grabbed his outstretched palm and rose. Mo and Tale stood in front of their tent, their attention directed toward the waterhole. The wind had risen, and a steady breeze coming from the direction of the water amplified the sound. As Alexa's eyes adjusted to the dark, she saw that the two men also gripped rifles in their hands.

"Right now, those jokers don't know we're up here. We need to find someplace to lay low." Tale spoke in a hushed tone.

"We could abandon camp and drive away, call for help when we get down the road a few kilometers," Mo suggested.

"This could be the poachers. They came in from the other side, maybe from the river. They have no idea we're here. Shouldn't we try to get some information about them? Driving away is a risk. They'll hear our engine; that could send them after us," Harry urged.

"As long as we stay out of sight, we could take a look. If it is poachers, they'll need light to harvest the tusks. I say, yes," Tale nodded.

With reluctance, Mo responded, "Okay, but we're outmatched with these three rifles. That was automatic weapon fire earlier."

Alexa swallowed. She'd fled from men with guns once back home, moving instinctively to save her life. Their situation here was less immediate. It was likely the poachers had no idea that she and the others were camped here. So, they had a choice; to flee or to help nail these butchers. Although she was frightened, she thought Harry's idea was worth the risk. "If we can describe them to the BDF, that could help end the poaching." She shuddered as she envisioned the slaughter that was likely going on right now on the other side of the tree line.

"I get that driving out of here could draw them to us. Even though we're downwind, they'd certainly hear the engine. But why don't I try to contact BDF on the Sat phone or raise someone on the radio?" Mo pulled a phone out of his jacket pocket. "I'll head out to the Land Cruiser. If I sit on the other side of the vehicle, it will shield the sound of the call. If it doesn't work, I'll try the radio." Mo headed off in that direction, taking cautious steps as he disappeared into the dark.

"I'll go up into those trees, check it out while Mo calls this in. Why don't you two just stay here for now," Harry said to Alexa and Tale.

"Fine," Tale replied and lifted his rifle into a guard position.

Alexa said nothing. The four of them splitting up, even in a small area, didn't feel right to her. But she couldn't argue against the need to alert the outside world or the plan to try for a glimpse of the poachers. More for comfort than warmth, she wrapped her arms around her torso. Her chest tightened as she tried to catch her breath.

Harry took a step forward but stopped cold as another burst of gunfire crackled through the night. Just behind the line of trees, several elephants trumpeted a wild chorus of warning.

Alexa cocked her head as a strange sensation reverberated through her soles. She dropped onto one knee and touched the ground with her palm. The earth was shaking. She hissed, "Something's very wrong. Can you feel the vibration? It's like an earthquake."

"Bloody hell, those sods down there have caused a stampede. Take cover in the trees," Harry commanded. He grabbed Alexa's hand and fled toward the trees to the left. She sensed more than saw Tale sprint off toward the second row of trees and hoped that Mo would hear the stampede coming.

As she crashed over uneven ground and patches of brush, Alexa clung to Harry's hand and thrust her other upraised hand out to shield against branches. Visibility was near zero. All Alexa could make out ahead was the tall line of trees, a deeper, looming black with branches swaying against the charcoal sky.

Harry lurched, slowed for a second, then cursed and hopped on one foot.

"You okay?" Alexa asked as she heard something thump against the ground.

"Stepped in a hole. I'm fine. Let's go." With a tug, Harry leapt forward, and Alexa scrambled to keep up.

As they neared the trees, she plowed straight into a waist-high stump, probably from a tree that grazing elephants had toppled and stripped of branches. "Oomph." Alexa doubled over at the blow to her stomach and let go of Harry's hand as she fell to the ground. Gasping for breath, she dragged her body upright using the rough stump. She bit back a scream when she realized that the thundering in her ears was not from the pain of colliding with the stump. To the right, a moving wall of huge gray shapes burst through the gap between the two clumps of trees. The panicked elephants bore directly down on their tents.

Several elephants swerved and headed straight toward them. Alexa froze, unable to move until Harry yanked her hand. Sprinting at full speed, Alexa raced those last desperate yards toward shelter in the trees.

"Here." Harry stopped and pulled Alexa against the wide trunk of a towering tree, shielding her with his body.

Taking deep breaths, she pressed her back against the wood. Even after the thunder of rampaging elephants faded into the distance, it took several minutes for the pounding in her ears to subside. When the night became quiet, Alexa whispered against Harry's chest, "Is it safe?"

"From the elephants? I think that was the last of the herd. Let's move over to those bushes and get a lay of the land." Harry stepped back and peered into the darkness above them. "Beggars can't be choosers, but now I'm worried that this tree is home to a leopard or a snake."

When they'd moved behind some bushes to the left, Alexa asked, "Do you think the poachers followed the elephants up here?"

"No." Harry put his hands on Alexa's shoulders and turned her a little. "Look down there. I think they have their hands full with the ones they shot. The elephants that came through here," he waved to indicate the ones that had nearly run them down, "they were either part of the larger herd that escaped or a different family that bolted at the gunfire."

Down at the water, several men lugged long bundles toward a boat. Each bundle took two men to carry. A portable klieg light cast a weak glow over the scene, but not enough for Alexa to see the men's shadowed faces. Just outside the pool of light, huge boulders dotted the shallows of the waterhole, like the giant rocks often featured in Zen calendar scenes. But there'd been no rocks in the water earlier that night. And, even in the dim light, the bank glistened a deep red. Alexa felt sick to her stomach, knowing that she was looking at another elephant massacre.

As they watched, the remaining two men switched off the lamp and folded it into a case. The clouds had lifted, and the moon cast enough light that Alexa could see the workers' every move. One of the men carried the case toward the river while the other gathered tools and stuffed them into a duffel bag.

"Looks like they're getting ready to leave," Harry whispered in Alexa's ear.

Left alone, the last man paused to scan the area where the group had been working, as if checking to make sure they'd left nothing behind. He then turned toward the waterhole and did a slow visual sweep of the shoreline. Dropping the duffel bag, he ambled toward a long, narrow object on the ground near the water's edge. A tool of some sort.

"Oh my God," Harry said under his breath just as a dark shape burst from the shadows and leapt onto the back of the unsuspecting man. In a blur of motion, a second cat joined in, pinning the man to the ground. The man's high-pitched scream rose into the night, then choked off abruptly.

"We have to do something. Stop them somehow." Alexa's voice rose as her body shook with chills. Lions were killing a man right in front of their eyes.

"I dropped my rifle when I twisted my ankle. Unarmed, there's nothing we can do. Stay calm. We don't want to attract the lions' attention."

A series of snarls broke the silence. "It's too late anyway." Harry gestured toward the lions, who'd begun to feed on the poacher and were jostling for dominance. "Damn, that's a kind of karma I wouldn't wish on anyone."

"Look." Alexa motioned toward the river. A man stood on a rise in the path from the river, watching the lions hunch over his companion's body. In silence, he turned on his heel and fled. Seconds later, an engine, perhaps two, roared to life and headed into the distance.

CHAPTER FOURTEEN

HARRY LED ALEXA back to find Mo and Tale. He made slow progress, limping a little from his ankle injury. Still in shock from watching the lions kill the poacher, Alexa wrestled with nausea as she stumbled along behind him. Her stomach throbbed where she'd slammed into the tree stump. At least the sky remained clear; the moonlight made it easier to navigate. The wind had died, scudding away with the clouds.

"Look for the rifle I dropped," Harry instructed. "I'm going to try to retrace our steps to see if I can find it. I'd feel better if I had it in hand."

Alexa nodded. To avoid a misstep, she was paying close attention to the ground anyway. Still, a rifle might be hard to find in the grass, even in the bright moonlight.

"I hope Mo and Tale are okay. I'm worried that they didn't come looking for us," Alexa murmured as much to herself as to Harry.

He stopped to reply, taking the weight off his injured ankle. "We scattered in different directions. Perhaps they're waiting for us at camp or expecting that we'd all make our way back to the vehicle."

Although his words were encouraging, Alexa could tell from the tightness in his voice that Harry was concerned too. She continued to fret. "If Mo got through to BDF, seems like their helicopter would have been here by now."

"Maybe. Depends on where they were flying from, Maun or their northern camp. They could be out on a mission somewhere." Harry hit a button on his watch to activate the screen. "It seems like hours since those first gunshots. It's more like twenty-five minutes."

"That's all?" Alexa shook her head in disbelief. It seemed like this nightmare had been going on forever.

They slowed to search the general area where Harry had dropped his rifle but couldn't find the gun. "I'll come back after daylight. Mo and Tale have rifles, too, if it comes to that. But the poachers seem long gone. And the chance of the lions wandering up here is slim."

Alexa stumbled and swallowed hard at the thought of encountering the lions fresh off their kill of a human. Looking over her shoulder but seeing nothing, she rushed to catch up to Harry.

A few minutes later, they found what was left of the tents. The elephants had run right over them, smashing all three into the ground. Scraps of tent fabric, sleeping bags, and a few supplies formed a ragged trail across the ground, a snarl of ripped nylon marking the path the elephants had taken.

"We can see if there's anything to salvage after daybreak," Harry sighed. "Maybe Mo and Tale are waiting at the vehicle."

Alexa couldn't wrest her horrified gaze from the tattered tents. "What if we hadn't gotten out in time?" She shuddered.

Harry wrapped an arm around Alexa's shoulders and hugged her to his side. "You can't dwell on the what-ifs. We did get out. We're safe." He planted a comforting kiss on the top of her head, then released her and moved toward the SUV.

As Alexa trudged up the ridge, she was frantic with worry. Still no Tale or Mo. Mo would have had a tough trek back to the SUV. The gullies. No flashlight. When the shooting started, things had happened so fast. Why hadn't she thought about any of these obstacles when Mo said he'd go make the call?

She and Harry reached the top of the slight ridge and paused. Alexa peered toward the shadowy form of the Land Cruiser. No sign of movement.

Then, Harry touched Alexa's arm and said in a choked voice, "You should stay here."

She looked at Harry in confusion, then followed his gaze to a spot about twenty yards away. Tale sat in a sea of trampled grass, hunched over, head in hands, a rectangular bag next to him. But it was the form splayed on the ground by his side that Alexa focused on.

"Oh no. No, no, no," she wailed. "The elephants."

"Stay here. You don't need to see this." Harry's bleak words barely pierced the fog of horror that enveloped Alexa. "I was in a village where an elephant trampled a man. It was," his voice caught, "brutal."

"I'm coming. It's Mo."

At their approach, Tale snapped out of his stupor. He leapt to his feet; rifle pointed in their direction.

"It's us, Tale. Harry and Alexa," she called out.

"Thank God. I thought you'd both been killed too. You didn't come back, so I went looking for Mo. He was still alive, but before I got back from the vehicle . . ." His voice faltered as he gestured at the medical bag. "I wanted to give him morphine. For the pain. Nothing could have saved him."

Alexa gazed down at the bloody, broken body. Too battered to identify as Mokapi. Tears streaming down her face, she said, "What about his family? He was going home in a few days. What will they do?"

Skirting a deep gully, Harry strode the few short yards to the Land Cruiser. Moments later, he returned with a blanket and bottles of water. He handed a water to Alexa. "Drink. We're dehydrated. And it's going to be a long day."

While Harry and Tale covered Mo's battered body, Alexa gulped half the bottle of water. Moments later she dashed into the tall grass to throw up. Stomach still cramping, she straightened up and wiped her mouth. Automatic gunfire, an elephant stampede, poachers, lions devouring a man. Each was over-whelming on its own. But nothing compared to the devastation of Mo's death. Cheerful, brilliant Mokapi. She had failed him. He was out here, all alone. Had he tried to outrace the elephants, aware of his coming death? Her body trembled as she tried to deal with the night's horror.

Alexa took several deep breaths as her nausea subsided a bit. Looking out across the glowing plain, she noticed that the sun had risen. *When had that happened?* Tilting her head back, she looked up with dull eyes and recoiled. The crimson morning sky was thick with circling vultures, drawn to the bloodbath at the waterhole. *And Mo*, her mind whimpered.

After a few more deep breaths, Alexa rinsed her mouth again. Then, she squared her shoulders and shambled back to Harry and Tale.

"Are you okay?" Harry asked.

Alexa nodded, avoiding looking at the woefully slight shape beneath the blanket. "Not okay, but I'll manage."

Tale swayed on his feet. Seeing the nasty gash on his forehead in the grow-ing light, Alexa cried, "You're hurt. Let me clean and bandage that cut. You should get off your feet before you collapse."

Harry grabbed his elbow. "She's right, mate." To Alexa, he said, "I filled Tale in on everything we saw at the waterhole."

Tale closed his eyes for a moment, then slipped his elbow from Harry's grasp. "I took cover in the other stand of trees. Banged my head on a low-hanging branch in the dark. Then, climbed up and held on until the herd passed. I went to the tents. What's left. Then came out here, looking for Mo . . ."

"Hey. You need to sit down." Harry hooked an arm around Tale's shoulders. "We need to get help. We know now that Mo never got through to anyone."

"No. It's clear he was making a run for the Land Cruiser. His rifle was next to him, but I found his phone back there." Tale pointed toward the ridge.

Alexa shot him a hopeful look. Her heart sank at his reply.

"The remains of the phone. Smashed it to pieces. Oddly, the rifle seems to be in good working order."

"My Sat phone's in the vehicle. I left it in my binocular case last night. Didn't realize until we got to the tents. Decided it could stay there until this morning. I just hope it has a charge." Harry released Tale, picked up Mo's rifle, and took a few steps toward the vehicle.

"Why didn't you mention this before?" Alexa's relief couldn't overcome her annoyance.

"Mo had his phone. He didn't need mine." Harry stopped short. "Even if it's lost juice, in just a few minutes I can charge it enough for a call. I know Mo couldn't connect with anyone by radio late yesterday, but we could try that as a second option. Even drive until we get into range. I guess Mo had the keys?"

Tale reached into his pocket, then held out a key chain. "I found this in Mo's jacket. They don't seem damaged." He leaned over to pick up his vet bag and followed Harry. Alexa paused to scan the area for animals. Several vultures perched on a nearby tree, waiting.

"Back off, you ghouls," she muttered, then hurried to catch up to Tale and Harry.

When they reached the SUV, Harry opened the passenger door and retrieved his binocular case. Extracting the phone, he looked at it. "Yes! I still have power." He leaned against the vehicle and punched in a number.

Slipping by Harry, Tale climbed into the passenger seat and collapsed. "There's a first-aid kit in my bag," he moaned.

Alexa rummaged through Tale's vet bag and located the standard first-aid kit with a big red cross on the canvas cover. Harry had reached someone and was describing their situation as she cleaned the gash on Tale's forehead and applied a large bandage.

"That will keep the dirt out. I think a doctor should look at it," Alexa told Tale.

"Thanks. I have antibiotics in my bag too."

"Human or animal antibiotics?"

Tale managed a wan smile. "Sometimes they're the same for humans and animals, but I always carry a broad-spectrum antibiotic for humans when I'm in the bush. Let's wait to see how quickly help arrives."

"We'll stay here with Mokapi's body and wait for your arrival. Please get here as soon as possible." Harry clicked off the phone and said, "I reached BDF. Called that special poaching task force number they set up. Then, I got in touch with Noka Camp. Emma answered the phone. Nick's in Maun, but she's going to send someone out here to help.

"I expect investigators will come too. This is going to turn into a complete shitshow," Harry predicted. "We should try to rest before they get here."

"That gel stove is in the back. Shall I make some tea? I'm not really very hungry, but there are some biscuits." Alexa turned toward the rear compartment but hesitated. "I should call Reese first. Tell him about Mo. Africa Trust may have procedures or something for a situation like this."

Harry handed her the phone. "Here. I'll set up the stove."

He looked at Tale. "Do you want to call your wife?"

Tale shook his head. "Maybe later. She'll only worry if I tell her what happened. I'll call when we leave here."

As Alexa dialed, she was seized with a sudden longing for the comfort of Reese's voice. Then, she remembered that Reese had no idea that she and Mo were out here in the bush. *Was it just yesterday that she'd been fired up about the prospect of lording this adventure in the wild over him? Making him regret he'd sent her on this assignment alone?* Now, she steeled herself for this conversation. Not only had she been in mortal danger, but Mo had died an unimaginably horrible death. Reese would be devastated.

Listening to the phone ring, Alexa let out a long, ragged sigh. *'Shitshow' doesn't even begin to describe this disaster.*

CHAPTER FIFTEEN

ALEXA SAT IN the vehicle, sipping a tin mug of tea and eyeing herds of zebra and impala in the distance. Out there on the plain, life went on. To the zebra and impala, death was a daily gamble. Predators stalked the unwary or the weak. Those who stayed alert most often escaped death until, one day, they stumbled or wandered too close to danger. Had Mo or the dead poacher been careless, or had they simply been outmatched by the animals that killed them? She sighed and closed her eyes. Her entire body felt like lead, except for the dull ache in her stomach. Foggy from lack of sleep and a deep malaise, Alexa felt as if she'd fallen into a dark, endless pit after a night of spiking adrenalin, terror, and grief.

The image of Mo's body flashed into her mind. Crumpled, almost unrecognizable as human let alone her friend. Alexa rubbed her forehead in an attempt to banish the terrible picture. Then, she broke down, shaking with silent tears.

Harry slid over and wrapped his arms around her. He murmured, "Let it out, princess. We're all due a good cry after a night like this one. There, there."

As she wept into his chest, a wap-wap-wap echoed on the distant air.

In the front seat, Tale sat forward and opened the passenger door. He shuffled to the front of the vehicle and shot a flare gun into the air.

Alexa watched the red flare shoot skyward for a moment. Then, she wiped her face on her sleeve as Harry released her and edged away from her side. She flashed him a wan smile. "Thank you. I swore to myself that I wouldn't fall apart."

Harry's voice was soft. "You were cool under extreme pressure. Last night. This morning. That's when it counted. This has been a bloody rough experience. You lost a friend." He gave a rueful smile. "You're entitled to a few tears. Most people would be basket cases at this point."

Two helicopters hovered into view, scattering the grazing herds. Harry climbed out and circled the SUV. He steadied Alexa with two arms as she made her careful descent down the side crossbars of the Land Cruiser.

When her feet hit the ground, Alexa looked up at Harry. "Thank you. For everything. You saved my life last night. If you hadn't dragged me into the trees, I might be lying back there like Mo. And I was ready to lose it when the lions attacked that poacher. You kept me sane."

"Alexa, you're what those old American films call a tough cookie. We saved each other." His voice caught as he dropped his hands from her shoulder. "And I'd hate for anything bad to happen to you."

"Thanks, mate." Alexa touched Harry's whiskered cheek and gently mocked him with one of his go-to phrases. "I'm glad you're still here too."

She turned toward the clatter of rotors as the helicopters touched down on the dusty road. Alexa and Harry moved forward to join Tale just outside the range of the rotor wash. As the larger helicopter's blades slowed, the door opened, and men in camouflage with guns poured out. The final passenger exited clutching what looked like a medical bag.

Preoccupied with the BDF's arrival, Alexa paid little attention to the second, smaller chopper. Her knees buckled when she looked beyond the scrum of soldiers and saw Reese hurrying toward her. Nick and two other men in khakis trailed behind. Harry caught Alexa by the elbow to steady her until she broke loose and ran on wobbly legs to her boyfriend.

Reese caught Alexa in his arms. "Lexie. Thank God. Are you okay? I've been so worried." He let her go and stepped back to examine her. "You're so pale. What about this blow to your stomach?"

"It hurts. A lot. I don't think it's anything major. Nothing compared to Mo . . ." Alexa's eyes brimmed with tears.

He kissed her forehead. "I'm heartsick about Mo. And thinking about what could have happened to you," Reese replied in an anguished tone. "I had no idea you were all out here. So remote." He folded her into his arms again.

Alexa clung to Reese for a few more seconds, soaking in his strength. She hadn't realized how desperate she'd been to see this man. He was a rock in times of trouble, always calm and steady. She wiped the moisture from the corner of each eye and stood taller, comforted by his presence. Then, she stepped back. "What are you doing here? You said you'd meet me when the BDF flew us back to Maun."

"When you called, I had just arrived at the Africa Trust house. I jumped in the car and drove over to the Delta Wild office. Emma had just contacted them about all of this. Nick happened to be at the office for a meeting today. Everyone was concerned about Harry. Many of them know Mo and Tale. The head of Delta Wild sent Nick up here because this is on the Noka Concession." Reese stopped his tumble of words. "Sorry to rattle on. Bottom line, I hopped a ride on their helicopter.

"We crossed paths on the way with the BDF chopper. Our pilot followed it here."

A haggard-looking Nick walked over and asked Alexa, "Do you need medical attention? What a horrible business this all is. Where's Harry? And the vet? I understand Mokapi didn't make it? I'm so sorry." He frowned. "An elephant stampede, was it?"

"I'll get the medic to check me out soon," Alexa replied. "Tale's the one I'm worried about; he has a gash on his head and a possible concussion." She looked back toward the vehicle.

"Looks like Harry's talking to the BDF. Is that Colonel Shonga? We should go find out their game plan." Nick rushed away.

Reese whispered to Alexa, "Nick's taking this hard. He feels responsible for greenlighting this trip up here."

Alexa bristled. "I know Nick has responsibility for this concession, but how could anyone have known something like this would happen? If we'd found the lions earlier, we might have camped elsewhere. If Mo hadn't set off for the Land Cruiser, he could have run to the trees when the elephants came. If, if, if . . ." Alexa stopped abruptly. "I'm sorry. Nick's done nothing wrong. I've been doing this if-only thing for hours, and I just can't do it anymore. Sometimes life throws terrible things at you, and the test is not whether you anticipated the pitch, but how you handle the catch."

"You're doing fine, Lexie," Reese murmured and hooked an arm around her shoulders. "You're doing fine."

Alexa almost believed him.

Alexa, Tale, and Reese briefed Colonel Shonga and the investigators on all the events of the previous night. Harry volunteered to lead the group out to the waterhole. Alexa had planned to go out with them. After another glimpse of the circling vultures, now darkening the sky and trees, she balked. She wasn't ready to face the horror again.

Colonel Shonga insisted the three survivors see the medic immediately after the briefing. The medic quickly taped up Harry's ankle, but the guide had brushed away any further examination. "Later," he'd grumbled and pushed outside to the waiting group of BDF soldiers.

When the medic looked up, Alexa pointed at Tale. "Check him first. He has a head injury. He's been a little groggy for the past few hours."

Tale threw her a grateful look. "Thanks. My head is throbbing."

Reese called to Harry. "Hold on a minute. I can't leave until the doc examines Alexa."

When the medic called Alexa into his makeshift exam room, Reese followed, holding her hand.

"My God. I thought you said it was nothing major," Reese exclaimed when she shed her shirt and long underwear top.

"Tell me if this hurts." The medic gave her swollen midsection a series of gentle pokes.

"Ouch. Ouch. Damn, that's tender," Alexa grimaced. "But it only throbs a little when no one's prodding it."

"There's some swelling. You should expect pain. Likely bruising in the next day or two." He frowned. "You'll need a few tests to rule out any internal injuries."

Reese looked at Alexa in alarm. "Internal injuries? Do we need to fly her to the hospital?"

The medic shook his head. "She needs to get there today, but I don't believe it's urgent. I just want the tests as a precaution."

He turned to Alexa, "In the meantime, take this paracetamol for the pain. Continue to hydrate. Try to eat something. We have sandwiches and more."

"Thanks, Doc." Alexa smiled. "I might be able to eat a sandwich."

Outside, Colonel Shonga's group, including Nick and Harry, waited, ready to head to the waterhole. Alexa looked at Reese, hovering over her. She could tell he was torn. "Go ahead. You need to be out there. So you can see what happened to Mo. And there are the lions. No matter how much he deserved it, they've now attacked a human. I'm sure there'll be fallout from that."

"Right. Maneaters. They'll want to put them down, but I want to make sure it's warranted. Are you sure you're okay with me leaving?" Reese asked.

"Go. I'll be here when you get back. Then, we can fly to the hospital. Be careful."

When Reese kissed Alexa on the cheek, she grabbed his hand for a second. "Thank you for flying up here. It means a lot that you came. Now, go."

An hour later, Alexa sat in the shade of the BDF helicopter, picking at a ham sandwich, amazed that she had any appetite at all. She'd retrieved a camp stool from the SUV and carried it to a dusty patch of road on the far side of the aircraft, looking over the plain. Away from the investigative team photographing the destroyed campsite. Away from the forensic team huddled over Mo's broken body.

Behind her, Tale rested on a cot they'd unfolded in the roomy hold of the military helicopter. The medic had stitched the gash and put him on a saline drip before radioing the medical helicopter service for an airlift to the clinic in Maun.

Alexa had asked again about calling his wife, but Tale refused. "When I'm out in the field, I don't call her. Right now, she has no reason to worry about me. I'll call her when they take me to Maun."

Her mind numb, Alexa barely registered the flock of guinea fowl scurrying around the base of a nearby termite mound. All the activity—helicopters, people fanning out through the bush on the search for the poachers—must have scattered all the other animals. Nothing moved out on the plain except tall grass dancing in the light breeze. Then Alexa caught a glimpse of motion in the distance. A herd of elephants headed toward the river, walking head-to-tail in a long line.

Seeing the huge beasts elicited mixed emotions. She hated that butchers were killing these noble animals, attacking them with guns and axes and chainsaws for ivory. For blood money. But she was still coming to grips with how dangerous the power of the charging herd had been last night. And what they'd done to Mo. She understood that the elephants who'd trampled him had been frightened by the poachers. It was possible they hadn't even seen him in their panic to escape. Or maybe they'd regarded Mo as another threat, one of the humans killing members of their clan. One thing was certain: She'd never look at elephants in quite the same way again.

Roused from her reverie by the sound of an engine, Alexa rose and walked to the road. She unbuttoned her outer shirt in the heat of the late-morning sun.

A mini-convoy approached with a BDF transport truck leading the way. Lagging well behind the truck's dust trail were two Land Cruisers with BDF seals on their sides. One pulled a jon boat on a trailer. Minutes later, a Delta Wild Land Cruiser coasted to a stop next to the Africa Trust vehicle that had brought Alexa's group to the waterhole-turned-crime scene.

As armed soldiers filed out of the BDF vehicles, Alexa carved a path through the mass of camouflaged men and walked to greet the guide from Delta Wild. She knew him from her visits to Noka as one of Mo's bunkmates and go-to radio guy for information on big cat activity. He was the friend who'd steered Mo to this waterhole.

"Otsile," she said. "Thank you for driving out here to help."

The Noka guide shook his head back and forth in a slow sweeping motion of grief. Tears filled his eyes. "I could not believe this bad business. That my friend, Mo, is gone." Instead of shaking Alexa's extended hand, he enclosed it between two roughened palms. "How could such a good man anger his ancestors so much that they'd send elephants to end his life? You know that the elephant was Mo's clan totem?"

"Yes. But the elephants didn't single out Mo. He was just in the wrong place when they fled the poachers. It was a horrible accident." Alexa hoped Mo's clan wouldn't interpret his death the same way that Otsile had. She considered how little she knew about many aspects of Mo's life, even though she considered him a friend. In his late twenties, the researcher had been a pleasant companion with an unerring ability to track down lions and leopards. Reese often remarked on Mo's scholarly expertise not only about big cats but African wildlife in general. He'd graduated with top honors from the University of Botswana.

In the many hours they'd spent together in the field, Alexa had discovered his quiet sense of humor and fascination with seventies American rock and roll. She recalled that he came from one of Botswana's minority tribes, the Basubiya, and lived in a village near Kasane. Each tribe had an animal totem that loomed large in their tribal customs and connection to the natural world. But they'd never talked about any of this other than the time Mo had mentioned that the elephant was his family totem.

"Were you hurt, miss? Or Harry?" Otsile asked in a less-emotional tone. He'd stopped the head motion and released her hand.

"We're both a little battered but will be fine. The vet who is with us, Tale Dema, has a head injury."

"Did you find the lions? I am wishing now that I had never told Mo about them."

"Last night after dark. We were going to try to collar one this morning." Alexa swallowed. "Harry and I saw them again after the elephants charged. They attacked and killed one of the poachers."

Otsile frowned. "Maneaters? Oh my. This is not good."

"No, it isn't. I'm sure Harry will talk with all of you at Noka about the lions. And Nick. Did I tell you that Nick flew in by helicopter? They're both out with the BDF at the waterhole." Alexa waved her hand in that direction. "That's what panicked the elephant herd. Poachers shot another family of elephants." She could tell Otsile had more questions, but she was too exhausted to answer them.

"Hungry? There's food in the helicopter. Harry and Nick should be back soon. They've been out there for hours."

"I could eat something." Otsile swallowed. "First, I would like to bid my friend, Mo, farewell."

Alexa reeled at the unexpected request. "His body's still in the field. See that first group of investigators?" She pointed. "They're doing their work and can't be disturbed now. You'll have to speak to the authorities about paying your respects.

"For now, come with me. We'll get you something to eat."

Over the next two hours, the staging area by the two helicopters was the site of constant activity. The new BDF arrivals received instructions and drove their vehicles off in different directions. The medical helicopter arrived to collect Tale. In the interim, the investigation team had wrapped up their work and prevailed upon the air ambulance to transport Mo's body to Maun. A stoic Otsile helped them carry the body bag.

Alexa's heart went out to Mo's distraught friend as they loaded the body bag into the bright-red helicopter. She also shuddered at the thought of the wounded veterinarian, Tale, having to lie next to Mo on his final flight. An investigator climbed in beside Tale, and the helicopter ascended in a whirl of dust.

With tears running down her face yet again, Alexa retreated to the Land Cruiser for some sleep. As she closed her eyes, she remembered Mo's delight when they'd found the lions. What was the saying he'd used? *However long the night, the dawn will break.* Alexa shook her head with a deep sigh. *What bitter irony that Mo never got a chance to see the dawn this morning.*

She woke up a half hour later, in time to watch Reese and Harry emerge from the gap between the trees and trudge back to the helicopters. She could read the anguish in Reese's solemn expression. Still limping, Harry looked drained, his face ashen beneath his tan, his eyes smudged with exhaustion.

Alexa climbed down from the vehicle, wincing at the flare of pain in her abdomen. Shrugging it off, she walked to greet them. "You both look as if you need food and drink."

"A bottle of St. Louis would hit the old spot." Harry's voice was too tired to carry off the joke.

"There might be some left in the cooler, although I doubt they're very cold at this stage." Alexa opened the rear compartment and rummaged through the cooler until she found two beers.

Reese gave her a fleeting smile and a brief hug as he accepted his bottle. "Ah, things like this are why I love you, Lexie. Nothing like a bottle of St. Louis to wash away a few terrible hours."

Alexa studied her boyfriend with concern. He had been pale with worry when he'd arrived here on the scene. Now, he looked beat, his shoulders slumped.

"*Pula*," Reese said as he and Harry clinked their bottles in a toast. The Setswana word for rain did triple purpose in mostly arid Botswana, also serving as the word for money and a favorite toast.

"Pula," Harry echoed, his eyes as bleak as Reese's.

"Why don't both of you sit down." Alexa grabbed two of the folding seats from the back and placed them in the shade. "I'll get you some sandwiches." She took Reese's hand and gave it a squeeze before she walked away.

When Alexa returned with food, Harry was leaning against the side of the vehicle. Reese was gazing at the ground. Neither man appeared to have moved.

"Sit," she said. "Ham was all they had."

The men tackled their sandwiches as she asked, "What have you and the BDF been doing down there?"

Harry shook his head, "It was even worse in the daylight than last night. I'm glad you stayed here. I walked them through everything that happened." His troubled eyes met Alexa's, and her chest tightened. For a moment, the terror of the past night flared brightly between them in that shared gaze.

Reese jumped in when the guide trailed off. "My God, what a scene. The poachers killed five adult elephants. BDF found three youngsters of various ages huddled nearby in the thorn brush, alive. They're worried about contamination of the waterhole from the carcasses as they decompose, but the scavengers may take care of that. The number of vultures was incredible. They're waiting to swoop in after the hyenas have done their work. That won't happen until the BDF packs up and moves out. Too much activity."

Alexa was glad she'd decided not to go. Reese's shock was even greater than at the first poaching site they'd seen. "What about the dead poacher?" Alexa asked, remembering her panic when the lions attacked the man.

Harry replied, "Not much left. Just some of the skull, pants, and the sole of a shoe."

Alexa tried not to gag. "Just one sole?"

"Yeah."

"Any sign of the lions?"

Reese said, "Colonel Shonga assigned a group to track them on foot. When the second group of soldiers showed, he added a vehicle to the search. If they don't find the lions by dusk, they'll have to stop. Given the smell of blood in the air, every predator within sixty kilometers likely has moved into the area. And now that the lions have broken that barrier and eaten a human, they're particularly dangerous."

"Will they kill them?"

"Probably." Reese tapped his foot in agitation. "I stressed the importance of making sure they have the right lions. I don't want them to gun down some random males they might stumble across. Several prides live in this general area." He looked at Alexa. "Harry said you may have gotten a few photos?"

"Not sure how helpful they'd be. Even if they did survive. They were red-light photos. Very grainy." Alexa stopped. She knew how much Reese loved big cats. He'd be devastated if the wrong lions were killed. Her tone gentled. "My camera was in the tent. A woman from the investigations unit told me they'd collected a few things from the tents that survived the stampede. Said they were evidence and had to be processed before they released them. I was thinking about my wallet and a few toiletries. Forgot all about the camera."

She looked at Harry. "They found your rifle. I think it's evidence now."

Harry sighed. "Glad it was recovered."

Reese straightened his shoulders and rose to his feet. "The colonel will be back here in a few minutes after he checks on the teams searching for the poachers. He has a few more questions, then you and Harry can leave." He put an arm around Alexa's shoulders, drew her close, and leaned his forehead against hers. "We're going to fly you to the clinic in Maun. Both of you."

CHAPTER SIXTEEN

THE CLINIC DOCTOR warned, "You could have pain for the next few days, but it should be manageable. I can give you a prescription to help with that. Then, switch to paracetamol. If the pain becomes intense, let me know right away. Although the CAT-scan and other tests look clear, the spleen or liver could be damaged. And you're dehydrated, so drink plenty of fluids."

"I'll take it easy," Alexa promised. "At this point, I could sleep for at least two days."

A few minutes later, Reese ushered her from the exam room with a packet of pain pills in hand. He handled her gingerly, shortening his stride to match her steps.

Alexa giggled and gently extracted her arm. "I'm fine, Reese. You're treating me like a porcelain doll or something. My tummy hurts, but I'm not going to break."

"You are my doll, Doll." Reese mimicked a Roaring Twenties gangster but took a few steps back.

"Thank you," she whispered. "I can't imagine what today would have been like without you riding to the rescue."

Harry stood as they entered the waiting room. "Everything top shape?" he asked.

"I'll be hurting for a few days, but nothing serious. And you?"

Harry extended his foot encased in a brace. "I didn't do the ankle any favors by walking through the bush all morning long. The doc wants me to wear this monkey business for a few days. I have a feeling I'll be doing paperwork for at least a week anyway, so no problem. I'm glad Nick saw the aftermath with his own eyes. This way he can confirm my report to Delta Wild management."

Reese smiled. "I was surprised he decided to drive the Africa Trust Land Cruiser back to Noka Camp. Otsile could have done it on his own. Sort of a wasted trip for Otsile."

"Not really," Harry said. "Otsile and Mo were very good friends. I think he wanted to see what happened for himself. Pay his respects. Poor guy feels responsible since he told Mo about the male lions. But, Otsile had nothing to do with the disaster our trip turned into."

Alexa asked, "Have you seen Tale?"

Harry shook his head. "The nurse at the desk told me that they flew him to hospital in Gaborone for observation. His wife went with him."

"That doesn't sound good. Maybe we can call for an update from the hospital later."

Reese looked at Harry. "Can we drop you at home?"

"The Delta Wild office would be better. I need to fill everyone in on details. Get started on those reports. Someone will give me a ride home from there."

When they got into the car, Alexa told Harry, "You take the front. Extra room for your ankle."

In the back seat, Alexa fought sleep, her eyes closing as Reese drove through Maun. She jerked awake when Reese stopped the car in front of the Delta Wild office. Sighing, she climbed out to take the front seat.

Harry exited the car and leaned in the open door to address Reese, "Thanks for the lift. Let me know when you hear the details of Mo's funeral." Then, he held the door for Alexa.

She paused and clasped Harry's hand. "Thanks again. Like I said this morning, you saved my life."

"And as I said, you're exaggerating. We both did the best we could."

Alexa dropped Harry's hand and embraced him in a swift hug. "Take care of yourself. Get some sleep." With that, she slid into the car.

When Harry closed the door and tapped the roof twice, Reese pulled into traffic. He put a gentle hand on Alexa's arm. "Let's get you home."

With Reese by her side, Alexa tottered up the few stairs to the verandah of the Africa Trust house to the waiting Sophie and Sally. Sally said, with tears in her eyes, "We are so sad to hear about our Mokapi. What a tragedy. That boy was so young."

Sophie cried, "Poor Mo. I just can't . . ." She waved her hand in distress then bustled toward Alexa. "What did the doctor say about your injury? Can you take some chicken broth? Sally has been cooking since we got the call about this disaster."

"Broth sounds wonderful. And then bed."

The women fussed over Alexa as they led her to the kitchen, leaving Reese to trail a few steps behind.

Sally served the soup, plus homemade bread and some cold chicken for Reese, at the table on the screened porch where Alexa and her boyfriend spent so much time. Then, the women went back to their work, leaving Alexa and Reese alone for the first time since he'd flown to her rescue in the bush.

"This tastes wonderful. I was still queasy when I had that sandwich this morning. It's been two days since I had a proper meal." Alexa leaned back in her chair and took a sip of water.

"It's been a very long day. And, for you, a long, difficult night before that." After a few minutes' silence, Reese said in a low voice, "I'm just glad that we're here together. That you're safe and sound. I heard what you said to Harry, that he saved your life?"

Alexa looked at him, puzzled by his tone, which sounded more resentful than grateful. "He did. He pulled me toward the trees when the elephants came barreling through. Twice, I stumbled, but he dragged me to my feet and kept me running. I might have made it on my own. But it was so disorienting. The dark. The ground literally shaking beneath our feet. It was terrifying."

"I'm so glad you made it." Reese's voice caught. "When you called this morning, I panicked. You said you were safe, but all I could think about was Mo being killed . . . and how you could have died too."

Alexa's eyes welled at Reese's concern. He rarely put his emotions out there so plainly.

He continued, "And I'm the one that sent you out there alone. You've been doing great on this Africa assignment, but you don't have the training. If I'd known that Mo was taking you out to collar a lion, I'd . . ."

"Reese. I'm sorry I worried you. None of this is your fault. I'll admit I was a little nervous about collaring the lion. But the vet was along. And then Nick insisted that Harry come with us. And I've always felt safe with Mo." Alexa paused and took a deep breath to keep her voice from shaking. "Turns out we never got to the collaring part. Who could have imagined the rest? It was total chance that we tracked the lions to a spot the poachers targeted."

"At the very least, I should have been there. Instead, you had to turn to Harry." Reese's last words were delivered as a subtle snipe.

Alexa rubbed her forehead. Somewhere this conversation had taken an unexpected turn. Her voice took on an edge.

"What are you saying? That I'm not capable of functioning on my own? Or that you're jealous of Harry? I'm not following. Maybe I'm just too tired and in too much pain."

"No, that's not what I meant," Reese protested.

Alexa held up a hand. "I can't do this. Not now. I'm exhausted." She summoned a half-smile as she stood. "Thank you for coming out there today. Having you there helped me hold it together. But I've reached my limit. I have to go to bed before I collapse."

Reese jumped up and followed Alexa to their bedroom. She stripped off her clothes and walked into the shower. When she emerged, wrapped in a towel, he pulled a fresh sleep tee over her head. Then, he peeled back the sheets.

"I'm sorry. I didn't mean to upset you. I've been so worried; everything came out the wrong way when I tried to talk about it. I love you, Lexie. I'm still reeling from the thought that I almost lost you." He pulled back the mosquito net, and Alexa crawled onto the bed. With a gentle hand, Reese covered Alexa with the top sheet and a light blanket and kissed her on the forehead.

"I'll check on you later," he whispered as he closed the mosquito netting. "Sleep tight. You need to rest. You need to heal."

Alexa closed her eyes and then opened them again. "Will you be here at the house?"

"Yes. I'm not going anywhere." Reese's expression darkened. "I have to call Mo's parents. Sophie gave me their number. The investigators sent someone out from Kasane to tell them about his death in person. But I was his boss. I need to speak to them myself."

"Mo," Alexa murmured as she fell asleep. "Those damn poachers killed him as surely as they killed the elephants."

CHAPTER SEVENTEEN

ALEXA WOKE LATE the next morning. She opened her eyes and lay in bed, listening to the sounds of bee-eaters through the open window. A colony nested in the near bank of the Thamalakane River, and the colorful birds often flew to the tall grass outside the house to harvest insects. After a few minutes, she slid her feet to the floor, igniting a firestorm of pain in her abdomen.

With small, careful steps she shuffled to the bathroom for a shower. When she gingerly lifted her arms to wash her hair, the quick stab of misery in her midsection brought tears to her eyes. She remembered Mo, the horror of the night in the wild, and the tears blossomed into sobs. Alexa leaned her forehead against the shower stall as the hot water and tears spilled over her face in a stream of grief.

When Alexa emerged from the bathroom, she felt better. The teary shower had helped both cleanse her anguish and loosen the tightness in her bruised stomach. She curled her lips into a rueful smile. *Good that Reese wasn't here to see me break down like this. He's already freaking out.* She remembered the conversation last night, which she'd had trouble processing through the fog of exhaustion. She knew Reese felt responsible, somehow, for what had happened. But there was something weird wrapped up there about Harry too. She needed to get to the bottom of that.

As she dressed, Alexa continued to discover how central the abdomen is to mundane tasks like leaning over to pull on khakis or donning a tee shirt. She needed a few minutes after she was fully clothed to sit in the corner chair and regroup. When the pain subsided, she shambled out to the kitchen.

"Good morning." Sally greeted Alexa with a look of concern. "How are you feeling? I'll make you some tea. Eggs and toast?"

"Just tea and toast for now, thank you." Alexa touched her stomach. "It definitely still hurts. I'm going to take this one step at a time."

"Go sit on the couch, dear. I'll bring this out to you."

Alexa smiled. "Thank you. I'm a little woozy from the medicine the doctor gave me." She started out the door, then stopped to ask, "Is Reese around?"

The housekeeper replied, "I think he's in the office. I'll tell him you're awake."

Stretching out on the living room couch, Alexa drifted off to sleep for a few minutes, rousing when Sally brought breakfast.

"Reese is on a call. He'll be in soon. Do you need anything else for now?" When Alexa winced as she tried to sit up, Sally leaned over to help. She arranged some pillows behind Alexa's back and pulled the tea table closer.

"You might want this." Sally handed Alexa her laptop before she returned to the kitchen.

Alexa scrolled through her email as she nibbled on the toast, opening a message from her best friend, Melissa.

Wow. Melissa and Jim would be flying to Johannesburg next week. This African sabbatical was fast coming to an end for Reese and Alexa. They were scheduled to finish their assignment with Africa Trust in—Alexa looked at the calendar in shock—less than two weeks. That's when they would join Melissa and Jim for the final ten days of the couple's safari.

Then, a few days back in Maun for the transition with Gary. Alexa smiled. Then, home. Back to Carlisle and her cabin in the woods. Back to her English mastiff, Scout. Back to her parents, yoga, and her life as an attorney. That was going to be some reentry!

Alexa poured another cup of tea, trying to ignore her fear that Reese wouldn't want to return to the States. That his love for Africa was stronger than his commitment to her. He'd left Africa and returned to Pennsylvania once for her. Would he do it again?

Perhaps she was more vulnerable to these creeping doubts because she was drugged up and feeling lousy. Her thoughts returned to last night's conversation with Reese. How should she view his jumbled reaction to her near-death experience? On one hand, he had been genuinely frightened for her. But he seemed to be blaming himself for putting her in a dangerous situation. And, somewhere along the line, that concern had become tinged with resentment aimed at Harry.

Had she given him cause to be jealous of Harry? Alexa shook her head. Not really. She'd joined the good-looking guide in a little harmless flirting. And she'd secretly admired those dazzling green eyes. But it wasn't like Reese to worry about her friendships with other men. Harry was his friend too.

She was more prone to jealousy than Reese. Look at how she'd had doubts about him and that barely legal Danish pop-tart, Karla. To be honest, Alexa still had a few doubts. Maybe Reese's reaction to Harry was the result of a guilty conscience.

"Be fair," Alexa murmured aloud. "You know you're probably reading too much into the Karla thing because you're scared that Reese will want to stay here. That he'll choose Africa with a side of pop-tart."

Reese's voice startled her. "What's that about pop-tarts? Are you still hungry?"

"Nothing. Just talking to myself. Everything's a little fuzzy with these pain pills."

Reese sat next to Alexa on the couch and kissed her tea-stained lips. "How are you feeling?"

"I've had better days. I could sleep some more, but I have things to do today. Call my parents. See about retrieving my camera and anything else the investigators salvaged. And I'm hoping to receive an email about the status of the Commission recommendations. Dr. Kopo was going full steam ahead. I didn't expect that protest was going to throw the process off track for so long."

Alexa shifted her position so she could see Reese's face. "You know we're done with this Africa Trust gig in just under two weeks."

"Yeah. I'm really feeling the pressure to finish a few more status reports before I hand the reins back to Gary." Reese shrugged. "In the end, I get done what I get done, I guess."

Breathing a sigh of relief, Alexa put her arms around him in a heartfelt hug. He'd shown no hesitation about leaving.

"I'll help set up a Skype with your parents. I guess they deserve to know you're hurt. By now, they should be used to hearing about the scrapes you get into."

"Maybe." Alexa laughed. "You know that doesn't make them any happier about it. They should be home from Italy now. Just in time for the dog transfer. Scout will be sad to leave Melissa and Jim, but he'll adjust quickly. You've seen how Dad pampers the big beast."

"No kidding. Biscuits and walks. Lots of biscuits and lots of walks." Reese nodded.

He drew Alexa closer and used a gentle tone. "As to your belongings. I already called the investigators. They have your camera. Didn't say how battered it might be. They also found items in each of the tents. I was going to run over today and identify your things."

Alexa bit her lip as she recalled the ruin the elephants had left. "The main thing I'd like back is my wallet. I'd rather not spend the next few days trying to cancel credit card numbers and getting new documents. Forget the toothbrush, toiletries, and the few clothes; I don't want them back after a herd of elephants ran over them anyway."

She tried to focus on something tangible to tear her thoughts away from the elephant stampede. "Did they say whether they'd been able to download the photos from the camera? I seem to remember giving them permission, but it's all a little hazy."

"The SD card was destroyed, so they got nothing."

Alexa had been leery of seeing the faces of the two maneaters again, even in a photo. Now she didn't have to worry. "It's hard to imagine the camera still functions if the card was broken."

Reese narrowed his eyes in concern. "Look. I know that dealing with this has to be difficult. I'll collect all the stuff, then we can figure out whether to trash it. You don't even have to look at it unless you want to." He paused. "They found a small backpack tangled in what remained of the larger tent."

"Mo and Tale shared that tent."

"I'll try to determine if it's Mo's."

At the mention of Mo, Alexa's eyes filled with tears again.

"I miss him, too, Lexie. I can't imagine seeing his body, after . . ." Reese took his thumb and brushed away a tear that had spilled onto her cheek. "It's going to take time to come to grips with all this. Not just Mo. All the rest. Even for someone as strong as you."

"I know. But these painkillers have made me weepy," Alexa wiped her eyes and gingerly leaned forward to pour more tea. The pot was empty. "Could you get me more tea, please?"

While Reese went to the kitchen, Alexa searched for Commission emails, finding two. She looked up as Reese returned.

"Sally will bring the tea when it's steeped."

"She's been so kind. Thank you." Alexa tapped on the computer screen. "Finally got word from the Commission. There's a meeting next week to take another run at the recommendations. Tuesday in Gaborone. I should be recovered by then. I hope. But the memo was a little sketchy on the details about what's happened since the last session fell apart. Seems like Dr. Kopo has been talking behind the scenes with Mama Botswana and a few others about the hunting ban. It's not clear if they've reached an agreement or plan to present a compromise. I would love for this to wrap up next week while I'm still part of the group. Do we know yet when Gary arrives back in Botswana? I want to brief him before we leave."

"I'm still waiting for an exact date. I'll email him again. He should have booked a flight from the States by now."

Alexa said, "Back to the Commission. I forgot to mention that Tad Dorsey's group, SAWA, has lost its seat at the table because of the disruption. As far as I know, Tad and a few of the ringleaders are still in jail."

Reese shook his head. "Tad really stepped in it. Yesterday, the colonel mentioned that they're looking into the rumor that Tad and SAWA may be behind the poaching. That they're killing elephants and staging the deaths to look like it's poachers. To create grassroots support for the harsher anti-poaching provisions the Commission is recommending."

Alexa frowned. "I heard the same thing. I don't believe it. No doubt SAWA takes its activism to the extreme. And they're willing to be thrown in jail for their stunts, like storming the Commission meeting. I heard they sat in front of bulldozers a few years back to protest a road being constructed through a game reserve. Apparently, they actually managed to stop the road. The government rerouted it.

"But they love wildlife. Protecting it is their whole mission in life. I can't see them suddenly going all Lenin on poaching."

Reese raised an eyebrow. "Lenin?"

"You know. You can't end poaching without killing a few elephants." She'd used Harry's analogy but belatedly remembered Reese hadn't been part of that conversation. Aloud, she said, "That's just not Tad."

Chuckling, Reese said, "Lenin gets all the credit, but the omelet/eggs quote actually goes back to Robespierre and the French Revolution. Still, I get your point. Not to mention, there've now been at least five poaching incidents. Killing one herd after another and taking the ivory every time? That goes well beyond what's necessary to ignite public sympathy for elephants."

"And those men Harry and I saw the other night. They didn't act like amateurs. They had their routine down pat."

"Except for leaving a man alone in the bush."

"Yeah, getting killed and eaten by lions couldn't have been part of their standard playbook." Alexa shuddered at the memory. She cradled her aching abdomen. "Have they found the lions?"

He shook his head. "They stopped the search not long after we left yesterday. Well before dark. They picked up paw prints heading north and planned to send trackers back out today. Colonel Shonga said he'd contact me when they find them. Assuming that they're even following the right lions. The closest resident pride up there includes two males.

"Nothing on the poachers either. I don't know how they handle all that ivory on boats, but using the river is a slick move. Makes it really hard for BDF to follow their trail. Of course, they have to get off the river somewhere."

"I hope BDF finds the poachers. This has to stop."

Sally came into the room carrying a pot and more toast on a tray. "Here's your tea, Alexa. And I've made you more toast. You must stay strong to heal properly."

"Thanks so much, Sally. You have been so good to me. Is any of that chicken broth left for later?"

"Of course. I'm going home soon. I'll leave it in the fridge."

When the housekeeper returned to the kitchen, Reese asked Alexa, "Are you going to be okay here? I have some work to do in the office. And then, I'll go collect your stuff from the investigators."

"I'm fine."

He stood. "I'll check in later."

Alexa took a sip of tea. "I'll be in bed. I'm already fading, and I haven't even taken my next pill."

"Sleep, babe. It will help you get better." Reese leaned over to kiss her forehead and left the room.

Alexa was surprised by the huge crowd. The funeral service was planned for the small white church at the edge of Mo's modest village, but it looked like they'd moved it outside to accommodate the large number of guests. She and Reese had traveled here with Harry and several others from Maun in the Delta Wild helicopter.

First, they paid their respects to Mo's parents. Mo's father spoke better English than his wife, but the language barrier made a painful conversation even more difficult.

Reese expressed condolences, and Mo's father nodded. "Our son loved his job with the wildlife study. Always since a little boy, animals, animals."

"Tale Dema, the veterinarian who tried to save your son's life, asked me to convey his sorrow," Reese continued. "He was also injured that night and is still recuperating."

Introducing Alexa and Harry, he said, "These two were also working with Mokapi when he died."

With a tear in his eye, the father asked, "You were there that night?"

Alexa nodded, "Yes. It was a terrible situation."

"Did he anger the elephants? Our totem."

"Oh, no. Not at all," Alexa replied and gave an inward sigh of gratitude when Harry jumped in to respond in what she assumed was Setswana. She knew that this tribe's primary language was Subiya but had never heard it spoken.

Harry spoke to the old man for a few minutes and shook the mother's hand before their group moved on. As they walked away, Harry muttered, "How can you explain something like this to grieving parents? I'm sorry, but your son was trampled by frightened elephants and there's nothing we could have done to stop it."

"It's the truth," Reese responded.

Alexa shook her head. "That doesn't make it any easier for us, let alone his parents. Wasn't Mo their only child?"

Reese nodded. "He was."

On the way to find seats for the service, Harry shook his head. "I wish I could say this was the first memorial I've attended in a while, but HIV/AIDS has taken several friends and Delta Wild staff. Things are getting better, but there for a while, people saved their Saturdays just for funerals. At least Mo's death was quick; not the long, painful decline of full-blown AIDS."

The memorial service was both familiar and unlike any service Alexa had attended in the States. Since the event was conducted primarily in Setswana, she tuned into the tone of the speakers and the emotions of the mourners. A minister dressed in a white robe led the service and read from a Bible at times. Several people spoke. Only a professor from the university and Reese delivered their remarks in English.

Alexa's eyes welled with tears as Reese spoke about Mo's excellence in wild-life research and gave several anecdotes about his work for Africa Trust. He ended by saying, "I know, as a big Dylan fan, that Mo has already knocked on Heaven's door and was welcomed through." The younger people in the audience chuckled, although Alexa could tell that many of the older villagers didn't understand the reference. She was proud of Reese's eulogy and glad he'd included a nod to Mo's abiding love of rock and roll.

After all the remarks ended, a group of women wearing the traditional dress of the region sang and danced, their flounced tops bouncing. When the service concluded, the family led a walking procession to a nearby cemetery. On that brief trip, Alexa spied a number of familiar faces in the crowd, primarily Africa Trust staff and guides she'd met from various camps.

Afterward, village women served an assortment of local food. Huge iron pots of the stewed meat dish *seswaa*, maize-based *pap*, and the wild spinach *morogo*. The type of traditional Batswana fare that Mo had loved.

Emma joined Alexa, Reese, and Harry at one of the long plank tables set up in the dusty outdoor space near the church. Alexa picked at her plate, looking up at Emma's question.

"How are you feeling? Nick said you needed medical attention after," Emma's voice lowered, "the incident."

"I had two rough days, but then I stopped the pain meds. They made me sleep all the time. Now, the pain is almost gone, although the bruise is a thing of beauty." Alexa laughed. "Yesterday, I got some work done. Mostly packing. Our friends from home arrive soon for our safari." Alexa smiled.

"That's right," Emma cried. "You'll be staying with us for a few nights. Maybe we'll assign Harry as your guide. Only the best for the best."

Reese shot Alexa an enigmatic look as he replied, "That would be great. We've spent all our time at Noka concentrating on the cats. I'm sure Harry can show us the animals we've been missing."

Harry kept his gaze trained on Reese. "Sure. This is your friends' first safari, right? I'll show them all the best spots in Noka."

He turned to Alexa with a stricken look. "And since it's your farewell to Botswana, we'll want to do it up right."

Emma had been glancing back and forth between Reese, Harry, and Alexa with a confused look on her face. Suddenly, her eyes widened, and she trilled, "Such a sad day today. I tried to tell Nick he should come with me, that the staff could manage the camp for part of the day. Since Otsile wanted to pay his respects, Nick stayed back to guide for the day."

"Really?" Harry raised his eyebrows. "It's been a long time since Nick went out with guests, hasn't it?"

Emma smiled. "I think he was quite looking forward to it. Even so, we're still short-staffed in the guide department."

"I'll be back tomorrow," Harry said.

"Oh, I'm not complaining about you staying in Maun for the week. You had things to do. A bum ankle." Emma paused. "In a few weeks, we'll be back at full staff. People return from leave. The new guide will pick up some slack. Not long after, guest volume will fall off with the start of the short rains. Everything always works out."

A few minutes later, Emma put down her fork and looked around. "I must visit the Ladies. Alexa, could you walk with me? Sometimes these village toilets are quite open-air affairs. I might need a guard at the entrance or help chasing off a random cow."

"Um, sure." Alexa rolled her eyes at Reese.

"Good idea." He looked at his watch. "It's almost time to leave."

Harry rose. "Let me check in with our other passengers, make sure they're still okay with the two o'clock flight time?"

As Emma led Alexa to a modern, enclosed toilet on the far side of the church, she murmured, "What is going on with you and Reese and Harry? The tension was so thick I could have cut it with a knife."

Alexa shook her head. "I'm not one hundred percent sure. I think it has less to do with Harry and more to do with the fact that he was there to rescue me from the elephants and Reese wasn't. Some sort of wounded male pride thing? I tried to talk about it, but Reese just shut me down."

Emma stopped short and snorted. "So, Harry's crush on you has nothing to do with it?"

"What crush? We're good friends. We developed a stronger bond," Alexa's voice caught, "that terrible night."

"Girl, you can't be that blind. Harry has been carrying a torch for you since you showed up in Botswana. And you certainly haven't discouraged him."

Alexa sighed. "No doubt he's good-looking. And can turn on the charm—I assumed charming is just his natural state. As I got to know him better, I discovered a genuinely interesting guy beneath that glib surface. And I've probably responded to that. Lately, Reese has been away a lot; preoccupied with this project in Zimbabwe."

Emma raised an eyebrow.

Alexa shook her head. "I didn't mean to give Harry any ideas. I'm committed to Reese. After all, I dropped everything at home and followed him across the world to come here." She scrunched up her face. "Why would Harry be interested in me anyway? He meets tons of glamorous women on these safaris. Wasn't he a private guide for that movie star, Lili Reynolds, earlier this summer?"

"You're selling yourself short, love, and you know it," Emma frowned. "You're attractive. Look at all those curls. You're smart as a whip. An attorney. Working on this commission with the government. And you've got a spine. I'd be curled into the fetal position for months after that night in the bush when Mo was killed. Bloody hell," Emma laughed and poked Alexa's arm, "I believe I have a crush on you too."

On the way back, Emma chattered on. "You say Reese has been a bit moody. Welcome to the club. Nicky has been an absolute bear for the past few months. And now, he's taking this incident with you and Mo so hard. Delta Wild hasn't criticized Nick or me. They understand that it was a routine research activity that just went bad. Things happen in the bush. In fact, management even praised Nick for sending a guide from Noka with you. And they know Harry's one of their best. But Nicky's been so unhappy. When I ask, he just says he blames himself." Emma snickered. "And they say women are the emotional ones."

Alexa and Emma were still laughing when they returned to the table. Reese was sitting with the other helicopter passengers.

"Where's Harry?" Emma asked. "I need to ask him something before you leave. Camp business."

"Off somewhere. Said he'd be back in a few minutes." Reese shrugged and went back to his conversation with the Delta Wild managers.

Glancing around, Alexa spotted Harry beneath one of the few trees she'd seen in the dusty village. He towered above most of the crowd, his red hair a bright beacon, even in the shade. She was about to point him out to Emma but paused. Harry looked to be in an animated discussion with Mo's good friend, Otsile, and Sammy, the Africa Trust researcher she'd hit with a cricket bat. What an unlikely trio. With an angry slash of his hand, Harry stalked away, still limping a bit.

Alexa turned her head, but not quick enough to miss the eyebrow that Harry raised in her direction. As he approached, she fended off the inevitable question with, "Emma was looking for you."

"Oh?" Harry turned to Emma.

"You said you'll be back to Noka tomorrow but didn't say when. Can we put you on the schedule for the afternoon?"

"Yes, I have a morning flight," Harry replied, then looked at the rest of the group. "Ready to leave for Maun?"

Reese and the Delta Wild managers nodded and stood as Alexa turned to Emma. "You're going back to Noka?"

"Yes. A driver is waiting to take me back to the airport. I'm on a late-afternoon flight with a group of guests coming in from Victoria Falls."

Alexa welcomed the headsets on the flight back to Maun. The crew insisted passengers wear them to hear directions and warnings in the noisy helicopter; they also forestalled any idle conversation. Instead, Alexa pondered Emma's statement that Harry had a crush on her. Maybe he did. He'd always sought her out when their paths had crossed. And he'd crept up to the verge of something—a declaration, a kiss?—the night he'd walked her to her tent at Noka. Maybe she had encouraged him; especially when she'd had that flash of jealousy over Reese and Karla. No doubt she'd turned to him for help and comfort the night of the elephant stampede.

If Emma was correct about Harry's feelings, Alexa hadn't really been fair to him. But was Emma simply stirring the pot because she was looking for a distraction from Nick's bad moods? She glanced at Reese, who was staring out the window. *Of course. He sensed it too. That's why he'd flipped out after that terrible night.* It wasn't so much that Harry had been the one to rescue Alexa. It was more that Harry was even traveling with her in the first place.

Do I talk to Harry or do I just let it slide? Alexa debated. *I'll be gone in a few weeks, and that will be the end of it. But Harry saved my life. Would it be more honorable to discuss the issue? Or would that just embarrass him? He's such a decent guy, very open and honest.*

Then Alexa considered the furtive discussion he'd been having with Otsile and Sammy. Maybe she didn't know Harry as well as she thought.

The pilot's voice interrupted. "Prepare for landing. We'll be touching down in five minutes."

"What a heartbreaking day." Reese shook his head as he handed Alexa a glass of wine. "I still can't believe Mo's dead."

"How devastating for his parents. They're overwhelmed with grief."

"Mo told me they were so proud he was accepted to university. One of the first in his village to reach university levels." Reese sank into the chaise next to Alexa. Once again, they had the Maun house to themselves for the weekend and had come out to the screened porch to watch the sunset. "Oh. I didn't want to bring it up at the funeral, but I heard yesterday that the prosecutors have closed the inquiry into Mo's death. The magistrate ruled it accidental."

"That was fast. Does it mean the poachers won't be charged with manslaughter?"

"Correct. It's likely the poachers' gunfire caused the elephants to run. Problem is that can't be proved as a certainty. And there's no evidence that the poachers knew you were up there on the hill. They may not be aware of that fact, even today."

"And still no word on the bachelor boys, the man-eating lions?"

"No. The Delta Wild guys said the BDF assumes they crossed into Zimbabwe, frightened by the tracking teams. No one has seen them in any of the concessions on this side of the border."

Alexa and Reese were quiet for a few minutes, listening to the first tentative tinkles of the bell frogs as the sun sank over the river.

"I'll miss this porch. Maybe we should add a screened porch to the cabin when we get home," Alexa broke the silence.

"And bring along the river and the bell frogs? Not sure we can recreate this *ambience*," Reese drawled the last word, "in the woods of Pennsylvania."

Alexa gave his arm a gentle punch. "Point taken. Although I love the peepers at home, nothing quite matches the sound of these tiny frogs."

Wunh, wunh, wunh.

At the deep call of a bullfrog, Alexa and Reese both laughed.

"How about pizza for dinner? I can call for delivery," he suggested.

"Perfect. Comfort food. I want pepperoni."

"Of course you do." Reese smiled, then touched Alexa's arm. "How are you holding up after all of today's activity? Does your stomach hurt?"

"No." She grimaced. "The only time I felt any pain was when I whacked myself with the buckle from the seat harness in the helicopter. Right where the bruise is the worst. I'm good. The few days of rest really helped."

Reese swung his legs toward Alexa and sat upright on the chaise. "Hey, I need to apologize."

"For what?"

"I acted like a jerk when we came back here after the clinic that day. You were still in shock, in pain, and falling asleep on your feet. And instead of telling you how much I love you and how worried I'd been, I jumped all over you about Harry. I'll admit. I'm a little jealous of the guy. But he helped you survive a dangerous situation. I should have been pampering you and thanking the man who helped keep you safe."

Alexa reached for Reese's hand. "Thank you. The fact that you care is important to me. And believe me. I can relate to the occasional pang of jealousy. I've had my moments over you and young Karla from Denmark."

"Karla?" Reese frowned. "Seriously? She's just a kid."

"Yeah, seriously. And you have no more reason to be jealous of Harry than I do of Karla. I like him a lot, and I'll be forever grateful that he got me through that terrible night safe and mostly sound. But I love you." Alexa kissed Reese's hand. "You."

Reese stood and pulled Alexa to her feet. "Maybe that pizza can wait." He brought his mouth to hers in a long, simmering kiss.

She rose to her tiptoes and leaned into the kiss. "Maybe it can," she breathed. Taking Reese's hand, Alexa led him down the hall, pink with gathering dusk, to their bedroom.

CHAPTER EIGHTEEN

"MISS WILLIAMS," THE chauffeur said as he opened the door.

"Hello, Big Boy," Alexa replied as she climbed into the black SUV.

The guard at the gate was the same man on duty as the first time Big Boy had taken Alexa to visit Mama Botswana. This time, he smiled and bowed as they drove out of the hotel lot. Had Alexa been imagining his consternation that night? Perhaps this trip in the middle of a bright, sunny afternoon was at a more acceptable hour?

As Alexa settled back into the seat, Big Boy said, "We are going to Mama's office near the hospital, so we will be there very soon."

"Fine," Alexa responded while she fretted again over whether she should have agreed to this meeting. The fact that it was in Mama's business office was one of the reasons she'd said yes. More importantly, she'd made a promise to help with Mama's draft sex-trafficking legislation. The advance copy that had been emailed to her incorporated some key concepts from Alexa's Pennsylvania task force. And the bill had real promise.

But the icon's abrupt defection from endorsing the pivotal hunting ban had made Alexa wary of the woman. It wasn't so much the policy position of wanting a shorter period for the ban. It was more the underhanded way Mama had gone about it—agreeing to the proposal in the workgroup session and then torpedoing it in the critical Commission meeting just one day later.

In the end, Alexa went with the good cause, deciding any contribution she could make to help prevent the sex trafficking of vulnerable women and children was well worth it. Even if it meant working with a woman she could no longer trust.

I won't let her dazzle me this time, Alexa vowed. *Just because she's famous doesn't mean she's everything she pretends to be. Sometimes public image is a mirage. I've read that even Mother Theresa could be a real hard-ass.*

Big Boy crawled through the neighborhood of Princess Marina Hospital, Gaborone's major public medical center. Pedestrians filled the wide streets, many of them wearing medical uniforms, many of them clearly patients. Several modern clinic buildings surrounding the multistory hospital and its outbuildings had familiar names, like Botswana-Harvard AIDS Institute Partnership and Botswana-Baylor Children's Clinical Centre of Excellence. Alexa had learned that additional US and international medical institutions such as the University of Pennsylvania and Children's Hospital of Philadelphia also had partnered with the government hospital. Like the shiny government office buildings in several sections of the city, parts of the medical district reflected the recent money that had been invested in Gaborone infrastructure. Then Big Boy turned onto a narrower street where the outlying clinics and medical offices showed wear and tear.

The SUV took another right and traveled another block before Big Boy stopped in front of a tidy stone cottage. Quite a contrast to Mama's swanky home, this tiny gem looked like it had been built by a homesick Englishman during Bechuanaland's days as a British protectorate. A blazing fuchsia bougainvillea climbing up the left side of the small stoop provided enough charm to overshadow the unkempt patches of dirt on either side of the stone walk.

Big Boy hurried out of the SUV and opened Alexa's door. His huge bulk threw a shadow over the curb, so she exited cautiously onto the unfamiliar pavement.

"Through the front door. The girl there will take you to Mama." Big Boy pointed toward the house.

Stepping inside, Alexa walked up to the young woman sitting at the front desk. "Hello. I'm Alexa Williams. Here to see Mama Nkala. She's expecting me."

"*Dumela, Mma,*" the receptionist replied with a smile. Big Boy had not been far wrong in calling her a girl. She looked quite young. At least she wasn't wearing a white pinafore. The office was a little less *Downton Abbey* than Mama's home turf. "Please take a seat. I will tell Mama that you are here."

A few minutes later the receptionist ushered Alexa into a large office where three people sat at a conference table. Mama Botswana rose to greet her.

"Come in, come in," she said with a huge smile. "This is Alexa Williams, our American expert on sex-trafficking legislation."

To Alexa, she said, "Please sit. Can we get you something to drink?"

"No, thank you." Alexa made her way to the table as Mama introduced her staff, a man and a woman. She still felt a little off-balance about coming here. The last time she'd seen Mama, the advocate had been railing against the proposed hunting ban in the Commission meeting. Once again, she felt her hackles rise. How could she ignore that?

Alexa bit her lip, then went with her earlier decision. The anti-trafficking work was what was important.

When seated, she used a neutral tone. "I reviewed your draft legislation. As I said in my comments, it looks fairly comprehensive to me. You said you wanted to go over the feedback I sent?"

Mama leaned back, an amused smile on her lips. "Oh my, yes. We were honored to receive your comments. But we have some very specific questions, to make sure we are clear on your thoughts."

As they began walking through the comments and the meeting fell into a familiar rhythm, Alexa's uneasiness receded.

Almost an hour later, Mama said, "Well, this has been so helpful. Thank you. We hope to present this draft to a friend in parliament who may be willing to introduce the legislation." She waved her hand at the staffers. "Can you work in these points and get me a new draft by tomorrow?"

Nodding, the two staffers left, clutching copies of Alexa's comments and copious notes of her answers to their questions.

As Alexa rose, Mama asked, "Could you stay a few minutes? I'd like to talk about the hunting ban. And perhaps you'd enjoy a cold drink before Big Boy takes you back to your hotel. Or wherever you'd like."

Alexa hesitated for a moment, then sat back down, feeling trapped. Her mother had raised her to be unfailingly polite. And despite their differences on the hunting issue, this woman was respected the world over. An ally in the fight against sex trafficking, she had a voice with influence well outside Botswana on this important issue. Alexa stifled an imperceptible sigh. "A Coke would be great if you have it."

Mama rang the little bell that sat in the center of the battered conference table, and the receptionist appeared. "Two Cokes, please."

"Right away, Mma."

Mama pointed to a sitting area in the corner of the room, beyond the desk. "Let's enjoy our drinks over there. Too much sitting in these wooden chairs is hard on my back." Twisting her waist as if to work out kinks, she crossed the room and sat in an armchair.

As Alexa perched on the edge of a faded chintz loveseat, the receptionist handed her a cold glass of soda. She took a sip and glanced around the room, a stark contrast from Mama's designer home. Worn furniture and an ancient carpet that looked as if they'd been old long before Bechuanaland declared independence from Britain in the mid-1960s and became Botswana. The single bright spot and only hint of native Africa in the room was the collection of colorful posters that lined the walls. They advertised various HIV/AIDS education campaigns, some in English, some in Setswana.

Mama drank from her glass and said, "Have you recovered from your injuries? Terrible business, that, up north. Sorry about the young man from your research team who was killed. What a trying experience."

"I'm fine now. My injuries were minor. Thank you for your condolences. Mokapi was a good man. A friend. We all mourn his loss." Alexa's initial surprise that Mama knew about the incident at the waterhole faded as fast as it arose. There had been some press coverage. And Alexa had learned to appreciate the power of Botswana's grapevine. In a country with some fairly remote areas, news traveled remarkably fast. And bad news? Warp speed.

Mama swallowed hard, "I once saw a man trampled by a wild elephant. He was trying to stop it from raiding his garden. I'll never forget it . . ." Her voice trailed off into silence, then she shook her head. "Distressing situation with these poachers. I am sure Colonel Shonga will soon have them in hand."

"I hope." Alexa grimaced. "They've killed far too many elephants. Now their actions have caused the death of my friend. In my experience, violence, once unleashed, can take unexpected paths."

Mama Nkala frowned. "I agree. But what can a girl like you know of violence?"

"You'd be surprised," Alexa responded. She'd been touched by Mama's emotional story about seeing an elephant trample a friend. It seemed to come from the heart, as if she might understand Alexa's own trauma over Mo's death. Then the woman had insulted her "American" experience and destroyed that tentative connection.

Alexa became wary again. "Perhaps a story for another day. I heard Tad Dorsey is under investigation. A theory that SAWA was staging poaching incidents to drum up support for anti-poaching proposals in the Commission report?"

"An odd theory, but Tad Dorsey and SAWA did paint a target on their own backs with that ridiculous protest. Word is the investigation now has been dropped."

"Never made much sense to me. They love animals too much," Alexa responded. "So, you wanted to discuss the hunting ban?"

"Ah, yes. The hunting ban." Mama placed her drink on the small table between them. "I know that many in our workgroup may have been surprised that I expressed reservations at the Commission meeting. Before I had a chance to fully explain my new position, things went off track. Because of the protest." She smiled. "I was one who headed for the door to avoid the tear gas.

"In the end, it may have worked out for the best. Dr. Kopo and I and a few others have been talking. We have a compromise to present tomorrow. Instead of ten years, we're proposing a ban for five, with an option to renew it for another five. It includes a new project for villagers who earned a living from hunting-related operations. To train them in alternative wildlife-focused jobs. And, it adds some funding to study animal population trends."

Mama continued, "I think it's a good compromise. It's a solution that can make a real difference to the villages. It allows us all a chance to assess the impacts of a ban on both employment and the animal populations. It doesn't lock us into a path for an entire decade. And, most important, it is something that the citizen groups can live with while achieving the same goal that the conservationists have been pushing."

Alexa moved back in her seat as Mama expounded. It felt like Mama was doing a dry run of tomorrow's speech to see how it played. She had to admit, as described, it didn't sound like a terrible deal. Lack of employment in the villages was an ongoing problem, so this could help. At the very least, it gave them a stake in the hunting ban extension. What was missing? Alexa kept waiting for the catch.

"How's the village employment project going to be funded?" Alexa asked when Mama stopped to take a breath.

"The increased concession fees. We will propose that a portion goes to this village project and the rest to conservation as anticipated."

Alexa angled her head as she thought this through. *The conservation groups may go for this compromise, but they'd be worried that money was being diverted from projects that benefit wildlife.*

Mama continued. "To address any concerns, there has been some discussion about asking for an international contribution toward the preservation of our wildlife resources that could help offset any lost hunting revenue. The Chinese have been ramping up investment in Botswana. And the United States and other European nations have always been there when we've needed them for projects like the HIV/AIDS initiatives."

There it was. The catch. Alexa sat up straight. "You think the Chinese would provide grants for wildlife preservation? The same China that's the destination for most of the illegal wildlife parts taken here in Botswana and the rest of Southern Africa?"

With an enigmatic smile, Mama said, "Perhaps our Chinese investors realize they need to rehabilitate their image. There have been a number of issues of shoddy construction, some with government buildings. And they know that most Batswana want to protect our wildlife. We don't like foreign theft of our natural resources."

"Not that I'm opposed to more conservation money, but it sounds like China thinks they can buy favor. And what? Continue to traffic in wildlife products? I'd rather see them go further in outlawing the import of wildlife parts—and enforcing those bans." Alexa leaned forward, clenching her fists.

"You're familiar with this Chinese saying, 'A journey of a thousand miles begins with a single step'? This idea of conservation funding may just turn out to be that single step. I believe Dr. Kopo is open to the experiment."

Alexa pursed her lips. "In America, we also have a saying, 'The fix is in.' Not to be too cynical here, but I thought you were lobbying me for support of this change. Now it sounds like I'm hearing about a done deal."

Mama frowned. "Oh, no. Dr. Kopo will be sharing this information tomorrow and asking for the Commission's endorsement. Nothing is a 'done deal,' as you call it. I admit that I'd like your vote on both shortening the length of the ban and the village program. I imagine this idea of accepting Chinese money is a decision to be made at high levels of government."

"Do you know if anyone's talked to the American embassy about this fund idea?"

"No, that would be for Dr. Kopo or others to handle, I expect."

Alexa stood. "Thanks for giving me a heads up. I'm surprised Dr. Kopo didn't send out a memo about this prior to the meeting tomorrow."

"Perhaps, given that this proposal has never before been discussed, he thought it needed a fuller, face-to-face explanation." Mama rose from her chair.

"I thought it important to fill you in. You've been so helpful to us on the sex-trafficking front." Mama lowered her voice. "And, frankly, I realize that it must have seemed ungracious that I didn't give you advance notice of my change in position at the last meeting. At our dinner that night, I was still getting input from a number of my advisers. Our position was not yet firm."

The attempt at an apology surprised Alexa. *Perhaps this isn't as done a deal as I'd thought.* "This gives me a chance to bounce these ideas off others at Africa Trust before tomorrow. They might be willing to compromise on the hunting ban. I can't predict their thoughts on this conservation fund. Is the money worth it if it gives the Chinese cover for importing animal parts?"

Mama nodded with a sage expression. "A legitimate concern. I've also heard some hesitation about accepting funds from the States and other countries that allow trophy hunting within their own borders or allow imported trophies from African nations. So many complicated ethical and practical issues. My mother used to say, 'When weaving a basket, choose the strongest blades of grass and cast the others aside.' Of course, the choosing takes experience and sound judgment."

Alexa smiled. "I suppose we'll be discussing this further tomorrow. Good luck with the trafficking legislation."

"Thank you, my dear. We appreciate your help. Big Boy will take you wherever you'd like to go from here."

On the brief ride back to her hotel, Alexa pondered whether she'd misjudged Mama. During the discussion on sex trafficking, she could tell that the woman had a true passion for helping trafficking victims and that her anti-AIDS crusade was heartfelt. Even her explanation for the abrupt change in position on the hunting ban at the last Commission meeting had the ring of truth.

Until now, Alexa hadn't appreciated the depth of Mama's involvement in Botswana politics. She'd seen politicians, lobbyists, and other players at work back home; Mama reminded Alexa of those who were masters at the game. Not surprising, really. One didn't get the level of government and international funding for HIV/AIDS work that Mama had obtained without serious political skills. Alexa knew there was more to this Chinese conservation fund than Mama had revealed. Although she had no specific reason to doubt the woman's motives, it would be a mistake to take anything about Mama Botswana at face value.

"Houston, we have a problem. It was out of my control, but I feel like I failed to complete my mission," Alexa moaned from her seat on the couch. She'd just arrived back in Maun from the Commission meeting in Gaborone and was consoling herself with a rare bag of potato chips.

Reese tossed some files into a wastebasket. "Hey, Gary knows more about Botswana conservation politics than we do. Last month, he was shocked that the Commission was considering a set of final recommendations so soon—almost like he expected things to fall apart."

"'Fall apart' is one way to put it. Torpedoed is more like it. We were so close. We resolved the financial questions, and even the enforcement provisions were endorsed with only slight modification. The group could have reached agreement on the shorter period for the hunting ban too. I feel certain we were close. But this international conservation fund. Chinese involvement. People just couldn't deal with an eleventh-hour proposal that was so controversial.

"You should have seen the uproar. It was almost as bad as the session the protestors interrupted. This time, the screaming was coming from the Commission members. People are up in arms about the elephant poaching, and they know that China is still a major black-market destination for ivory. The timing couldn't have been worse. That's why I say torpedo. It's like someone deliberately threw a bomb into the Commission's work."

"Who?" Reese asked. "Where'd the proposal come from? Hey. Any chips left?"

Alexa rolled off the couch and walked the chip bag over to Reese at his desk. "That's still not clear. Dr. Kopo wouldn't say. When I first heard about it from Mama Botswana, she talked vaguely about Chinese investors being interested. I don't know if they approached Dr. Kopo or if someone else floated the idea to them. Two of the Commission members speculated that the minister or even the president himself are involved. Who knows if that's true or whether they were just talking smack?" She perched on the wooden chair next to Reese.

He sampled the chips before he said, "I spoke to a few people at our embassy like you requested. They were aware of the international fund idea. Like you, they think it might have been floated to slow down any final Commission report until after this session of parliament. Sounds like they're trying to assess if it's even a legitimate proposal."

"Wow. It never occurred to me that the fund idea might not be serious." Alexa frowned. "If that's the case, they snookered Dr. Kopo. He'd never deliberately derail the Commission's work. The man's poured his heart and soul into this report."

Reese shrugged his shoulders. "The best you can do at this point is write up a summary for Gary. Tell him where the recommendations stand. Describe the fund and the reaction. And what the next steps will be. You said that the Commission won't meet again until October?"

"Right. Dr. Kopo was going to tell the minister that the report will be delayed. And it might be for the best that Gary is stepping back in. Like you said, he understands the nuances of Botswana politics better than I."

Alexa's tone became thoughtful, "You know I was outraged by Mama's about-face on the recommendations. As I've thought about it, perhaps my attitude says more about me than her."

With a puzzled expression, Reese asked, "And that would be?"

"I was looking more at the image than the real woman. You know, Mama Botswana, the Mother Theresa of the nation. I forgot that there's always a real person beneath the image. I think she cares a lot about victims of HIV/AIDS. But believe me, she didn't rise to international icon status without political skills. I'm not sure what her real goal is with conservation policy. I wouldn't be surprised if she's playing a larger game with trade-offs between her AIDS work and the Conservation Commission. In some ways, I respect that even though I might not agree with this fund idea." Alexa grabbed her laptop from the desk. "I'll work on the summary while the meeting's still fresh in my mind."

"Please take these chips too. I thought we stopped eating chips?" Reese handed her the bag. "I'm going to finish cleaning up here. It's the last window I'll have before we meet Jim and Melissa." Reese snapped his fingers. "I didn't get a chance to tell you since you went straight to bed when you returned from Gabs. I have to head out to Zimbabwe again tomorrow. Like you, I hope to finish the village project before I leave. Can you do this last trip to the Moremi on your own? Sammy knows which prides we're targeting."

Another surprise trip to Zimbabwe, Alexa thought. *A chance to say farewell to Karla?* She shook off that jealous notion, but as the clock ticked down to their departure, she worried still that Reese might find an excuse to stay in Africa.

Suddenly, the Sammy part of Reese's request registered. Alexa stopped in the middle of the living room and turned to her boyfriend. "Sammy? The guy I attacked with a cricket bat the last time we met?" Alexa winced and placed her laptop and the chips on the table. "With you along, I had a buffer. I hope he doesn't hold a grudge."

"He apologized for scaring you that night. It will be fine. Maybe you'll even get a chance to see that new leopard." Reese gave her an apologetic smile. "Sorry to dump this on you. This is a standard trip; nothing dangerous like the last one. No lion collaring. Just observation like we've done many times."

"No problem," Alexa said, suppressing a queasy feeling in the pit of her stomach as she wondered again what Sammy had dragged up from the river that night. She wasn't hesitant to go back out in the field, with or without Reese. Yet she still felt uneasy about Sammy. And about Karla the pop-tart waiting for Reese in Zimbabwe. She opened up the chips and inhaled another handful.

"I'll be back here Friday. Can you believe it?" Reese crowed. "Next, we head out on our official safari."

"The safari should be fun. And then, home." Alexa's smile was wistful. "I'm looking forward to seeing Scout, Mom and Dad, our cabin."

"Yep. My parents want us to visit soon after we're home. And I'm anxious to get back out on the rugby field. The fall season is already underway, but I might make a few games before the playoffs." Reese sighed. "It will be tough to go back to my Africa Trust desk job, but I've loved every minute of our time here. Kenya was great, but Botswana is even more spectacular. Seems like we just got here."

Alexa walked back to Reese, still seated at his desk, and gave him a hug. She decided to confront her nagging concern head-on. "I'm glad we came. But I've been worried that you wouldn't leave," she murmured into his cheek.

"What?" Reese turned. "We always knew this was temporary. A few months, then back home."

"But I lost you to Africa once before." Alexa stood and stepped back. "I've seen how much you love it here."

Reese stood and took her hands. "And I made my choice. I came back home because I love you. That hasn't changed. Yes, these few months in Botswana have been fantastic. Even though we've had a few bumps to contend with, I would be happy to stay longer. But only if you were with me. I tried Kenya alone the last time, and it didn't work. So, we'll be going home together. Because you're my home, Lexie."

With tears in her eyes, Alexa stepped into Reese's arms.

CHAPTER NINETEEN

WHEN SAMMY PICKED Alexa up at the airstrip, he plunged into a detailed explanation of the schedule for the afternoon and the next day. Although she had feared some tension, Sammy's tone was light and breezy. "This afternoon we'll look for the Lediba Pride. They like to hang out near the camp, not far from where the guides take guests on mokoro rides. Tomorrow, we'll drive to the Gomoti Plains and scout out the pride there. That will take the whole day."

"Sounds good. I'm here for the extra set of eyes and to sub for Reese on the annual survey. I know he was here a few months ago, but I've never been to this concession. I'm glad to get the chance to see it. You know that Gary will be back soon, and Reese and I will be returning to the States." Alexa caught herself babbling, as if that would cover any awkwardness between her and Sammy.

"Yes. I am knowing about Gary's return."

Alexa detected a sulky undertone in the researcher's voice. Despite his welcoming manner today, something about the guy continued to make her uneasy.

"Look, sable. A small herd, but such beautiful animals." Sammy pointed to the left at four glossy black males, big as horses, with two-foot horns that curved back over the animals' heads.

"They are handsome. My favorite antelope. Most I've seen are quite shy, but we don't seem to be bothering these fellows."

"No. They are used to the vehicles here. Camp is only a few minutes away."

"Sammy," Alexa bit her lip. "I wanted to apologize again for whacking you with the cricket bat that night."

"No problem, *Mma*. I was drinking *Chibuku* with my friends." At Alexa's puzzled look, he explained, "One of our traditional beers. I was not thinking so clear. I should have knocked. Please, do not mention it again." He waved a hand as if to dismiss the issue.

"Still, I overreacted," Alexa responded. "Can we call it even?"

Sammy wrinkled his face in confusion.

"Let's say we were both wrong," Alexa clarified. "And, as you suggest, not discuss it again."

"Good, Mma." Sammy looked bored with the entire discussion as he pulled the vehicle into the roundabout in front of the thatched common area of the camp. "I'll go park. Someone will show you to your tent. Let's meet here for brunch at ten-thirty. I'd like to head out soon after that to find the Lediba Pride before the guide vehicles could send them running into the brush."

As Alexa climbed the stairs to the common area, she shook her head and wondered. Was Sammy truly unfazed by their run-in at the Africa Trust house? Or was he a very good actor? She really couldn't tell.

Later that afternoon, Alexa wandered up to the common area to watch the sun set over the flooded river. She liked the low-key feel of this camp with its line of tents tucked away in a swath of trees facing the river. On their afternoon drive, Sammy had told her that the current high water was seasonal—part of the yearly flood that raised the water level in the Okavango and surrounding areas. In an annual cycle old as time, rains that fell months earlier in the distant highlands of Angola reached Botswana, seeping slowly into the ground and reaching peak level from June through August. The waters turned the Delta's rich vegetation green and sustained the animals that relied on the water. When the floods reached the Kalahari Plain south of the Delta, the water's flow vanished in the deep sands. Over a several-month period, the water levels in the Delta receded and much of the vegetation faded to yellow and tan. At this camp and elsewhere, the river abandoned the floodplain and returned to its core channel to wait for the dance to begin again the next year.

Earlier, Sammy had pointed to a line of three canoes carrying camp guests being poled by guides standing in the back. "See these mokoros gliding through the channels? In a few months, the water will be too low."

Now, as Alexa gazed at the expanse of river below the deck of the common building, she tried to imagine what it looked like when the water receded. On the far bank, a herd of elephants made its way to the water, each animal breaking into a run as it neared the channel. With an uneasy smile, she remembered similar behavior in the elephants at the waterhole, the evening before Mo was trampled.

"Can I get you a drink, miss?"

Startled, Alexa looked up at the server. "Yes, please. White wine would be lovely."

"We have a South African chardonnay?"

"Perfect."

The setting sun turned the sky a kaleidoscope of reds and pinks as its final rays painted the evening clouds. Then, the sun dropped into the river and darkness fell. Several vehicles unloaded camp guests at the main entrance, and a thirsty crowd assembled at the bar. A few minutes later, Sammy plopped into the chair at her side.

"I'm starving," he said. "They're having beef tonight. The chef here cooks the beef all afternoon in a thick gravy." Sammy clasped a hand to his heart. "It makes my mouth water just thinking about it."

Laughing, Alexa said, "Sounds good."

One of the staff rang a bell by the bar. "Dinner is served."

Sammy jumped to his feet. "Here, things are casual. Everyone sits at a single table, and they serve family style. Let's find a seat." He led her to an empty chair in the middle of the group of twenty or so. When things settled down, he introduced her to a few of their dining companions, including one of the two female camp managers and several guides.

Alexa was still trying to remember all the new names when the tall Batswana guide across from her leaned forward and spoke in hushed tones. "Did you hear about the latest poaching?"

"No," exclaimed Sammy as Alexa shook her head.

The manager, Nyana, motioned with her hand for Sammy to keep his voice down. "This one's bad. No need to upset the guests," she murmured.

"What happened?" Alexa asked.

The guide replied, "Several elephant carcasses were found on the edge of Makgadikgadi Pans, stripped of their tusks. The devils doused them in Temik. That killed a lot of vultures, hyenas, and jackals. A ranger I know said it looked like a war zone of dead animals."

"Temik?"

The guide to her right said, "A poison. Made for agricultural use but it kills anything it touches. It was banned years ago, but there are still old supplies around. Heard about poachers using it in South Africa and Zim. First I've heard of it used here."

Sammy shook his head. "Why sprinkle it on the dead elephants?"

Nyana responded, "To cover their tracks. Gives them time to get well clear of the area. They didn't want a guide or ranger to notice the birds of prey circling. A vulture takes a chunk of meat laced with Temik—instant death."

"My God, how savage." Alexa put a hand to her mouth in shock.

The first guide nodded. "Exactly. These criminals need to be tracked down and put away for a good long time."

"Or shot," muttered the second guide. "They're no better than mass murderers."

Alexa's stomach clenched. The beef on her plate looked less appetizing than it had a few seconds before. "This seems like a change in pattern. The poachers never used poison before. The other killings have all been near a river. There's no river near the Makgadikgadi Pans, is there? Just shallow seasonal pools."

"These dead elephants were nowhere near a river," Nyana responded. "Are you sure that the others were all by water?"

"Africa Trust has been following these incidents very closely. I'm certain that at least three of the five other incidents were near rivers." Alexa didn't share that she'd seen those three sites with her own eyes.

Sammy said nothing. Instead, he reached for another helping of beef.

Alexa picked at the food on her plate as the conversation turned away from the poaching and onto the animal sightings of the day. She only half tuned in to the conversation as she thought about this new twist in the poaching onslaught. Had the poachers simply taken a more diabolical turn with this latest incident? Their willingness to treat scores of other bird and animal deaths as collateral damage showed a callous disregard for life that went well beyond the transactional nature of killing an elephant for ivory. The latter she could understand, if not condone. But, to kill scavengers to delay the discovery of the carcasses was really cold-blooded.

Maybe this was a copycat. Another set of poachers who saw that the first group hadn't gotten caught and concluded, why not make some money too? Disgusted at either option, Alexa's shoulders drooped in dejection.

"I'm going to skip dessert," she said to Sammy.

His face dropped in disappointment. "Okay. I'll walk you back to your tent."

The guide next to Alexa said, "Stay put and finish your meal, mate. I'm heading back and can drop the lady by her tent."

Sammy smiled. "All right." He looked at Alexa. "We'll head out right after breakfast tomorrow. Sleep well, *Mma*."

As they left the dining area, the guide chuckled. "For such a scrawny little bugger, Sammy does like his food. But he's a decent guy. Dedicated researcher. We all have our quirks, don't we?"

Alexa responded with a half-smile but couldn't help wondering: Sammy had been remarkably blasé about tonight's poaching news for a man whose profession was wildlife research. Perhaps he truly loved the beef. Perhaps she was holding him to the impossibly high standard of her dead friend Mo. But something about this guy struck her as odd. Maybe he just wasn't that into his job?

The next morning, Sammy had already finished breakfast by the time Alexa arrived. "Just give me a few minutes," she said as he rose from the table.

"No rush. I have to round up our lunch and drinks from the kitchen. If we leave in the next half hour, that gives us plenty of time."

After finishing her meal, Alexa grabbed a cup of tea to go from the breakfast bar. Carrying the lidded metal cup and her backpack, she headed toward the vehicle. As she approached, a man in a staff uniform handed Sammy a big bag, which he placed in the rear compartment of the Toyota. From the way Sammy's arm dipped on the hand-off, Alexa could tell that the bag's contents were hefty. The man noticed her, said something to the researcher, then strode away with a last glance at Alexa. *Probably just a heads up to let Sammy know I'm approaching—or could it have been a warning?*

Sammy turned with a smile, "Ready? Today will be a fairly long drive, but the Gomoti Pride is quite large. And it is a beautiful open plain. One of my favorite areas."

"Looking forward to it," Alexa replied and slid into the passenger seat. As Sammy pulled away from camp, Alexa assembled her binoculars, camera, and notebooks so they'd be easily available. By now, the routine had become second nature. With a pang, Alexa reflected that this would likely be her last research trip in Botswana. She'd miss the time outdoors in Botswana's wild beauty.

The drive passed mostly in silence. Sammy spoke only to point out wildlife in the distance. Without his keen eye, Alexa would have missed several animals that blended almost seamlessly into their arid surroundings. A jackal, his fur a mottled beige, standing right by the road. A herd of giraffes with desert tan coats in the midst of a grove of thorny acacia. A pair of bat-eared foxes tumbling over each other as they played in the sand.

The passing landscape captivated Alexa. Early on, they slogged through kilometers of sandy flatland punctuated by stands of tall palms and spindly bare bushes. Sammy told her that the bushes were dormant and would revive with the late-October rains. For much of the drive, Sammy made frequent downshifts into low range as deep sand grabbed the Land Cruiser tires. When the vehicle rocked like a bronco as it powered through the relentless powder, Alexa had to grab the dash for stability.

Alexa sat forward in relief when they emerged onto a lush grassy plain. She'd enjoyed the stark, desert-like scenery, but she was happy to take a breather from all the rocking.

"Look." She pointed to a honey badger that darted across their path. As she watched, the fierce beast disappeared into one of the mounds of young, stubby palms dotting the landscape like small islands. Her eyes lifted to the wide plain beyond where a herd of zebra filled the horizon.

"This is prime honey badger territory. I wouldn't be surprised if we see more," Sammy said, then wiped his forehead. "I could use a break. Want to stop for tea?"

"Sure." Although still mid-morning, it was quite warm. The dearth of tall, shady trees in this area meant there was little protection from the morning sun. Alexa peeled off her jacket, glad for the canvas roof of the SUV.

Anxious to stretch her legs, Alexa circled the vehicle a few times while Sammy assembled the tea. When he handed her a steaming cup of Earl Grey, Alexa said, "Thank you. At home, I drink several cups of tea each morning. I'm so glad that the custom out here in the bush is to have mid-morning tea as well." She looked at Sammy's cup. "Or coffee."

"Yes. I'm a coffee drinker, now. We only drank tea at home. When I went to uni, a friend introduced me to coffee. He called it java. At first, I thought it was too bitter. But now, I can't get enough of it."

Spurred by this small exchange of personal information, Alexa said, "I don't know much about you, Sammy, except that you're from Botswana. How long have you been with Africa Trust?"

"Just a year, Mma. I live in Maun, which is where I grew up. I went to university there and did an internship for Batswana Conserve in community education. I had planned to go there and work full-time on that project after I graduated, but they lost their funding. So, I applied to Africa Trust."

"Do you like the job?"

"I like being out in the bush, but I don't like being away from my family so much. I am saving to start a cultural center in Maun. A place that tourists can come to learn about Botswana's tribal history. That way I can be home to help my parents. They take care of my brother's children."

"Full-time?"

"Yes. Both my brother and his wife have passed from the disease."

"HIV?"

"Yes." Sammy hung his head. "We thank God that the children were not infected. My brother worked in the diamond mines. Away from home for weeks at a time. He brought the disease home to his wife the year after their youngest child was born. My parents are happy to raise their grandchildren, but two extra mouths to feed is a struggle." Sammy flashed a shy smile. "That's why this job is so important to me, even though I have future plans."

"The cultural center sounds like an interesting idea," Alexa responded. "Wouldn't it cost a lot of money to get off the ground?"

"Yes, but I will apply for a government grant. It will take me at least another year to save the money I need. Maybe longer."

"Good luck on your project."

"Thank you." Sammy emptied the hot water and mugs and packed them into a basket. "Shall we go?" he said. "It's not far to the Gomoti Pride's territory."

After another short drive, Sammy stopped the Land Cruiser on a small rise and said, "The Gomoti Plain. The pride has a favorite spot on the other side of the river. We'll go there first."

Alexa looked down at the broad floodplain that spread below them. Zebra, wildebeest, elephants, impala, and red lechwe grazed on the short grasses. A small river meandered through the middle. She was surprised when a hippo surfaced, sending a water bird into flight. The bird, a heron of some sort, landed a short distance away, unfazed by a croc sunning on the bank.

"How beautiful," Alexa exclaimed. She took several photos as Sammy slowly descended the slope, but this spectacular scene was one that even her brand-new camera could not fully capture. It was like a real-life Garden of Eden. Too bad Reese wasn't here to see this lovely slice of Botswana.

After dinner that evening, Alexa and Sammy joined guests and staff around a roaring campfire. The day had been successful. They'd found, cataloged, and photographed the lively Gomoti Pride and then made the long drive back to camp, arriving just after nightfall.

Sammy was chatting with the guest next to him. Left to her own thoughts, Alexa stared into the fire and replayed the sights of the Gomoti Plain in her mind. When a guide approached Sammy from behind their chairs, Alexa roused from her sleepy trance. She came fully awake when the man passed Sammy a bag, which looked fairly heavy from the way he was handling it. *What was with these bags? First, the guy this morning. Now, this guide.*

When the man left, Sammy turned to Alexa and answered her unspoken question, "Palm nuts. Staff here collect them for me. I pay them for each nut. I take them home and my father carves them into decorations like Christmas tree ornaments. He sells them to a tourist shop in Maun."

A light bulb went on in Alexa's mind. "Did you drag a bag of these up from the river that night we had our run-in? I saw a groove in the dirt the next morning."

Sammy laughed. "I did. I tossed them against the house, then tripped over a garden chair. Next morning, my friend drove me home, and I delivered the bag to my father."

Alexa shook her head in bemusement, remembering all the wild theories she'd concocted about what Sammy had smuggled from the Thamalakane River. Ivory or some other contraband? No. Palm nuts. Elephants loved to shake real fan palm trees for their nuts, a delicacy for the giant beasts. The elephants digested the outer layer of the nuts, excreting the hard, plum-sized centers. She'd seen the work of local carvers who turned the nuts, often called vegetable ivory, into handicrafts. Sammy's big secret wasn't a secret at all.

"There's no rule against it," Sammy said in a defensive voice. "The camp managers know I take these home to Maun. There are still thousands left on the ground that grow into palms. Gary questioned me about it once though. He said I shouldn't take natural resources from the concessions. That Delta Wild might object."

"Do they object?"

"Nyana or the others never said anything."

Alexa shrugged her shoulders. This wasn't her battle. "I just couldn't figure out what was in these bags people kept handing you. Sounds like your father is a real artist. I understand that those nuts are as hard to carve as ivory."

"Maybe harder," Sammy said. "My father's work is much admired. I worry that I may not be able to bring him so many palm nuts in the future. Mokapi would collect them for me at Noka. At his funeral, I asked his friend Otsile if he would be willing to gather nuts for me instead. To take on his friend's obligation. Otsile and the tall, red-haired guide became angry with me. They said I shouldn't be talking about such things at Mo's funeral. I was not offended. I believe their anger was more about Mo's death than the palm nuts. I will miss Mo, just as I miss my brother. Still, the living must go on while the dead rest."

"Maybe you'll find someone else to help gather the nuts," Alexa replied as she remembered the argument between Harry, Otsile, and Sammy. It had seemed so suspicious but instead was totally mundane.

In her spacious tent for the night, Alexa made sure the window flaps were rolled up for airflow. This place was one of the roomiest staff tents she'd stayed in, more like a canvas-walled junior suite with a couch and sitting area. Too bad she was here for such a short stay.

Alexa climbed into the four-poster bed and pulled the mosquito netting into place. As she set the alarm on her phone, she thought about Sammy's palm nuts and giggled. The giggles expanded into uncontrollable laughter until tears ran down Alexa's cheeks and her bruised stomach gave a twinge of protest. Then a laugh caught in her throat and became something closer to a sob.

"It's time. It's time to go home," she whispered. Alexa had to admit that she wasn't fully healed from Mo's violent death, from that feeling of terror when she and Harry fled from the elephants. Dead friends. Dead elephants. Dead poachers. Monsters who would kill scores of birds and scavengers to conceal the slaughter of elephants for ivory.

Despite her love for Botswana, she was reeling, seeing evil around every corner. Imagining Sammy was up to no good. Wondering if Harry was involved in something fishy. Looking for nefarious motives in the woman Botswana considered a saint. All but accusing Reese of cheating on her with that blonde teenage Dane.

She needed to take a step back. Reuniting and going on safari with Melissa and Jim would be wonderful. But the ultimate cure was on the horizon: her cabin in the woods; her dog, Scout; and time to just chill with Reese.

Alexa shivered with embarrassment. *Have I become one of those self-absorbed prima donnas, weak and needy, making everything about me, me, me?* Upon consideration, she decided to give herself a break. Maybe she was just homesick.

Exhausted from her emotional outburst and the day's long drive, Alexa turned off the light and went to sleep.

CHAPTER TWENTY

"LOOK AT YOU two, all tan and khaki-clad. Sun-streaked hair. I barely recognize you." Her auburn locks bouncing in a wild halo around her beaming face, Melissa rushed forward to hug Alexa.

Tall, burly Jim trailed behind, pushing a cart full of luggage. With a broad grin, he and Reese gave each other awkward man-pats then sprang apart. "Dude," he said. "It's been a while."

"It has," Reese nodded. "Seems a little surreal to see you two here in Botswana."

Alexa asked, "How's your safari been so far?"

"Great." Jim returned to his cart.

"Fantastic," Melissa enthused. "Can't believe how luxurious Ebony Camp was. We've been pampered and spoiled beyond . . ."

A group of exuberant tourists barged between Alexa and her companions, cutting off Melissa's reply.

The three paused until Alexa caught up, then Reese said, "This airport's always a madhouse. They can't get the expansion finished too soon. Let's get out of here, and then we can talk."

Twenty minutes later, they arrived at the Africa Trust house, where Melissa and Jim would spend two nights. Then, Alexa and Reese would join them on the rest of their safari.

Sally had insisted on coming in Saturday morning to prepare for the guests. She served soup and sandwiches to the four friends at the makeshift table on the screened porch.

"This soup is so good." Melissa took another spoonful. "I can't place the flavor?"

"Pumpkin." Alexa giggled and shot Reese a knowing glance. "At any meal, there's a ninety percent chance that the soup is pumpkin. I think it should be named Botswana's national vegetable."

"Could be that it's more popular on the safari circuit than in local homes," Reese commented.

"Isn't pumpkin a fruit?" Jim asked with a mournful glance at his empty bowl.

"Yes. But everyone thinks it's a veggie," Melissa laughed.

"Best soup I've had since we started this vacation," Jim said. "Great lunch."

"Knowing Sally, there's more . . . fruit soup." Grinning, Alexa reached for his bowl. "I'll get you a refill."

"No, I remember where the kitchen is." Jim rose, bowl in hand, and wandered into the house.

Melissa looked toward the river where polers steered a pair of mokoros down the Thamalakane. The laughter of the passengers and the splash of the long poles through water murmured in gentle melody as if the river were babbling a soft tune. "Wow," she said. "What a wonderful place to live."

Before Alexa could answer, Reese replied. "We've spent about half of our time here in Maun, half out in the bush. It's been a pretty amazing few months. But both Lexie and I have missed the cabin. And it's great that we'll make it home in time for autumn. I would hate to miss the leaves turning."

Alexa added, "Part of my regular assignment took me to Botswana's capital, Gaborone, several times. It's not the most memorable city in the world, but, still, an interesting experience. A real mix that ranges from super-modern to one-room, tin-roofed shacks."

Melissa shook her head. "You spent a decade in New York City, so I imagine all other cities pale in comparison."

"New York makes Gabs look like a small town. The tallest building is maybe thirty floors. And that building is both fairly new and unique in its height. Comparing New York to Gaborone? Comparing apples to oranges."

"Uh, I guess you mean Big Apples, right?" Melissa broke into peals of laughter and reminded Alexa how much she'd missed her best friend.

That evening, Alexa and Reese took their friends to Chapman's for a taste of the party side of Maun. Both the bar and restaurant were packed, but Pretty found them a table.

"I hear you go home to America soon," she said as she handed around menus. "We will miss you."

"We leave in about two weeks. We might make it back in here before we go." Reese smiled. "One more Baobab Burger for the road."

"I hope so." Pretty tittered. "Can I get you drinks?"

While they chatted and waited for their meals, Colonel Shonga appeared out of nowhere and strode toward the table. "Michaels, I heard you were here," he barked, then nodded to Alexa and threw a quick glance toward Melissa and Jim.

Reese said, "Colonel Shonga, meet our friends Melissa and Jim from the States. Jim and I were forest rangers together." He looked at the guests. "Colonel Shonga is head of the Botswana Defence Force anti-poaching efforts. The BDF has one of the best track records for deterring poaching in the entire continent."

Pretty rushed up with an empty chair, and the colonel sat. He leaned forward and spoke in a low voice, "I know you are leaving Botswana soon. I will be sorry to see you leave. You've both been quite helpful in providing information about this latest rash of incidents."

The colonel held Alexa's eyes as he asked, "Are you fully recovered, my dear?"

"Physically, yes. I think it will take a while for the nightmares to go away. In time, I know they will fade. Of course, Mokapi doesn't have that luxury."

"Yes. A tragedy. I hear his parents will receive compensation for the young man's death. Money is hardly an adequate substitute for the loss of a son, however.

"I have some good news. Our unit down south near the Makgadikgadi Pans caught three poachers this morning. They were armed with high-powered rifles, *okapi* knives, and Temik. We believe they are certainly the men responsible for the last poaching where poison was used. Perhaps the others as well. The Public Prosecutor's Office believes it unlikely that we would have two large-scale poaching operations at work at the same time, given our recent success in deterrence. I am not entirely convinced, but I hope they are correct."

Reese sighed. "That *is* good news. These bastards have been escalating. Yes, that first massacre was shocking. But now they're endangering the entire ecosystem with the poison. The ramifications go well beyond the elephant populations."

"Are they locals?" Alexa asked.

"They have Francistown addresses, but we believe they're originally from Zambia. The investigators have just begun to sort through that as well as trying to identify their buyer for the ivory. I can't say much more at this time."

"Will they reopen the case and charge them with Mokapi's murder?" Reese asked in a bitter tone.

"That will be up to the director of public prosecutors." The colonel grimaced. "Like you, I believe the poachers are responsible for inciting the elephant stampede that killed your researcher. Murder? Unlikely. Even manslaughter would be hard to prove. And tricky since they closed the case."

He looked at Alexa. "I assume you would be willing to return to testify at a trial for the poachers, if needed?"

"Yes. The investigators have my contact information in the States."

Colonel Shonga straightened. "I must get back to my dinner meeting. But I wanted to thank you personally, and the Africa Trust organization, for your support of strong anti-poaching measures." He turned to Alexa. "When we first met, I did not make the connection that you were sitting on the Conservation Commission. I understand that you've been an ardent advocate for the stronger enforcement provisions and extended hunting ban."

"That has been Africa Trust's position. I've tried to represent it as best I could. You might know that the Commission's effort has gone off track. Now, they seem to be going down a rabbit hole with this Chinese and international compensation fund idea."

The colonel tilted his head. "Rabbit hole?"

"Sorry. A reference to the children's book *Alice in Wonderland*. I mean that this funding idea has been introduced at the last minute and it's leading the Commission down a longer path. Perhaps it's an idea that could work and add funding for conservation. Perhaps it's a distraction to derail the Commission's final recommendations. I don't know enough about Botswana politics to judge."

The colonel's eyes crinkled, and he pursed his lips in something approaching a smile. "We have a proverb that says, 'If you live in a mud hut, beware of the rain.' I believe you understand Botswana politics all too well, Miss Williams. This offer of Chinese *pula*, assuming it is real, comes with invisible strings that may have little to do with protecting wildlife. Considering the Asian predilection for ivory and more, it may be the exact opposite. This battle will be fought outside the Commission at the highest levels of government. And, when it is resolved, the Commission can resume its work."

Reese said, "We'll be in country for two more weeks, Colonel. I hope that you'll have the information to charge these poachers before we leave."

"If you wish, check in with Major Bisi for an update." Colonel Shonga pushed back his chair, rose, and strode from the room.

As he left, Alexa glanced around. The attention of the entire restaurant was riveted on their table. The gawkers included Nick Fuller, who was hugging a barstool next to his friend, the tall man who'd been wearing the white suit on their last visit to Chapman's. Tonight, the man was wearing a sky-blue designer jogging outfit, which stood out even more starkly against the sea of khaki and blue jeans than his previous linen number. When the colonel exited the room, Nick and his friend swung their stools back to the bar and plunged into an animated conversation.

Alexa raised an eyebrow as she thought: *Emma is worried about another woman. Perhaps she should be worrying about this flamboyant man. One never knows about sexual preferences.*

Melissa's voice drew her back to the table. "Well, that's an imposing man. Colonel . . . didn't catch the last name? He's the guy in charge, I take it?"

"What's the story on this poaching?" Jim asked. "One of the guides at Ebony mentioned an elephant kill but then clammed up when the camp manager walked by. Are you two wrapped up in that somehow?"

"Colonel Shonga," Reese clarified. "Yes, he's second in command of the army here, which is dedicated almost entirely to anti-poaching efforts. Alexa and I stumbled upon the first poaching incident when we were out in the field."

"Of course you did," Melissa groaned, rolling her eyes. "Alexa has a knack for finding trouble. Why would this African paradise be any different? Did I hear you say someone was murdered? You didn't find another dead body, did you?" She looked at Alexa in disbelief.

Alexa and Reese spent most of the meal recounting their brushes with the poachers' work and Alexa's frightening night when she, Harry, and Tale had observed them in the act—the night that Mo had been killed by elephants fleeing the poachers' rifles.

The story was interrupted by several friends who stopped at the table to say goodbye. Then Jim went back to the poaching discussion. Having arrested a few out-of-season deer hunters at home in the Michaux State Forest, he was fascinated by the challenge of tracking down people who would wipe out an entire herd of elephants. He peppered Reese with detailed questions.

When Jim and Reese launched into a discussion of the technical aspects of Temik poisoning on the food chain, Alexa's attention wandered. She looked to see if Nick was still at the bar. Both he and his well-dressed friend had vanished, their seats now filled by two guys who worked for one of the mokoro outfitters.

Jim was still asking questions of Reese when Pretty brought the bill. Jim stopped talking long enough to pick up the tab. "We'd never have scheduled this safari if you two hadn't lured us to Botswana. We owe you," he said.

"Yes. It's been wonderful. Lucky for us, we've not seen any poaching," Melissa chirped.

Alexa smiled. "Sounds like the bad guys are in jail. No one's going to have to worry about poaching—at least in the immediate future."

"And the adventure is just about to kick into high gear. We have tomorrow to hang out and ten more days on safari." Reese pushed back his chair. "Let's go back to the house. We'll take you on a mini-tour of Maun tomorrow, but otherwise, let's take it easy. We have to get ready for those early mornings out in the bush."

Alexa threw herself into their safari with abandon. She'd worried that the vacation with Melissa and Jim would feel like an extension of the last four months in the field. So, she was surprised by how much fun she was having. And how different it was to be driven by a guide; to have a wide focus on all of Botswana's many animals and not just the big cats. Even the meals in camp took on a fresh aspect as the friends focused not on research but on enjoying each other's company and recounting the day's animal sightings. Of course, seeing Botswana through the eyes of their best friends was also a treat. This was the first trip to the African wilds for both Melissa and Jim, and they were loving the experience.

Their first camp was in the Kalahari Desert. Although Reese had made a quick trip to the Central Kalahari early in their stint in Botswana, the stark but beautiful landscape was new to Alexa. She had expected a desert of sand like the pictures she'd seen of the Sahara. The Kalahari was very dry and sandy, but some of it was covered in hardy grasses that reminded Alexa a little of wheat before harvest time at home. Elsewhere, clumps of shrubs, grasses, and cactus dotted large expanses of hardpacked sand. Yet another type of acacia tree, the small, umbrella-shaped camelthorn, was the most common tree in the area. These ubiquitous trees paled in comparison to a towering baobab they visited the first day. It dwarfed any they'd seen on the Delta.

The desert wildlife included some unique species. Their guide found two prides of the famous black-maned lions of the Kalahari. They saw a family of cheetah hunting one morning, and the area teemed with honey badgers, oryx, springbok, brown hyenas, and intriguing birds like the pale chanting goshawk and massive kori bustards.

"I can't believe the baobab tree was two thousand years old," Melissa marveled that night at dinner. "I got some interesting shots of the limbs against the sky. They really do look more like roots on top than branches. I'm disappointed though. The tree was just too large to capture in my lens."

"Definitely ginormous and impressive." Jim nodded as he cut a piece of meat on his plate. "Like this kudu. Tastes just like beef."

"I'm glad our guide took a photo of us standing in front of the tree. But we're going to look like ants compared to the size of that trunk." Alexa laughed.

Reese nodded. "He had to walk out over a hundred yards to fit the tree in his shot. When we get home, we'll have to circle the four of us in the picture so people know we're there."

"It's sad that the elephants are destroying the baobabs." Jim shook his head. "The trees piled around it to block the ellies. Seems like a losing game. The elephants must be relentless."

Reese shrugged his shoulders. "The bark retains moisture in the dry season." He waved his hand at the plain in front of the camp. "Water's scarce out here, so you can't blame them."

"But they're such magnificent trees. And now so rare. Just think. If that granddaddy out there dies, it will be two thousand years before a seedling reaches that size." Melissa frowned.

"You've just summed up the dilemma that faces so many aspects of conservation in Africa," Alexa said. "This commission I've been part of, we're trying to update some of Botswana's conservation policies. And so much comes down to balance. To tradeoffs."

Jim nodded his head. "Same thing, different issues at home. For instance, how many deer are too many? How long should the hunting season be to thin the herd but not go overboard?"

Alexa smiled. "Exactly. Here, it's do we protect elephants at all costs, because the population is under threat on this continent, even though their numbers here in Botswana are larger than anywhere in Africa? Or do we allow some hunting? Elephants are ravaging crops in some of the villages, where a season's harvest can mean food for the next year."

"I've been dealing with a similar issue over in Zimbabwe, near Hwange National Park, involving a lion." Reese put down his fork. "He was raiding goats and cattle from a village. They were afraid he'd turn to kids next. Or an adult in the wrong place at the wrong time. The traditional village response would be to poison the lion. We negotiated a compromise and are funding a few villagers to act as lion protectors. The concept's based on one that a University of Oxford program out here called WildCRU has modeled successfully. They research lions too.

"Anyway, the protectors will watch for the lion and scare him away from the village with noisemakers and other techniques. They'll also work with the villagers on safety measures like penning their livestock at night. And educate them about the importance of lion conservation."

Jim leaned toward Reese, "You'll have to fill me in on the details. Sounds like a great approach."

He shifted his attention to Alexa. "We have some of these same animal/human dilemmas at home. To a larger scale in some of the Western states. To a smaller scale in Pennsylvania. Can't imagine how tough it must be in Botswana and other African countries with their wildlife density. I don't envy the policymakers."

Alexa smiled. "In our brief time here, we've just scratched the surface. But you're right. They are hard issues with hard choices, but the long-term consequences can be enormous."

On the second night of their stay, the camp staff made up a bed on an elevated deck over their tent. Bundled in down blankets to ward off the near-freezing desert night, Alexa and Reese lay on the plush mattress and marveled at the spectacular night sky.

"I've never seen so many stars," Alexa breathed. "This is truly amazing. The sky's so vast. Yet, it seems like I could reach out and touch a constellation."

"Absolutely. It's all flat land out there so the horizon seems endless. Look at the depth of the Milky Way. I think that's the Southern Cross." Reese pointed to a spot on the right.

"It's too beautiful out here to sleep."

"We're miles and miles from any source of light pollution. And no moon tonight," Reese said. "This must be one of the best spots in the world, at least on land, for star-gazing."

"I hope Melissa and Jim are sleeping out too. Jim was trying to convince her that leopards wouldn't climb over the gate and up the stairs."

"Look." Reese pointed. "A shooting star."

Alexa smiled at the trail of light as the star traveled across the enormous sky. "Make a wish."

"I have everything I've wished for right here," he murmured and turned to kiss Alexa.

"I love you," she whispered.

"Wow, look how fast my wish was granted," he teased. "Let's look for more falling stars."

Snuggling onto Reese's shoulder, Alexa gazed at the sky in wonder for quite a while. At some point, she felt her boyfriend slip into the steady breathing that signaled sleep. Eventually, Alexa closed her eyes and joined him. Even the most memorable night sky she'd ever seen couldn't compete with a tiring day spent in the midday heat and fresh air of the Kalahari.

Their second stop was a dry camp on the western edge of the Delta, rich with wildlife in its grasslands and small forests. Between the early morning and late-afternoon game drives, the four friends fell into the habit of long brunches, in which they shared their experiences over the past four months. Alexa couldn't hear enough stories about Scout, and his adventures with Ansel while in Melissa and Jim's care.

"It was great of your parents to take both of the dogs while we are on our trip," Melissa said. "My parents are so flighty; I'd worry about our little Frenchie all the time if we'd left him with them."

"Melissa, your parents might live their life like it's still the sixties, but they would take perfect care of Ansel."

"You're right. But Ansel and Scout have been a team for the last four months. Keeping them together was less disruptive. Did I tell you about the mini-exhibit I did at the gallery with photos of the two of them?"

As Alexa leaned back and listened to Melissa chatter about the dogs and then launch into a story about the latest exhibit at her photo gallery, she smiled. She and Melissa had been friends since elementary school. It was one of those friendships that remained strong even after periods of separation. The longest hiatus had been during Alexa's years in New York City, at Columbia for college and law school, then followed by a few years at a big corporate law firm. She and Melissa had kept in touch and seen each other just a few times during those years. When Alexa returned to her hometown, they slipped back into hanging out together, just as they had as kids.

When Jim jumped into Melissa's monologue to suggest some rest time in their tent, Reese's amused eyes met Alexa's across the table. Alexa knew he was still surprised that his outdoorsy former housemate had found happiness with the artistic, flamboyant Melissa.

"Sounds like a good idea. I could use a nap," Reese said. "We're doing a night drive, right? That means a late dinner."

"I hope we see bush babies," Alexa said. "They're hard to spot because they're so small and they jump from branch to branch. But they have these huge eyes."

Melissa raised an eyebrow, "Bush babies sound totally adorbs, but is it scary out there at night? Aren't the predators out hunting then?"

"As long as we stay in the vehicle they won't bother us. I hope we do see some lions or hyenas on the prowl. The guide will have a red light so we can spot the night animals." Reese made no effort to restrain his enthusiasm for the upcoming night drive.

Jim took Melissa's hand. "It will be great. Just wait."

When Reese mentioned lions on the prowl, Alexa felt the temperature drop. In that instant, she was back on a remote ridge in the cool of night, watching two lions leap onto a man's back.

"Ready to leave, Lexie?"

Reese's question brought Alexa back to the present. She looked up in surprise. Her three companions had all risen from the table and were waiting for her.

On the way back to their tents, the group had to stop on the raised boardwalk to allow a small family of elephants to cross in front of them. The boardwalk dipped down to the ground for a short distance to provide a path for elephants and other animals that wandered through camp.

At first sight of the elephants, Alexa's stomach tightened. She imagined that the boards beneath her feet were shaking. One of the larger females at the rear of the line halted in the middle of the crosswalk and turned her head to trumpet at the four humans. Alexa recognized this as a warning call. The elephant was just telling them to stay clear of the youngsters in the herd. Still, she recoiled and grabbed the wooden rail as sweat beaded on her forehead.

"Should we back off?" Melissa whispered. "Will it charge?"

"No. We're fine. Let's just wait until they're well clear of the area," Reese reassured her while Alexa white-knuckled the handrail. "It's okay, Lexie," he murmured. "They're moving on. There's no danger."

Jim and Melissa had moved to the far side of the boardwalk and were laughing at the antics of the tiniest elephant in the departing herd.

"Wow." Alexa shook her head. "How many elephants have we seen from the vehicles, and I've been fine? But, this time, the smell of elephant and dust. I was back in that night, running for the trees." She didn't mention her earlier flashback to the lion attack.

Reese put his arm around Alexa's shoulders. "You had a frightening experience. It's going to take time."

As Melissa and Jim turned, Alexa let go of the rail and took a deep breath. "All clear?" she asked.

Jim replied, "They've moved out in front of the dining tent. All clear."

"Yes, what's that expression? This, too, shall pass." With a kiss on his hand, Alexa slipped out of Reese's protective embrace and stepped forward, hoping the trite expression applied to elephant-induced PTSD and the other trauma that still lingered from that fateful night in the bush.

CHAPTER TWENTY-ONE

As the small plane made its slow descent, beneath them, a convoy of three black cargo trucks turned from a narrow road onto an unpaved highway and headed east. Alexa shook her head in amazement at what she'd heard was a long, bumpy drive to Maun or Kasane. It could take as long as one or two full days, requiring drivers of these rigs to be a hardy lot.

The pilot made a wide pass over the airfield below, circled back, and angled into his approach. Alexa smiled at the word 'Noka' outlined in white-painted rocks on a bank next to the runway. She was glad they'd chosen Noka as their final camp. She'd done more research work here than at any other site in Botswana. Coming back gave her a chance to say farewell to a spot she'd grown to love.

Plus, she had unfinished business. She wanted to say goodbye to Harry, the man who'd saved her life, and Emma, who'd become a good friend. Less concrete but still important, Alexa had never returned here after she, Harry, Tale, and Mo had driven out to their unexpected rendezvous with terror. Noka staff had packed the things she'd left in the tent and sent them back to Maun. Alexa was bothered by a nagging feeling of something left incomplete, a broken circle that needed to be made whole before she could move on from that night. She'd tried to explain it to Reese last week but could see that he really didn't get it. Although solicitous about her injuries and traumatic experience, he was a down-to-earth type of guy who didn't always relate to vague feelings or impulses. Heck, she barely understood this urge to come back to Noka herself. She just knew that returning would help her heal.

When they climbed out of the plane, Harry stood on the dusty runway to meet them. He greeted Alexa with an enigmatic half-smile before he turned to the group. Shouting over the engine noise of the plane's hot landing, he yelled for everyone to head to the vehicle. He collected their bags as a group of six departing guests filed past to board the plane. Harry threw the bags into the back seat as Alexa, Melissa, and Jim clambered into the Land Cruiser.

Reese helped Harry stow the bags in the vehicle. "You're a brave man taking on the task of guiding this crew," he said with a good-natured grin before he climbed into the SUV. "But I'm glad that you did."

Harry jumped into the driver's seat and yelled, "Let me get out of here before the plane takes off." He gunned the vehicle into motion and drove away just as the pilot moved the plane forward and a huge cloud of dust from the dirt runway drifted downwind in their direction. Harry drove for about three minutes, then pulled to a stop.

"All right then," he said as he turned to look at his passengers. "Sorry for the speedy exit. I didn't want you to start off your visit to Noka covered in dust. Winds are a little tricky today."

He smiled at Reese and Alexa. "These two know me, but you must be Melissa and Jim, right? I'm Harry DeJongh. I'll be your guide here at Noka. Would anyone like a drink? Water? A soft drink?" Following four refusals, he said, "It's about fifteen minutes to camp. We'll get you checked in, have brunch, and then talk about options for this afternoon." With that canned introduction, the guide pulled back out onto the road.

Remembering Reese's brief bout of jealousy over Harry, Alexa had been a bit wary about how this part of the Noka trip would play out. But the three had started out as friends, and Reese and Alexa both had accepted Harry's offer to guide them. After all, he was one of the best guides in the entire Delta Wild system. She breathed a sigh of relief. They'd cleared the first hurdle with no signs of awkwardness. Her worries had been unnecessary.

"Is that an eland?" Jim asked.

Harry stopped the vehicle and launched into an overview of elands, then impalas, as a bachelor herd came into view on the right.

While her companions admired the two species of antelope, Alexa studied the red-haired guide and smiled at the enthusiasm he showed for animals he encountered day after day. Harry was such a great guy, but, on reflection, she'd begun to doubt this theory that he had a crush on her. He was a congenital flirt, who would probably spend most of this evening trying to charm Melissa.

Then, as Reese pointed out to Jim and Melissa a second eland in the distance, Harry turned and held Alexa's gaze. He flashed her a look so poignant that Alexa caught her breath. She couldn't deny it. She loved Reese. She wanted to spend the rest of her life with Reese. At the same time, what lay between Harry and her was more than a passing attraction. On that deadly night near the Chobe, they'd formed an indelible bond. These next few days might be more complicated than she'd imagined.

"This is quite an upgrade from the pilot's quarters," Reese joked as they walked into their luxury tent facing a quiet lagoon. "Look, an indoor shower, an outdoor shower, and a bathtub."

Alexa opened the door to look at the outdoor shower. "It's open to the lagoon."

"Showering with an audience of hippos should be interesting."

"And a slipper bathtub, no less." Alexa closed the door and pointed to the elegant tub.

"Although I'm not quite sure what a slipper bathtub is, it's clear, given all our options, we will be very, very clean here at Noka."

"And very calm. Look at this view." Alexa slid open the door of their room, which was less a tent and more a rustic suite; a canvas-walled palace with a bedroom, living room area, and multiple baths. Native baskets and huge photos of wild animals covered the walls, connecting the interior with the wild outside of the screened windows. Leather camp chairs and a carved wooden chest and coffee table cemented the exotic African safari vibe.

Alexa stepped out onto the wooden deck, sank into one of two chairs, and looked out over the water. "How serene. So many water lilies. Strange that I never fully appreciated that Noka is primarily a water camp. We're actually sitting over the water right now." She peered through the cracks between the wooden floorboards at the lagoon beneath the deck.

"It's on an island," Reese teased as he sank into the chair next to her.

"Really, oh my gosh," she replied in an impish voice. "What I meant was I know we always crossed the footbridge to the main reception area and dining tent. But we stayed off-island in the staff quarters. And all of our work was done in the bush, out on dry land. Here, where the guests stay on the lagoon, it's absolutely lovely." Alexa took in the broad pool of water ringed by a total of eight tents including theirs. Linked by boardwalks, the tents fanned out in a curve from a central walkway, with four tents on each side. The designer had done a masterful job of assuring privacy. Melissa and Jim were in the adjacent tent, but Alexa could only see a corner of their deck.

Reese took her hand. "I'm so glad we did this safari. We needed some downtime together before we go back home. And this has been great." He fell quiet and gazed out at the lagoon. "Remember Archer's Camp in Kenya?"

"How could I forget? This place actually reminds me of that wonderful, exotic tent at Archer's." Her lips curved in a slow, intimate smile. "We spent a lot of time in that tent, as I recall."

"That is also my recollection, Counselor," Reese said in a mock-serious tone.

Alexa tightened her grip on his hand. "Samburu and Archer's Camp. I hadn't seen you in months and wasn't sure you even wanted me there in Kenya. We had a perfect few days of safari. A perfect romantic reunion. And then, during our last perfect night together, we decided that we were free to go our separate ways."

"Well, we know how that worked out, don't we? It took me a while, but I came to my senses and came home. Best decision I've ever made." Reese kissed Alexa's hand.

"I'll always remember what you told me, just before I left Archer's. You quoted an African proverb: 'Love never gets lost; it's only kept.' And you said that you'd always keep me in your heart."

"I have. I always will." Reese paused before he said, "I want to tell you again that I'm sorry I doubted you . . . more like doubted me. Worried that I'd failed you. I know you and Harry are tight. You went through an experience together that would turn any friendship deeper. And the guy's a little dazzled by you. Believe me, I can relate. But you and me. We're good, right?"

"Very good. You, Reese Michaels, are the man I keep in my heart," Alexa said without hesitation. It was true. As much as she was drawn to Harry, Reese was the one she loved.

The two sat in companionable silence, gazing out at the water for several minutes. At the sound of a splash, Reese said, "Look. Is that a waterbuck?" He pointed toward an expanse of reeds in the distance. Just before the reeds, a large, darkish antelope with thick horns waded into the water.

"I could sit here for hours."

"Don't get comfortable." Reese looked at his watch. "Brunch starts in five minutes. We should have time to relax out here this afternoon before our game drive."

"Wonderful." Alexa laughed. "I call dibs on this chair."

As they walked the central boardwalk toward the dining tent, a mongoose on the ground below scurried away from the noise of their footsteps. The elevated walkway and the common buildings all stood on solid ground. From this angle, Alexa could see the layout of the areas of camp she was most familiar with. To the left were the common buildings, a kitchen, and the camp managers' tent. Straight ahead, a footbridge over water led to the staff quarters and the equipment sheds. Farther to right, Alexa knew there was a boat dock that she couldn't see. Someone had pointed it out on an earlier visit, although she'd never been on the water here.

Melissa and Jim were already going through the buffet line when Alexa and Reese entered the dining hall. Melissa waved and pointed toward a table with a jacket hanging on one of the chairs.

Reese said, "I'll get us some tea if you want to go ahead."

"Sure, I'm starving," Alexa said and headed toward the food. Halfway across the room, she saw Emma enter from the kitchen area.

"Alexa. Staff told me you'd arrived." The camp manager bustled over and enveloped Alexa in a quick hug. "I'm so happy you're staying with us for a few days. Especially since you're leaving the country soon. I'm sad to see you go. Of course, Nicky and I will be heading out for England shortly ourselves. Are those your friends over there with Reese?"

When Emma finally paused for a breath, Alexa responded, "Yes, Melissa and Jim. Come, let me introduce you."

"I'd love to meet them, but it must be later. There's a crisis brewing in the kitchen. And, of course, Nicky is off somewhere. That's right, he's with a crew readying the new equipment shed. I just popped out to say hello. Are you settled? Everything fine with your tent?"

"Everything is perfect. Four nights here will be bliss." Alexa smiled. "Go take care of your crisis."

"Ta," Emma said and scurried away. She turned back just before the kitchen door. "All of you will sit with Nicky and me at dinner. Talk to you then."

Chuckling at Emma's whirlwind appearance, Alexa made her way through the buffet, piling her plate with eggs, toast, and fruit before she joined her group at their table.

Dinner that evening was billed as Okavango Night. During the cocktail hour, Noka staff entertained the guests with a program of tribal songs and dances. The meal featured the traditional Botswana dish, seswaa—a stew of meat, peppers, and onion served over polenta. It was a slightly more gourmet version of the dish served at Mo's funeral. The chef also had set up a barbeque, cooked over a huge wood-fired grill just outside the dining tent. The soup, however, was served at the table.

"Pumpkin soup?" Jim asked after his first spoonful.

"It's one of our chef's specialties," Emma answered with no hint of irony. "I hear you spotted wild dogs this afternoon. What a treat."

"It was so interesting to see the way they worked as a team tracking that impala," Melissa remarked.

Harry nodded. "Every animal in the pack has a job. Even the ones who lag behind and take care of the pups."

"Their killing method is brutal though. I wasn't that sorry to miss the actual takedown. The impala was dead by the time we got there," Reese added.

"Hmm, perhaps not the best dinner table topic," Nick interjected. "I hear that Harry is taking you out on a motorboat tomorrow. Have you been on the Okavango's channels yet?" he asked Jim and Melissa.

"No, this will be a first," Jim said. "Should we expect to see a lot of animals, or is this more a scenic tour?"

"A little of both," Harry responded, "but we should see a good number of water-based animals. Crocs, hippos, elephants, red lechwe for sure. We never know what animals we'll find on the small islands we pass."

"Hippos at water level." Melissa gave a wary laugh. "That should be interesting."

Nick jumped in. "Jakes is going out with you, right?" At Harry's nod, he continued, "Jakes has been steering boats through Delta channels since he was eight years old. He won't let you get too close to hippos or any other animals for that matter. He knows these waters like the back of his hand."

Emma had fallen quiet. Concerned about her downcast expression, Alexa tried to draw her back into the conversation. "Remind me again when your leave begins?"

Emma smiled. "End of September. Just two weeks, and we're off to England. Nicky is coming home with me for a while, then we'll fly back to Zim and visit his uncle. Can't believe I'm looking forward to spending time in the rain and cold. When I close my eyes, I can almost feel the mist on my face. The exact weather I came here to escape." She tittered. "That's why Nicky has been working on getting everything ready here for the low season. So that Harry here won't have to deal with anything other than routine camp management while we're gone."

Alexa shot a puzzled glance at Harry, who responded with a lazy smile. She hadn't known he was going to fill in as camp manager here. Instead of pursuing it, she turned to Nick. "That's right. Emma said earlier today that you were working on the new maintenance equipment shed. That's the big new building over by the pilot's quarters, right?"

"The longest building project in the history of Botswana," Nick replied in a bored tone. "Supply problems, staffing problems, communication problems. I thought the project would never end. Miracle of miracles, it came in under budget. The building crew left today. And they actually did quite a decent job in the end."

Remembering her strange encounter with the man outside the shed, Alexa said, "You say you had communication problems. I took a walk near the building one time I stayed here. A man, I guess one of the workers, shooed me away."

A look of consternation passed over Nick's face. "Did you go into the building? It was a construction zone, so could've been dangerous. Was he rude? That's simply unacceptable. You should have mentioned it so we could deal with it."

"No problem. I was just walking by. I figured he'd been told to guard the place and I strayed too close. But I couldn't understand what he was saying. He might have been speaking Setswana, but it sounded a little different. Perhaps another tribal dialect."

"Some of the crew was from Angola, and at least one worker came from somewhere else. The language barriers got in the way several times according to the crew boss," Nick said.

"Well, their trucks pulled out today. So, that's one less problem to deal with. And the new shed really expands our storage capacity for equipment in the rainy seasons," Emma added.

"I saw trucks on the main road as we flew in," Alexa said.

"I did too," Melissa cried. "Three big black trucks. I wondered what they were hauling."

"Men and tools, but not much else on the way out," Nick commented. "They used those trucks heavily during the project, however. Every board, nail, and piece of roofing tin was brought in on them. They had to make multiple trips."

The server who had brought the soup approached the table and said, "Ladies, gentlemen, the main course is ready, please."

Emma said, "Nick."

When Nick rose, Reese pushed back his chair and said, "I'm ready for some of that barbeque. Those ribs look delicious."

Jim stood too. "Count me in."

"I won't be far behind," Alexa said, glancing at her best friend. "I'll wait until Melissa finishes her soup."

When they left the table, Harry looked at Alexa and asked, "So, princess. Are you fully recovered? You seem to be moving fine."

"The pain is gone." Alexa curled her lip in a half-smile. "Could be a year or so before the bruise goes away. I can't even begin to describe the current shade of purple. And you?"

"Fit as a fiddle," Harry replied in a light tone.

Emma put a hand to her mouth, "Oh my. I should have asked about your injury first thing, Alexa. You were still hurting at Mokapi's funeral. I'm glad to see you're fully recovered."

Returning with brimming plates, Reese and Jim sat down. Nick had barely placed his meal on the table before he said, "I hear they may have caught the poachers." He turned to Reese. "I saw you the other night in a confab with Colonel Shonga at Chapman's. Maybe you have the latest on that subject?"

Reese shook his head. "Nothing more, really. The police have detained some suspects. Caught virtually red-handed down near the Makgadikgadi Pans somewhere. I don't know the details, although it sounded like authorities think these are the ones responsible. I hope they are."

"These criminals have a lot to account for. They should be jailed for a long, long time." Nick slapped the table with his palm each time he said 'long.' "Too bad that shoot-to-kill rule isn't in place yet."

"What?" Melissa exclaimed. "Why would anyone poach knowing they could get killed?"

Jim said in a dry tone, "That's sort of the idea, Melissa. Deterrence."

"Money's the driving force. And even though Botswana's fairly well-off compared to many other African nations, the average annual income is less than twenty thousand dollars. So, especially in some of the poorer rural villages, people need money. And, like everywhere in the world, some of those people turn to crime. Hell, even rich people turn to crime," Reese elaborated.

Harry added, "Word is that a single elephant tusk can bring as much as fifty to seventy-five thousand US dollars, depending upon size. With this series of elephant kills, these wankers have bagged . . ." He paused for a moment as if counting in his mind. "Somewhere around fifty elephants. Maybe more."

Melissa silently did the math. "Wow, we're talking millions, right?"

Nick took a bandanna from his pocket and wiped his forehead as he said, "A small fortune, even divided among a group of poachers."

Emma looked at her fiancé and laughed. "My word, Nicky. Does the very thought of that much money make you break out in a sweat?"

He rolled his eyes. "No, love. I put too much Tabasco on the seswaa."

Reese ignored their bantering and said, "For someone who's poor or desperate or doesn't give a damn about wildlife, that level of riches might be enough reason to risk capture or death."

"Even for some mother-f-er who's just plain greedy," Melissa replied.

Alexa caught Emma's look of shock and Nick's ashen face, even though Melissa had stopped short of letting the full curse word fly. She stifled a smile as she rose for the main course. My, how she'd missed her uninhibited best friend.

After a cup of tea and a biscuit, their group boarded an aluminum motorboat as dawn broke the next morning. Alexa zipped her lightweight down jacket to her neck and tugged a beanie over her ears as Jakes, the boatman, left the narrow channel and headed across the open lagoon.

At first, Alexa thought he was headed right into a bank of reeds. Then, as they neared, she spied a four-foot opening in the wall of soaring green plants. Soon they were traveling a narrow passageway, almost like a tunnel. When Alexa tilted her head back, she could see the dawn sky, alabaster with a hint of pink. On both sides rose unbroken expanses of green reeds at least twelve feet tall, and papyrus, a slender plant topped with a lacy spray.

Jakes slowed the boat to a stop, and Harry said, "Much of the wet part of the Delta is just like this. The vegetation that you see on either side isn't growing on soil. These dense mats float on top of the water. Reeds and papyrus are the predominant vegetation. As the sun rises higher, we'll see dragonflies, birds, frogs, and many more small creatures. These narrow channels widen as they pass larger islands. That's where we'll spot most of the big wildlife. Today's our chance to experience Delta life at water level." Harry nodded to Jakes, and they motored forward at a leisurely pace.

After Nick's assurance that Jakes was a veteran navigating these waters, Alexa had expected Noka's expert boatman to be a wizened old man. She'd been surprised to find the guy was so young. But Jakes said he'd grown up on the Delta and had been piloting the channels since he was a kid. Working at Noka for over five years, he clearly knew each twist and turn of this watery labyrinth.

Alexa loved the boat trip. Even with the sound of the outboard motor, the morning was serene. Jakes guided them from channel to channel, through spacious lagoons, past palm-dotted islands, and into open areas where the towering reeds gave way to low, marshy grasses. Harry identified scores of birds. Alexa didn't even try to retain all the names, but Jim, the biologist, was completing a checklist with each new sighting.

"Which heron is that?" Melissa pointed.

"Squacco, right?" Jim replied with a questioning look at Harry. "Same as on that last island."

"Ahead, on that tree to the left. Another African fish eagle," Harry indicated. "As they passed, the eagle spiraled into the air with a piercing cry.

"Do you see something?" Melissa asked as Alexa leaned over the side to peer at a branch.

"Nope, it flew." Alexa laughed. "I'm really jonesing on the Malachite kingfishers." These tiny birds perched on reeds or small branches before they dove into the water for fish, their iridescent teal-blue feathers glistening in the sun.

Reese broke an extended silence. "There's one. On that branch ahead." He'd been quiet for much of the trip, eyes alert for wildlife but seemingly content to just enjoy the morning on the water.

The Malachite took to the air as the group motored by. When the boat rounded a curve in the reeds, the water widened into a pool. A pod of hippos clustered against the left bank. They seemed placid as their eyes followed the boat, although Jakes steered in a wide arc to avoid them. Several grunted in the boat's wake.

"That's the sound that kept me awake last night," Melissa declared. "Are there hippos at the camp?"

Harry gave her an amused smile. "We often see hippos in the lagoon. And they can get pretty noisy at night. Of course, many of them go out on land at night to feed. Not that hippos climb onto the boardwalks at camp, but you never want to approach a hippo on land. They're the animals that kill more people than any other in Africa. Often that happens at night when they're feeding and some poor soul stumbles into their path. On the positive side, hippos are largely responsible for all these channels in the Delta. They clear the vegetation as they travel from area to area."

A few minutes later, Jakes slowed again as one of the giant animals surfaced not far from the boat. Just its eyes showed above the waterline. Then another emerged from the depths to join the first. Jakes hugged the right bank as he chugged by, then accelerated when the second hippo thrust his entire head above the water and opened his mouth wide.

"Whoa," Jim said, looking back at the hippos as they receded from view. "Was that guy pissed?"

Harry nodded, "Probably just warning us off. It's possible that there were other hippos from the pod underwater. Anytime hippos are involved, it's best to give them a wide berth. Those teeth are lethal. And they may look lazy, but they can move fast. On land, they can run almost thirty kilometers—that's twenty miles—per hour. In water, they don't actually swim. They run along the bottom and push off. Even then, they can travel five miles an hour."

"Faster than me, that's for sure," Melissa said in an impressed tone.

"Jakes runs into some nasty hippos out here from time to time," Harry said.

"Oh, yes. The single males are the most dangerous," Jakes agreed. "They be angry from being kicked out of the herd. And they don't like the lonely life. So, they often get nasty and aggressive. Sometimes, I must turn around and take another channel if we run into a rogue male."

"They've been known to capsize boats and attack the passengers who fall in the water," Harry said.

"Eek," Melissa cried. "Will there be hippos where we're doing the mokoro rides tomorrow?"

"No. We drive out to a place where the water is very shallow. Too shallow to attract hippos at this time of year when the Delta is still high. Don't worry." Harry smiled. "Delta Wild's goal is to have all our guests leave unscathed at the end of their stay."

Reese leaned forward with a serious look. "Jakes and Harry will do everything they can to keep us safe from hippos. And crocs." He gestured to a pair sunning on a sandy island to the left. "And everything else we might encounter.

But always remember that we're out here in a wilderness that's chock full of dangerous animals. We're the intruders. The Okavango is their home. Always be alert in the bush."

"Melissa and I understand that, buddy," Jim said. "However, it never hurts to get a periodic reminder. From you." He smiled. "And, even more compelling, from that hippo. Did you see the incisors on that baby? They must have been two feet long."

After a brief stop on a large sandy island for tea and a bathroom break, they got back into the boat and motored on. Alexa had stripped off her down jacket before tea, but she took off the next layer of fleece as they reached an open pool in full sun.

"Look." Harry waved toward a line of palm trees bordering the marsh. "Red lechwe coming in our direction."

"Did something startle them?" Reese asked as the small herd barreled closer.

"Possible. Everything beyond that tree line is solid ground. They might be running out into the marsh to avoid a predator." Harry told Jim and Melissa, "This species of antelope has elongated hooves to navigate watery terrain. Out here they have the advantage over most predators."

Alexa smiled as the lechwe approached, soaring several feet above the marsh grass in a series of running bounds.

"Lions. You were right, Reese," Harry said, binoculars at his eyes.

Reese whipped his binoculars from his backpack to study the lions. "Three females. One's knee-deep in the water. No, she's turning back. I wonder which pride?"

With an indulgent smile at Reese's excitement at the first lions of the day, Alexa said, "I have no idea where we are in the concession. Out here on the water, with all the twists and turns of the channels, I've lost my bearings."

Harry pulled a map from his shirt pocket. "I suspect that it's the Lesego Pride. We're near this part of the concession." He put his finger on the map. "Here is where the Lesego Pride hangs out. Those rocks that they like to nap on are just on the other side of those palms. This is the main road that takes you there from camp."

He moved his finger. "Over here is the BDF outpost. And the wide-open plains where the Marula Pride lives. This road," Harry paused, raised his eyes, and looked directly at Alexa, "this is the road we took northeast to look for the bachelor boys. Here's the river."

Reese raised his binoculars and returned his attention to the lions.

"They're moving closer, along the tree line," Jim told him. He'd paid no attention to the map discussion, keeping his eyes on the lions the entire time.

"Thanks," Alexa said to Harry. "I can't believe I've paid so little heed to all this water that runs right through the middle of the concession. Mo always knew where we were headed. I guess I should have paid closer attention on all those drives . . ." Her voice trailing off, Alexa touched the place on the map where Mo had died.

"Farewell, Mo," she mouthed silently. Looking up, she met Harry's eyes.

He touched her shoulder gently. "Whatever works, princess," he murmured, folding the map. Then Harry turned back to the men and the lions.

With a deep breath, Alexa straightened and saw Melissa watching her with a concerned expression. Her friend leaned across the boat and whispered, "We need to have a talk. Soon."

Jakes retraced their route on the ride back to camp. Alexa was surprised at how quickly they covered the same territory without all the stops they'd made on the outbound trip. They did pause for several minutes to watch a herd of elephants drinking at the hippo pool. The hippos had relocated to a quiet corner to give the elephants a wide berth. Jakes idled the motor so they could get photos of the elephants, including two tiny babies playing on shore.

As they headed away, Alexa breathed a sigh of relief. She hadn't panicked at seeing this herd so close. Maybe all she needed were more elephant encounters. Something from a college psychology class popped into her mind. A technique for treating phobias. What had her professor called it? Systematic desensitization.

Harry interrupted her thoughts when he gestured toward a wide-mouthed channel. A dead palm trunk marked the near corner. "That's the channel that takes you to the BDF outpost. So, out there is Marula Pride territory."

And beyond that, the waterhole where the bachelor boys had made their mark, Alexa thought but didn't say. It was time to start letting the trauma go.

As they finished brunch, Melissa said to Alexa, "Let's go to the gift shop. I need to buy something for my new assistant at the gallery."

"Sure."

"I can skip this little shopping expedition, right?" Jim asked with a hopeful expression.

"Count me out too," Reese said. Then, with mock concern, "Remember, our luggage is full. All those baskets you bought."

"Yes, dear," Alexa said sweetly.

"All right. Just us girls," Melissa high-fived Alexa.

After extensive browsing, Melissa settled on a set of glass African trading beads that were small enough in diameter to be worn as a necklace.

Alexa giggled at her choice. "I already have two strands that I plan to use as home decor. Mine are too big to wear."

Clutching her purchase, Melissa took Alexa's elbow and steered her out of the shop and into a corner of the empty lounge. "I did need the gift, but it was mainly an excuse to talk to you alone."

Alexa looked up as a waiter approached. "A Coke, please."

"And one for me." Melissa sank into a chair.

Sighing, Alexa sat too. "What exactly did you need to talk to me about?"

"Men, of course. What is going on with you and Harry and Reese?" Melissa tilted her head. "Oh, no. Don't even try that what-are-you-talking-about look with me. We've been through this too many times before.

"I suspected something was going on from the minute Harry picked us up at the airstrip. All those stolen glances. 'Princess' this, brushing your arm that. And what was going on in the boat this morning? Granted, the man is gorgeous. All that red hair, green eyes, and rugged manliness. What is that dreamy accent?"

"South African, although he's a Botswana citizen now," Alexa muttered.

"South African. Thought he might be British. Regardless, Reese manages to treat him like a good friend, all the while barely speaking to the guy. So, I know there's something not quite right between those two. Still, I can't figure out what's going on with you, Lexie.

"I can tell you've been downplaying whatever happened out there in the bush when your researcher friend was killed. And, I gather, Harry was part of that. But, Lexie. When you left Pennsylvania, you were head over heels in love with Reese. Hell, you put everything in your life on hold to follow him to

Botswana. Where does this wild South African fit in with the man you called the love of your life?"

Alexa broke into peals of laughter when her friend finally paused to take a breath. "Melissa, I'm so glad we had this talk," she sputtered, stopping only because the waiter brought their drinks.

When he left, Melissa scowled at Alexa and said, "I'm serious. I know there's something wrong. I don't know if it's with you and Reese. Or if this Harry has anything to do with it. I just know you're not yourself, Lexie."

"You're right. I can't quite get over that night out in the bush. The elephants trampled Mo, but they could have killed us all. Harry saved my life that night. He literally dragged me to safety. And he was there when we saw one of the poachers killed by lions, and through the long hours while we waited for help. I owe him. Big time.

"Reese sent me out on the assignment alone because he had something else come up, but he didn't know it'd be as intense as a lion collar. I think his guilt for not being there got mixed up with anger about Harry being the one to save me."

"It's more than that, though, isn't it?"

"It is." Alexa gave a reluctant nod. "I've been lonely here. It's been a great experience, but all of this—doing wildlife research, a new country with new customs, navigating the politics of the Commission—it's been a bigger transition for me than Reese. He's done this type of thing in Kenya twice before. Plus, Reese was often off in Zimbabwe or at another camp. Or preoccupied with managing Africa Trust even when we were together.

"Harry's had a bit of a thing for me since we first met. At first, I thought he was just a flirt, and it was fun to play the game. After that night when he saved my life, I started to figure out his feelings for me might be deeper. Believe me, Harry would be an easy guy to fall for. But, I haven't. I won't. I'm committed to Reese. He's still the love of my life. We've talked all this through. Still, he's not blind. He knows that Harry has a thing for me and that we share an experience that's tied us together forever."

Melissa had calmed down. She patted Alexa's arm. "You'll heal from this trauma, this near-death experience, when you get home. Take a few more weeks before you return to work. Graham won't mind. He's been running the law practice without you for months already. But, honey. Shouldn't you have a little talk with Harry? I think he's got it bad for you, and you're going to walk out of the man's life forever. You need to tell him it was never going to happen. That Reese is the man for you."

"Really? You think I should confront this? Bring it out in the open?"

"I do, Lexie. I do."

The next day, Alexa and Reese sat on their deck, reading during the break before the afternoon game drive. From time to time, she glanced, unperturbed, at two elephants feeding on the marshy edge of the lagoon less than twenty feet away.

"This safari has been good for me. For us. A chance to unwind before we have to adjust to life back home. Wow. Only one more full day," Alexa ventured.

Reese looked up from his book. "These days at Noka Camp have been wonderful. When we come back to Botswana someday, we need to stay here again."

"Great idea." Alexa closed her book and rose. "Maybe we can do a grand tour of Africa, highlighting all the camps where we made our best memories. Archer's, Noka, the Kalahari." She put her hands on the arms of his chair and leaned forward to kiss Reese's forehead.

He swept her onto his lap and pulled her close in a long kiss. "Okay, grand tour it is. Maybe we'll add some new places into the mix. Jim and Melissa seemed to love Ebony Camp. We never made it to Mana Pools in Zimbabwe either."

"Why not? The more the merrier." Alexa gave her boyfriend a swift hug and looked at her watch. "Oh. Time for me to head up for my farewell tea with Emma. She's been very kind to me during these past months. She says she'll miss my visits to Noka Camp. And I'm sad to say goodbye to her." She rose from Reese's arms.

"Still haven't figured out what she sees in Nick. The guy's nice enough, but he tries too hard. Like he's pretending to be an English lord or something, what's the word he'd use? Posh."

"Posh Nick, the sixth Spice Girl," Alexa spluttered.

Reese laughed. "Were there five Spice Girls? I was more into REM and the Chili Peppers when I was a teen. Although I do remember one of my friends had a poster of Victoria Beckham."

"That's right. She was the one called Posh Spice. So, I guess that title's already taken. Sorry, Nicky." Alexa giggled. "I did listen to them when I was about ten years old. By the time I reached teenybopper status, I'd moved on to Nine Inch Nails."

"What?"

"Just kidding. I was always borrowing Graham's Neil Young CDs." Alexa flashed Reese a big smile before she went inside to get her backpack and camera. A few minutes later she was heading to the main tent. On the way, she stopped to watch a mongoose darting around in the underbrush. A second appeared, and the two ran beneath the walk. Alexa went to the other side, smiling as the two tumbled over each other in play. Then they scampered down a dirt path beneath the boardwalk.

When Alexa entered the main tent, Emma hadn't yet arrived. Harry was sitting at a far table, reading a book. She slowed, then moved forward when he looked up and smiled.

"It's a bit early for tea," he said.

"Emma asked me to meet her for a chat. A chance to say our goodbyes before we go our separate ways."

"I'm waiting for Nick. He's on a call with the head office in Maun. Said he'd send word when he was ready. We've been spending a bit of time together on the hand-off. You know they're on leave soon, and I'm filling in?"

"Yes, it was mentioned the other night at dinner. Is this just a one-time thing or are you thinking of moving out of guiding and into camp management?"

"I'm not ready to stop guiding. I enjoy the group tours and the occasional longer stint at a camp like I'm doing here. The chaps at Delta Wild asked me to get some experience as a camp manager too. They want me to come in from the field and bump me up to corporate management. I told them I'm not ready to leave the bush yet, but I'd start broadening my experience."

Alexa tilted her head. "I was going to say I can't imagine you anywhere but out here in the wild. On second thought, I can see you in management, as long as it has an outdoor element. You have a broad perspective that would be valuable to Delta Wild. In Maun?"

"God, yes. I don't know if I'd ever want to move back to South Africa. And even Maun could be a couple of years away." Harry's tone was agitated.

"Whatever path you take, Harry," Alexa said. "I wish you well. I'll never forget that you saved my life and what a good friend you've been to me—to Reese and me—during our time here."

"I'll miss you, princess." His voice softened, "I think you know my feelings for you go a bit deeper than friendship. I've never met a woman quite like you."

He sat back; his voice tinged with regret. "I also know you're attached at the hip to Reese. Lucky sod that he is." His tone lightened: "I may never get over you, darlin'."

"Ah, but you will." Alexa smiled and spoke in a rueful tone. "I could say another time, another place. If only I'd met you before Reese. And all of it would be true. But you're right. As irresistible as you are, Harry DeJongh, I'm committed to Reese. And we'll be gone in just a few days."

Harry put his hand over Alexa's. "I wish you well. Send me an email every once in a while." He grinned. "If ever you decide to dump the bloke, let me know and I'll be on the next plane. I've always wanted to see America."

"There you are, Alexa. Sorry I'm late. I was on a business call with Nick," Emma called from across the room.

Alexa turned her hand to clasp Harry's, palm to palm, and held his eyes for a long moment. Then she rose and turned toward her friend.

"Nick's ready for your meeting, Harry," Emma said as she neared.

To Alexa, she said, "Staff is laying out our tea in the library. We still have a half hour before guests start flocking in."

"I'll see you, ladies. Enjoy your tea and your gossip." Harry stood, squeezed Alexa on the shoulder, and walked toward the office.

That evening after dinner, Alexa and Reese prepared for the morning game drive. They'd found it was easier to have everything ready to go when the alarm went off at five-thirty, well before daybreak.

"It's been great to watch Melissa and Jim on their first safari," Alexa said as she checked her camera battery. "Even an animal as common as an impala becomes interesting when you hear Melissa gush over it."

"Their eyes are just so soulful. Like liquid pools of amber," Reese mimicked Melissa in a feminine tone of voice.

"Stop it." Alexa laughed. "She's sincere, and you know how artsy Melissa is. Everything is more in her world. More beautiful, more unique, more photogenic. I'll bet she's taken thousands of photos. I'm anxious to see the exhibit she creates for her gallery."

"I'm joking, but you're right. I've enjoyed their enthusiasm. Jim's whole life is wildlife and the outdoors. He's loving every minute of this trip." Reese placed his backpack on the chest at the foot of the bed and stretched out on the bed.

"One more day here at Noka, then they head back home. And we're not far behind." Alexa kicked off her shoes and joined Reese.

"A few days in Maun with Gary. Then, *go siame* to Botswana." Reese ran a thumb over Alexa's cheek. "Should we turn in? We need to be well-rested for our last big day on safari."

Alexa snuggled closer and said, "Soon. But first . . ." She kissed Reese and unfastened the top button of his shirt.

CHAPTER TWENTY-TWO

ALEXA DOUBLE-KNOTTED HER shoelaces, pulled on her lightweight down jacket, and switched off the bedside light. Reese had left for breakfast a few minutes ago to use the only Wi-Fi, in the main tent, to check his email. The guest tents offered no internet or cell phone service. And they'd left the Africa Trust satellite phone back in Maun. Reese was anxious to learn the details of Gary's arrival back in Botswana. They were becoming concerned at his continuing silence.

In the half-light of breaking dawn, Alexa stood and slung her backpack over her shoulder when the shot split the quiet morning. At first, she thought she'd cracked the bedpost with the pack and winced, thinking about her brand-new camera. Then, a volley of shots rang out. The rapid fire of an automatic weapon. Screams came from the direction of the main tent.

Alexa dropped to the floor, gasping for breath. She flashed back to the night of the poachers and the elephant stampede. That had started with gunfire too. How could this be happening again? Why would poachers be hunting elephants here at Noka Camp? *Wait. The investigators had arrested the poachers.* Her mind darted frantically, trying to figure out what was going on. Nothing she imagined was reassuring.

Reese. He must be in the midst of the shooting. And Melissa and Jim. *Why had I continued to encourage them to come on safari after all that had happened?* She saw more faces in her mind. Harry. Emma. Nick. That nice couple from Cincinnati they'd met last night. Most everyone would be at breakfast by now. Dizzy, she rested her cheek against the cold floor.

The shooting stopped. Now, Alexa could hear shouting and the clatter of running footsteps on the boardwalks. She lifted her head from the floor, eyes damp with tears. Trembling, she took her heavy camera out of her backpack and pushed it under the bed. She battled her instinct to dash up to the main tent and find out what was going on.

Instead, Alexa crawled to the back of the tent where a bathroom window gave a partial view of the dining tent. As the yelling continued, a man's voice rose above the noise. The tone was commanding, but she couldn't make out any words. She couldn't see anything that was happening up there. One thing was clear though: It was not good.

She bit her lip, trying to decide what to do. Go up there and risk being shot? Or hide?

Two men with guns burst out of the common area and thudded down the boardwalk. Even in the dim light, she could see they were wearing camouflage. They ducked into the first tent, shouting. Might have been Setswana. Definitely a tribal language. Seconds later, one came out, manhandling two guests. It could've been the couple from Cincinnati, but she wasn't sure if that was their tent. The man pushed the pair toward the main tent, prodding the weeping woman with hard jabs of his rifle.

His companion emerged from the tent and stormed down the walk to the second tent. One more tent left before he'd reach Alexa's door. She dropped back to the floor, tucked her pant legs into her hiking shoes, and scrambled out to the bed. Picking up her backpack, she crawled to the door of the outdoor shower. Easing it open, she slid outside, back against the canvas wall. Then, she reached up to close the door shut behind her. Click.

With a deep breath, Alexa crawled to the front edge of the shower where it overlooked the lagoon. On the left, a privacy wall shielded the shower area from the front deck. Peering over the lagoon-facing edge, she searched for dry land below. At the corner of the deck, it looked like solid ground, but less than a foot out, the water's edge was obscured by marsh grass.

God knows what's down there. Alexa shuddered. Snakes, crocs, scorpions? Then, footsteps pounded out on the walkway, and another woman screamed. Alexa slipped her shoulders into her backpack and slithered over the edge, back turned to the lagoon. *Ooof.* She bit her lip in pain as the sharp edge of the floorboard scraped over her bruised abdomen, reawakening an ache that had all but disappeared. She ignored the discomfort as her feet dangled, searching for the patch of solid ground. Then, she took a deep breath, let go of the railing, and dropped.

Alexa landed on her feet in knee-high grass. The surface beneath her feet felt spongey. When she looked down, water was rising around her thick rubber soles. Eyeing the sandy soil beneath the deck, she took two steps forward over the springy mat of grass and hopped onto firm ground. She was surprised to see a small structure beneath the tent platform, a rough wooden enclosure containing some equipment. Maybe a water pump? A tall person might have to bend over to walk under the shower deck, but Alexa had a few inches above her head to spare.

She tiptoed forward, scanning the area for snakes or other creatures. The sandy ground was relatively clear and well-trodden. Maybe camp staff did regular maintenance down here? At the sound of footsteps approaching on the boardwalk above, Alexa slipped into the pump enclosure and crouched low to the ground. She held her breath for a moment. Above her, the noise of the front door sliding open was followed by a loud bellow, the words similar to those she'd heard from the men at the first tent.

As the sound of boots searching the tent pounded over her head, Alexa froze. A second set of footsteps boomed down the boardwalk. They stopped on the front deck and a man asked a question. The person in the tent moved onto the deck and said, "*Ninguém.*"

Even after the footsteps had receded far down the boardwalk, Alexa continued to crouch beneath the tent. Her limbs heavy, she couldn't force them to unfold. Rooted in place, feeling trapped, her breath came out in short gasps. She pictured Reese lying dead, shot by one of the camouflaged men. Then, she closed her eyes in a silent chant, one that had guided her once in a life-threatening situation back home. "Panic is death. Panic is death. Panic is death." Soon, the mantra helped steady her fear, and Alexa's breath flowed evenly.

A plan. She needed a plan.

Could she get close enough to the main tent to find out what was going on but still remain hidden? She had no weapons, but maybe she could help somehow. Who were the men in camouflage anyway? She knew the uniforms of the BDF and the rangers. The men she'd seen in the distance wore clothes that looked more like what you'd buy in an Army Surplus store in the States. Not an official Botswana military uniform. But clearly armed and dangerous.

Maybe a recon mission to get a better handle on what was going on? Gritting her teeth, Alexa rose and left the illusion of safety the enclosure had provided. Swiveling her head in every direction, she walked a diagonal to the back corner of the tent base, feeling completely exposed. A rustle in the weeds at the water's edge made her jump then hustle forward as she saw a crocodile lumber onto the sand nearby and plop down.

At the back edge of the tent base, Alexa discovered an opening in the tall grass. A trail underneath the boardwalk. As she moved toward it, she remembered seeing a path on the ground below the raised walk. Was this it? She stopped and pulled a brown patterned handkerchief out of her pocket and knotted it like a scarf to cover her hair. Although still hidden by the main tent, the sun had risen high enough to tint the sky with a rosy glow. *Red sky at morning.* Alexa twisted her lips into a bitter smile.

Even though the early morning sky had lightened, the boardwalk threw a shadow on the ground beneath. This worked to her advantage but could change as the sun climbed higher. Better to move out now. Alexa inched forward with careful steps, following the path that wove beneath the walkway and then along its far side, away from the main tent. A tangle of grasses and shrubs carpeted the surrounding area, but the path was soft sand. She saw no animals. Even the mongoose family had fled, likely frightened away by the gunfire and raised voices.

As Alexa approached the point where the two guest boardwalks merged into a passage leading to the dining tent, she slowed. She needed to be at a higher level to see into the main tent. But if she tried to scale a post onto the boardwalk, she'd be visible. Looking at the post that rose above her head, she was doubtful she'd be able to shimmy up there anyway.

A burst of automatic rifle fire rang out. More shouts and screams split the air. Alexa dove to the ground until the gunfire stopped. That's when she spied the staircase on the other branch of the guest walkway. Probably how staff accessed this maintenance path. She hadn't noticed it before, perhaps because she and Reese had never walked to that row of tents. She edged forward on the path, alert for more gunfire, but heard only raised voices. An argument of some sort.

Alexa reached the foot of the staircase and crept upward. Stair. Pause and listen. Stair. Pause and listen. If someone approached on the walkway, she was poised to take cover. About halfway up the stairs, she felt a burning sensation between her shoulders. Was someone watching her? If these intruders had anyone stationed behind her, she was screwed. With a quick glance around, she forced herself to continue the climb.

At the top step, Alexa flattened her body, trying to melt into the staircase while hugging the shadow cast by a huge log post that supported the deck. She raised her head just high enough to get a look into the main tent.

What appeared to be the entire staff and all the Noka guests were crowded into the dining area. Most sat at tables. Some on the floor. Several men wearing the camouflage she'd seen earlier stood guard over them with automatic rifles.

On an empty table farthest from the hostages sat a pile of what Alexa could barely make out as cell phones, tablets, and a couple of laptops—these criminals had been thorough. Closer to her, three men stood in the lounge, arguing. Nick was one. The other two wore the standard camouflage. In a jarring note, one of them had on a baseball cap that glinted metallic in the lamplight. The way he carried himself seemed familiar to Alexa, but the brim of his cap shadowed his face.

As she struggled to keep her head low to the boardwalk, the shadow man grabbed Nick's arm and bellowed at him. Nick hung his head. Then, the shadow man spoke to his companion, who dashed to a nearby table and seized a thin blonde girl. One of the British birders who'd arrived yesterday.

Two guests leapt up as if to intervene, but a guard moved in with his rifle and motioned the tall men back to their seats. Reese and Harry. Alexa sighed in relief. Both were still unhurt. Were Melissa and Jim sitting just behind them? In the gloom, she couldn't be sure.

Shadow man's flunky dragged the girl to the edge of the lounge. She presented little resistance, her entire body jerking in spasms as she cried.

Then, shadow man barked something at Nick, who opened his palms wide and shook his head.

In a flash, shadow man looked at his companion and nodded.

Nick yelled, "Nooooo!" at the same time the flunky raised a pistol and shot the blonde.

Recoiling, Alexa slithered down several steps, then crept back to the ground, the vision of the girl's limp body falling off the deck and hitting the dirt instantly imprinted in her mind. She hid behind one of the deck supports and tried to take deep breaths. Her body was a clammy cold, but sweat poured off her face.

Coming up here, she'd had two ideas. One involved her staging some sort of dramatic rescue. That was laughable. Clearly out of the question. She was unarmed. Even if she had a weapon, she'd be outmanned and outgunned. These bandits, or whatever they were, meant business.

Her second idea had been to get close enough to the main tent Wi-Fi to call, text, or email for help. The rest of this island had no cell phone reception so guests could get away from it all. But the Wi-Fi idea wouldn't work either. Even if she could get a signal out here on the steps, she couldn't risk cell phone sounds alerting these murderers to her presence.

She had just a single advantage. Since these men hadn't waged an all-out search for her, perhaps they didn't know they were missing a guest. Maybe no one had mentioned it yet.

Hands shaking, Alexa pondered her options and came up with one. Only one. A boat. All the camp vehicles were parked on the mainland. The walking bridge, the only way to get there, was in clear sight of the main tent. And, even if she got across, she had no idea whether they'd left guards over there too. Or where the keys were for the vehicles. The boats, however, were tied up around the bend from where she stood. Here on the island. If she could get there unseen, she might have a chance to take one and go for help.

Once she'd made the decision, Alexa buried her worries for Reese and her friends and headed for the docks. This was where they'd left for their boat trip two days ago. The main boardwalk led to a pergola that sat on the channel between the island and the mainland, so Alexa still had cover as she hurried beneath it. The sandy path to the boat dock started at the bottom of the stairs near the pergola. The last forty yards or so were on open ground.

When she reached the dock path, Alexa paused to listen. The quiet was eerie. Even sound from the main tent had disappeared. With a pit in her stomach, she looked at the sky. The growing daylight was not her friend. She darted forward, walking at a rapid pace toward a stand of tall bushes that shielded her from camp. When she reached the cover of the bushes, Alexa raced down the last leg of the path.

Seconds later, she approached the dock. Lines from two motorboats wrapped around dock cleats on the far side. She could see a flash of aluminum from one of the motorboats. The other was hidden by the dock structure. A single mokoro lay, bottom-up, on the bank. Alexa stopped by the bushes while she scanned the area. It was almost full daylight now, and she'd be a sitting duck the minute she walked onto the dock.

With one more quick look around, she steeled herself and strode directly to the dock, scooping up the pole lying next to the mokoro as she passed. She paused on the dock only long enough to determine the position of the boats and slide the pole onto the boards. Then, facing the dock, she lowered her feet into the bow of the nearest boat, clinging to the piling for stability. Gasping for breath, more from fear than exertion, Alexa clung to the dock for a few seconds.

"Unhhh."

A loud groan sent a chill racing down Alexa's spine.

CHAPTER TWENTY-THREE

THE GROAN CAME from right behind her. Spinning around, fear of the bandits or a wild animal flashed through her head. Instead, Alexa looked into the pain-wracked eyes of Jakes, the boatman. He was soaked, lying in a pool of reddish water, his back propped up against a middle seat. His hand clutched a wound in his abdomen.

"Jakes," Alexa whispered. "They shot you?"

"Yes," he whispered. "Left me for dead in the shallows. I was able to climb into the boat, but that took all my strength. I can't . . ." His eyes closed and his voice trailed off.

A single shot pierced the air. Alexa stiffened. It had come from the main tent. With effort, she pushed aside worries about Reese, about another execution, and turned back to the task at hand. Jakes' eyes were open again, watching her.

"We need to get away from here. Then, I'll see if I can stop your bleeding," Alexa whispered. She pointed beyond the stern of the boat, the way they'd traveled into the Delta channels two days earlier. "That's the only way out, right?"

Jakes nodded.

Alexa rose to untie the boat and eased the mokoro pole off the dock and into her hands. Keeping low, she scrambled past Jakes to the rear of the boat and used the pole to push the boat from the dock. She'd watched polers propel mokoros on several boat trips, but the long narrow pole felt clumsy in her hands. Leaning against the side, she slid the pole into the water, hoping the channel was shallow enough that she would reach the bottom. Alexa held her breath. *Yes.* The pole, at least ten feet long, touched bottom, and she held it there while the boat swung around on the slight current until its prow faced forward. Then she gave a strong heave to give the boat momentum.

Push. Push. Push. The wide aluminum motorboat wasn't built to be poled, but Alexa couldn't risk turning on the outboard motor this close to camp. And she doubted her ability to move Jakes aside and row the boat even though there were oars on the sodden floor.

Alexa gasped and her arms burned as she rounded the end of the island. Pausing for a moment, she let the boat drift by the first tent. These were the tents opposite where she and Reese had been staying. They were farthest from the common area, where the bandits were holding everyone. Alexa worried that sentries might be patrolling the area, but she saw no activity on land.

Back to the pole. Push. Push. Alexa's tiring arms quivered. She moved from the floor to the seat to get better purchase as she poled. She was afraid she'd tumble over the side if she tried to stand. As she passed the third tent, the open lagoon yawned ahead. Alexa blanched. The expanse of water looked huge. But she had to cross it to enter the Delta channels. This was the only path to help. Completely exposed on the open water.

A burst of shouting came from the island. Alexa ducked as if lowering her profile in the boat would protect her. Glancing toward shore, she saw no one. The noise sounded like it came from farther away, from the main tent.

With a burst of panic-fueled adrenalin, Alexa ventured out into the lagoon, aiming toward the break in the reeds. Push. Push. Push. Push. With one last frantic heave of the pole, the boat slipped between the walls of towering reeds. Even though she was now hidden from the camp, Alexa pushed onward down the channel with a few more thrusts of the pole. Then, she crawled forward to Jakes. Tearing off her hair scarf and jacket, she made a makeshift bandage to wrap around his midsection.

He whimpered when she tied the sleeves of the jacket into a knot. "Sorry, but the wound's still bleeding. This will put some pressure on it." She was concerned by the gray undertone of his dark skin. She pulled her water bottle from her backpack and gave Jakes a few sips.

"I'm going to start the motor now and hope we're far enough into the reeds that they won't hear."

Jakes nodded and turned a thumb up.

"Damn. I should have disabled the other boat." Alexa slapped her knee in frustration, leaving a bloody palmprint on her pants, then plowed on. "Hold tight, Jakes. We need to move on. I'll need your help to find the BDF camp. What I remember is: right at the end of this channel, then right again. Then look for the channel on the right?"

Jakes nodded in silence.

Alexa touched his shoulder in reassurance as she scrambled back to the stern. Once there, she lowered the outboard into the water, pulled the choke, and cranked the ignition. To her great relief, it started without a problem. She eased into gear and headed down the channel.

The first ten or so minutes passed with few challenges. As Alexa steered through the narrow channel, she played the morning's events over again and again in her mind. Reese sticking his head into the bathroom as she brushed her teeth, saying, "I'm going to head up early to check my email. See you up there in a few?"

Alexa had just nodded, her mouth foaming with toothpaste. She hadn't even kissed him goodbye. And, now, she may never see Reese alive again. She choked on a sob as tears streamed down her cheeks. Melissa and Jim. They'd never even be here in Botswana if she hadn't encouraged them to come on safari. And Harry. The man who'd saved her life was now at risk of losing his own.

Angry that she'd given in to emotion, Alexa wiped the tears away and revved up the speed a notch. Then, Jakes raised his hand and waved it in a patting motion. He was telling her to slow back down. She eased off and looked ahead in consternation. In the distance, the channel split into three. She didn't remember this place. On their earlier outing, Alexa hadn't paid much attention to the route. She'd been a passenger, safe in the knowledge that Jakes and Harry could navigate their way through this labyrinth of channels, pools, and islands. And that trip had been punctuated by stops at almost every turn to examine an interesting bird, plant, or animal.

Very different from this desperate trip to get help for people trapped by murderous men. Up to now, Alexa hadn't had time to dwell on who this band of killers in camouflage could be. Now, she tried to figure it out. Terrorists? Robbers targeting rich tourists? Something about the man in the shiny hat jostled at a memory, but Alexa's mind skittered away before it could make a connection. Whoever these monsters were, she needed to get help. To save her friends. These men had shown that they had no qualms about killing their hostages.

As they approached the three-way split, Alexa called to Jakes, "Do we take the right?"

Once again, he raised his thumb in the okay signal.

This channel widened into a pool. A line of crocodiles was sunning on the island to their left, their mouths open to regulate their temperature in the now-bright sun. Reacting to the power of suggestion, Alexa opened the buttons of her quick-dry shirt against the growing warmth. She also dug sunglasses out of her backpack and slipped them on to lessen the glare from the water.

As fragmented thoughts raced through her mind, Alexa began to obsess again on the notion of rivers. *Here I am again on a river, headed toward an important destination. So many of the dark things here have happened next to rivers. But, this time, the darkness is behind me, at Noka. And I'm headed upriver toward the light, toward help.* With a sob, she faced the hard, cold fact: *If I don't reach that destination, more people could die.*

After five more minutes of motoring, Alexa bit her lip and studied the channel ahead. If they reached the hippo pool, she'd gone too far and passed the channel to the BDF outpost. She spotted a stand of palms in the distance. Hadn't they been at the entrance of the large hippo pool? She wiped her forehead with a sleeve, wracked with uncertainty.

Concentrating on the palms ahead, she almost missed a narrow channel to the right. Was this the one she was looking for? Alexa turned the engine to idle and called to Jakes. "Is that the channel to BDF?"

Jakes gave no response. His hand slid from the seat he rested against and lay motionless in the crimson water on the boat floor.

Alexa crawled forward, gripping the side of the boat as it rocked. Jakes' eyes were closed. His entire body crumpled against the seat. He was out cold, probably from loss of blood. *Or,* Alexa swallowed, *was he dead?*

"Jakes," she said, hoping her voice would wake him. "Jakes." Still no response, so she reached out to touch his neck, searching for a pulse. "Thank you," she said aloud. The boatman's pulse was weak, but it was there. She couldn't bear for another good man to die on her watch.

Back at the helm, Alexa considered her dilemma. Did this tiny channel lead to the BDF camp? With Jakes unconscious, she was on her own out here, with no time to waste. She studied the channel to the right again and rejected it. Too narrow. The BDF channel had been wider. And something else about it was unique. Alexa pressed her temples, trying to remember. A landmark of some sort. *That's it.* It came to her. A dead palm tree sticking out of the water at the mouth of the channel. It must be up ahead.

Alexa put the outboard into gear and moved forward, eyes peeled for the BDF channel. She was so focused that she almost missed two elephants that stood at the edge of an island, the one with the row of palms she'd seen earlier. They watched her with curious eyes until she veered into another channel so narrow that the reeds and papyrus formed a tunnel over her head.

As she emerged from the tunnel, the channel took an abrupt turn to the right. The hippo charged the moment she rounded the bend. Alexa gasped. Because of the curve, she'd been unable to see the solitary hippopotamus lurking ahead in a spot where the channel fanned out into a wide pool.

The animal stopped his charge about ten feet away from the boat. Head thrown back, the massive hippo opened his giant mouth and roared.

Alexa's heart leapt into her throat. This was not the placid pod of hippos they'd passed two days ago. Or even the male in the smaller group that had grunted a warning. This was a single animal all alone. And he looked very angry.

Heart pounding, Alexa idled the motor, assessing the situation. This solitary animal could be one of the rogue males that Harry and Jakes had described. Jakes would know what to do, but he was unconscious. And Alexa only knew one way to get to the BDF outpost. Straight ahead until she found the side channel.

The hippo retreated briefly but soon took another run at the boat. Alexa was shocked at how fast such an ungainly-looking animal could speed through the water. He stopped short again and furiously shook his head. This time, the beast was so close to the boat that the spray spiraling off his neck dampened Alexa's face. She wiped away the water and put her hand on the gears, ready to click the engine into reverse. The animal's teeth were enormous, and Alexa couldn't forget Harry's warning that hippos killed more people than any other animal in Africa. On edge, waiting for the hippo's next move, Alexa reflected on the bitter irony of this confrontation. How sad would it be to escape armed bandits only to be killed by a strung-out hippo?

The animal sank beneath the surface, and Alexa searched frantically for a sign of where he had gone. Was he swimming beneath her? Would he upend the boat and throw her and Jakes into the water? She gave the engine just enough juice to edge the boat next to the tall reeds, cutting off the animal's access on one side.

Then she waited. Each second stretched out like an hour as she scanned the pool for the beast. She breathed a little easier when he surfaced farther away, in the middle of the pool ahead. Still, she couldn't risk trying to pass. Her attention riveted on the hippo, Alexa continued to wait, alert for an opening. After a third feint toward the boat, the animal retreated to a spot directly ahead, blocking the right side of the channel. He looked as if he was preparing to charge.

Alexa had to do something. Drifting here, she was a sitting duck. She revved up the engine and sped the boat across the pool to the left, into the shallows of a small island. She positioned the boat stern to shore and studied the hippo. The beast stared back. This monster meant business. He kept making deliberate moves to block her passage through the channel, each charge punctuated by loud roars. Alexa waited for him to settle down and back off. The water below her should be shallow enough to prevent the hippo from swimming beneath and capsizing the boat. But what did she really know about rogue hippos? Did they settle down once they reached full fury like this guy? Or did they live in a continual pissed-off state?

She looked around for a tree to climb if he rammed the boat. She saw nothing substantial enough to scale. Even if she tried, how could she leave Jakes? He was still slumped unconscious, and the ever-deepening crimson of the water indicated he continued to lose blood. As Alexa waited and assessed the situation, she kept coming to the same inescapable conclusion: She was in terrible danger here. She gritted her teeth to avoid surrendering to panic.

Moments later, the hippo launched an explosive new charge. This time, the enraged animal actually leapt out of the water, half of his body thrusting into the air just a few yards from the side of the boat. All Alexa could focus on was the beast's gaping mouth full of teeth. The two lower canines had a nasty curve and must have measured two feet long. She braced herself for the animal to hit the boat.

At that moment, the furious hippo's head and shoulders smashed back down into the water, creating a small tsunami that slammed the boat. Alexa grabbed the gunwale as the boat tilted to the right, then rocked back down into the resulting trough on the left. The seesaw motion catapulted Jakes' limp form into the water. The counter wave from the lurch of the boat propelled his body directly toward the angry animal. In a flash, the hippo impaled the boatman on his huge tusks and submerged beneath the pool with Jakes' body in his grip. As the animal swam to the head of the pool, to the place Alexa had first entered from the channel, a trail of red bubbles rose to the surface to mark the beast's course.

Time stood still. Stunned, Alexa could barely process what had just happened. In the dreadful quiet, a kingfisher swooped by with a plaintive cry. The bird spurred her into action. She could do nothing for Jakes. He was already gone. But she could still try to save all those people back at Noka.

Sobbing, Alexa slammed the engine into gear and sped forward, leaving the hippo and the remains of Jakes' body behind. Just a few minutes later, she reached the dead palm and the channel on the right. She eased into this new waterway, wiping her eyes with her sleeve. Soon, she pulled up to a dock.

Two men in BDF uniforms ran onto the dock. One of them held out a hand and said, "Off limits. You must turn around. This is a military facility."

Alexa lifted her tear-streaked face to look him in the eye. "I know. I need help. Noka Camp has been attacked. They're holding everyone hostage."

The English-speaking soldier turned to his companion and rattled off several sentences in Setswana. Alexa assumed he was translating her plea for help.

He nodded at her. The English-speaker said, "Of course we help. Tell the lieutenant this. His English be better than mine. Come."

As Alexa tried to hoist herself onto the dock, she started to shake uncontrollably and slid back into the boat. The two soldiers leaned over to lift her up and grabbed her backpack, red with Jakes' blood. After she stopped wobbling on her feet, they rushed her into the nearby command tent.

CHAPTER TWENTY-FOUR

THE NEXT TWO hours passed in a blur. Alexa would remember some of what happened. Some parts would always remain hazy.

After she explained the situation to Lieutenant Ketayi, he'd radioed the main BDF headquarters about the crisis. Then, the twelve men at the outpost had jumped into their vehicles and sped toward Noka. They'd wanted Alexa to remain in camp with their medic, who had plied her with rehydration salts in water as she told her story. Instead, she'd insisted on coming with them. They gave her a BDF tee shirt to replace the blood-splattered one she was wearing and found a seat for her in an SUV. As they approached Noka, a BDF helicopter flew overhead and descended just beyond the staff quarters. Alexa suspected the chopper would land in the staff soccer field.

Lieutenant Ketayi yelled over the road noise to Alexa, "This won't be a stealth operation. They heard the helicopter land. They're on an island. It would be difficult to surround without them knowing. So, we will overwhelm them with force."

As the driver skidded to a stop, the men in the back climbed out of the SUV, guns in hand. The troops in the second SUV followed. A larger force of soldiers from the helicopter had already arrived at the edge of the trees near the footbridge. The group from the outpost waded into the shallow water behind the camp manager tent and headed for the island. Their path kept them out of sight from the main dining hall.

"Stay here," the lieutenant directed. "We need to concentrate on the hostages."

Alexa obeyed his command, pacing back and forth as she watched the rescue unfold. She worried that the bandits would shoot their hostages when faced with capture by the BDF. Even worse, she feared they could already be dead. Her heart ached for Reese and her friends.

The island was quiet. No gunfire. No voices. Was anyone still alive?

The outpost group of soldiers had reached the island and circled the managers' tent. When they slipped into the kitchen compound, Alexa lost sight of them. A blast of static ripped through her tension. To her left, a voice, amplified by an electronic speaker, said, "We have you surrounded. Drop your guns and walk across the footbridge. Do not think of harming the hostages. Our numbers are much greater than yours. You have no choice but to surrender." The same voice spoke again in Setswana, likely the same message.

Alexa searched for the speaker, but he was among the soldiers assembled along the tree line, hidden in the shadows of the forest.

When the soldier finished speaking, Alexa held her breath, waiting for a reply. The silence lengthened, uninterrupted by the typical sounds of birds and insects. It was as if the entire bush had paused, waiting to hear the bandits' response. But no one shouted out a surrender. No one emerged from the main tent to cross the footbridge.

The soldier used the electronic megaphone to broadcast his message again. The other soldiers stayed in the forest, waiting for a reaction.

As the minutes ticked by with no response, the absolute silence became ominous. Fearing the worst, Alexa's shoulders slumped. Had the bandits killed everyone? She'd read of attacks in East Africa, al-Shabab, the Children's Army. Had terrorism come to Botswana? How could she survive without Reese? Without her best friend?

In a sudden burst of activity, BDF soldiers emerged from the main tent and shouted, "We have the hostages. The hostiles are gone."

Alexa ran toward the footbridge. The soldiers from the tree line beat her across, and the last man grabbed her when she hit the island.

"Please. You must wait, miss. It still may not be safe." The soldier gestured toward a tree swing on the bank of the channel. "Please, sit over there for now."

Alexa twisted in his grip but stopped when she caught sight of several bodies on the ground at the edge of the tent. She'd seen them shoot one woman, the birder. That hostage hadn't been the last. Alexa's heart leapt when she saw no auburn hair; Melissa was not among the dead. Then, she burned with shame knowing there were friends and family who would mourn these women too.

The soldier watched as the emotions played over her face. His expression softened. "I will try to find your friends."

"My name's Alexa. Tell them Alexa is here." She choked back a sob and trudged toward the tree swing. As she sat looking at the mainland, Alexa tried to reassure herself. None of those bodies—maybe three—looked big enough to be Reese or Jim or Harry. Then, once again, she remonstrated her callous selfishness. How sick was it to hope that these dead people were not her loved ones? Certainly, someone out there loved each of those souls and would be devastated by their deaths.

At the sound of another approaching helicopter, Alexa raised her eyes. For the first time, she spotted the inevitable vultures perched on a large dead tree across the water. The helicopter was bringing help to the living, but the vultures were there for the dead.

"Lexie! Oh my God, I've been so worried about you."

Alexa turned at the sound of Reese's voice, rose, and flew into his arms.

Alexa's eyes brimmed with tears again when she said, "I thought they were going to kill you. Kill everybody."

"And I was going out of my mind, Lexie. For all I knew, you were lying dead or bleeding alone in our tent." Reese's voice caught. "Not knowing about you. All the while waiting for those sick savages to kill the next hostage."

Alexa pulled his head to hers until their foreheads touched. "We survived. We're fine. We're the lucky ones."

"I hear some of that is thanks to you. How did you bring the BDF?" When Alexa started to answer, Reese said, "No, wait. Tell us all at the same time."

He led Alexa into the main lounge where Melissa, Jim, and Harry waited. After a round of hugs, Alexa sat and looked around in a daze. The other guests and staff filled the chairs there and in the adjacent dining room. Someone had thrown tablecloths over the bodies on the ground. Two of the staff were pouring tea and coffee at the buffet line for the group of shaken hostages and their rescuers.

Many of the soldiers had fanned out through the camp, searching the guest tents. Others had rushed to the BDF helicopter, which rose into the air soon after the other copter landed. Alexa was surprised to spot Colonel Shonga standing in the back of the dining area. She hadn't known he was leading the BDF force that had arrived from the main base. A group of men rushed across the footbridge and headed toward the colonel.

Alexa tuned out the bustle of activity around her and took a sip of tea, savoring its soothing warmth. Then, she turned to Reese. "What happened? Where are the men who attacked the camp? What did they want? Is Emma okay? And Nick?"

Reese gave her a tired smile. "We'll give you the whole story. Or at least as much as we know. And you'll have to tell us how you managed to arrive with the cavalry to rescue us. Those thugs bound our wrists and ankles. Put duct tape over our mouths and locked us in the kitchen storage area. The pantry's huge, but we were still packed in like sardines."

"I was afraid you were all dead. Especially when no one answered the soldier's command."

Reese put his arm around Alexa's shoulders and pulled her close. "We're fine. Mostly."

A weary-looking Harry jumped in. "Let's start at the beginning. The men attacked at breakfast. No one saw them coming until they stormed this area, armed to the teeth."

"Were they terrorists? Bandits?" Alexa asked.

"Poachers." Reese, Harry, and Jim all spoke the word at the same time.

"What? These were the guys who've been poaching elephants? I thought they were in jail." Alexa wrinkled her face as she tried to process this startling information.

Reese shrugged his shoulders. "We're not sure if these goons are part of a larger group that includes the men in jail. Or the Francistown guys could have been running a separate operation down in the Makgadikgadi."

"Okay, so these poachers. Why would they come here?" Alexa asked.

Harry spat out a name. "Nick."

Reese continued. "Turns out Nick is the mastermind behind all this poaching. The guys who carried out the actual killing of the elephants were the work crew that's been here at Noka for the past few months."

"Yeah," Harry's tone was sardonic. "While they built the new equipment shed during the day, the wankers slipped out at night for a spot of poaching. They stored the ivory in the shed and smuggled it out on their supply runs."

Alexa remembered her run-in with the worker at the shed and shivered. She'd been closer to danger on that aimless walk than she could ever have imagined. Then, she thought about the metallic hat she'd seen the man wearing this morning in the dining tent. That was the same guy. He'd been wearing one of those silver Mickey Mouse baseball caps when he'd chased her away from the shed that day. Apparently, he spoke English after all. Then, another dot connected. Was he also there that day they'd gone upriver to investigate the four dead elephants? One of the men she'd seen in the boat nearby had been wearing a metallic cap.

But Nick? Involved in poaching? Alexa had trouble wrapping her head around that idea.

Jim said, "They must have transported the final load of ivory out of here a few days ago. Emma mentioned that this construction project was just finished."

"We saw the trucks leaving when we landed here." Alexa shook her head in confusion, still trying to absorb this startling information. "Three, no four days ago. Why would they come back?"

Reese's voice dripped with disdain. "Seems like old Nicky boy stiffed them on the payment. When they crossed the Zim border and transferred the ivory to the buyer, he paid only half of what they expected. Turns out the buyer had already paid Nicky the first half. Nick thought he could get away with it since the men were headed to their homes up north and he'd escape to England with the extra money."

"We got the impression that they were all from Angola and the DRC. Somehow, Nick lured them down here for the poaching job," Harry added.

"How did you learn all of this?" Alexa asked.

He answered, "Hard not to. While his pack of thugs kept us in our seats at gunpoint, the head guy and his righthand man raged at Nick. Apparently, Nick's Bantu, Swahili, and Portuguese are nonexistent. So, their conversation was in English."

Jim nodded. "After a while, everyone in earshot figured out why these crooks were here. They were dead set on collecting the money from Nick."

Melissa finally spoke, eyes brimming with tears. "Nick said he didn't have the cash at Noka. They didn't believe him. So, that monster, the one in charge, decided that the way to get Nick to cough up their cut of the money was to shoot the tourists. First, that young woman from England. The one who was a birder. Then, an old lady. I think she was German. Then, the woman we spoke to last night. The one from Cincinnati. Thank God there were no children here. They dragged the executions out over an hour or more. Gave Nick plenty of time to stew between each new dead tourist."

Alexa had seen the first execution. She tried to imagine how terrifying it would be to sit, trapped by these evil men, wondering if you'd be next.

"Finally, the fucker wises up and realizes maybe Nicky doesn't really give two shits about these random tourist women. After all, it's unlikely that he'll still have a job here as camp manager after a day like this. So, why not hit him where it hurts? His fiancée?" Melissa's anger burned through each word. Alexa had never seen her friend so bitter, so shaken.

"Emma? Oh no." Alexa glanced around the room again but couldn't see Emma anywhere. She looked toward the bodies under the tablecloth. "Is she . . . ?"

Reese sighed. "Emma's fine. At least physically. Nick still has a sliver of heart left. When the poachers threatened her, he broke down. Swore he didn't have the cash. He sent it to his uncle in Zimbabwe. Said he'd give it to them if they spared Emma and the rest of us. That's when they tied us up and left, taking Nick with them."

Jim said, "Emma completely lost it when the guy threatened to shoot her. Kept looking at Nick like he'd turned into the Devil himself. Then, she passed out when they tied us up. It was like she completely shut down. The BDF medic got her to open her eyes, but she's in shock or something. I don't really know the woman, but I'd wager she had no idea what Nick was up to."

"At our tea the other day, Emma confided that she feared he had another woman in Maun. She thought that's why he was always away and distracted when he was here at Noka." Alexa shook her head. "Poor, sweet Emma. Another woman would have been infinitely easier to deal with than this." She waved her hands at the disastrous situation.

Melissa eyed Alexa. "The entire time, we were frantic about what had happened to you. We heard some shooting early on, down near the boat dock. But we knew you were in your room. When they searched the tents, we expected they'd bring you here. We were shocked when they came back without you but hoped you found a place to hide. No one mentioned you were missing. I was thrilled you'd slipped their grasp. That at least one of us might survive," her voice cracked.

Reese drew Alexa close and kissed her forehead. "We were all hoping."

"You escaped and made it to the BDF outpost to alert them?" Harry's glance was warm with a mixture of admiration and relief.

"Jakes helped me, but he'd been shot." Alexa shuddered at the image of the boatman being dragged beneath the water in the jaws of the rogue hippo. "He didn't make it." She paused, then took a deep breath. "It was horrible. Let me tell you the entire story."

The BDF and investigators quarantined all the guests and staff at Noka through the following morning, with two exceptions. The husband of the elderly woman who'd been killed experienced chest pains. And Emma was still in deep shock. So, the authorities sent them both to the hospital on a medical helicopter. BDF medics patched up the minor cuts and bruises of the others.

The soldiers sent out a party to look for Jakes' body. In a private meeting in the small library, Colonel Shonga personally informed Alexa—and Harry, as Delta Wild's senior person on-site—that his men had recovered some of the boatman's remains. The colonel withheld any details.

"It all happened so fast. I feel like I should have been able to save him," Alexa's eyes brimmed with tears as she relived the horrific moment Jakes' body flew into the hippo's mouth.

"You said the young man was unconscious from loss of blood," Colonel Shonga responded. "You were trying to get him medical attention. The bush is an unforgiving place, as you have already learned firsthand while in our country, Miss Williams. Sometimes courage and determination are not enough to prevail against the wild."

Harry added, "Don't forget, it was the poachers who shot him in the first place. If he hadn't been wounded, Jakes would have been steering you and the boat to safety."

A single tear spilled as Alexa thought, *What both men had said was true, but neither had been there at that horrible moment in the channel.*

When the colonel left the room, Harry lifted a hand to caress Alexa's damp cheek. "I'm so glad you survived, princess," he murmured.

She clasped his hand and looked into those caring green eyes. "I was worried about you too, mate."

Alexa shook her head in disbelief. "I wanted to come back to Noka one last time before we left Botswana. I felt like I had unfinished business here after the elephant stampede. I needed to honor Mo at his favorite camp. To say goodbye to Emma." Her voice caught, "To see you. What does it say about the Universe that, instead of completing the circle, providing resolution, it hit me with more violence and death?"

"Don't ask me to interpret the Universe, princess. But I suspect you'll figure it out. You're a strong, resourceful woman; one that I'm happy to have traveled with, even if just for a while. I would never have wished for any of this disaster." He motioned toward the dining hall. "But I'm glad we got a chance to say goodbye."

Harry kissed Alexa's forehead. "I need to get back to the staff. There's so much to deal with. I'll see you and Reese at dinner." His expression changing from wistful to resolute, Harry wheeled around and walked back into the lounge.

🐘

The authorities spent the rest of the day interviewing each person about the morning's events. Harry stepped in to get the camp back into gear. He was also working with management in Maun, who had to find spaces in other camps for incoming guests. Authorities had informed Delta Wild that Noka would be closed for several days while they processed the scene for this hostage incident and the equipment shed for signs of poached ivory.

Although wildlife activities ceased, the staff worked around their interviews and went back to their duties, cranking out meals and cleaning rooms. After their formal interviews, Alexa and Reese went to their tent and fell into bed. Exhausted, they slept until dinner.

Jim took the evening meal to Melissa in their tent. She had told him she couldn't step into the dining area without thinking about the terrible events of the morning. Alexa was worried about Melissa, whose brash confidence some-times fell apart when confronted with dangerous or emotional situations. She was glad that her friend could count on her husband's calm support. Alexa had never seen the steady forest ranger become ruffled, even though she'd seen him face some dicey situations.

Reese, Alexa, and Harry found a quiet table in the lounge where they picked at omelets during a mostly silent dinner. Listless, Alexa had nothing more to give. The voyage for help. Her fear that Reese and her friends could die. Jakes' macabre death. The long interviews with authorities. Even the depressing news that Nick was the head poacher. This taxing day had drained away both her energy and emotion.

Her fatigue was shadowed by a grim sense of déjà vu. Here she was again, sitting with Reese and Harry, trying to process a tragedy and running out of words to deal with the outrage. They sat in Noka Camp's lounge on comfy chairs rather than camp stools in the bush, but the feeling of despair mixed with a hint of guilty elation at being alive—that was the same.

From the desolate looks he sent her way, Alexa knew that Harry was reliv-ing the night in the bush too. Reese might not have experienced that night with them, but he'd seen the immediate aftermath. And he'd been right in the midst of this hellish day. She knew they were both struggling.

Alexa's escape was harrowing, especially when the hippo attacked and she'd lost Jakes. But, Reese and Harry, both used to taking action, had been in an impossible situation. Helpless to intervene in the face of so many men with automatic rifles, they had to watch one woman after another die. In a strange way, the shared ordeal seemed to have knit their frayed friendship back together. Alexa sensed a new brothers-in-arms vibe between the two men.

That night, Alexa lay awake, listening to the hippos grunting in the lagoon and thinking about those awful seconds when Jakes tumbled into the water. Like the elephants she'd encountered, the hippos appeared so harmless. But she'd seen firsthand what the 'wild' in wild animals could lead to if they were provoked.

The next morning, Delta Wild management appeared at breakfast to begin damage control. Guests had been killed in one of their premier camps. And one of their camp managers had not only been at the heart of the incident but had been unmasked as the poacher reviled throughout Botswana. Harry said that it was going to be a setback for the safari company but thought that its stellar reputation would protect the outfit from lasting harm.

By mid-afternoon, Alexa, Reese, Jim, and Melissa had returned to Maun. The broad outline of what had happened at Noka had spread like wildfire. So, Sophie and Sally were waiting for them when they returned to the Africa Trust house. Reese and Alexa spent time filling them in and sending out updates to the Africa Trust network.

Now the four friends were sprawled in the living room, revisiting the events of the past two days. Sally popped in periodically to ply them with food and drink. Alexa's stomach was in knots, so she sipped a Coke but refused the offers of food.

"Are you feeling any better?" Alexa asked Melissa. Her friend had been pale and nauseated since yesterday.

"I'm okay." Melissa's smile was wan. "I think it's just nerves. You remember when we found Cecily Townes dead at her house. I didn't cope well that time either."

Jim kissed his wife on her forehead. "We've all been through a lot. There's no shame in feeling off-balance. With the flight postponed until tomorrow afternoon, we can just chill here with Alexa and Reese. I bet you'll be in fine shape to travel by then. Plus, we're basically going to climb on a plane and sleep for twelve hours."

Reese said, "I'm glad that Gary has been delayed. Something about an additional doctor's appointment in the States. Works out because that leaves the guest bedroom open. Plus, Lexie and I can use the free day to decompress."

"He'll be here before we head out on Wednesday, right?" Alexa asked.

Reese looked at his phone. "The email says he'll arrive late evening on Sunday. That still gives us two full days to do the transition. We'll just have to make our briefings concise. So, it's all good. Given the circumstances, I couldn't imagine focusing enough today to give him anything coherent."

Melissa had been staring at a spot on the couch, unengaged in the group conversation. She mumbled, "It's going to take me a long time to get past watching those women die, one after another." She raised her voice in anguish. "Those monsters. It's always the women, isn't it?"

"They killed Mo and Jakes too. Maybe not directly, but the poachers are just as responsible for their deaths."

Melissa's eyes met Alexa's. "You know what I mean, Lexie. Your friend, Mo. Jakes. Their deaths are no less tragic. But they were killed in the heat of battle, so to speak. The executions of those three women though. Just like all the sex traffickers, when they look to target someone, the fuckers always choose the women."

Alexa nodded. "I know exactly what you're saying. And to be right there in the room when those women were killed. It must have been heartbreaking."

Melissa stood. "Yes. Heartbreaking is one word for it. I'm going to lie down for a while." She took a few steps toward their bedroom.

"Wait, honey. A rest sounds like an excellent idea," Jim said with a concerned expression as he followed his wife down the hall.

Alexa looked at Reese. "She's right, you know. Melissa's more attuned to it because of her anti-sex-trafficking work with RESIST. And I know they traffic boys too. Bottom line, jerks like those poachers find it easy to prey on women. They see us as more vulnerable. And, often, physically, we are." She pursed her lips in a rueful smile. "Even those of us who learn Krav Maga."

Reese edged closer to her on the couch. "I know, although those murderous bastards would have killed any one of us, male or female, to get their money. I wish I could have done something to save those women," he said with a despairing look.

"You were in a no-win situation. They had guns and made it clear that they had no qualms about murdering innocents. I saw you and Harry try to stop the first execution. If you hadn't stood down, they would have killed you too." Alexa touched Reese's cheek.

"Knowing that doesn't make it any easier to live with. I kept thinking they'd let down their guard. That we'd get a chance to make a move. But they were relentless."

Reese shook his head, then said with a ghost of a smile, "If those cretins had stayed around just a little longer, they would have found out that a tough-as-nails woman was leading the charge to take them down. Even though they fled, you put the BDF on the poachers' trail early. I hope they catch them."

He kissed Alexa, then rose. "If it's okay with you, I'm going to do some work. Prioritize what we discuss with Gary now that we have less time."

Alexa appreciated Reese's ability to roll with the punches. She knew that the experience at Noka had shaken him, but part of her love's personality allowed him to compartmentalize and move on. Sometimes, she wished she had that same capacity to shrug off trouble. Other times, like now, when she was still processing yesterday's tragedy, she questioned how Reese found it so easy.

"Okay. I'm going to check my emails. Then maybe read a book. I considered calling Mom and Dad, telling them about what happened at Noka. But why worry them? We'll be home in a few days. We can tell them then; spin it as an African adventure. Even if they hear about an incident in the news, they won't know we were involved."

"Sure." Reese's sarcasm was evident from his tone. "I agree. There's no need to tell them or my parents about this mess until we're home. Even then, they'll worry despite knowing we arrived home safe and sound."

Reese's cell phone rang. "Hello. Reese Michaels." After a few seconds of listening, his face took on a grim look.

When Reese pressed end-call, he announced with a deep sigh, "BDF caught up to the poachers and Nick, not far from the Zimbabwe border. Things went south. There was a gun battle. All the poachers are dead."

"And Nick?"

"Dead."

"My God. Nick's dead," Alexa shook her head in disbelief.

"Almost like an after-the-fact shoot-to-kill." Reese shrugged.

Alexa asked, "Are you suggesting . . . ?"

"Not really. Well, maybe. Easier than a trial. They were all foreign nationals, even Nick. It's a tidy solution."

"I don't want to believe it. By law, the deaths must be investigated by the director of public prosecutions. The truth should come out. But, now, they won't be able to get information about the buyers," Alexa complained. "That's almost as important as stopping the poachers."

Reese rubbed his forehead. "I always sensed something a little off about Nick. I wrote it off as him being a poser. Trying to pass as an upper-class guy and not quite nailing it. But it never crossed my mind that he could be behind this poaching. When the elephants killed Mo, we traveled up there together. He seemed so distraught and concerned."

"Yeah. Now we know he was probably concerned about his team of poachers getting caught and wanted to be on the inside of the BDF hunt for them. Granted, I had no clue either. I just knew Emma was too good for him." Alexa shook her head. "Poor Emma. I hope she makes it through this. It's going to be a hard road. People will be suspicious. I really like her, but even I'm suspicious. And you well know that I was snookered by Caleb Browne, a guy I thought I knew. So, if *I* have questions . . ." Alexa paused, then asked, "Could she have lived with this guy and truly had no idea about what he was involved in? Or did she just turn a blind eye?"

"I don't know, Lexie. We only saw their relationship from the outside. I'm inclined to give Emma the benefit of the doubt, but the police will get to the bottom of it."

Alexa looked at Reese with bemused eyes, "I wouldn't expect anything less from you. One part of me wants to reach out to Emma, but I guess it's not the right time. She's probably still hospitalized."

"Or in custody. Let's see how this plays out. Okay?" Reese returned to his laptop.

"Okay." Nick had caused so much pain and death. Perhaps a violent demise was the karma he deserved. But a part of Alexa felt sad for the waste the man had made of his life. To stop the thoughts whirling through her mind, she picked up her phone and paged through the news.

A few minutes later, Alexa interrupted Reese. "Only a day since everything went down at Noka, but there's already an editorial here about how all this might affect the Commission work. The author urges swift action on the hunting ban and advocates for a clear shoot-to-kill mandate. Wonder if today's news will make a difference?"

"Hard to tell. Will the deaths of nine poachers, including Nick, seem like too high a price for fifty or so felled elephants? Or will public sentiment get behind BDF and validate their actions?"

"A lot depends on the minister and the president."

"Probably. What about your friend, Mama Botswana? Will she bend to public sentiment if opinion shifts?"

"Who knows. I'm still not clear what's behind her sudden affection for international funding for conservation—especially from the Chinese. Get this.

I just read she's coming to Maun on Sunday to open a new HIV/AIDS clinic and give a luncheon speech. I might run over there. Say goodbye and find out what she's thinking if I can. Any information will be a help to Gary when he steps back into our seat on the Commission. Plus, my last meeting with Mama ended on an ambivalent note. It might be a good idea for Africa Trust if I try to mend fences a bit." Alexa flashed an impish smile. "It's never a good idea to piss off an international icon."

"If you think it's helpful—and you're feeling up to it—go for it."

CHAPTER TWENTY-FIVE

By Sunday, Alexa was prepared for their return to the States. She'd spent the day after Melissa and Jim left washing clothes from their safari, doing her final packing, and finishing the summary on her work with the Commission. She was glad to keep busy. When she sat idle, her thoughts turned to her boat trip on the Delta and Jakes' horrible death. That led to her dwelling on Mo and all the other needless deaths she'd seen during their stay. The poacher killed by the lion. Elephant after elephant cut down for pure greed. And the shock of finding out that the man she'd joked with, dined with, and regarded as a friend was at his core a soulless poacher.

Work kept Alexa's mind occupied. She was tired of obsessing on death and destruction. On the whole, Botswana had been a wonderful experience. Spending almost every waking hour in the outdoors, seeing the animals, learning a new kind of work—it had given her a new perspective. She wanted that joy to be the feeling she took home from this once-in-a-lifetime sabbatical, not the darkness.

Reese was preoccupied with writing final reports for Gary. Frankly, he was going overboard in creating transition documents for Africa Trust's Maun executive director. Yes, he'd been gone for four months. But Gary's entire research team would still be here to brief him on the current status of their work. Alexa had come to realize that writing these meticulous reports was a way for Reese to detach from Botswana.

She tried to put it in perspective. Only a few weeks ago, she'd been concerned that her love wouldn't want to come home to Pennsylvania, that he'd choose Africa over her once again. What was the big deal if Reese wanted to dot all the i's and cross all the t's? Still, she couldn't help being annoyed. Not only had he seemingly moved right past the Noka Camp disaster but also he was spending their last hours in Botswana hunched over a computer.

At breakfast, Alexa told Reese, "I'm going to drive over to that AIDS center opening that Mama Botswana is doing." Already knowing the answer, she asked, "Want to come along?"

"Do you mind if I stay here? I just have one more project to organize. Since Gary's arriving tonight, I want to have everything complete." He reached for her hand. "Sorry I've been so wrapped up in paperwork. I expect we'll both be tied up tomorrow with this transition. But let's make sure we spend most of our last day here out on the Delta. Maybe take a boat ride or drive somewhere?"

"I'm going to hold you to that. I'd like to get out in the bush one more time before we leave. It will be like getting back on the horse that threw you."

Reese gave Alexa a puzzled look.

"I don't want my last experience in the Botswana bush to be the nightmare of that boat trip to get help." Alexa's response was sharp.

"Oh, right. That makes sense," Reese mumbled and picked up some papers.

With a glance at her watch, Alexa said, "I don't expect this Mama Botswana thing will last more than a few hours. The dedication is first. Then she's giving the speech." Alexa giggled. "You won't believe where."

Reese gave her a blank look.

"At Chapman's."

Laughing, Reese said, "Well, they manage to handle large crowds on a regular basis. What better venue for a Maun event?"

"The ad said you can buy tickets at the door. I better get ready." Alexa downed the last of her tea and headed toward the bedroom.

By the time Alexa found parking at the nearby supermarket, a large crowd had gathered at the new AIDS education center. The proud staff was offering tours, so Alexa dutifully joined a walk-through of the small building. The tour guide made clear that this was not a clinic site, although they had two exam rooms. The local public and private hospitals served the Maun area's AIDS patients' medical needs. This center would primarily provide preventive education and encourage testing and treatment.

After the tour, everyone was hustled into the dusty parking lot where the crowd had assembled. A woman at the entrance of the center cut off people who were about to enter for the next tour, announcing that the dedication was about to begin. Alexa turned toward the makeshift stage to the right of the center door.

Out here, the pounding late-morning sun reminded Alexa that the hottest month of the year was only weeks away. She was glad she'd dressed for the heat in a tan linen pantsuit, rose shell, and flats. However, the woman who tottered to the microphone had misjudged the weather. Dressed in a wool business suit and high heels, she looked very uncomfortable, her face bathed in perspiration. With a squawk of the public address system, she spoke. "Welcome to the new Maun Center for Education and Hope. We are so pleased that the leader who has been so important in Botswana's fight against HIV/AIDS has joined us to launch our new project. She is known throughout the world for her courageous and tireless work. I, like all of Botswana, hold this woman in my heart, Mama Nkala."

One of the aides Alexa had met at Mama's office steadied her boss as she climbed the few steps onto the stage. Then, the aide disappeared into the crowd as Mama walked slowly to the lectern. The crowd went wild with cheering, clapping, and ululation.

Mama smiled and gestured with her hands to quiet the noise. "*Dumela*, my friends. What a fine day to celebrate this blessing to the Maun community. It makes me proud to see the hard work and," she smiled, "hard *pula* of so many people here and in our government result in such a fine center for those in need. Our children, our mothers, our fathers, our friends, our neighbors will all have a place to go for education about the disease that is devasting our country. And they can learn that there is hope. Diagnosis and treatment for those who are already ill. Advice for those who have family members with HIV. Education so our brothers and sisters can avoid becoming infected.

"This center and its wonderful, caring staff open its doors today and invite everyone in. More important, we invite you to join us in bringing HIV and AIDS out of the shadows. It is a terrible disease but cannot be beaten unless we name it, educate about it, encourage prevention, and accept medical treatment without fear or shame.

"We wouldn't be here today without . . ." As Mama launched into a series of thank yous for donors and other key players in building the clinic, Alexa checked the time. The lunch event at Chapman's started in less than an hour. She wanted to get there early enough to get a ticket. With a deep breath, she edged her way through the thick crowd. She was glad she had tucked a few items into a small crossbody bag. A big pocketbook would have impeded her crawl through the crush of tight-packed bodies. Alexa paused at a burst of sudden applause.

She turned to see a beaming Mama Nkala whisk away a cloth that had been hiding a large poster with the new clinic logo. With that, Mama and the first speaker left the stage to be replaced by a group of dancers wearing the animal skin costumes of San Bushmen. At the beat of a drum, they rocked forward into the first steps of a native dance.

Alexa reached the edge of the crowd and ran into Mama's aide. "Hello. What a nice event. I expect the center will do wonderful work."

"Miss Williams, I did not expect to see you. I'd forgotten you were based in Maun. I was going to send you an email next week updating you on the progress we've made with our draft trafficking legislation. I thought you might want to see the final version."

"I'd like that. I'm heading back home to the States in a few days. My email address won't change. I'll watch for your message and give you my feedback."

"Thank you." The young staffer smiled. "Are you coming to the luncheon, I hope?"

"I'm heading over there now to get a ticket."

"No need. I have a few extra tickets for friends and donors. Please take this," she said and held out a printed card.

"Thank you so much. I'll see you at the lunch. I'm looking forward to Mama's speech."

"I must get back to her now. See you there."

Alexa walked back to her car. The restaurant had a great deck next to the water. She'd head over there and have a drink before lunch. Now that she had a ticket, Alexa could avoid standing in line.

The deck at Chapman's was almost empty. Alexa ordered a coke and sat looking at the water, the same Thamalakane River that ran by the Africa Trust house. Here, the restaurant was perched right on the riverbank and had taken advantage of the canopy provided by several huge trees to shade the outdoor deck.

Such a lovely day, Alexa thought. *I will miss Botswana.*

Since she'd been here, images of the towering pine trees near her cabin in Pennsylvania had filled many a night's slumber. Would the Thamalakane and the waters of the Delta flow through her dreams when she returned home?

A small motorboat packed with teenage boys puttered by. Their laughter floated behind as they disappeared down the river. Alexa hoped that only good memories would visit her during the night, not that desperate boat trip that killed Jakes nor the elephant stampede that had taken Mo. She still felt responsible for both deaths. If only she had been more skilled in dealing with rogue hippos, she might have been able to avoid the confrontation and get Jakes the medical attention he needed. In the most rational kernel of her mind, she understood she could have done little to save Mo. She'd escaped only because of Harry's help. But losing Mo still hurt.

At the thought of Harry, Alexa sighed. He was everything a girl could want. Unless that girl was already head over heels in love with Reese Michaels. When they'd parted at Noka, Alexa had kissed Harry on the cheek and asked him to keep in touch. Then, she, Reese, Melissa, and Jim had walked away, leaving Harry to clean up the physical, emotional, and business mess that Nick and his gang of cutthroats had left behind. She knew he was the man for the job, but she'd still felt like they were abandoning him. Alexa twisted her mouth in a smile. Somehow, someday, she expected they'd see Harry again.

The cry of a heron on the far bank of the river nudged Alexa from her reverie. She checked her watch. Twenty minutes until lunch. Plenty of time for a visit to the restroom. As Alexa meandered down the corridor, she glanced into the dining area. A few people were already seated, and more streamed in the front door, so she quickened her pace.

When Alexa exited the ladies' room, a waitress with an empty tray stepped out of a door to the left and into her path.

"Oh, I'm so sorry, miss," she said.

"No worries." Alexa sidestepped the server and glanced into the room the woman had just exited. In the near-collision, the server hadn't fully closed the door. Mama Nkala was sitting at a table with a teacup in front of her. Thinking that the woman was resting alone before her talk, Alexa decided to pop in for a quick goodbye. She knocked on the half-open door as she pushed it open.

"Sorry to intrude, but . . ." Alexa stopped speaking and came to a halt when she stepped into the room. Mama was not alone. Two men were with her, sitting at the far end of the table where they'd been hidden from view. One was small with Asian features. He was dressed in a safari outfit that looked fresh off the rack of a high-end tailor. The other man, in a white linen suit, was very tall. Alexa did a double-take when she recognized him as Nick's fashionable buddy. The guy she'd seen twice with Nick at the bar out front.

Alexa took in Mama's companions in an instant as she babbled her apologies, "I'm so sorry, Mama. I saw you sitting in here and just wanted to say goodbye. I'm leaving for home in a few days. I had no idea you were in a meeting." Alexa backed out the door.

"Don't apologize, child," Mama said. "We were just finishing." Although the activist downplayed Alexa's interruption, the expression in her eyes was wary. Alexa could tell that Mama had picked up on her recognition of the tall man.

"Are you staying for the luncheon? Perhaps we can spend a few moments together after my talk?"

"I am." Alexa stopped at the threshold.

Mama looked down the table and spoke to her companions. "Alexa Williams has been a temporary member of the Conservation Commission, representing Africa Trust. I expect she will have mixed feelings about her few months in Botswana. She has been involved in two tragic incidents involving these poachers who were just brought to justice."

Mama turned back to Alexa. "I hear that you escaped and managed to bring in the BDF to rescue the hostages at Noka Camp. I imagine the BDF could not have picked up the poachers' trail so quickly without your brave actions."

"It was a frightening situation. I did the best that I could."

"Indeed," Mama replied in a careful voice. "You are quite a resourceful young woman."

Mama was making Alexa uncomfortable. While her words expressed polite admiration, she spoke with an icy undertone. *She must be really pissed that I walked in on this discussion*, Alexa concluded.

"Perhaps we'll have a chance to speak later. Again, my apologies for interrupting." Alexa backed out into the hallway and closed the door behind her.

Alexa walked straight to the dining room and took the first empty seat. After nodding to the people gathered around the table, she leaned back in her chair, shaking her head. *Way to screw things up, Alexa*. She'd made a point of coming here and to the dedication today in hopes of mending fences with Mama Botswana, world HIV/AIDS icon. Instead, she'd barged into the woman's private meeting and royally pissed off said icon. It didn't escape Alexa's notice that Mama had made a point of introducing Alexa but had pointedly not shared her companions' names.

Alexa would just leave quietly at the end of the luncheon. After that debacle, she was sure Mama had no great desire to wish her a fond farewell.

"May I bring you a drink?"

Alexa looked up at the question. "Pretty, I should have expected you'd be working today. Yes, thank you. I'd like a Coke, please."

When Pretty returned with the drink, she said, "You and Reese must be leaving Botswana soon?"

"On Wednesday. We'll certainly miss you and Chapman's."

The server put a hand over her mouth to stifle laughter. "I wish you well, Mma. Pula."

The women around Alexa chattered away as if they knew each other well. She made no attempt to get involved in their conversation but let the stream of Setswana wash over her as her mind returned to the encounter with Mama. She couldn't stifle her curiosity about the woman's meeting.

Chinese and Southeast Asians were common in Botswana. As with other African nations, the Chinese were making concerted efforts to become invaluable partners to Botswana's government and business. Africa was a relatively untapped bonanza of natural resources and a developing market for commerce. Botswana was a particular target as one of the continent's most stable economies. But Alexa was not aware of significant Asian interest in subsidizing HIV/AIDS or other healthcare programs. Of course, China dipping a toe into the conservation grant business had been a surprise too.

Nick's buddy was the real mystery. Botswana wasn't that big a country, so it wouldn't be unusual for one guy to be acquainted with both Nick and Mama. For example, he could be an HIV specialty doctor who liked to party with Nick when he was in Maun. Still, Nick had pulled the wool over a lot of peoples' eyes, masquerading as a camp manager and defender of wildlife, all while running a huge elephant poaching operation. Alexa had speculated that the tall man was one of Nick's womanizing buddies or even that he and Nick were lovers. Now she knew that Nick hadn't been stepping out on Emma. His betrayal had been criminal, not romantic.

Of course, that didn't mean the tall man was involved in any of Nick's shady business. Then Alexa thought about something Reese had said at dinner the night following the hostage situation at Noka. He'd thrown up his hands and said, "The thing I still can't wrap my head around is Nick as the mastermind behind this whole poaching operation."

Harry had agreed. "Yeah. The part that's more Nick's style is toppling the whole thing. If he hadn't gotten greedy, his hired help would have gone back to Angola and the DRC. He could have sat on his blood money for a while, then quit his job and swanned off to Zim or England a rich man. Screwing it up sounds more like the Nick I know than Nick, the head of a successful criminal enterprise."

What if tall guy was the mastermind, and Nick met him here in Maun to get his marching orders? Then, Alexa laughed at her crazy imagination. Like they'd meet in public, at Chapman's of all places. And wouldn't the investigators have discovered if Nick had accomplices?

Alexa took a sip of her drink. Servers were bringing out soup to the far tables. Good. Now that she'd messed this up with Mama, Alexa wanted to get this lunch over and head back to Reese.

"Miss."

The woman to her right turned and looked up, then nudged Alexa's elbow. "Miss Williams."

Alexa swiveled to see Big Boy standing behind the table. She had to lean back a bit to see his face.

"Big Boy. Hello," she said in surprise.

"Miss, may I speak to you?" the chauffeur asked.

"Sure." As Alexa rose, Big Boy stepped into the empty hall.

"Dumela, miss. Mama Nkala asks if you could come talk to her for a few minutes. She has a short time until she will make her speech. She was hoping that you could meet now. Something about saying goodbye?"

"Okay." Alexa looked regretfully at the bowls of pumpkin soup that Pretty was serving, then started down the hall.

"Not that way," Big Boy said. "Mama is sitting in the car. She wanted to make sure you wouldn't be interrupted."

As if anyone would interrupt her in a private meeting room. With a twinge of shame, Alexa followed Big Boy to the edge of the parking lot and to Mama's big black SUV. Since it was unlikely Mama had traveled the eight-plus hours from Gaborone by car, it appeared she'd rented an SUV that was identical to the one she used at home. And Big Boy was wearing his uniform with the gold-braided cuffs. Had he flown on a plane in this outfit?

The chauffeur opened the door, and Alexa slid into the back seat next to Mama. The car was running, and the automatic locks clicked into place. Air conditioning in this shady spot seemed unnecessary to Alexa, but then she hadn't yet reached that certain age where hot flashes were a constant challenge.

"Thank you for letting me pull you away from your lunch, dear. We'll get you back to your companions soon." Mama exuded charm. Her earlier icy mood had vanished.

"I'm here on my own," Alexa responded. "My boyfriend is working, so I jumped on the opportunity to come out and hear you speak."

"I am flattered, dear. And I'm so glad you could meet today."

"I'm sorry I barged into your meeting."

"Don't be. If you hadn't walked in like that, I might not have realized that I had some loose ends to tie up. I wouldn't want you back in the States before I had a chance to deal with them."

Alexa was a little confused about Mama's loose ends but wrote it off to language issues. She'd noticed that even the best English speakers in Botswana often misused idioms. She wasn't about to complain since her grasp of Setswana was still limited to less than twenty words.

Mama continued, "I want to thank you one last time before you leave us. Your help on the sex-trafficking bill has been invaluable to our efforts. I will always be grateful, dear."

"I was happy to help," Alexa smiled.

"In that way, we're much alike. We're both willing to go above and beyond for the causes we're passionate about. I noticed that about you when you first came to the Commission. And in our discussions about sex trafficking. We are also both women with boundless curiosity and enough courage to get us into trouble."

Alexa tilted her head, surprised at the personal turn the conversation had taken. "I'm not sure we know each other well enough to reach a conclusion like that, Mama. But I'm flattered that you see similarities in our characters." When Alexa noted that she'd lapsed into the careful language of a lawyer, she tuned into her subconscious. This conversation was becoming uncomfortable, even a little frightening. Time to leave.

She looked pointedly at her watch. "Oh my. I better get back to lunch. I'm sure you want to prepare for your remarks."

Mama ignored Alexa's hint and said, "As a lawyer, I know that it's part of your profession to take threads and weave them together. I wouldn't be surprised if you've already wondered about today's meeting. To speculate about my tall friend's connection to Nick Fuller. He recognized you from an evening here at Chapman's. Nick told him your name. And I'm certain that, even back in your home in the United States, you won't let it rest. You won't stop weaving."

With mounting panic, Alexa understood that something was very wrong here. One look at Mama's implacable face hammered that point home. Why would Mama be talking about Nick? About the poaching?

Then she remembered Nick mentioning that he'd met Mama but down-playing any connection when questioned. Something about Mama and his uncle? *My God.* It hit her at last. It wasn't the tall man. It was Mama. Mama was the mastermind. Reese and Harry had been right that Nick didn't have the skill to pull the poaching scheme off on his own.

Alexa reached for the door handle, but it was locked.

Mama patted Alexa's shoulder. "I'm sorry, dear. I think we could have been wonderful friends under different circumstances. However, one makes choices in life. And I've made HIV/AIDS my life's work. I can't go forward wondering when some bright young attorney in the States is finally going to weave all those threads together and stop my momentum. There are just too many lives to save. And the need for money is never-ending. Like I said, we all must make choices. Like with the ivory, my choice here is clear. It's for the greater good."

Alexa didn't have to be the brilliant lawyer Mama was describing to figure out the unspoken implication here. The greater good meant Alexa's death. Her eyes darted around the SUV for a way out. The locks were engaged. No weapon in sight. Alexa shivered. Suddenly, the air-conditioned car felt like a cold black tomb.

"Big Boy," she pleaded. "You seem like a reasonable man. You don't want to be part of this. Let me go. Just open the door. I'll tell the investigators that you helped me."

The big man's eyes met hers in the rearview mirror, but he gave no response.

Mama smiled and shook her head. "It's no use, my dear. Big Boy is as committed to the cause as I am. He was only a small boy, so our mother's slow, painful death affected him even more greatly than me. He sat by her bedside for hours, listening to each agonizing breath. Many years later, he was the one who made our stepfather pay for bringing HIV into our mother's bed. Make your peace, Alexa."

Mama leaned forward. "Big Boy, it's time for my speech. I'll see you back here."

Big Boy opened the lock to Mama's door, and she slid out.

Alexa scrambled toward that side of the car in an effort to follow Mama, but Big Boy clicked the lock shut before she reached the door. When she looked up, his eyes found Alexa in the rearview mirror.

"Miss. I'll need your bag and phone."

Alexa hesitated, considering. Could she dial for help before he could take the phone from her?

"Don't make this harder, Mma," he said.

Alexa eased the phone from her jacket pocket and held it by her side. With her left hand, she looped the cross-body purse up over her head but deliberately caught the strap beneath her jacket collar. As she tugged at the purse, she hung her head and snuffled. What she'd intended as fake turned into real tears. She leaned forward and sobbed. As she exaggerated her cries, she plowed through her very real fear to call Reese. She used her body to shield her right hand as she unlocked the phone with her index finger, toggled the volume down on the side, then tapped on the first contact saved to her home screen.

Big Boy turned around. "Pull yourself together and give me your things. Or I'll come back there and get them."

Alexa used her sleeve to wipe her eyes. Then she leaned forward and slid the purse strap over her head. She slipped the phone, face forward into the sleeve on the outside of the bag, straightened up, and handed it to Big Boy.

Please go through, call. And, Reese, please answer. But don't shout into the phone when you get the call. Alexa closed her eyes. *Not much to ask, right?*

"Thank you," he said, tossing the purse on the seat beside him. Then, Big Boy put the SUV into gear and drove forward.

"Where are you taking me? Are you going to kill me, Big Boy? You don't have to obey Mama Nkala's orders. I won't tell anyone what she's done. I'm going home to America soon. What do I care about what happens here in Botswana with poaching?" Alexa shouted at the chauffeur, hoping that Reese was hearing this, or it would record on his voicemail.

"Be quiet," Big Boy commanded.

Alexa stopped shouting and looked around the parking lot for help. It was empty except for a young man in khakis who'd just arrived on a motorcycle. She hit the window button. It slid open but stopped just a few inches down. The child lock button. "Help," she screamed. "Help!"

The instant Alexa yelled, Big Boy raised the window with the master controls. The young man looked up as if he'd heard her cry. But, as Big Boy sped out of the parking lot, the biker turned and walked into the restaurant.

CHAPTER TWENTY-SIX

As Big Boy drove at a sedate pace down the road, Alexa's thoughts raced. Now that Mama had connected some of the dots, a new picture had emerged about the poaching. Mama and, probably, Nick's Zimbabwean uncle were behind the poaching. Nick had been the operations manager, using cheap labor from Angola and the DRC to do the dirty work. Alexa assumed that Mama or the uncle had the connection with the buyers. And, remembering the Asian man at Chapman's, that Mama's sudden interest in Chinese money was somehow connected to this whole scheme.

Alexa reined in her speculation. *What difference does solving this mystery make if I'm dead,* she raged in her mind. She understood that she was using the puzzle of the poaching scheme as a distraction because thinking about her current situation was too frightening.

You have to concentrate. Think, Alexa. How will you get out of this? Can you get out of this?

It came to her that Mama and Big Boy couldn't have planned her abduction in advance. They hadn't even known she'd be attending the luncheon. Alexa stumbling in on Mama's meeting and seeing her two companions had been pure chance. All due to random timing and the server leaving an open door. So, they'd improvised this kidnap-and-murder scheme in the few minutes after she'd left for the dining room.

Alexa also surmised it likely that Big Boy had not carried a gun on the plane and so had none in this rental SUV. He'd be relying on his huge size for whatever violence he intended.

She looked out the window. "Where are we going, Big Boy?" she asked. "It looks like we've crossed the river and are heading away from Maun. Are we heading east?" She glanced briefly at the sun, which was almost directly overhead and therefore of no help to her.

"Why do you care? You should be praying to God in your final hours," Big Boy admonished her.

"God? Do you think God would approve of you driving a woman out into the bush somewhere and killing her? And, God aside. Do you think the United States government is going to let one of its citizens die without tracking down her killer? And the Botswana government. I have become good friends with Colonel Shonga in the Botswana Defence Force. He will hunt you and arrest you for murder. If you think your sister can save you, think again. Even the world-famous Mama Botswana can't get away with murder."

"Stop your talking. I must do as Mama wishes. I'm not happy with you anyway. If it hadn't been for you, Nicky might still be alive. He was my friend." Big Boy hesitated and mumbled more to himself than to Alexa, "I used to take little Nicky fishing at the farm when he visited."

Alexa fought a sinking feeling in the pit of her stomach. It was a given; she couldn't beat this giant of a man in a physical contest. And it was becoming clear she couldn't throw him off course or undermine his resolve. She hadn't been able to pierce his slavish devotion to his older sister. Plus, there was something a bit strange about Big Boy that hadn't been fully apparent in her early encounters with him. He wasn't simple-minded, yet he didn't seem to have all the faculties of a typical adult. Her options, if you could call them that, were two at most.

One. Maybe Reese picked up the phone call and was listening. And he'd alerted the investigators or the BDF. Cell reception was good around Maun, so if the call had gone through, it should be transmitting. Maybe.

But she couldn't rely on Reese. Even if he got the call, he still had to find her. That could take time. Time she didn't have.

So, that really left only option two. Seize an opening. Any opening. And run like hell.

The road turned from gravel to sand. With each kilometer, the surroundings became more desolate. Alexa leaned toward the window to check out a large wooden sign ahead, marking a lane to the left. The battered sign read " ingfisher S fari Lod e." Behind it, the lane was blocked by a peeling wooden gate. It had clearly been years since either kingfishers or safari guests had spent any time here. With a mournful smile, Alexa recalled the bright teal Malachite kingfishers she'd admired just a week ago on the Delta.

"Kingfisher Safari Lodge? Looks like they should change the name to Vulture Lodge." She shuddered as she noticed several scavengers tearing apart the carcass of a small animal near the roadside.

"Be quiet. I said no more talking," Big Boy admonished.

Alexa closed her eyes in despair.

Several minutes later, Big Boy turned the SUV off the road at a fenced property. She could see the river in the distance. They must have been driving parallel to the winding path of the river this entire time.

He pulled right up to the gate and punched some numbers into a keyboard on the entrance wall. They drove a short distance on a sandy drive that wound through a well-manicured forest before stopping in front of a sprawling stone-and-wood lodge. The stone patio was littered with leaves and debris, giving the place a deserted look. A window shutter hanging askew and an overturned deck chair added to the general air of abandonment.

Alexa looked at the house with bleak eyes. Was this the place where her life would end? The neglected second home of one of Mama Nkala's rich cronies—likely someone who would never sanction the murder of a young American woman but who would also certainly fail to report any signs of such a murder to the authorities if found on their next visit to the lodge?

Big Boy got out of the car and walked to the stone balustrade at the front of the patio. When he paused, Alexa heard a beep as the door locks engaged. She tried the handle in the back seat anyway. Still locked.

After some searching under several dilapidated pots, Big Boy came up with a key and used it to open the lodge door, which swung inward with a loud creak. Then, he unlocked the car, slipped the key fob into his pocket, and pulled Alexa out. The minute her feet hit the ground, she poised to run.

She looked for an opportunity to flee, waging her desperation and physical fitness against Big Boy's bulk. She was going with the gamble that he had no weapon to shoot her. As if reading her thoughts, Big Boy tightened his iron grip on her upper arm as he shuffled Alexa into the lodge.

Inside, the rooms were dim behind closed curtains. Big Boy shut the door behind them and tried the switches, but the electricity must have been turned off. He grunted angrily, then cracked open the front door for light. A smell of dry dust and decay hung in the gloom. The furniture was sheathed in grimy sheets that made Alexa think of burial shrouds.

As Big Boy dragged her from living room to shadowy sitting room to murky dining room, Alexa gasped for breath. She had trouble matching the huge man's stride, but more than that, she was panicking. Running out of time. It was only a matter of minutes before he killed her. Alexa couldn't figure out why he hadn't already tried, why he'd dragged her into this house. She tried to muster her mantra, "Panic is death," which had willed her on in the past when things seemed desperate. Trying to focus her mind on the phrase, this time the words splintered and disappeared into the vortex of her fear.

Even as hope faded, Alexa stayed alert to the smallest opening for escape. When Big Boy dragged her into the bright kitchen, she blinked at the sudden light, then reeled in fear. *He was going for a knife. He planned to stab her to death.* Alexa wobbled on her feet and almost collapsed.

Big Boy kept her upright by tightening his grip on her arm. In the merciless light of the bare window, Alexa had no problem seeing his fierce glare. "Walk," he barked as he dragged her past a block of knives on a kitchen counter and toward a door in the wall. He opened the door and pushed Alexa into a pantry, blocking her exit with his body and rifling through boxes on a nearby shelf.

Alexa shrank back into the corner, sizing up the cans of vegetables and fruits on the shelf as potential weapons. She spied an open toolbox tucked behind some boxes at her elbow. When Big Boy bent over to get something from a lower shelf, she grabbed a screwdriver and slipped it into her jacket pocket.

Big Boy straightened, holding a length of rough rope. "Come," he beckoned. "You have a few more hours to think about your life on earth and pray for grace. People will notice if I'm not there to pick Mama up after her speech. And I cannot have a mess on my uniform. Mama says we cannot draw attention to ourselves with anything out of the ordinary. So, I will leave you here for now. I'll be back tonight to end things."

Alexa breathed a sigh of relief, followed by the bitter realization that she'd reached a point so low that she was celebrating even a few hours' reprieve from death. Momentarily overcoming her terror, Alexa stepped forward, realizing that Big Boy planned to tie her up. This was her opportunity. She had to act.

"Can I use the bathroom first? I really have to go, and you don't want a mess in your friend's house, do you?"

Big Boy looked uncomfortable, like he was affronted that women had to use the bathroom from time to time. "All right." His tone was reluctant. "The toilet is near the sitting room." He seized her arm again with a vise grip and push-dragged Alexa down a small hall. Stopping at a door, he opened it and said, "The window is too small to climb out, but I'm going to leave the door open while you go." His voice turned prissy, "I'll turn my back, so you'll have privacy."

Alexa swallowed a harsh laugh. This man was hours away from ending her life but worried about bathroom propriety for ladies. *What a gentleman.*

Big Boy thrust her into the small water closet and turned his back as promised. Alexa sat on the toilet, which was tucked away to the left of the door, and urinated. She hadn't been lying. She had to go. As she finished, Big Boy shifted on his feet.

"Please," she protested. "I'm not decent yet." Big Boy turned away and shuffled a few steps away from the door as if embarrassed. When Alexa rose and fastened her slacks, she slipped the screwdriver into her hand, then stepped to the sink, turning on the faucet. With the water still running, she turned in silence and tore through the opening between the doorframe and Big Boy's back.

Alexa's shoulder brushed Big Boy's lower back as she leapt forward and raced for the front door. The giant grabbed for her but missed. As he gave chase, Alexa shoved a small table in his path and sped toward the open door. Big Boy stumbled but recovered quickly. Alexa could hear his footsteps pounding behind her on the wooden floorboards, getting closer and closer. A few feet shy of the exit, he seized her left arm. Without breaking stride, she stabbed the screwdriver into his hand, deep enough that the tool stuck fast.

"Owww," he yelped and let Alexa go.

Alexa's heart leapt as she surged through the doorway. Big Boy had left the key in the lock. She skidded to a stop, pulled the door shut behind her, and turned the key. He'd be able to open the door from inside, but having to unlock it might slow him down a few beats.

Alexa sprinted to the SUV and opened the passenger door. She grabbed her phone from the seat and bolted into the woods. She thought furiously as she ran. She'd made it out of the house, but she was still trapped. If the front of the property was any indication, the entire grounds were enclosed by a high fence, topped by barbed wire. She wasn't sure she could scale the wire barrier. If she could make it to the front gate, though, she had a good chance of getting out. She'd seen this type of gate before, and most required no combination to exit.

Big Boy would certainly head for the gate first. So, she decided to go left and figure out how best to approach her exit attempt. Behind her, the loud creak of the front door opening sent her pulse into overdrive. She ran faster, fallen leaves crunching under her feet, wondering how far it was to the perimeter of the grounds. Ahead, she could see the silvery glint of a chain-link fence and next to it a small herd of giraffes browsing on a stand of acacia—inside the fence.

It had never occurred to Alexa that there would be animals in this compound. Most farms here used fencing to keep animals out. She veered to the right to avoid the giraffes, scanning the forest for other wildlife. Surely the owners of this property wouldn't keep predators in here?

Soon, she'd reached the fence and followed it until she found a brushy area that would help conceal her from Big Boy's view. Panting, she crouched down and tried to catch her breath. Mopane bees buzzed around her face, attracted by the sweat. She slapped them away as, in the distance, a car engine started. During Alexa's flight, the wind had picked up. The steady cross-breeze muffled the sound, but she could hear the SUV moving to the left. Big Boy was doing as she expected and driving to the gate.

When he found no sign of her there, would he assume that she'd made it out? Or would he start driving through the open woods, searching the compound?

She yanked the phone from her pocket. If the surreptitious call she'd placed to Reese had gone through, it was no longer connected. She dialed him once again, heart bursting when he answered.

"Alexa, where are you? Are you in trouble? I heard part of your call. I could tell right away there was something wrong. Most of it was garbled and muffled, then it cut out right after you said something about crossing the river and heading east."

Her eyes moistened at the sound of his voice, but she had no time to waste on emotion. "I'm in big trouble. Mama Nkala's chauffeur, Big Boy, kidnapped me and drove me to a compound outside Maun. It took us about fifteen minutes from Chapman's. Over the river and to the east. It's a vacant lodge surrounded by a chain-link fence. Someone's weekend home. Probably a friend of Mama's. I got away from Big Boy, but I'm trapped in the compound. He's going to kill me if he finds me." Alexa raised her voice to compete with loud noise in the background on Reese's end. "Where are you?"

"In Colonel Shonga's chopper. He picked me up at Chapman's. Pretty told me that you'd been there but disappeared at the beginning of the lunch service. A man at the bar said he heard a shout when a black SUV left the parking lot, but he wrote it off as someone fooling around. We've been circling, looking for black SUVs on the eastern side of the river."

"We passed a boarded-up safari lodge called the Kingfisher. That road came directly past the place I am now. This compound is a little farther on the right. Not far from the river."

Reese talked to someone, then came back on the line. "The colonel knows where this Kingfisher Camp is located. He thinks he even knows where you might be. Lay low. Keep the phone on."

"Wait, I think Big Boy is driving in this direction," Alexa interjected. "I have to turn the volume down, but I'll try to keep the line open."

To her right, the giraffes took off in a canter, frightened by the approach of the SUV. Alexa burrowed farther into the acacia, worrying about thorns and snakes. When one of the long thorns snagged her knit shell, Alexa moved to unhook it and gasped. She'd forgotten she was wearing the bright rose blouse. Keeping low, she scuttled back, slipped out of her jacket, and tore the shell over her head. She shrugged the linen jacket back on, fastening the buttons with shaky hands. As the SUV turned and headed in her direction, Alexa buried her ruined designer top beneath a pile of leaves. A smell, almost like balsam, came from the crushed leaves and calmed her. The scent reminded her of the pines at home.

She held her breath as the SUV passed in front of the acacia bushes and kept going to the right. Then, Big Boy stopped and did a wide turn, circling back toward her. Alexa feared she'd been spotted. She leapt up and tore along the fence to the left, then headed back out into the forest, running toward the gate. Behind her, the roar of an engine telegraphed that Big Boy was pulling forward. He'd found her and was on her tail.

Alexa ran in an uneven path, aiming for trees set close together. The forest was open enough for the SUV to drive through, but scattered clumps of trees offered her sporadic protection from the oncoming vehicle.

Alexa hoped to replicate what she'd done in the lodge. Make it through the gate and close it behind her before Big Boy could drive through. He would have to stop the SUV and walk to the gate to open it. Even a few seconds out of the giant's sight could give her time to disappear somewhere outside the compound. He would surely give chase. But he would have at least a fifty percent chance of choosing the wrong direction. As the SUV rocketed around a clump of trees, trying to cut her off, fifty-fifty odds sounded pretty good.

She dashed toward another small copse of trees, holding the growing stitch in her side. Even the breeze couldn't offset the relentless heat reflecting off the sandy ground. Looking ahead as she ran, Alexa quailed. One more thick group of trees ahead, but the long, long final slog to the gate was open ground.

The SUV closed in as Alexa reached the trees. Big Boy was getting better at navigating tight turns. This time he caught her. Big Boy pulled parallel to

Alexa, then made a sharp left in front of her and slammed on the brakes. He'd cut off her path to escape.

Alexa took a long, anguished look at that last open stretch to the gate and collapsed against a tree in a gesture of surrender. She'd nearly made it.

With the motor still running, Big Boy barreled out of the car.

The minute he put both feet on the ground, Alexa pushed off the tree and broke for the gate. *Faster, faster*, she told herself one more time. Racing forward, she no longer felt the stitch in her side. Adrenalin spiked through her veins. This was her last chance.

When he'd stepped out of the SUV, the scowl on Big Boy's face had been thunderous. Chasing Alexa through the forest hadn't been part of his plan. It was clear he was no longer in a polite mood. If Big Boy seized her, Alexa was dead. Now.

Behind her, a car door slammed. Back in the SUV, Big Boy gunned the engine. Then, forest debris exploded in sharp pops beneath the tires as he drove after her. Alexa summoned all she had to put on a final burst of speed. But Big Boy closed the gap in seconds. Alexa glanced over her shoulder as the SUV leapt forward. She threw her body to the left just in time. The fender grazed her hand before she fell headlong into the sand. When the SUV backed up, she sprang to her feet and confronted the vehicle.

The hulking form of Big Boy loomed behind the wheel. She stood frozen in place, poised to jump again. He revved the engine and rocketed forward. Alexa reacted as she had to. This time, she jumped to the right and landed with a wobble on her feet. She recovered her balance and circled behind the SUV as it streaked by, then she flew toward the gate.

As Big Boy reversed the SUV, the air filled with unbearable noise. Dust, grit, and dead leaves rose from the ground and swirled as a helicopter touched down between Alexa and the SUV. Several uniformed men with guns jumped from the chopper and moved toward the vehicle before the blades stopped whirling.

Just yards from the gate, Alexa leaned over to escape the rotor wash, hands protecting her face. Then, her shaking knees buckled, and she collapsed into the dust, chest heaving with exhaustion. When the helicopter shut down, Alexa rolled over and looked up, drinking in the flawless blue of the sky. Reese rushed toward her, and she burst into tears.

EPILOGUE

ALEXA STRETCHED OUT on the chaise and listened to the autumn breeze sigh through the old-growth pines in front of the cabin. Scout nudged her hand, and she scratched his head again. Since she'd arrived home several days ago, Scout had followed her everywhere. Her fears that the English mastiff might have forgotten her had been groundless. The dog was ecstatic to see Alexa home and to settle back into life at the cabin.

Scout wasn't the only one. Alexa was treasuring this time alone. The first days after her return from Botswana had been busy with catching up. Her parents. Her brother and his family. Good friends Tyrell and Haley. There'd been a steady stream of welcome home visits.

When Jim and Melissa stopped by, Scout had been happy to see his temporary roommate, Ansel. He and the little French bulldog played while Alexa, Melissa, and Jim sat on the deck and rehashed their safari and the assault on Noka Camp. But when Melissa and Jim walked to their car, Scout had high-tailed it to the cabin door.

"Oh, buddy. You're staying here," Alexa consoled the dog.

Melissa laughed. "Should we be insulted that Scout doesn't want to spend another few months with us? Look at the poor baby. He's so glad you're home."

"I don't think it's anything personal," Alexa replied. Then she gave Melissa a somber look. "I'm so glad you've recovered your balance."

"Me too. But it might be a while before I'm ready for another safari," Melissa replied with a shaky laugh.

As her friends drove away, Alexa gave Scout a big hug and whispered, "I'm as glad to be home as you are, buddy."

After seeing friends and family, it was great to just savor life at the cabin and ease back into the groove. Her brother, Graham, the lead partner in their law firm, had agreed that Alexa should postpone her return to work for another week. She needed time to unpack and do mundane household chores like fill the empty refrigerator. More importantly, she needed time to regroup. She liked to think that she would have escaped Big Boy and his deadly SUV. In her heart, she knew that it could just as likely have gone the other way. That she could be lying in some shallow grave in the Botswana bush and have never again seen all these beloved family and friends who'd welcomed her home.

The authorities had arrested Mama Nkala and Big Boy. They'd also identified the tall man who fancied linen suits and Mama's Asian friend as black-market ivory buyers. Colonel Shonga expected to arrest both men quite soon. Nick's uncle in Zimbabwe would be taken into custody as well. Botswana authorities were working on issues like jurisdiction and extradition with their counterparts in Zim.

The police had dug into the connection between Mama, Big Boy, and Nick. They unearthed a tale of two families that became intertwined in the long, violent shadow of the Rhodesian Bush Wars and Zimbabwe's turmoil after independence.

For many years before she was born, Mama's parents worked for Nick's uncle, Duncan, the outfitter who ran trophy hunting safaris in Zimbabwe. When she was a child, Mama's father left to join the rebels fighting Rhodesia's Ian Smith regime. He was killed in a battle with government forces, leaving his family at risk. So, Duncan sent the family—mother, young Mama, and toddler Big Boy—to safety and a new job at his brother's farm across the border in Botswana. The mother remarried and, a few years later, died of HIV. But Mama and Big Boy stayed on at the farm after their mother's death and even after their stepfather's subsequent demise. Mama's comment about Big Boy making the stepfather pay for their mother's HIV suggested he'd not died of natural causes.

Even as young adults, Mama and Big Boy regarded the farm as their home until, during one of their visits, an elephant raiding the garden trampled their benefactor, Duncan's brother. Duncan continued to take an interest in Mama, paying for some of her educational expenses and trips abroad as her public profile and influence in Botswana politics increased. When Mama needed HIV program funding, Duncan introduced his protégé to the lucrative black market for wild animal parts.

Nick's years in his uncle Duncan's care began long after Mama and Big Boy had fled for Botswana. But Nick visited his other uncle's farm in Botswana many times as a child and knew both Mama and Big Boy. *Well enough*, thought Alexa, *for Big Boy to take young Nick fishing. And who better for Uncle Duncan and Mama to enlist to manage their new poaching venture than Nick, situated in the middle of Botswana's elephant-rich Okavango Delta?*

When the police recounted these details to Alexa and Reese, she'd shaken her head. At various times, Nick, Mama, and Big Boy had all shared tiny pieces of this story with her. But, with neither names nor any reason to imagine a connection, the pieces of the puzzle had never come together.

Poor Emma appeared to be collateral damage in all of this. The police had cleared her—at least enough for her parents to swoop in from England and take their traumatized daughter back home. Alexa had sent a brief note of sympathy to her friend but had not yet received a reply.

After her rescue from Big Boy, Alexa had remained in Maun for another week before she was permitted to return home. She spent most of that time in interviews with investigators and prosecutors. Ripples of shock were still spreading through Botswana and the international AIDS community over Mama's arrest for poaching, ivory trafficking, and attempted murder. It was possible she'd also be charged tangentially in the deaths of Jakes and the tourists at Noka Camp.

Alexa suspected that the story of this respected woman—so dedicated to a cause that she'd run completely off the rails—would be a cautionary tale in social justice circles for years to come. It was sad that her AIDS organization would likely collapse because Mama had funneled dirty money into the program.

Dr. Kopo had flown into Maun to get Alexa's take on how the Mama situation would impact the Conservation Commission work. Mama's actions had thrown suspicion on all her proposals to the committee. Dr. Kopo was inclined to dismiss Mama's suggestions about the hunting ban change and the foreign-sponsored conservation fund. But it was anyone's guess how the unprecedented spate of poaching, the deaths of both citizens and poachers, and the resulting uproar would play out in either public opinion or the government.

Alexa sighed and tuned into the beauty of the crimson and orange leaves all around her. She would continue to follow these Botswana issues. She'd invested too much time and emotion not to remain interested. However, her role now had shifted to observer from afar. It was time to focus on life back at home.

"Hey, buddy," Alexa said to Scout. "Do you want to take a walk? Let's go to Weaver's Pond. That's one of the things I missed in Africa. Out in the bush, you can't just take a casual stroll. You have to be on alert for dangerous wild animals all the time."

The dog jumped up at the word 'walk' and trotted down the steps. Alexa locked the house, grabbed her phone, and followed. Strolling into the cathedral of towering pines, she breathed in the comforting scent of the evergreens, and the traumas of the last few months begin to slip away.

The brutal elephant slaughter, Mo, Jakes, the dead poacher, the senseless killing of the tourists at Noka, Alexa's own near murder. That turmoil and grief had been a horrible part of her Botswana experience, one she'd never expected to encounter. And she'd never forget the horror or the violence of those deaths. Yet, she knew she'd be able to put them in balance and also remember all the wonder of her months in Botswana. Eventually.

Alexa and Scout emerged from the tall pines and headed down the trail to Weaver's Pond. As they walked, her thoughts turned to Reese. He was still in Botswana. While she was off getting kidnapped by Big Boy, Gary had called Reese. On the day before his return flight to Botswana, the man had reinjured the shoulder he'd just had repaired. Something about a heavy suitcase. The surgeon had put him in a sling and ordered several weeks of new physical therapy.

So, Alexa had flown home, and Reese had stayed on in Botswana. In a way, her fears had come true. At least in the short term, Reese had chosen Africa again. It was only a few weeks, he said. Africa Trust had asked him to stay on until Gary returned. What could he do?

To be fair, Alexa had agreed that it was reasonable for Reese to remain on as interim executive director for just a little while longer. Still, she missed him desperately. She'd dreamed of the two of them coming home together. Easing back into the comfortable life they'd carved out as a couple before the months in Botswana.

Reese had been so loving and solicitous after Big Boy's attempt on her life. He'd been with her constantly during that last week in Botswana, showering her with support in the wake of the latest ordeal. With a smile, she remembered their last night together in the mosquito-netted bed in Maun. Just thinking about their tender lovemaking made her heart catch. Yet, he'd let her come back home alone. And Alexa couldn't shake a nagging worry that she might lose him to the lure of Africa yet again.

Alexa had reached the log that served as her seat at the pond. She sat and gazed at the serene water as Scout snuffled about, revisiting familiar territory. She laughed as he disturbed a bullfrog that sailed into the pond with a splash. Soon, the frogs would burrow in for the winter.

Her thoughts returned to her time in Botswana. What an adventure those four months had been. A lot more excitement and danger than she'd expected. Alexa was so grateful that first Harry, then Reese had been there for her when things got dicey. She'd never be able to fully thank Harry. And her love for Reese went so much deeper than gratitude. The two of them were destined to always keep each other in their hearts no matter where their paths took them.

But Alexa knew that her own toughness and resilience had more than met the multiple challenges that Botswana had thrown at her. She'd survived an elephant stampede, a murder attempt, and helped save the hostages at Noka.

But now. Oh, how she was looking forward to a calm fall and winter. A soothing routine in which the only skills she'd need to use were in family law, hiking, and yoga. With a rueful twist of her lips, Alexa thought, *Right, Lexie. That's always the plan, just before you stumble face-first into some new calamity.*

"Not this time," she declared aloud. "I need a break. A long break."

Rising, she called to the mastiff, "Scout, come. Let's go home." Side by side, Alexa and the dog headed back to the serenity of her familiar cabin.

AFTERWORD

DEAD ON THE DELTA is a work of fiction, and its characters are drawn from my imagination. Any resemblance to actual people, organizations, or companies is purely coincidental. The only exceptions are public or historical figures, such as various heads of state.

Many of my references are based in fact. Wild animal populations are shrinking across Africa, with elephants, lions, and other species becoming threatened and even endangered. Poaching, human-animal conflict, economic issues, and climate change are all factors. For many years, Botswana has been at the forefront of animal conservation and anti-poaching efforts, resulting in the largest elephant population in Africa. The Botswana Defence Force remains the backbone of the country's anti-poaching efforts. However, changes in the country's elected leadership have brought shifts in approach to conservation policy. This book is not intended to reflect the political or conservation situations on the ground in Botswana at any given point in time. Rather, I've tried to create a fictional scenario that recognizes the complex realities that Botswana and many other African nations face as they attempt to conserve the unique wild animal populations that are beloved around the world, yet also meet the economic needs and realities of their citizens.

Poaching is very real, and some poachers use methods described in the book—or worse. Despite international treaties banning ivory sales and other multi-national efforts to discourage sales of wild animal parts, a thriving black-market trade for these products continues to exist primarily but not exclusively in Asian/Southeast Asian countries. Trophy hunting continues to be a controversial topic in Botswana, other African countries, and internationally. Many argue against hunting animals where the species population is shrinking. Others argue that trophy hunting may end the lives of a limited number of animals, but the economic benefits help preserve the species as a whole. A number of nations outside of the African continent have tried to reduce trophy hunting by banning imports of animal remains. The United States was one of those nations but has loosened restrictions in the past few years (as of this writing).

The Okavango Delta, one of the most beautiful places on earth, exists, as do some of the places mentioned such as the Moremi and the Kalahari. But don't try to plot the camps and rivers on a Botswana map. I've created a Delta with fictional camps and a generalized geography for purposes of the story. Similarly, Gaborone is the capital of Botswana and Maun is the gateway town to the Delta, but don't look for Mama Nkala's house in Phakalane Estates or the Africa Trust headquarters on the outskirts of Maun.

The specific political drama over conservation legislation is fiction, although I've accurately reflected Botswana's general governmental structure. There is no conservation organization called Africa Trust. Similarly, the other organizations named in the book do not exist. However, there are numerous local, regional, and international conservation organizations and research projects in Botswana and neighboring countries, which focus on preserving the wild species of Africa and do enormous good in working with governmental organizations to protect African wildlife. See the Acknowledgments for one such organization, Wild-CRU, which provided me with generous assistance in researching this book.

ACKNOWLEDGMENTS

ALMOST FIFTEEN YEARS ago, my husband and I went on safari for the first time. After that introduction to the African wild, we returned again and again and again, with Botswana becoming our favorite destination. In an earlier novel, *Dead of Summer*, I tried to capture some that experience when I sent Alexa Williams on a brief safari in East Africa. Writing *Dead on the Delta* gave me the chance to set an entire Alexa book in Botswana while highlighting the important issue of endangered and threatened species on the African continent.

I owe a huge debt of gratitude to a number of people and organizations who helped me with my research for *Dead on the Delta*. I want to acknowledge their kind assistance.

First, I want to thank the University of Oxford and its Wildlife Conservation Research Unit (WildCRU) for generously permitting me to engage with lion researcher Robynne Kotze for a few days in the field. Robynne is Botswana Research Coordinator for the Trans-Kalahari Predator Programme and is currently working on a PhD based on lion research in the Okavango Delta. She educated me about the WildCRU mission, their big cat research, and the day-to-day life and tasks of a wildlife researcher in the wilds of Botswana. Talking to and observing Robynne at work helped me ground the book in reality.

WildCRU, which is part of the University of Oxford, is tackling the emerging biodiversity crisis and wider environmental issues by bridging the gap between academic theory and practical problem-solving. WildCRU has grown to be one of the largest and most productive conservation research institutes in the world. Their projects have a broad, international reach, ranging from the Scottish Highlands to Mongolia, West Africa, and Borneo.

The Trans-Kalahari Predator Programme is one of WildCRU's largest projects, focused on the predators of southern Africa and their conservation and interactions with people. Initiated in 1999 with the Hwange Lion Research Project in Zimbabwe, it was extended into neighboring Botswana in 2013 to form the Trans-Kalahari Predator Programme. The program encompasses ecological research with a focus on African lions (and increasingly other predators), ecologically sustainable transboundary land use management in the Kavango-Zambezi Transfrontier Conservation Area, and the promotion of coexistence of humans and predators to simultaneously improve human livelihoods and safeguard globally threatened lion populations.

In addition to Robynne Kotze's help, I obtained background information from a book written by Director of the Trans-Kalahari Predator Programme and University of Oxford Research Fellow Doctor Andrew Loveridge. That book, *Lion Hearted: The Life and Death of Cecil & the Future of Africa's Iconic Cats* outlines his work with lion research, including the famous Cecil, in Zimbabwe.

If you are interested in supporting WildCRU's lion research and conservation efforts, they welcome donations at https://www.oxfordna.org/donate (a 501c3 registered charity). Select *WildCRU* under the *I would like my gift to be used for* tab, and then in the *Further information* box, specify that the funds should be donated to the *Trans-Kalahari Predator Programme, Botswana*.

I also want to thank Dave Luck, an excellent guide with Wilderness Safaris, for helping me with questions about African wildlife and much more about Botswana. His long expertise in the bush made him a valuable resource.

Wilderness Safaris' wonderful camps have always been our destination when my husband and I go on safari in Botswana, Zimbabwe, and Zambia. The company, which supports WildCRU's field research in a number of ways, was particularly helpful in arranging my time with Robynne Kotze. Simon Stobbs, the Wilderness Business Manager for North America, went above and beyond to help.

Similarly, I'd like to thank the US-based adventure travel company International Expeditions for arranging our research trip to Botswana as well as our other previous trips to Africa. Kim Guth has always arranged exciting safaris that keep the Knowltons returning for more. Steve Cox was particularly accommodating in assisting me on this latest research trip.

And I'd like to thank my guide in Gaborone, Tendai Chikangaidze of Maroon Tours, for helping orient me to Botswana's capital city.

I want to give a shoutout to my regular support team for all the Alexa Williams books. My husband, Mike, who supports my writing and in so many ways is my rock. He reads my early drafts, gives me sound advice, and copes gracefully with all the hours I spend writing. And, in this case, spent over a month in Africa with me doing research and provided the lion photo that is the foundation for the cover of *Dead on the Delta*.

I also want to thank the Knowlton/Kuehn clan, who give me feedback on manuscripts, moral support, and more. This group includes my son, Josh; daughter-in-law, Laura; Steve, Pam, Dave, and Nancy Knowlton; and Denny and Coe Kuehn.

I owe a big debt of gratitude to Val Muller, a fellow author and teacher, who gave me insightful feedback on *Dead on the Delta* in its final stages. Thanks also go out to a group of fellow authors who give me consistent input on my work: Joan West, Pat LaMarche, Phyllis Orenyo, Andrew Carey, and Alma Bond.

I also want to thank the crew at Sunbury Press: Publisher Lawrence Knorr, who continues to support the Alexa Williams series and played a very hands-on role by designing the cover for this book; Jennifer Cappello, whose amazing editing helps enhance each book and brings continuity to the series; and Crystal Devine, who is adept at the technical aspect of production. And I can't forget my marketing team, Adrian Stouffer and Kim Lehman, who help me place each new Alexa Williams book in the public eye.

Thanks to all of these generous people who have helped me make *Dead on the Delta* more accurate. If I've misinterpreted any information, the fault is purely mine.

Finally, I want to thank all my readers. Your continuing interest in the Alexa Williams series is gratifying and inspires me to keep writing. I would like to ask my readers to help spread the word about my novels by leaving a brief review of *Dead on the Delta* and my other Alexa Williams books on Amazon, Goodreads, Barnes & Noble, Indie Bound, Book Bub, or Sunbury Press. And, of course, tell your friends. Thank you.

ABOUT THE AUTHOR

Sherry Knowlton is the award-winning author of the Alexa Williams suspense novels, including *Dead of Autumn, Dead of Summer, Dead of Spring, Dead of Winter,* and *Dead on the Delta.* Her lifelong passion for books started as a child when she would sneak a flashlight to bed so she could read beneath the covers. All the local librarians knew her by name.

Now retired from executive positions in government and the health insurance industry, Sherry is "rewriting retirement" by turning her passion for writing into a new career. She draws on her professional background and global travel experiences as inspiration for her novels. She also uses her writing as a platform to shed light on social issues affecting our world today.

Sherry and her husband, Mike, began their journey together in the days of peace and music when they traversed the country in a hippie van. Embracing the travel experience, they continue to explore far-flung places around the globe.

Sherry lives in the mountains of Southcentral Pennsylvania, where the Alexa Williams suspense series is set.

STAY IN TOUCH WITH SHERRY KNOWLTON

Read more about Sherry Knowlton's Alexa Williams suspense series, upcoming books, events, podcasts, and book club guides, and sign up for her newsletter at:

www.sherryknowlton.com

Get Social with Sherry!

Newsletter Sign-up:
www.sherryknowlton.com/contact

Facebook:
@sherry.knowltonbooks

Instagram:
www.instagram.com/sherryknowltonbooks/

Twitter:
@KnowltonSBooks

LinkedIn:
www.linkedin.com/in/sherryknowlton/

Pinterest:
www.pinterest.com/knowlton0706/

YouTube:
https://www.youtube.com/channel/UC6OiC0fqu2t_OPZxdpFkkjA

Goodreads:
www.goodreads.com/sherryknowltonbooks

Amazon Author Page:
amazon.com/author/sherryknowlton

www.ingramcontent.com/pod-product-compliance
Lightning Source LLC
Chambersburg PA
CBHW020550020726
47494CB00006B/2004